BEHIND THE SHADOWS

A SHADOWS STANDALONE

J.A. OWENBY

FREE PALATE CLEANSER EBOOK

SIGN UP FOR J.A. OWENBY'S NEWSLETTER and download your FREE palate cleanser Ebook, Love & Sins. Stay up to date concerning exclusive bonus scenes, updates on upcoming releases, and more. Visit www.authorjaowenby.com or Click Here.

TRIGGER AND CONTENT WARNINGS

Please visit https://authorjaowenby.com/pages/content-warnings for triggers, content warnings, and tropes.

Please do not proceed reading if these are potential triggers. Your mental health is too important.

xoxo,
J.A. Owenby

PLAYLIST

Liquor Talkin' by Don Louis
Ghost by Teo
Paper Bag by Fiona Apple
God Needs the Devil by Jonah Kagen
Cry Later by NateTaylorr and Mellina Tey
The Death of Peace of Mind" by Bad Omens
Killed Me by XV Nauthiz
God's Gonna Cut You Down by Empara Mi
Me and the Devil by Gil Scott-Heron
Click here for the full playlist.

You think I'm unholy? You have no idea. I'll have you reading with one hand between your thighs, my name on your lips, begging to be ruined again and again. Say yes, and when I'm done, you'll never look at a cross the same—and you'll kneel only to me.

For Hollie.
You made my world a better place. I miss you.

PROLOGUE ~ KIP

The sharp clang of my shovel reverberated through the silent graveyard as it pierced the earth. The oppressive Eastern Oregon heat clung to my skin like a suffocating blanket, but I couldn't stop when I was so close to the truth. My mind raced with dark thoughts as I dug deeper into the ground, each clump of dirt threatening to reveal a new layer of depravity inside me. I laughed to myself. If people only knew how fucked up I really was.

My attention briefly drifted to home. I was anxious to return to Portland before anyone missed me. Plus, I was eager to see the pretty little thing who had captured my attention at the coffee shop yesterday. My cock throbbed at the thought of her hips swaying in her jeans as she strolled to the pastry display. Her long, blonde hair flowed past her shoulders and down her back while I envisioned wrapping it around my hand and forcing her to her knees. I'd fucked a lot of women, and none of them meant a damn thing to me. She wouldn't be any different. Ignoring the intrusive thought, I smirked, sick amusement bubbling up inside me. I chuckled at the irony of being turned on while desecrating the resting place of the dead.

As the shovel bit deeper, the soil grew colder and damper. The sky darkened, the once-bright moon was quickly obscured by thick clouds that materialized out of nowhere. The air turned sharp, like ice against my lungs, and a sense of unease settled in the pit of my stomach. On high alert, I glanced around, certain that I was being watched from the shadows of the tombstones.

While I focused on the job, thirsting for answers and revenge, I couldn't escape the smothering weight of betrayal. Each hour that passed only fueled my burning desire to confront the past, which refused to stay buried. Lies and betrayal had led me here, and I could trust no one—especially not ...

Shaking my head, I pressed my lips into a thin line. They had molded and manipulated me into a monster, stripping away my humanity until all that remained was a vessel for darkness and vengeance.

My nostrils flared as the memories assaulted my senses. They were the reason why I was in the graveyard, digging up a goddamn body. If I got caught, my life as I knew it would be over, and that couldn't happen. At the same time, I would go to any length for answers—even if it meant murder.

A sudden chill slithered down my spine, and I tried to shake off the foreboding feeling, attributing it to the lateness of the hour and the eerie surroundings. But as my shovel gathered another pile of dirt, a glint of something metallic buried in the earth caught my focus. Brushing off the soil, I realized with growing horror that it was a rusted old locket, its chain tangled with decaying roots. My jaw twitched, blood pounding in my skull. The name blurred under my gaze, carving itself into my brain.

I staggered backward, dropping the necklace as if it had burned my hands. My pulse jackhammered in my throat as I stared into the night. A corner of the coffin grabbed my attention, and I hurried back to the pit.

The sharp edge of the shovel blade sliced through the last layer of soil, and I leaped into the gaping hole. With cautious steps, I made my way to the front of the casket and uncovered the rest of the ornate wooden box.

My heart thundered inside my ribcage as I wiped away sweat from my stinging eyes. I inhaled deeply, trying to ignore the pungent scent of earth that threatened to choke me. As I reached for the lid, I braced myself for what I would find inside. I lifted it slowly, the creak of the hinges breaking the otherwise silent night.

I froze, staring at the satin lining interior of the box. My mouth hung open while my brain scrambled to make sense of the sight in front of me. The son of a bitch mocked me as my chest heaved with anger. The casket was ... empty.

THE GHOST ~ KIP PRESENT DAY

The darkness was suffocating, swallowing me whole until I couldn't even make out the outline of my hand right in front of my face. When would this relentless madness finally end? I was a grown man, yet evil shackled me, unyielding and merciless. I pressed against the wall, the frigid cement gnawing into my bare back like icy teeth. There had to be an escape, a different existence out there, shimmering on the horizon. But every time hope dared to flicker in my mind, the rancid stench of my true nature tore viciously at my soul.

The door cracked open with a jarring creak, unleashing a blinding stream of light that sliced through the blackness of the room. I shot to my feet, my pulse pounding in my neck, and furiously clawed at my arm, where the needle marks seared and itched, like a thousand tiny fires—relentless, unforgiving.

She glided in, the light framing her as if she wore a halo.

"Kip." Her voice was hollow but held a familiar tone.

"Yeah?" I straightened to my full six-foot-three height and squared my shoulders.

She strode toward me, her stare avoiding mine, while her long hair cascaded like a waterfall down her back. The white dress, with its scooped neckline and a row of buttons that seemed to strain against her curves, clung to her figure with an allure that was impossible to ignore. My body reacted instantly, tension coiling within me as my gaze devoured the sight of her large breasts and the mesmerizing sway of her hips. My worn, grimy, gray sweatpants hung precariously low, utterly incapable of concealing the desire that surged through me. Her slender fingers reached out with intent, tracing a path between my pecs, dancing tantalizingly along my abs, before teasing the edge of my waistband.

"You're happy to see me." A soft giggle filled the room, and an eerie echo bounced off the walls.

The hair on my neck bristled, a primal jolt clawing at the edges of my consciousness. But it vanished in an instant when she yanked my sweats down, liberating my throbbing cock. Her petite hand engulfed me, stroking with a deliberate rhythm that sent waves of pleasure shivering through me.

I gasped, my breath hitching as she sank to her knees, her lips brushing against the tip of my cock with a tantalizing softness. A feral hunger ignited deep within me, swirling like a storm in the pit of my stomach as she took my length into her velvety mouth, drawing me deeper into the depths of ecstasy.

"That's it," I muttered as I cupped the back of her head and moved her closer.

My eyes slammed shut, blocking out the chaos that threatened to consume me. I concentrated solely on the intense sensation of her mouth moving with fervent precision. But why was she here? Who was she? I banished the intrusive thoughts, shoving them deep into the recesses of my mind. I would deal with them later—right now, they had no place here.

"Suck my cock, my pretty little whore." My hips bucked as she pumped me with her hand, her saliva coating me as she worked her magic. Her grip grew firm, and I couldn't help but grin.

"You like being my dirty slut?"

I continued to fuck her mouth, a primal growl escaping me as she gagged. My fingers tangled in her hair, grasping roughly, and I twisted the long strands around my fist, yanking her head back to take me in deeper.

"That mouth of yours is hot, but what about that pussy of yours?" I growled. I pulled out and forced her to look at me. Her facial features blurred in and out, and I blinked several times in a vain attempt to bring her into focus. It was no use, though.

I yanked her to her feet, and a little yelp escaped her.

"Why are you here? Who sent you?" I asked, running my knuckles down her slender throat.

"You called me." The corners of her mouth turned up into a smile, but her face remained blurry.

I loomed over her petite figure, casting a shadow that swallowed her whole. "You should be terrified, my little toy. The things I want to do to you ... "

She laughed, a sound like mocking bells. "What makes you think I don't crave every twisted part of you? All of your darkness. Every ounce of your sin?"

With a swift, decisive motion, I grabbed the fabric of her dress, tearing it open down the front with a forceful rip. The tiny pearl buttons exploded in every direction, ricocheting off the floor and skittering away like scattered marbles. Her exposed breasts rose and fell with her ragged exhales. I descended upon her, my mouth colliding with hers in a passionate clash. Her lips parted eagerly, her tongue dancing provocatively with mine as she pressed against me. Her hardened nipples grazed my chest, sending electric currents of heat racing up and down my spine, igniting every nerve inside me.

I traced down her naked back and over the curve of her ass. Her skin was soft and smooth, shockingly warm in the chill of the cell. I grabbed her ass, squeezed, and pawed at her until she grinned. With a quick move, I pinned her against the wall, and my cock hammered against her stomach. Her body was so fucking small. Our kisses grew more desperate while I moved my hand between her parted legs. She wanted me to fuck her. I could tell from the wild thump of the pulse in her neck, the wet slickness between her thighs when I lifted her and she wrapped her legs around my waist. I positioned my hands beneath her ass cheeks and held her as the tip of my cock pressed against her entrance.

She lowered her head and sank her teeth into my earlobe with such ferocity that blood trickled down my neck.

A sinister chuckle reverberated around the room—mine. If she believed she could hurt me, she was sorely mistaken. The scars on my back were jagged, crimson reminders of agony, barely healed, each one a testament to suffering. Nothing compared to the excruciating torment, a deliberate, drawn-out pain designed to shatter my mind long before it would break my body.

With a surge of raw energy, I lifted her and drove my cock into her with unrestrained force. "Your cunt is soaking wet."

"Fuck me, Kip. Fuck me hard." She seized the short strands of my hair with a forceful intensity as I plunged into her relentlessly. By the end, every inch of her would bear the marks of our time together. The rough cement blocks tore at her bare back, each scrape igniting a primal thrill inside me. The vision of her skin breaking, the crimson droplets forming, spurred my thrusts, feeding a hunger that roared with an insatiable desire.

"Just like that," she whispered in my ear.

Her tight walls clenched around me as she braced against the wall, her breasts heaving with each relentless thrust. But still, it wasn't enough. I demanded her cries, her screams echoing my name as I drove her to the brink, pushing beyond the limits of her imagination.

"Do you want to play a game, dirty girl?" I asked, slowing my pace. Our gazes connected, and a spark of interest flickered to life in her blue eyes.

She sank her teeth into her lower lip and peered at me through long eyelashes. I was about to fuck that innocent look right off her.

"I love games." She placed her palms on my shoulders and dug her nails into my skin as I lifted her up and off my cock. I glanced over at the only so-called furniture in the far corner of the room. Before she could ask questions, I led her over to the bench and motioned for her to sit down.

"Part your legs and show me that sweet little cunt."

Her breath caught, her full tits moving with the motion.

I placed my fingers beneath her chin and forced her to look at me. If she wanted to resist me, she wouldn't much longer. "Is there a problem?" I growled.

She shook her head and with a submissive gesture she knelt for me like she'd done it a thousand times—like her body remembered even if her face was a blur. I had no fucking idea who she was. Not really. Just a ghost stitched together by my broken mind.

But she was mine.

"You're my little whore," I growled, my hand tangled in her hair as I tilted her head back. "Say it."

Her lips parted, and her reply was soft but obedient. "I'm your little whore."

The way she says it... reverent. The word burned through me, a prayer I don't deserve but took anyway. My pulse slammed in my throat, and I couldn't breathe around the aching need to own every sound she makes.

I dragged my thumb along the seam of her mouth and shoved it between her lips. She sucked without hesitation—hungry, submissive, worshipful. My chest tightened. My cock throbbed. It felt like she was offering me more than obedience; she was handing me her trust, her devotion, and it was fucking intoxicating. For a moment, I wasn't just a monster. I was her god. Her executioner. Her salvation.

"Good girl," I murmured. "Open wider."

She obeyed. Of course she did. I held all the power. I always did.

"It's time. Lay on the bench." I walked across the small room to the dark corner where I kept my most treasured possession. My only possession.

It hung from a thick, blackened silver chain—a gothic crucifix, ornate and imposing. The cross was forged from dark steel, etched with filigree that twisted like smoke, delicate and dangerous. But beneath the beauty was the threat: a hidden blade, sharp enough to slice skin, buried where divinity should've been.

It wasn't just a weapon.

It was a promise.

Too heavy to be a trinket. Too wicked to be holy.

I wore it like a badge of sin—around my neck or always within reach. When I pressed it into my palm, my cock bobbed with excitement. Slowly, I turned back to her, my attention raking over her naked body as she waited for my return. I stood at the end of the bench and licked my lips.

"I bet you taste absolutely sinful." I chuckled, the eerie sound echoing through the cold room. "I have something special for you." I held the cross up, then located the edge of the blade buried in the longer part of it. Removing it, I ran my finger over the edge and grinned as blood bloomed on it.

Fear twisted her mouth, and she grabbed the edge of the bench. "What are you going to do to me?"

"Don't worry, you'll love it and beg me for more." I reached out, spreading her lips apart and ran my tongue along her cunt, her taste exploding in my mouth. A soft, airy moan escaped her as I nipped and licked her swollen clit as she writhed beneath me, responding to each flick of my tongue. I took the cool, smooth end of the cross, running it along her entrance, and her body arched to meet it.

When I dragged the cool metal over her skin, pressed the edge deep enough to blur the line between pain and pleasure—she stopped being my good filthy slut.

She became my sacrifice.

I pressed the crucifix against her pussy lips. A sick twist of devotion—something stolen from my past, corrupted into satisfaction. She whimpered like it was a blessing. Like she was grateful.

"I'm going to fuck you with this cross while you choke on prayers that won't save you from the way I will break you."

I feasted on her, and her juices dripping down my chin while I dragged the crucifix up her quivering thigh. A scream tore from her *throat as I began to fuck her with the cross, plunging it in and out of her with a relentless fury. I seized my cock, stroking it as she thrashed against the cold metal invading her. Seeing her cunt devour the cross, stretching around it like some obscene, sacred desecration, sent me spiraling toward the edge. The sight was fucking transcendent. Profane. A brutal, carnal communion—everything I craved.*

I buried my face between her legs and licked her clit as I fucked her harder and harder. Cries of pain and ecstasy reached my ears as she struggled against me, trying to pull away. But she didn't want to. Not really. She thrived on the pain as much as I thrived on giving it to her.

Her panting filled the room, and I knew she was close to coming. But not yet.

I stood and took one of her hands and placed it on the cross.

"Fuck yourself."

"No."

Without a word, I yanked the object from her flesh and turned it around. The blade's tip gleamed menacingly in the dim light, a wicked promise of what was to come. I dragged the knife over the silky skin of her thigh, slicing with deliberate precision, enough to draw crimson tears from her flesh. I observed her frantic struggle against me, her sobs echoing the agony I inflicted. She thought she knew pain, but this was a mere whisper of the torment I could unleash.

Her chin trembled before she said, "You're a monster."

I threw my head back and laughed. "Yes, I am. Now, fuck yourself." Grabbing her hand, I wrapped it around the handle and shoved it into her pussy again.

She didn't dare defy me this time, and she eased the cross in and out of her center. I stepped back enough to watch the glorious show in front of me. Gripping my cock, I stroked with a fierce hunger, matching her intense pace. Her tears evaporated, replaced with gasps of pure pleasure, the echoes of pain forgotten in the heat of her lust-filled frenzy.

"You like it. I knew you would. Fuck that cunt for me."

"Say it," I demanded, my voice low and commanding.

"You're my monster."

"Again."

"You're my monster," she repeated, breathless. Desperate. Like she loved it.

I watched the way her hips rose off the bench to meet the crucifix. Her ecstasy was agony. Beautiful. Dangerous. I wanted to destroy her and keep her forever.

She bit her lower lip and said, "Does my monster like to watch?"

"Your monster loves to watch." My hold tightened around my dick as I stroked faster while she neared the edge of her orgasm. "That's right, little whore, where is your god now? I'm your god tonight, the only one worthy of your devotion. Surrender to me. Come so I can lick your juices off your pussy when you're finished."

Her head fell back, and ebony hair cascaded down her shoulders like a dark waterfall as she guided the object and pumped it against her. Her hips moved in a frantic, desperate rhythm. Her eyelids were closed and lips parted. "This is for my monster," she murmured, her hips bucking wildly against the cold, unyielding metal.

My body tensed as I looked at her, my desire throbbing and pulsing in tandem with her movements. I could feel the heat building, the pressure rising, the electric tingle at the base of my spine. I released myself as she collapsed back onto the rough stone bench, heaving.

As I approached her slowly, my footsteps echoing in the quiet room, the air thick with the scent of sweat, sex, and desperation. I could see the goosebumps on her flesh and the sheen of perspiration on her forehead. I removed the cross from her, and her skin was flushed and warm to the touch.

Parting her legs, I thrust into her, her center hot and slick. She screamed, the sound raw while her back scraped against the cement bench. The red streaks from her thigh smeared against my side, sticky and warm, as I moved against her, my hips driving into her at a brutal, relentless pace. I dug my fingers into her hips and drove deep enough to make her arch against me. We moved together with a kind of animalistic logic, the slap of skin against skin and her little gasps punctuating the silence. I lost myself in it, let it erase the rest—the stench, the filth, the gnawing disgust—until nothing remained but the rhythm and the feeling and the raw, selfish need.

Her fingernails dug into my shoulders as she came again, her breath hot against my ear, and I felt her tremor.

I grabbed her neck and cut off her air. "Say it," I demanded, my voice low and commanding. I released her enough for her to gasp air.

"You're my monster."

"Again."

"You're my monster," she repeated. Desperate. Like she loved it.

Her head tilted. Something ancient stirred behind her murky blue irises—like a memory fighting its way to the surface. For a flash, her features sharpened—high cheekbones, her full lips trembling, and freckles splattered across her nose. Familiar. Impossible.

I seized her jaw, dragging her up to meet my mouth, and kissed her like I wanted to devour the last bit of her soul.

I was close. So fucking close to the release I so desperately craved.

And then a whisper in the background said my name. "You did this, Kip."

Higher. Sharper. Twisted.

My rhythm faltered. She was still under me, but her eyes were gone now—glassy, vacant.

"You did this," the echo in the distance said again. "Run, little girl, before it's too late."

Her skin, colder. Crimson fluid seeped up from the cement, soaking my hands.

The words rattled me, too sharp, too familiar. My mother's voice. For a split second, it almost sounded like she wasn't condemning me at all, but warning someone else. Protecting her. But that couldn't be right. My mother never saved anyone.

I blinked and jerked back, chest heaving, cursing.

I didn't come.

I couldn't.

Suddenly, she faded. She was gone. Again. Her body slipped through my grasp like smoke.

And I woke up—hard, sweating, and furious. I shook as I glanced at my ragged, chewed-down fingernails. I reached for the cross on my nightstand, clutched it until the sharp points dug into my palm—grounding myself in the present.

The cold steel bit deeper. My stomach twisted. It always did, but I never knew why.

Until the flashes started.

Hands. A voice. My mother's voice? "You did this, Kip."

I blinked, but the image smeared across my vision like bad film stock—grainy, cruel, and wrong.

I don't remember that night. But the needle always came after the screams.

I stared into nothing, my skin prickling with shame.

There was no peace in my head—only the rush of blood and the echoes of her laughter.

The darkness wasn't done with me.

She was still gone.

And I?

I was still the monster.

1

———

KIP

"What's up, motherfucker?" I slapped one of my best friends, Hal, aka Dope, on the back before I settled onto the loveseat in the basement of his house, or as his friends referred to it, his dungeon.

Dope leaned over and turned down the music, "Liquor Talkin'" by Don Louis. He shoved his hand through his red hair and rolled his computer chair back. "Locating the next family." He raised a light eyebrow. "And of course the son of a bitch that deserves a long, torturous death. Some monsters don't deserve redemption," Dope muttered.

I gave him a look but didn't argue. Absolution was a fantasy for those who still believed they could be forgiven. I wasn't one of them. I used to believe in saving people. Now I made sure the predators were put down before they hurt others.

But sometimes I wondered if I was simply cleaning up a mess I'd helped create.

There were nights I couldn't sleep. Ghosts I couldn't forget.

And one I couldn't quite remember—only the sound of her screaming.

I leaned back, stretching my legs in front of me. "What do you have so far? Death is getting restless."

Death, a notorious serial killer and childhood friend of ours, had killed multiple people in the Portland area and across the country, leaving a trail of victims and attracting unwanted attention from the authorities. Once Safe Horizon, an underground operation that helped women and children leave horrible, warped living situations, had been established, Dope and I realized Death would get caught soon if left to his own devices. We took it upon ourselves to protect him. We gave the police misinformation, planted evidence, cleaned crime scenes, and fed him sick fucks to murder. It was all planned so we could manage and sidestep the authorities. It was our job to cover his tracks and point him toward the bastards who sold kids and beat their wives. Most of those vile pieces of shit were identified when we found the right families to help.

Not only did Death get what he needed, but the men who hurt and tortured women and children were punished for their crimes. We used the society to feed a serial killer his victims. It was fucked up and twisted, but no one had a clue how alike Death and I really were. I fed on the aftermath and cleaned up the murder scenes, but lately it had turned into more. The beast inside me had awakened with an insatiable hunger, consuming my every thought and toying with my emotions. As hard as I tried to keep the memories buried in the back of my mind, they continued to emerge through the cracks and crevices, haunting me with reminders of my past and taunting me with uncertainty about my future.

A part of me was driven by selfish motives. By doing good deeds, I wished I could somehow redeem myself for the sins of my past. But deep down, I knew it was too late for me. My humanity had been stripped away over the years, and once it was gone there was nothing to put back into that empty space. Still, working with these vulnerable individuals and seeing the glimmer of hope in their gazes was the only thing that kept me going, an anchor in the blackest corners of my soul.

"Sorry, what did you ask?" Dope gave me a lopsided grin. It was the same one he gave his friends when he knew he'd been caught not paying attention.

"I asked what you have so far. Death is getting irritable. He needs his next victim."

He rubbed his palms together, nearly giddy. "As always, I've got his back. We need to hop over to Ohio and help a mom of three. She's tried to leave her husband, Collin, twice, and he's made her pay for it." Dope folded his arms across his chest, his expression twisted with fury. "The bastard is trading guns for girls to sell. He's in deep, so we have to watch our asses on this one. He's connected with a shit ton of powerful men."

"Understood. At least we can put an end to Collin. If someone else comes after us, then Death will have another victim. We can keep feeding his dark side." Grinning, I laced my fingers behind my head.

Dope's hands flew over the keyboard, then he said, "Is Riley going to cover the bar at Velvet Vortex while you're gone?"

"We need more people than her. I'll work on changing the schedule. It's a little more difficult covering the bar and restaurant since Bass left."

Sebastian, who we called Bass, my other best friend and business partner, had moved to New York with his wife, Ella, for a while, but after serious shit went down, they'd returned to Portland. Even though Bass loved to cover the bar and chat up the customers, his situation had changed, and he ran the club behind the scenes the majority of the time.

"It's not only Collin's enemies we have to watch for. We've made enemies while working at Safe Horizon, and not to mention the other crazy motherfucker that's now in our lives." Dope pretended to play a flute and raised his brows at me. We hated mentioning the sick fuck's name, so we skirted around it as often as possible.

He didn't need to mention who he was talking about. I would never forget the cold, knowing stare that shot straight through me when

I first came face-to-face with the Pied Piper—a notorious serial killer and one of the most dangerous men I'd ever met. He'd taken an interest in Sebastian's family, and now we were all looking over our shoulders.

Dope cracked his knuckles before he rolled his chair forward and returned to his computer. Multiple screens covered his workspace, so he could work as fast as his brain moved, unless he was super stoned.

"Want some?" Dope reached for the rolled joint tucked behind his ear and stuck it between his lips.

"I'm good, man." Weed wasn't my friend. It opened some fucked-up shit in my head that I preferred to leave alone. Lately, memories were surfacing without my permission, and the last fucking thing I needed was to open the door and invite them in.

"You seem distracted again. What gives?" Dope's fingers tapped a few keys on the keyboard. "There it is," he mumbled while he shook his head, then grabbed his lighter and lit up.

"Nothing for you to be concerned about." I had to mask my thoughts better. Absentmindedly, I rubbed my arm where the faint scars of my heroin days still taunted me.

Dope didn't miss my movements. He blew out the smoke and asked, "How long have you been clean now?"

"Fucking years, man. It's in my rearview mirror. Don't sweat it."

"Easy to say, but you're coming apart at the seams, dude. Either tell me what the fuck is eating you alive, or I'm going to keep asking."

I stood, not in the mood to deal with his meddling questions. It was none of his fucking business. Smoothing my navy polo shirt, I tipped my chin at him. "Gotta go. I'll make sure Velvet Vortex is covered, but I need to know when we're taking care of Collin's family."

"In three days. Be ready."

"I will. I have to visit Mother and make sure she's taken care of while I'm gone."

Dope's shoulders visibly tensed. "How's she doing? Sometimes I forget you're dealing with all of that."

I barked out a sarcastic laugh. "I wish I could forget. Until she fucking dies, she's once again my problem."

His forehead pinched as if his next words caused him pain. "Let me know if you need anything. Bass and I will do whatever we have to."

He didn't have to explain what he was suggesting. I knew exactly what that offer looked like, and I'd considered letting them help my mother disappear for good.

"I appreciate it, but it's my issue to deal with." Dope and Bass knew a few things about my past, but only enough for them to understand why I'd broken ties with my family ... until Mother got sick and there was no one to pay her medical bills. Since I was an only child, the responsibility fell on my shoulders. Lucky fucking me. Even though I would never say it out loud, some twisted part of me hoped she would one day forgive me. Maybe if she looked at me and saw more than a broken monster, I could find the redemption I was always chasing but could never hold on to.

"I'll be at the club working tonight but stop by if you want something to eat." I shoved my hand in my jeans pocket and headed up the stairs to the living room. "I'll lock the door behind me," I yelled at Dope. I doubted he heard what I said, but he had a bad habit of not locking his windows or doors. With the work we did, that was asking for trouble.

"GHOST" by Teo finished playing on the car stereo as I pulled into Mother's driveway and parked my car. I reached into my pocket and removed my contacts case, carefully removing my brown-colored lenses. I placed them in the container filled with solution and closed it with a click. As I tucked away the case, I felt for the familiar weight of the bulky, silver cross pendant hanging from my necklace. With a sigh, I slipped it beneath my T-shirt, a constant source of comfort and security for me.

I opened the screen door, my stomach churning at the idea of being here again. I hated being in her house. Every wall was a shrine to her obsession—Bible verses in gold lettering, cross-studded knickknacks, and framed photos of her with that smug pastor. To anyone else, it looked saintly. To me, it was all a lie. She was no better than the devils she pretended to condemn. Worse, she hid behind scripture while creating her own hell at home.

"Cynthia?" I called out to let the caregiver I'd hired know I was there. "Why isn't the screen door locked?"

A short, brown-haired woman appeared from the back of the home and gave me a warm smile. "Kip, the entire door is a screen. If someone wanted to come in, a little lock wouldn't keep them out. Besides, we're out here in the country, and if someone were sneaking around, Dog would start barking."

As if on cue, a German Sheperd appeared. I knelt and patted Dog. Mother never decided on a name, so I did. One I knew would irritate her since she named everything around her, including her houseplants. "You're a good boy, aren't you?" Dog licked my cheek as his tail wagged so hard his back feet bounced across the wood floor. "Are you taking good care of Cynthia and making sure she's safe?"

I glanced up at the caregiver, who arched a dark brow at me. "He keeps your mother safe too." She placed a hand on her hip and gave me a firm look.

"I know. I just like messing with you." I straightened and chuckled. "How's the patient today?"

"Cranky, but we both know that's nothing new." Cynthia snorted.

"I heard that, Cynthia! Tell my son to come see me," Mother called from her bedroom.

My stomach twisted, acid burning the back of my throat. Even after all these years, the sound of her voice could still cut me open like a dull blade.

"This place is too small to have any kind of private conversation." Cynthia wiped her forehead with the tissue she was holding. "Maybe we could get some air conditioning in here?"

I didn't miss the hope in her voice with her question.

"I'll have someone come out and install a few window units. It seems we're going to have a hotter summer than usual. The shade is usually enough to keep the place cool, but no such luck this year."

"Thank you, Kip. It will help her not be so pissy all the time too." Cynthia laughed. "We can hope anyway."

I grinned at her. "I'm not doing it for the old bag. It's for you."

"Kip?!" Her dry hacking cough echoed through the house after she attempted to yell at me.

I groaned at my mother's sharp tone. "Guess it's my turn. Take the afternoon off, and I'll see you later this evening." I squeezed Cynthia's shoulder as I passed her to locate the patient in her bedroom.

My footsteps announced my presence, and Mother lifted the oxygen mask from her nose and mouth. "It's about time. You have no idea what Cynthia is like when you're not here."

"Unless she's poisoning the food, I seriously doubt that she's mistreating you." I sank into the blue recliner in the corner of the room. The ceiling fan whirred on high, the chain clinking against the light as it spun.

When she had been diagnosed with pulmonary fibrosis, I'd invested in an adjustable bed for her, so she'd be more comfortable. What I hadn't planned on was her mean streak. Somehow it had gotten worse with age, and I hated spending any time with her. Not that I'd enjoyed her company when I was younger. Quite the opposite. The only person I'd liked was my uncle, but he was ...

"Where are your contacts?" Mother asked, interrupting my thoughts. "I've told you not to come around here with your demonic eyes. Put your lenses back in."

Inwardly, I grinned, knowing full well I was irritating the shit out of her. She hated that my eyes were so pale they looked colorless, swore it was the devil's curse, proof I was born of his blood and not any man's. For too damn long, I believed her. My uncle finally got sick of her screeching prayers and exorcisms, so he dragged me to get my first pair of colored contacts. Everything changed after that—at least outside the house. I made friends. Kissed a few girls. Pretended to be normal. But nothing changed with Mother, no matter how much I hoped it would.

"No. I can't wear contacts all the time. I need a break."

She scoffed. "The devil doing the devil's work." She glared at me before she leaned her head on her pillow.

"It's a good thing I do, or you'd be in a dilapidated nursing home being neglected. I know Cynthia is good to you. You like to bitch and make people feel like shit."

She huffed. "I'll pray for your rotten soul, then I'm going to take a nap. You're draining me."

I stood, glad our chat had offered an exit into another room. "Sleep well," I muttered as I walked away, leaving her alone. Unfortunately, it rarely mattered if I was around her or not. She was always in my fucking head. It had to stop, but I wasn't sure how to silence her.

Or maybe I did.

2

KIP

The stench of death and fear permeated the air, burning my nostrils as I swore under my breath. The abandoned warehouse room was splattered with blood, and entrails littered the concrete floor. Whoever the sorry bastard used to be, he was no longer recognizable.

"You're late," Death said, his gaze narrowing behind the grim reaper mask that molded to his face.

I'd known my friend for years, but the hair on the back of my neck still stood on end at times. This was one of those occasions.

"I'm here and that's what counts, you grumpy bastard." I placed my hands on my hips, the acrid tang of the slaughter still fresh in the room.

He stood still, his irises glinting dangerously behind the eyeholes of his disguise. "You've never been late before. What's the problem?" he growled.

I rolled my neck and stared at the ground, trying to dismiss the tension in the air. "I had to take care of some personal business. It took longer than anticipated. It doesn't matter now, though. There's a mess to clean up." I massaged my right shoulder. "What the fuck are you doing killing in Portland anyway? You're supposed to be lying low."

"It's been months since I played here. Plus, I'll be heading to the East Coast after we get this shit cleaned up."

I nodded, agreeing with his plan. "Good, stay the hell away for as long as you can. I can't keep covering for you if you continue your work here. It's not as if a serial killer stops drawing attention from the authorities."

As I approached the mutilated body, I wondered who the man was, and what led him to his gruesome fate. In this city, death was everywhere, and I was a mere shadow in the night.

I knelt, running my fingers through the congealed crimson fluid on the ground, feeling the slick texture beneath it. "Ready to get this shit done?" I asked, barely above a whisper.

My friend nodded slowly, the powerful energy of his presence swallowing any light that tried to enter the room. "Yeah," he replied.

We left to gather what we needed from my beat-up Mustang's trunk, leaving the foul stench of death behind us. As we walked, a sense of unease rose, a hint of dread that something was wrong. Portland was already suspicious of my friend, but it was my job to stay one step ahead of the authorities and protect him.

"Who was he?" I asked as we unloaded the tools from my car's trunk. If I was ever investigated, the chemicals would be a dead give-away. But thanks to some connections, there was never a paper trail. Those same people had taught me everything I needed to know to make any trace of a person disappear into thin air.

I chucked a respirator at him. "What was the son of a bitch's sin?"

He reached out with one hand and caught the safety gear midair. "Murdering his wife and two kids. He poisoned the wife over time, so it wouldn't look suspicious. Once she was gone and he got a big-ass life insurance policy, he smothered his kids in their sleep."

A twisted grin eased across his features. "The fucker never saw me coming."

I chuckled as I collected the needed supplies. "Is water still available in the building?"

"Yeah, can't clean up without it," he mumbled.

We walked quietly back into the warehouse, my mind focused on how to most efficiently eliminate the body and scrub away the evidence.

"You've not provided me with an update lately. Have you learned anything new from our contact about the case?" He swung open the door and held it for me.

Whenever I assisted Death, I gave him any details I had. I was one of the reasons he'd never been caught. Not only that, but he was a smart motherfucker—brilliant actually. It was one of the reasons we'd become friends in middle school. There was something different about him that drew me in. When I caught him torturing and killing someone, I knew we were made from the same all-consuming darkness.

"My connections say the investigators are struggling to put the pieces together," I said. "A few leads are pointing toward some fucker they want to pin the murders to. They haven't done anything yet, but they're catching heat for not arresting someone." I gave him a pair of gloves. "They were getting close, but I've managed to leave a few clues in the wrong direction to give you some more time to lay low. But when you do this shit in Portland, it makes my job a hell of a lot more difficult." I blew out a sigh, frustrated that he wasn't cooperating.

His expression remained stoic. "As long as there isn't any evidence, they won't find me."

I grimaced. "We try to make sure it's all destroyed, but we're only human. We're bound to fuck up at some point."

As we methodically dismantled the crime scene, I wondered how many more victims would become Death's prey. He had done what I'd only fantasized about. Wipe the earth of evil. It was what it was though, and he had my full support until we both went down, or we burned in hell. The city was a maze of secrets, and we were two threads in its complex tapestry, but one wrong move on our part would end everything.

"You think they'll ever catch us?" I asked as we continued our gruesome task.

He chuckled, a twisted sound that echoed through his respirator mask. "No. They won't. Let them chase the shadows. We'll stay one step ahead. At least we've been able to in the past." A flicker of doubt crept into his tone, but I didn't say anything.

"Just remember that I can't protect you if either of us is behind bars. If the police found out what I was doing for you, that would be the end of me."

Death paused, his gloves covered in blood and white, sticky bone shards. "If you got caught, I would wonder if you're still on my side, or if I had to add you to my list."

My brow arched. Even though I thought our friendship would hold true over the test of time and issues, I didn't think he would actually kill me. At least I was clear on where I stood with him if shit ever went down and I was arrested, but I refused to let those thoughts clutter my mind.

Before I responded, the corner of his lips kicked up in a grin. I knew him well enough to understand there was a warning in his words if I ever turned on him, but he was also fucking with me. One thing about Death, his sense of humor was dark, and sometimes it was hard to tell if he was serious or kidding.

"You're not getting rid of me, motherfucker. We're always a team. Besides, I might need you one day." I cleared my throat, ready to get the hell out of here and ditch the respirator. "I've had a lot of other crap to deal with too." I stopped myself before I told him about my mother. That would be a shitshow for another day.

Sweat dripped down my forehead and blurred my vision as I scrubbed the stained cement. Each swipe of the sponge brought me closer to erasing all traces of the dead guy who had lain here a few hours ago. As I worked, a sense of satisfaction washed over me, knowing my training was being put to good use. Not a single trace of the body was left behind.

A sharp, blinding pain shot through my head, the room tilting as her voice hit me. My fingers balled at my sides, blood pounding so hard in my ears it was like a war drum.

"You're sick, and you have to be punished, Kip."

"Don't, please!" I tugged at the collar around my neck in a vain attempt to loosen it to breathe better. Even without a shirt, the heat and stifling air were enough to suffocate me.

"It's time to read the scriptures and pray for redemption." Mother's expression shifted with a moment of fleeting compassion before it was replaced with disgust.

The heavy wooden door of the basement opened, and a pretty brunette who was close to my age was brought into the room by a man I didn't recognize. She smiled at me before she knelt with the Bible clutched to her side.

"2 Chronicles 7:14," she began. "If my people, who are called by my name, will humble themselves and pray and seek my face and turn from their wicked ways, then I will hear from heaven, and I will forgive their sin and heal them." She set the Bible on the dirty floor and folded her hands in her lap. "It's time to repent."

My gut twisted like barbed wire, and I clenched my jaw to brace myself. Mother reached into her pocket and removed a metal cross. Regardless of the appearance, that cross only brought me hell.

She walked over to me and jerked my chain so hard I dropped to my knees. The contact with the hard cement sent shooting pain through my entire body.

From the edge of my sight, I watched the bitch pull the knife blade out from the middle of the cross. She grabbed my hair and forced my head forward, allowing her better access to my back.

"For God so loved the world," she said as the tip of the blade carved into my back. "That he sent his only son."

I gritted my teeth, the pain excruciating as she continued to carve up my skin. Tears stung and blurred my vision, but I had to focus on the hate I felt for her. It was the only protection I had against her.

"Amen," Mother said, her cruel and vicious cleansing ceremony over. Even so, the pain would last for months.

"Take this time of solitude to continue ridding yourself of evil. Maybe God will have pity on you and restore the color of your eyes to what they should be."

I trembled violently, and I stared at the ground, refusing to look at her.

The girl got to her feet, and then the sound of footsteps climbing the basement stairs echoed in the dank room. With the pull of a string, the light went out, and I was swallowed by the abyss.

My pulse slammed in my throat as I struggled to grasp reality again. The room blurred in and out until I was present again.

"Ready?" Death gripped my shoulder.

"Yeah," I croaked out, attempting to cover the fact that I'd disappeared inside myself for a minute. I couldn't let him know my flashbacks had returned with full force. He would want to know what they were about, and that was something I wouldn't tell anyone. Ever.

A comfortable silence stretched between us as we walked through the abandoned warehouse, our combat boots the only noise on the concrete surface. We reached the door, and I opened it, then stepped outside. Dusk had fallen, and the sound of the crickets chirping in unison caught my attention. A hush fell over the area, broken by a flicker of movement—someone hiding behind a tree.

3
____

HOLLAND

Cami Hayes released a tired sigh as she plopped down in a chair behind the nurses' station, wisps of her long blonde hair escaping the bun on the top of her head. I leaned against the counter on the other side, watching her try to catch her breath. The constant drone of beeping machines and chatter that filled the air was punctuated by the occasional sound of someone screaming or crying. The emergency room had been busier than usual with two car accidents.

As part of my job, I evaluated patients with mental health concerns at the hospital twice a week. My years in Sacramento had given me the chance I'd always wanted—to help others. Tonight, I'd been called in to assess a young man with severe depression and violent tendencies. Cases like his could be draining, but every patient who found a way back to themselves made it worth every second.

Once, I'd needed that same kind of help. But no one had come. No one had heard me when the night terrors had clawed at the few hours of sleep I'd managed. Not until I'd found the two people who'd finally pulled me out of the dark. That was why I couldn't turn away. I wouldn't let someone else be left alone in their madness. Not if I could stop it. Not ever. Except maybe one person ...

Before heading home, I wanted to say hi to Cami. She had quickly befriended me when I'd moved back to Portland seven months ago from Sacramento. I'd returned to be closer to my family and start a new position with a top-rated psychologist and his business partner, and this role included time at St. Vincent Hospital.

I approached the nurses' station and planted my elbows on the front of the counter. "It's a wild night," I replied, taking a sip of my lukewarm soda, and scrunched my nose in disgust. I hated to throw it away since it was half-full, but flat all the same.

"No shit." Cami rolled her neck and massaged her shoulder.

My red strands fell into my face as I leaned against the counter. "You look tired. What time do you get off work?"

"Five in the morning." She glanced at her watch and grimaced. "Another three hours to go. I need coffee, and a lot of it." The corner of her mouth kicked up. "Do you think they have coffee in IV form?"

I arched a brow in agreement. "Shit, I wish. Maybe we should invent it, get rich, and retire early."

"Hell, yes. Sign me up." Cami grinned.

A loud outburst cut through the chaos, and I looked up to see the back of a tall man struggling against a nurse's grip near the entrance.

"Let go of me!" he yelled while his cheeks flushed with anger. The nurse attempted to calm him down while a doctor and a security officer rushed to assist her.

Cami shot me an inquisitive look as she casually remarked, "Looks like we have some entertainment. I should go help." She hopped out of her seat and hurried to assist.

I locked onto the man at the center of the chaos. My heart slammed in my chest, each beat echoing like a war drum as sheer terror cascaded through my veins. An all-consuming urge to run surged through me, threatening to consume me in a tide of panic.

The voice pierced through me like a serrated blade, sending icy tremors coursing down my spine and igniting a raw, primal terror that clawed at my insides.

My hands shook violently as I slammed the papers onto the

nurses' station. With nurses focused on the man screaming, no one noticed me slip down the hallway. Each step felt like I was wading through molasses, desperate to distance myself from him.

Dizziness swirled in my head, threatening to pull me under as I stumbled forward, slapping a palm against the stark white wall for support. The man's rage-filled screams echoed down the hallway, driving me toward the only escape in sight—an employee storage room door that promised temporary safety.

I fumbled for my ID card, shaking so violently that it took several tries to scan it properly. Finally, with a loud click, the door unlocked, and I practically threw myself into the room. The light snapped on, illuminating the printer paper, ink, pens, tablets, and other supplies. I flipped the switch, turning it off again and welcoming the silence. I desperately tried to calm my racing pulse and push away the flood of traumatic memories that threatened to pull me under.

My blood thundered through my veins as I whispered to myself, "How the hell is he here?" With wobbly legs, I hugged the cinder block wall and inched my way toward the corner of the small room. The panic attack ripped through me at Mach speed, each breath ragged and desperate.

I pressed my fingertips to my temple, willing myself to calm down. Gritting my teeth, I stifled a rush of self-hatred. I was a coward hiding in a room instead of owning my power. What happened to that grown woman with self-defense training and a concealed carry permit?

I hit the bullseye on a target almost every time.

"I can protect myself," I said in a hushed tone.

But those thoughts continued to taunt me. I covered my ears in a stupid attempt to block out the noise of the memories.

"Dammit, Holland. Get a fucking grip. This is a hospital," I reminded myself. "Security guards and colleagues are right outside. He can't hurt you here."

I wiped my sweaty palms against my black pants.

My emotions were a storm I had to push aside, yet they clung to me, refusing to be ignored. I rolled my neck and shoulders, staring into the blackness that mirrored my turmoil. No one could ever know about my past or the danger that haunted me now. I had painstakingly rebuilt my life, burying the trauma and embracing anonymity. But now, seeing that familiar face, all the memories surged back, threatening to unravel everything I had fought so hard to hide.

I leaned my head back against the wall, a twisted thought clawing its way to the forefront of my mind. My breathing hitched as I fought to regain control, pushing through the remaining tendrils of PTSD. With a sharp inhale, I straightened my spine and defiantly lifted my chin. That son of a bitch was on my territory this time.

I flipped on the overhead lights, squinting against the brightness. When my vision adjusted, I opened the door and strolled into the hall with a confidence I didn't feel. I focused on the sound of my high heels slapping against the white tile floors, which helped me remain in the present moment as I returned to the nurses' station. I scanned the emergency room, searching for any sign of him. Had he been caught and removed from the hospital? Or worse, had he seen me? The tension in my muscles tightened even further, twisting into painful knots as I searched the busy area.

"Girl, you missed it," Cami said, placing her hand on her hip as she approached me. Her pretty features flashed with mischief.

I rubbed my hands up and down my upper arms, as if trying to shake off the sudden cold seeping into my body—and hoping to hide the fact that I was upset. If Cami noticed my anxiety, she would demand explanations I wasn't prepared to give. Yet, a part of me longed to confide in her, while I wrestled with the fear of vulnerability and the desire for support. "I desperately needed to use the bathroom. What did I miss?"

Cami sucked on her lower lip and tilted her head to the side. I followed her nod, preparing to see that monster again.

"The cops showed up and hauled that guy out of the ER. They're talking to another nurse, Lyndsey, and Dr. Richton now." She turned slowly, grinning like a Cheshire cat about to pounce on an unsuspecting mouse.

I looked over at the two police officers engaged in conversation with Lyndsey and Dr. Richton.

"Oh, that's nice scenery," I said softly while I checked out the tall hottie with brown hair. His black pants clung to strong thighs and a gorgeous ass. I bit my lip, playing it up for Cami's sake. I wasn't interested in dating right now, but she didn't know that. "Is he new?" Over the last few months, I'd met several of the officers due to my job here, but I didn't recognize him.

His broad shoulders tensed beneath his blue shirt as he took notes, listening intently to Lyndsey.

"Girl, I don't know, but maybe we should introduce ourselves. Officer Jackson is hot, but the other one ... Hell, they both look like they walked off the cover of a magazine. They might be a fun night." She stifled her giggle. "You take your pick."

I wasn't the only newly single one. Cami was still reeling from a brutal breakup, the kind that leaves cracks you can't hide with lipstick and laughter. Her ex had been a cop too, which made it all the more surprising that she was willing to joke about dating another one.

"They certainly don't hurt my feelings any, but you know I've sworn off dating cops." Or anyone else involved with the law and with the ability to learn my secrets. Regardless, I was grateful for the fleeting distraction.

Cami squeezed my shoulder. "I think it could be good for you, babe. Getting under someone else could help you move on after Coop."

"I wish it were that simple," I said, unable to hide the pain in my tone. I still missed Cooper, but I would get over it. Over him. The relationship had been a constant rollercoaster, and I finally had to get off that wild ride. At least I'd left him in California, and the distance was good for my soul.

I watched as Officer Jackson's stern features softened slightly while speaking to Lyndsey.

As the conversation concluded, the new officer fixed his gaze on me, and my pulse pounded like a drum. His piercing brown stare pinned me in place with an intensity that stole my breath, sending an electrifying shiver racing down my spine. I hastily averted my attention, the heat of a blush burning my cheeks. Though I had no interest in a relationship, the whirlwind of fear and adrenaline from moments earlier had left me thrumming with energy, craving a release.

Apparently, I was infatuated with men in uniform, which was dangerous. Even Cooper had started digging too deep during our relationship, and I knew I had to sever ties before he unearthed my dark secrets. The thought of being near detectives or cops was worse than a nosy boyfriend, and it sent a jolt of panic through me. It was a gamble I couldn't afford to take.

The officers bid their farewells and headed toward the door, leaving a trail of staring nurses in their wake. My friend nudged me with a mischievous grin.

"Looks like the newbie has taken a liking to you," she teased.

I rolled my eyes. "As much as I'd love to stay and keep you entertained, I need to head to my place."

Cami gave me a big hug. "Be safe, and text me later."

I offered her a warm smile. "I will. Have a good one."

When Cami had learned I was a single woman in the big city, she'd made me promise to message her when I got home if I was out at night. She did the same with me and a few other friends. I appreciated the sense of safety it provided. Hell, we all did. Around the time I'd moved to Portland, there had been a serial killer on the loose, although there hadn't been any news recently. It was almost as if he'd disappeared into thin air without leaving a trace. I could hope, anyway.

Still on high alert from the unexpected visitor, I scanned my surroundings with a hawk-like intensity as I stalked down the deserted hallway toward the elevator. The oppressive weight of the parking garage always gnawed at me, yet I convinced myself it was a fortress compared to the vulnerability outside, especially at night.

A sharp chill raced up my spine, and the hair on the back of my neck stood rigid, prompting me to slow my pace and whip around, searching frantically for a sign of movement. But the corridor was empty, mocking my paranoia. I steeled myself with a mental pep talk and dashed to the elevator, jabbing the button with urgency. The doors abruptly parted with a mechanical sigh, revealing a somber woman and her small child. I mustered a warm smile as they passed, though the shadow of their sadness clung to the air. Had they experienced the cruel hand of loss, or was a loved one battling for life in that sterile place? My insatiable curiosity, usually an asset in my line of work, now served as a mere diversion from the lingering dread that had clawed its way into my being. A shudder worked its way through me, and I gave the painful memories of my past a swift kick in the ass. I softly hummed "Paper Bag" by Fiona Apple as I waited for the elevator to reach the correct floor.

Before I reached my level, I located my car keys and held them tightly. I nodded at the people waiting to enter the elevator before I stepped out and into the garage. The parking lot had been nearly full when I'd arrived, and I'd been forced to park on the opposite side of the building entrance. My footsteps echoed through the otherwise quiet area, and I couldn't shake the feeling that something was wrong. I walked faster past a row of vehicles, chiding myself for forgetting my weapon at home. I always carried when I worked at night, but I'd been in a rush to leave and had forgotten.

Thundering footsteps pounded behind me, sending a cold prickling sensation through my body. I whipped around, my chest squeezing tight, but there was nothing—no one—in sight. My mind raced with denial, refusing to accept the possibility that I was losing my grip on reality. "Who's there?" I called out, struggling to keep my voice steady. My legs shook as I attempted to keep my back covered, but there were too many rows of vehicles that could easily hide someone. I was exposed.

Instead of a response, a pair of strong arms wrapped around me from behind and a large palm covered my mouth, stifling my scream.

4

———

KIP

"Get back," I ordered Death and shut the door. "We've got someone watching us. I have no idea who it is, but you know the drill. Go! Now!"

When Death had acquired the decrepit, abandoned building—an old warehouse with peeling black paint and windows boarded up like blind eyes—we'd understood that someday we might get caught. Despite our relentless efforts to avoid it, we were human and fucked up. And today was that day. Even though Death and I had poured sweat and tears over the last few years carving a hidden tunnel beneath the building, we had never needed to use it—until now.

I whipped my head around, and my throat went dry as I watched my friend fade into the shadows. My stare locked onto the pathetic bastard lurking outside the shattered window. The corners of my lips curled like a man possessed, and I cracked my knuckles, ready for the chase. The thrill of terrifying someone was second nature to me. Honestly, I was glad Death had to leave. It was my opportunity to handle someone myself. An opportunity I'd denied myself for way too long.

I eased the heavy door open, searching for his hiding place. "It's your lucky day, motherfucker. Come out, come out wherever you are," I said in a singsong voice.

I walked outside, dry leaves and twigs crunching beneath my footsteps. Other than a few scattered trees, the field was open, and my new friend had few places to hide. I also knew the property like the back of my hand, which gave me a substantial advantage.

I reached a massive oak and every muscle tensed while I strained to catch the slightest sound that would betray the guy's hidden location. A flock of birds erupted from the field, shattering the silence. I released a low, devious chuckle. The dumb ass must be creeping along the ground, clumsily startling the birds. With predatory precision, I moved in the direction from which the birds had taken flight. Vivid, ruthless images of what I intended to do to him surged through my mind, and I fought to suppress a sinister grin.

"There's no use hiding, you stupid bastard. I'm going to catch you and when I do ..."

The tall grass rustled, then he launched himself across the field with desperate speed. It seemed he was hell-bent on reaching the sanctuary of the forest before I could close in. Fueled by adrenaline, I rushed forward, the wind slashing against my cheeks as I accelerated. In mere moments, I snatched the collar of his burgundy shirt and yanked him back with brute force. He crashed into me, and I coiled my arm around his neck with relentless pressure. His fingers clawed at my arm, a futile struggle for breath as he gasped and fought against me.

In a rough whisper, he said, "I didn't see anything, man. I was coming out here to smoke so my wife wouldn't catch me."

"Doesn't matter. You were at the wrong place at the wrong time. Nighty night, asshole." I locked in the chokehold, counting the seconds as his limbs twitched and then stilled. His weight sagged against me, deadweight. No resistance. No fight. Telling me he had passed out cold. I grunted as I turned his limp body, then tossed him over my shoulder. I'd carried plenty of bodies before, but this one was still alive. Adrenaline pumped through my veins, my pulse throbbing in my neck as the thrill of what was to come overshadowed any potential consequences.

Upon reaching one of the back rooms, I positioned my victim against a corner wall while I gathered the necessary ropes and tools. I had limited time before he regained consciousness, so I moved swiftly. I secured ropes to two pulleys on opposite sides of the room, then tied them around his wrists and ankles. Confident in my knots, I pulled him to the center of the room. He let out a groan as I turned the handles on the first and then the second pulley, watching as the ropes stretched him in all directions until he was upright. His head lolled to the side, his jeans and T-shirt grungy from the woods. I guessed he was in his late thirties and had lived a full life from the ink that covered his arms—fire, angels, snakes, and skull. My intuition told me he wasn't someone to let go. He would come back for me. *Sorry, motherfucker, not happening.*

His eyelids flickered open, and I watched as his features morphed from confusion to terror.

"Welcome back. Did you have a nice nap?"

He tugged on the restraints, frantic as his mind allowed him to fully take in the situation. "What the fuck is wrong with your eyes, man?"

Over the years, I'd thoroughly enjoyed fucking with people when necessary. I was well aware of how messed up my eyes were.

I pinned him with a sharp glare, ignoring his question. "What's your name?" I walked behind him while I waited for him to talk.

"Fuck you," he growled.

"Wrong answer." I stopped and reached into the back pocket of his dirt-covered blue jeans. Removing his wallet, I flipped it open and searched for his driver's license.

"Michael Ruppert Branson." My laugh echoed across the room. "Ruppert, huh? Bet you got teased while growing up."

Michael remained quiet, observing me as I paced the room. Although I could continue this indefinitely, time wasn't on my side. Turning to look at him, I felt the cross's weight pressing against my chest under my shirt. I reached in, took it out, and gripped it tightly, the sharp stainless-steel edges cutting into my hand. I flipped the blade out, and he recoiled in shock.

"I didn't see anything. I swear to fucking god!"

"I don't believe your bullshit story. You were too close to the building. If I were in your … restraints, I would lie too." I paced the room, pretending to be in deep thought. After another moment of silence, I approached him, my nose only a few inches from his. "If you tell me the truth, I'll let you go with a warning."

He stared in surprise, hope flickering to life in his eyes. Hope was a dangerous thing.

"You promise?" His chin trembled with the question.

"I'm a man of my word." I placed my palm on my chest directly over my heart, stifling the smirk that tried to emerge. In some ways I wasn't lying. Years ago, I had vowed to protect my best friend, Death, no matter the situation or consequences. That had been my word, and I would continue to honor it.

Michael blinked several times, then blurted, "There were guts and … I saw some fingers. But that was it. I didn't see who they belonged to, man. I swear. And you and the other dude had those masks on so I couldn't see anything. I promise. If you hadn't run after me, I wouldn't have seen who you were." He gulped several times, waiting for me to respond.

"But you can identify me. Then, they can track down my friend who was with me, and that shit simply can't happen."

"You're not going to let me go? I won't tell anyone, I promise … please." Panic clung to him as sweat beaded across his forehead.

I arched my brow at him. This fucker was gullible as hell to believe I would let him go, and he confessed so damn fast.

"Tell me, Michael, are you familiar with the blood eagle?"

"Never heard of it." He tugged on the ropes in a vain attempt to get loose.

"There are rumors about it. No one's sure if the Vikings actually used the form of torture or not. Those sons of bitches were ruthless, so I could see it being one of their favorite pastimes." I paused. "Basically, the person's back was slashed in order to allow access to the ribs. They were then broken and twisted upward to resemble wings. Often someone died before the ribs were even broken due to the loss of blood. It's debated if the ritual was only legend or if it was actually used. Regardless, it's going to be used today." I sneered as I watched his piss soak his jeans, then splatter on the concrete floor.

"I swear to god, I won't tell anyone! I have no idea who you or the other guy is. You can't fucking do this. I have a family, kids."

I laughed as he blubbered with every reason I shouldn't kill him.

"Your cries are falling on deaf ears. You were here at the wrong time. It's game over."

His sobs rang out through the room as I played with the blade from my cross. "First, I'll give you a tattoo on your back, so I know where to make the first cuts."

"You're a fucking psycho, man!"

An evil grin crept over my expression. "You have no idea, but you're about to find out."

HOURS FLEW by in a frenzy of skin and screams, and then I cleaned up the mess. Every cut I inflicted, every drop of Michael's blood that stained my hands, every one of his cries that echoed in my ears was worth it. I would do anything to protect Death—to protect those who meant the world to me—the ones I would murder for. Michael had been a thorn in our side, a problem that needed to be solved. And as I plunged my knife into his back, feeling the satisfying slickness of his flesh parting beneath it, I understood the thrill and power that Death must feel when he exacted justice.

A twisted sense of satisfaction washed over me, and for the first time, I understood the rush that came with taking a life. I'd assisted Death before, cleaned his messes, carried his burdens—but this kill was mine alone. The exhilaration was raw, dangerous, a demon inside me begging to be fed again. Mother would drag me to her church pastor if she knew. But it wasn't about justice. It was about survival—because if I didn't give my darkness somewhere to go, it would eat me alive. And staring down at Michael's lifeless body, I knew one thing with absolute certainty—I would do it again, without hesitation.

As the first rays of sunlight pierced through the early morning sky, I bid farewell to the warehouse and embarked on a leisurely drive back to the city. I rarely took the same way twice in case I was being followed. The quiet roads were bordered by lush green fields, their dewy blades sparkling in the warm golden light. As I approached, the skyline grew larger and more imposing, with towering buildings reaching toward the heavens like giants among men. The city pulsed with raw energy and life, a stark contrast to the place I had left behind.

I stifled a yawn and reminded myself to reach out to Death later to make sure he was on his way back east. Hopefully, he would stay there and not return to Portland for a while. His presence was complicating matters, and we had to be careful. When his bloodlust returned, it was with a vengeance. Would the same thing happen to me if I continued to kill? I barked out a laugh. Like I fucking cared. Since I was well trained as a cleaner by my uncle, I could get away with more than most. I'd never left any evidence behind when I'd cleaned for Death. I sure as hell wouldn't start now.

"God Needs the Devil" by Jonah Kagen played softly over the car speakers as I hopped on I-5 and approached the hospital. I slowed and obeyed the speed limit, since the last fucking thing I needed was to get pulled over for speeding with tools and chemicals in my trunk. It would take some time to clean up everything and hide the car in a back alley behind the surgery center.

I caught sight of a white Mercedes speeding out of the underground garage on a collision course with me. My heart kicked into overdrive while I swerved at the last possible second and slammed on the brakes, narrowly avoiding the impact.

"Goddammit! Watch where—" I started, but then I found myself looking directly at a redheaded woman in the driver's seat, her face frozen in terror.

The world spun around me as I was thrown against the seat belt. Confused and shaken, I hesitated, unsure whether to feel anger or relief. Moments later, with my mind still reeling, I drove into the side parking lot and stopped the car.

"Son of a bitch." My thoughts spun out like a whirlwind as I tried to convince myself that the driver of the Mercedes wasn't who I thought it was. It was literally fucking impossible. Yet, doubt gnawed at me.

An oppressive weight settled on my chest as I grappled with the idea that I might be losing my grip on reality, teetering dangerously close to the edge of sanity once more.

I climbed out of the car, the warm air chilling my sweat-slickened skin as the stomach-churning memories seeped into my head like a sickening fog, suffocating me with their gruesome details. I paced the length of the car and attempted to talk myself out of what I'd seen. She was only a mirage, my mind playing twisted tricks on me after I'd murdered someone like a cold psychopath. If this was what guilt felt like, maybe I did have a soul. It might be pitch black, but I'd take that over not having one at all.

But every time I rubbed my palms over my clammy skin in an attempt to scrub away the doubts, a different aspect of the woman's appearance jumped out at me—her fiery red hair, piercing blue eyes, and full lips. As hard as I tried to dismiss the woman, it didn't take long to realize my efforts were futile. That meant only one thing.

5

HOLLAND

The sharp sound blared from the small oval alarm clock on my nightstand. Sleep had completely eluded me. Every time I closed my eyes, the parking garage replayed in my mind like a nightmare stuck on repeat—the echo of my footsteps, the sudden grip from behind, the gloved hand clamping over my mouth. I couldn't shake the feeling of breath against my ear or the twisted thrill in his voice when he whispered, "I would kill, but where's the thrill in that? The hunt is what excites me, and there's something intoxicating about toying with my prey."

Instinct screamed at me to bolt back into the hospital, but that was impossible. Too many people. Too many questions I couldn't afford. If anyone dug too deep, they'd find out who I really was—what I'd survived, what I'd done. I couldn't risk that. Not here. Not at work. Better to take my chances in the garage, alone, than let my entire past unravel under fluorescent lights.

The moment I had broken free, I sprinted to my Mercedes in the parking garage. My legs shook as I fumbled with the keys.

Despite the chaos in my mind, fear fueled me, allowing me to start the engine and navigate out of the parking structure, narrowly avoiding an oncoming car.

Five minutes from the hospital, with no signs of pursuit, I pulled over. My legs were unsteady as I stepped out. A surge of nausea overtook me, twisting my moment of reprieve into fresh panic. I braced against the side of my Mercedes, caught between gratitude for my escape and the unsettling aftermath that left me tethered to both fear and freedom.

Even now, my skin crawled at the memory. My heart hadn't slowed since. I'd barely made it through the front door before locking every deadbolt and slumping to the floor in a shaking heap. Sleep wasn't just elusive; it felt impossible. How could I close my eyes knowing he was still out there, watching, waiting ... hunting?

I sat on the edge of my queen-size bed and placed my feet on the floor, forcing myself to believe I was safe as I shut off the alarm. In the past, I'd tried to wake myself up with a gentler tone, but I never heard it if I was in the grips of a night terror.

Inhaling deeply, I tried to clear my thoughts as my attention landed on the collage of picture frames that graced the top of my dresser. My throat tightened with regret and loneliness as I stared at the only picture I had of a tall, skinny, strawberry-blonde-haired girl. She had her arm slung over my shoulder, grinning as I glowered at her. My sister was two years older than I was, but we'd always been close ... until.

I swallowed over the lump in my throat, pushing the darkness away and forcing myself to look at the other pictures of a happier time with my parents, college graduation, and fun snapshots of Cami and other friends that I'd made since I'd moved to Portland. At least I was working from home today on client notes and a few virtual sessions. Thank God. After last night's scare, I couldn't shake what had happened at the hospital. I was almost certain the man in the garage was the same one I'd seen in the ER, but doubt gnawed at me. Maybe a shower would help calm me.

Forty-five minutes later, I was clean, dressed in a bright teal silk blouse and black slacks, and my makeup was in place. Next on my agenda were two shots of espresso and a cup of coffee with a dash of Snickers-flavored creamer.

"Alexa, play my soft jams playlist," I said as I entered the kitchen. "Cry Later," by NateTaylorr and Mellina Tey floated through the air.

As I sipped my espresso, my thoughts kept returning to last night's events. Who was that mysterious man who'd materialized out of thin air in the parking garage? As much as I wanted to, I couldn't shake off my suspicions. Could it really have been Draco who found me? If he saw me inside the hospital, then staying here was a risk.

"Keep it together. You've figured out how to hide until now. You've got this."

The kitchen was a stark contrast to my scattered and racing thoughts, with its pristine white cabinets, stainless steel appliances, and a row of potted herbs on the windowsill. I walked over to the refrigerator and pulled out a carton of eggs, contemplating making myself a healthy breakfast to distract myself from the whirlwind of emotions.

But as I cracked the eggs into a bowl, my mind once again drifted back to the hospital parking garage—to the feeling of someone watching me. My instincts were correct, and I had to stop second-guessing myself.

Once my food was ready, I climbed onto the barstool at the bar and tapped the screen of the iPad I kept on the counter. It was time I talked to my bestie and allowed my subconscious to work on the Draco problem.

Autumn's bright, beaming face appeared on the screen, her eyes crinkling at the corners as she smiled. Before she could speak, her phone bounced around.

"Sorry! I've got the baby in my arms." Her laugh filled the line before she was able to settle into her rocking chair.

"How's the nanny job going?"

"It's great. Baxter and Nina are amazing to work for. They treat me like family and spend a lot of time with Krista too. I was worried about that at first, but they're great parents. It's kind of crazy that I got this job through Cooper, though."

Ignoring her comment about Coop, I squinted at the screen, trying to identify what was on Krista's shirt. "Is that baby puke?" I snickered.

"Yup. Didn't you know that baby puke is in style this season?" She giggled, smoothing Krista's blonde fuzz on her head. "She's gassy and has been crying nonstop most nights. Her mom and I take turns trying to soothe her little belly. We sleep in shifts. Maybe soon Krista will sleep through better."

"Do you need me to visit? I have some vacation time, and I can be there to help." My chest ached. Autumn and I had been best friends since high school, and although it was wonderful to see her on the iPad, I missed her. At one point, I'd considered moving to Missouri to be closer to her, but something inside me wouldn't let me leave the Northwest.

"Have you called the pediatrician?" I propped my elbow on the counter, waiting for her to adjust Krista on her shoulder.

"It started a few days ago, but we're going to call tomorrow." She patted Krista's little back, then a big burp floated through my speaker.

I laughed. "I have no idea how such a big burp or fart can come out of such a little body."

"Right?" Autumn snickered.

"So, one of my coworkers recently got back from maternity leave. Her daughter had colic, and she mentioned there were drops you could put in the bottle to help with the gas. Do you want me to ask what she uses?"

"Oh. My. God. Is there such a thing?" Tears welled in Autumn's tired gaze.

"Apparently so. Maybe send your boss to pick some up at Target or Walmart, whatever you guys have out there."

"I'll call him as soon as we're done chatting." She placed a gentle kiss on the baby's little nose. "I miss you. Tell me how you're doing. Have you heard anything from Coop?"

I sighed, shoulders slumping with temporary defeat. No matter how hard I tried, I couldn't rid that man from my system.

"You know that we've gone our separate ways and are doing our own thing. I wouldn't count on us getting back together."

Autumn's forehead creased in concern. "You never told me why you broke things off with him. I mean bits and pieces but not the real reason."

I swallowed over my suddenly parched throat. "Secrets. It's always about secrets, isn't it?" *And you have your own. Secrets you can't ever risk getting out.* I bitch-slapped the whisper in my mind and returned my attention to my best friend.

I didn't miss the troubled expression in her gaze.

"What is it?" My forehead creased. "What do you know?"

She straightened in the rocker as Krista squirmed.

"Why would you think I know anything?"

I crossed my arms before I said, "Don't play innocent with me, Autumn O'Neill. You forget who you're talking to. I know you almost as well as I know myself. Now spill."

"Holland, you can't tell a soul. Not a fucking word, not even in your sleep. Promise me." Her lips thinned as she waited for my declaration of silence.

"I swear. Not a word to anyone." I placed my hand over my heart for emphasis.

"All I know is that Coop came up in conversation a few weeks ago. Baxter was on speaker with his brother and another friend, and they were discussing business for a while. The moment I heard Cooper's name, the volume was turned down, and then Malaki, Baxter's brother, closed his office door. I don't know what was said, but it wasn't for my ears. I think something is going on with Cooper, Holland. Maybe consider reaching out to him and seeing if he's okay."

"Why would you think he's gotten into some kind of trouble? My guess is that his gambling finally caught up to him." Before she could respond, I pressed my lips into a thin line. I broke up with him, he was no longer my problem. "No. Whatever he's gotten himself into, he can fix it on his own."

Her brows furrowed. "What do you mean gambling?"

I swore softly, realizing I'd given something away. "Autumn, he was disappearing in the middle of the night, and sometimes I wouldn't hear from him for a few days. He was distant and refused to talk to me about it. As you already know, when I hired a private detective, he returned with evidence that Cooper had messed up with some shady people and owed them a lot of money. I can't be in a relationship where I'm not considered a trusted and equal partner. Life is too short to wait to be cherished by someone." *But you loved the twisted games he played before he fucked you senseless.* Sinking my teeth into my lower lip until it caused me pain, I discarded the thoughts of what he did to me, like a used car he could trade in without a second thought. I had other shit to deal with, like the monster who showed up in the emergency room last night. I had to stop wasting my time wishing Cooper would change.

"You absolutely deserve better than that, babe. Now that you've shared what happened, I'm glad you're out. Stay away from the piece of shit." She paused, her expression turning wistful. "I just wish your information wasn't solid. He seemed like a good guy."

"That's the thing, people can present whatever mask they want, but eventually it will have to come off." I sighed and tucked my hair behind my ear. "If you learn he's dying or something serious, let me know. Other than that, I have no intention of reconnecting with him. My emotions are still too fragile." I hated admitting it to her, because when I spoke it out loud, I was also admitting it to myself. Cooper had broken my heart. I thought he was the one I'd spend my life with, but apparently, I was alone in that fantasy.

"I know. I'm sorry you're hurting. You know I'm always here for you." Autumn rocked the now quieter Krista.

"As soon as I have a long weekend, can I fly out to see you?"

My bestie nodded, grinning. "I'd love to see you."

"Perfect. I should get some work done. Love ya."

"Right back atcha, bitch. And for the record ... when the right guy shows up, I bet it will all be worth the tears and shitty times." Her sweet smile spoke volumes.

"I'll have to take your word for it." I winked at my bestie as a small wail pierced the air along with Autumn's ear. "Go take care of Krista, and I'll text you later."

We blew each other a kiss, then disconnected the video.

Leaning back in my chair, my mind immediately returned to Draco. If it really was him, he'd probably seen me get into my Mercedes when I left for work or ran errands. I couldn't take that chance—not if I wanted to stay hidden. I'd need to rent something different.

"Shit," I muttered. I couldn't take any more chances, which meant I couldn't drive my car.

AFTER I TOOK an Uber to the car rental place, I drove around for a while. Once I'd determined that no one was following me, including Draco, I steered the vehicle toward my destination. Forty minutes later, I directed the car into the alleyway and parked several houses down the street. Maybe I shouldn't go anywhere with Draco making an appearance, but I couldn't hide either. Granting him all the power was something I couldn't allow myself to do again, yet part of me hesitated, wondering if there was a way to manage the situation without losing control. I needed to be cautious and remain vigilant, but the pull of past mistakes still lingered.

I opened the driver's side door and climbed out of the rental before I smoothed out the wrinkles on my blouse. I couldn't shake the feeling of unease as I stood in front of the imposing two-story Victorian home. Every visit was a mixture of love and discomfort. The cracked sidewalk beneath me seemed to symbolize the fragile relationship between myself and the people inside. Squaring my shoulders, I walked, and my heels clicked against the concrete. The freshly manicured lawn tickled my nose, and I wiggled it, willing myself not to sneeze. As I walked up the porch steps and to the entryway, I noticed the outside had been freshly painted a blue-gray. It was a nice change from the dingy white that had started to peel away over the last few years.

I rang the doorbell and waited, my nerves tap-dancing along my spine. Thank God I'd stashed a travel-size deodorant in my purse for occasions like these.

The door swung open and a pretty face with big brown eyes lit up at the sight of me. Her perfectly styled hair and designer slacks and blouse told me she'd taken time to prepare for my biannual visit.

"Holland, it's so good to see you." She stood back, her slender frame appearing frail, but she was actually quite strong for her age.

I stepped inside, the lemon scent of Pledge lingering inside the home. The polished, light wood floors gleamed, and I was certain there wasn't a speck of dirt to be found.

"Hi, Mom." I leaned down and embraced her, allowing myself to briefly experience a sense of safety and security while she hugged me back. Our relationship was tumultuous with criticism and unsupportive looks, which spiked my anxiety any time I was around her.

"It's been too long. I know you're working a lot, but we won't always be around."

I looked away, irritated with the manipulation ploy. Granted, it was true they wouldn't be on the earth forever, but they were both in good health. The last year had been spent with patients and Autumn's family, who had needed me more.

I broke our embrace and gave her a pointed look. "What did we say about the guilt trips, Mom?"

"Well, honey, if you visited more often, then I wouldn't need to."

My jaw tightened. "I can leave. I want to be here, but not if it's going to be tense and stressful." At least I'd learned to put appropriate boundaries in place with her.

Her shoulders dropped slightly. "You're right. As you say, 'I'll knock that shit off.'"

I couldn't stop the tug at the corners of my mouth. Mom didn't swear often, and it always made me laugh. "Much better. I've missed you. I want to hear about all the things." I tipped my nose in the air. "Hmm."

The sound of heavy, purposeful footsteps echoed through the pristine foyer, accompanied by the smell of fresh bread and spices. A man emerged from the kitchen, his round figure obscured by a cloud of flour. He wiped his hands off on a white apron before spotting me and breaking into a wide grin.

"There's my girl!" Dad exclaimed as he made his way over to me. "You look as beautiful as ever, but ..." He tilted his head and studied me for a moment before tapping the tip of my nose with his index finger, leaving traces of flour on my skin. "You're a bit on the thin side. I'll have to send you home with some leftovers."

"Hi, Dad." I couldn't help but fling myself into his open arms. My dad was the reason I was here, in this warm and familiar place. I loved my parents dearly, but he'd saved my life in more ways than one. And for that, I would always be grateful.

Mom had tried her best to raise me to be a graceful lady, but it seemed that my rebellious nature had won out—evidenced by my tendency to swear like a sailor and engage in casual sex. Despite our differences, I couldn't deny that she had done her best to shape me into who I was today. And that was no easy feat considering what a difficult teen I'd been.

"Do you want to help?" Dad beamed at me.

"Of course."

"You two have fun. Let me know when it's time to eat." Mom squeezed my shoulder and disappeared to the library, where she spent a lot of time reading.

I beamed at Dad, and he led me into the kitchen, where he nodded to the blue apron sitting on top of the black granite counter.

"How have you been?" I slipped the apron over my head and tied it behind my waist.

"Good, but I've been missing my girl. Grab the potatoes and start peeling." He resumed his position near the ball of dough and began to knead it.

"I know. I miss you too. With work at the office and hospital over the last several months, I've barely had time to sit down." I glanced at him as sadness flickered through his brown-eyed gaze. "I'll do better now that life has settled down a bit." If only.

He looked over at me, a dark brow slightly raised. "I know your mother drives you crazy, but she loves you. We both do. We have since the moment you stumbled across the mall parking lot in our direction." His words were gentle and nonjudgmental. I'd always loved that about him. Even when the conversation was uncomfortable, he was kind ... unless you fucked with his family, then all bets were off, and the man literally transitioned into a beast right in front of you. *Just like someone else you know.* I swore to myself I would make better choices about men moving forward, then I brushed the thoughts of Coop out of my mind and focused on the potatoes.

Dammit, how had the conversation turned dark when we were talking about Mom? I hadn't even been here for ten minutes.

My hand froze in midair, hovering above the counter. "Dad." My voice cracked with emotion. "Please, I don't want to talk about it."

"Sweetie, look at me."

Reluctantly, I turned to him, gripping the handle of the peeler and imagining I could strangle the life force out of it. He stared into me, as if he could see all the pain and fear I was desperately trying to hide.

"I know something is wrong," he said gently. "You're like a porcupine, prickly and guarded. But you don't have to be afraid to talk to me. What is it?"

I leaned against the countertop, feeling vulnerable under his scrutiny. My tongue darted over my lower lip, and I wondered if he would accept the partial truth. "I miss Coop. That's all."

"I understand that. Matters of the heart aren't easy. But I think there's something else." He wiped off his apron, a trail of flour following his moves. "I know I'm prying, but I feel like something is off. Father's intuition." He winked at me.

Maybe I could talk to Dad, and he could help me put the irrational fears back in the box I'd buried deep inside my soul a long time ago. They weren't irrational with Draco around.

I focused on the next potato as the brown peels piled up in the sink. "It's someone from my past," I finally managed. My jaw clenched as I forced myself not to cry.

A beat of silence hung in the air while I waited for him to respond.

"Who?" His tone held a sharp edge, and I knew that he would do everything in his power to protect me.

That was the problem, though. My parents couldn't protect me no matter how hard they tried, because when the monster came out of the closet, it was only for one reason—to devour you.

"I know you haven't told us everything about what happened before we found you." His words were like a knife twisting in my gut, reopening old wounds and dredging up experiences I wanted to forget. "But if someone has found you, then I can help." He paused. "This would be a good time to install a security system in your home, honey. I would feel better if you did."

Security systems made my skin crawl. The idea of a third-party company watching, logging, controlling access just like when ... No, thanks. All it did was remind me of my past. I trusted myself, my aim, and my paranoia.

But looking at my dad, I felt the familiar ache in my chest. He'd already lost so much because of me, because of what had been done to me. And yet he was still here, steady, offering to shoulder a weight he didn't even fully understand. Part of me wanted to keep carrying it alone—to keep him safe in ignorance. But another part, the tired part, craved the comfort of not being the only one holding the truth anymore.

Maybe he couldn't protect me back then, but maybe now he deserved the chance to try. Even if it meant cracking open the past I'd buried so deep it still poisoned me in my sleep.

I nodded and rubbed my arms. "I know you would, and I understand. I can't tell you everything, but … you might want to sit down, Dad."

He pulled up a chair, his attention never leaving me.

"I think someone from my past has found me," I said, my voice shaking. "I can't say any more than that. I just needed you to know in case … in case anything happens to me."

His mouth opened like he was about to speak—then the kitchen phone rang, slicing the air between us.

6

———

KIP

I pulled into the alley behind Velvet Vortex, the neon lights casting a pink glow on my car. Before I climbed out, I slid my contacts over my eyes again, blinking several times until they settled in. My scuffed boots clicked on the concrete as I made my way to the back entrance of the building. As I pushed open the employee door, a blast of loud music greeted me. When Sebastian had offered me a partnership in the club, I didn't hesitate to accept. It was my escape from my troubled past. Plus, I met a lot of hot women and got laid whenever I wanted. It was a good life, and much better than what I'd left behind.

Not too long ago, we'd sunk a shit ton of money into a remodel, but it had been worth every penny. We'd quadrupled business.

Upon entering, a warm and inviting ambiance greeted customers. With a mix of wood and industrial metal elements, we'd put our own stamp on the place. The bar area featured a long, polished wooden counter with a backdrop of exposed brick, lined with a curated selection of craft spirits and local brews. Edison bulbs hung from the ceiling and provided a soft, amber glow, creating an intimate atmosphere.

The restaurant seating included cozy booths upholstered in rich, dark leather, alongside reclaimed wood tables. The walls showcased artwork from local artists, and the few potted plants added a touch of the Portland outdoors we were known for.

I popped my knuckles and blew out a sigh. I'd worked hard to leave unwanted memories in the rearview mirror, but when they'd looked me straight in the goddamn face a few days earlier, I had no choice but to deal with them head-on. Her red hair, blue eyes, and perky nose were unmistakable as she drove like a hellion out of the hospital parking garage. Terror was etched on her expression, and I wondered what she was running from. Regardless, she'd be running from me soon.

"Hey, Kip," Riley said from the bar over the music she was playing. "The Death of Peace of Mind" by Bad Omens quietly thumped through the speakers.

The restaurant and bar wouldn't open for a few hours, but we had to set up and make sure the alcohol was properly stocked.

"Hey. Are you okay covering for me soon? I'm waiting to hear from Dope when the next run for the society will be."

She folded her arms over her chest, staring at me. "You've gone the last several times. I want in on the action."

Riley had joined the Horizon Society not too long ago, and she was always asking to go on more of the missions. Maybe it was time I let her go. It would free me up to do other things, like dig into the mysterious woman's past.

"If you want to go, I'll talk to Dope. I'm fine staying behind."

Her features sparkled as she removed two of the alcohol bottles from the box and put them away on the shelf. She nodded, her long blonde ponytail swinging with her movement.

"That would be nice. I need a change of scenery anyway. Being behind the bar all the time gets old." She flashed a warm smile at me. "Besides, our work is important and being a part of something bigger than myself keeps me sane."

Riley had joined the Velvet Vortex team when she was seriously down on her luck. I watched her grow into a strong, young woman who I'd grown to respect as she pieced her life back together. Even though she never shared any details of how she'd landed on the streets, I suspected her shitty ex-boyfriend had something to do with it. Maybe he should be on our hit list. Riley was like a younger sister to me, and if he ever needed to be dealt with, I was game.

"I get it." She had no idea how much I really did. Helping women and children escape monsters was the only shot I had at redemption. But I wasn't blind to what I was—I carried the same darkness as the men we hunted. The difference was, I kept mine on a leash. I had lines I would never cross. Protecting kids was one of them. Maybe the only thing that kept me human.

I removed my phone from my back pocket and tapped out a quick text.

Me:
Riley and I are trading places on this one.

Black dots flickered as I waited for the response.

Dope:
I'll let the boss know. Riley's not been out in a while anyway. Can't have her getting rusty.

Me:
Agreed. Send her the details when you have them.

Dope responded with a thumbs-up emoji, and I shoved my cell back into my pocket.

"You're all set, Riley. Dope will reach out."

"Awesome. I can't wait. The missions are a helluva lot more rewarding than watching a bunch of drunk people." She laughed.

"No kidding. Dope thinks it's a good idea too. Plus, I have a bunch of shit to deal with."

Riley glanced at me, sympathy in her expression. "How's your mom?"

My lips pursed into a thin line. "Still a bitch and still alive. It's best if I stick close to her for now, so I appreciate you working with Dope on this one."

She picked up the empty box from the floor and plopped it on the black bar top. "I know you're not one to talk much, but if you need an ear, I'm here."

"I appreciate it. I need to work on the schedule if you're okay here?"

"Yup. I've got it under control." She grabbed the box and headed to the back, where we kept the inventory.

I'd lied to her. I had finished the schedule a few days ago, but I needed to do some research without anyone around, looking over my shoulder.

With every step down the hall to the office, my mind raced with thoughts of the mysterious woman in the car. Grateful for my close friendship with a skilled hacker, Dope, I had the means to uncover what I wanted to learn about her. With the knowledge he had imparted to me, I was ready to delve into her identity and expose any lies or secrets she may be hiding. But as I approached my computer, doubts crept in—what if I was wrong? What if this woman wasn't who I thought she was?

As I entered the dimly lit office and powered on my laptop, a sense of unease washed over me. Once I was settled in front of the desk, I connected to the dark web. It was a place of endless possibilities, both good and bad. And today, I needed it for the latter. I could find almost anything there, including some very screwed up shit about people, trafficking, drugs, murder, and more.

My first destination was the hospital staff. It was a shot in the dark, but I had a feeling the woman in the car was connected to them somehow. As I combed through countless pages, my shoulders tightened as I struggled to find anything about her.

But then, I found what I was looking for. Sacred Heart Hospital had recently hired a part-time psychiatrist from California—Holland Alder. A chill ran down my spine as I dug deeper into her credentials and experience. She seemed too perfect, almost too good to be true.

And when I thought I had hit a dead end with no photo to match her name, an additional search revealed that she also worked at an office in downtown Portland, Blaine and Kirchoff. My frustration grew as I realized she was intentionally hiding her identity. She wasn't making this easy for me, which only fueled my determination to continue.

An hour later, I had a name, occupation, home address, and more. I stared at the image in front of me. Either she had changed her name, or fate was screwing with me in a twisted and fucked up way. There had to be a mistake. Struggling to talk myself out of what I suspected, my mind raced with memories of her when we were younger. For some stupid reason, I couldn't remember exactly how old we were, though. However, the moment I saw her leaving the garage, the horror on her expression imprinted itself in my brain.

"Fuck. This is bad. Real bad," I muttered to myself, scrubbing my face with my hands as I questioned my sanity. My night terrors had haunted me for years, a toxic blend of hatred, fear, and confusion festering in my chest. One thing was certain—I had to find out if she was really the girl from my past, or if she just looked like her.

I read through the information again, trying to piece together what the articles weren't saying, but my brain kept returning to her career. "A fucking psychiatrist? How was this even possible?" If this woman was from my past, Holland wasn't her real name, so why was she using it? However, a much larger question hovered over me like a menacing storm cloud.

RILEY WASN'T PLEASED with me for leaving the club, but I

couldn't stop thinking about Holland. I needed to figure out what the hell was going on, and I was willing to risk it all.

As I approached her bungalow-style home, darkness shrouded the area. I expertly scaled her tall privacy fence and landed softly on the other side.

I crept toward the back of the house, my pulse hammering with adrenaline against my wrist. Looking around, I scanned the area for any signs of life in the eerily quiet neighborhood. The back entrance loomed ahead, taunting me with its familiarity from the countless images I had studied online. With steady fingers, I expertly picked the lock and pushed open the door, holding my breath as it gave a loud creak. Every nerve in my body was on high alert as I cautiously stepped inside, ready to confront her at any moment.

I listened intently for any noise—a TV playing, music, or voices talking—but there was only silence. With a sense of urgency, I walked into the kitchen, noting the immaculate countertops that gleamed under the moonlight filtering in through the windows.

"Who are you really, Holland Alder?"

Cautiously, I made my way through the home, noting the guest bedroom seemed untouched as did the hall bathroom. Her place lacked a personal touch, appearing as clinical as I assumed she was when she practiced her profession.

I arrived at her bedroom and hesitated before peeking inside, finding it unoccupied. The bed was neatly made with a light peach comforter and coordinating throw pillows, meticulously arranged against the large ones she slept on. My gaze wandered to a tall, dark dresser against the wall, where several picture frames caught my attention. As I moved closer, my focus settled on a photo of two young girls. The younger one seemed to be glaring at a taller girl who looked astonishingly like her, though clearly older.

I felt a twinge of confusion, caught in a tug-of-war between the comfort of the familiar picture and the unsettling anxiety that churned deep within my gut.

Is the older girl in the image the one I saw in the car? If so, then everything is true and you're a sick motherfucker.

"Do you have a sister?" I reached for the picture, examining it more closely. The resemblance of the older girl was strong enough to deepen my doubts, and I found myself truly questioning who I'd seen in the Mercedes. Was this the right girl, or could I be standing in her sister's house? The uncertainty gnawed at me, leaving me caught between my instincts and the nagging possibility that I might be mistaken.

My mind was spinning with different possibilities and names—Holland; it must be Samantha's sister's name.

I continued to examine the additional pictures, noticing the girls appeared to be around the same age as they were in the first image.

This wasn't adding up. Anger roared to life in the pit of my stomach. I'd gone through enough hell. All I needed was a goddamn yes or no about her identity. I didn't have time to deal with this shit.

The high-pitched squeak of hinges swinging open pierced the silence and reached my ears, sending a jolt of *hurry the fuck up* through me. I needed to get out of there and fast. The rhythmic, deliberate sound of approaching footsteps echoed in the hall, each step growing louder and closer, telling me that I didn't have time to get away. *Fuck!*

7

———

KIP

Growing up, I was surrounded by horror—real, visceral horror—not the kind splashed across a movie screen. It lived in my walls, my veins, my lungs. At thirteen, I was dragged into a world so warped, so vile, it rewrote my sense of reality. My uncle called it a rite of passage. To me, it was a descent—no, a free fall—into madness. And it never let go. It rewired me, taught me to spot the rot in people, the filth they hid behind fake smiles. But Holland's sins? They should've rotted in the ground with her. The woman drifting through this room wasn't supposed to exist. She was a fever dream, a cursed echo that clawed through my nights.

Nearly groaning at my bad timing, I slid into her closet and cracked the door, but only enough to see her. Just enough to breathe her in. As I scanned her room and waited, something coiled inside me. Whoever this woman really was ... she wasn't a ghost from my past—she was something else entirely. And she was hiding monsters.

Her entrance into the room was like a gust of fresh air, and she carelessly threw her purse onto the bench at the foot of her bed. She gracefully sat down and kicked off her black heels, revealing toned and shapely legs that seemed to go on for miles. That skirt didn't just hug her curves—it worshipped them.

With swift movements, her nimble fingers unbuttoned her cream silk blouse, revealing a delicate lace camisole underneath. The fabric draped over her like a second skin, accentuating every inch of her. I was entranced by her effortless beauty and confidence. *Jesus, she's beautiful.*

A rush of heat surged through me as she undressed, and I greedily soaked in every inch of her. She moved with a sensual grace, her lithe form slowly shedding layers until all that remained was a red thong that I desperately wanted to remove myself. The way the fabric hugged her hips and emphasized her curves made my cock painfully hard against my jeans. As she walked toward her bathroom, the cool air caused her pink nipples to harden and stand erect. My tongue darted over my lower lip.

She flipped on the light, and I could see her more clearly now—her long hair cascading past her shoulders, the smooth skin of her back glistening under the warm glow. Within seconds, I heard the shower turn on and steam began to swirl in the room. I couldn't remain there any longer, yet the soothing sound of water splashing on tile held me captive. Leaving wasn't an option either. The fact that she was so unaware, so exposed, while I watched from the shadows ... it lit a fire inside me.

The latch clicked softly while she opened it, and my instincts screamed at me to leave before she saw me leering. But my cock demanded more. I pushed the door wider, slow and deliberate, her shirts brushing my arm like they welcomed me there. I should've stayed hidden. The thought of her catching me—seeing me—was a high I couldn't resist.

Behind that transparent shower wall, every slick, glistening inch of her was on display. And I knew, without question, I'd found my next obsession.

A fierce hunger ripped through me, and I tore open my jeans, my cock springing free, pulsating with raw need. The grate of my lowering zipper filled the cramped space. She threw her head back, water running down the curve of her neck, streaming over her full tits.

I pictured stepping through the glass, hands spanning her waist, my fingers digging into the soft flesh as terror twisted her beautiful features. In my mind, I pressed her cheek to the tile wall, and her chin trembled. I could almost taste the humid heat of her breath fogging my skin, feel the electric spike of her nails scraping my thigh in protest. My cock twitched as I imagined shoving her to her knees with such force the grout of the tile floor would bite into her skin. She'd try to look back at me, but I'd only clench a fist, twisting her hair tighter.

My other hand slipped lower and stroked the evidence of my need, as I conjured every depraved scenario. I wanted to hear her beg for mercy, wanted to see her lip tremble, to watch tears mingle with the water on her face as I made her mine over and over.

Her jaw would ache with the force of my cock fucking her mouth. I would grasp her by the hinge of her jaw, keeping her open for me. Tongue flattened, drool slicking my shaft and running in strings down her chin to puddle on the shower floor. She would start to cry. I would make sure of it—tiny, silent tears diluted by the spray of the water, and I would watch them pour freely, a perfect blend of pain and devotion.

I would leave marks—red, sprawling handprints, teeth at the hollow of her throat, a bruise blooming across her skin. She would whimper, the sound muffled by the thick air. I would pull her head back, making her bend, making her obey. And even through the cascade of tears and denials, she would welcome every fucking second of it.

There was a depraved pleasure in her humiliation, in the knowledge that she would take exactly what I gave her—no questions, only aching, grateful obedience. I pictured the end, how I'd pull free and watch her collapse on all fours, wrists buckling while she coughed and spat and gasped for the oxygen she so desperately craved. I'd kneel next to her, my palm guiding her chin up, my thumb forcing her eyelids open to meet mine.

"Fuck, you look so good like this," I whispered, my voice ragged in the echoing tile chamber. In the fantasy, her lips would part for whatever came next—words, spit, my cock in her cunt—and she'd tremble, waiting, wanting, ruined.

I pressed my forehead to the wall and let myself pulse with the sick longing, body strung tight between the fantasy and the ache in my palm.

A sound from the shower pulled my attention back to her in time to see her bend over, her full ass tipped up in the air. A raging fire burned within me, threatening to consume every last ounce of self-control. My muscles tensed as I resisted the urge to burst out of the closet, slam her against the shower wall, and bury my cock inside her. The thought of plunging into her tight, sweet cunt until she was raw and screaming my name consumed me.

As my climax neared, my short, jagged nails clawed into the wall behind me, the cool plaster crumbling slightly beneath my urgent grasp. With a guttural growl, I erupted, thick ropes of cum painting one of her navy silk blouses. The satisfaction of marking her clothes filled me with a twisted pleasure.

I imagined her horror and fear as she discovered the stains, the shock rooting her to the spot as she clutched the soiled fabric. The thought of her gaze widening in disbelief and her lips parting in a silent scream was almost enough to bring me to the brink once again. The room spun around me as I panted, shaking from the intensity of my release and the forbidden thrill of my actions. Every nerve ending was alive and electric, my senses heightened to the point of overload. The world outside the closet faded away, and all that existed were my lust, my desire, and the echo of my ragged breaths.

Once I returned to earth, feeling the weight of reality settle back onto my shoulders, I carefully tucked myself back into my jeans and fastened them. The steady sound of the running water continued to echo softly in the background, a gentle reminder of the moment's serenity. I stepped out of the dimly lit space, the scent of freshly laundered clothes lingering in the air, and made my way toward the bathroom door. There, I peered at her from the corner, positioning myself just beyond the reach of my reflection in the mirror, observing her in a space where my presence remained unseen.

My attention remained fixed on her, unable to look away, and there was no doubt she was the same woman I had seen in the car. Yet, that fact no longer held as much importance.

Holland had become an intoxicating drug to me, coursing through my veins like a potent poison, consuming every fiber of my being. Her essence was like a dark, addictive elixir, and I was determined to possess her, regardless of the cost. My desire for her had quickly morphed into an obsession, a relentless hunger that would drive me to the ends of the earth to claim her as mine. It was merely a matter of time before I bent her will, forcing her to submit and serve me—serve her monster. Only then would I uncover the truth, even if it meant prying it from her lips with force.

Yet, the mystery remained unsolved. Who was the other girl in the photo? The question lodged itself in my skull like a splinter, impossible to ignore. Her identity held the key to a door I'd struggled to close, a chapter of my past that had haunted me for years. Once I uncovered her name, perhaps I could finally lay it all to rest and find the peace that had eluded me for so long.

I cautiously retreated from the doorway, ensuring that the sound of running water would mask my presence before she could finish her shower. Silently, I slipped into the kitchen, searching around the living room. There on the coffee table was a manila envelope. Smirking, I hurried over and picked it up. I had no idea what was inside, but she did, and that was all that mattered. The contents were a mystery to me, but she knew their importance, and that was my leverage. With a swift motion, I broke the seal and pulled out a few pages just enough to ensure they would catch her attention. I placed them on the counter by the kitchen sink in hopes she realized that someone had moved and opened the envelope.

In the meantime, whatever else I learned about her would decide the timing of my return, but next time I would be ready.

THE EVENING DRAGGED on as I worked with Riley at the bar, my mind consumed by thoughts of Holland. Memories flooded in, causing chaos and confusion as I tried to piece together what was real. Was the woman I saw truly Samantha, or could it be her sister, cousin, or some other relative in the picture with her? The uncertainty gnawed at me, making it hard to focus on anything else.

Riley nudged me in the side with her elbow. "Hey, your customer is calling you over." Her gaze narrowed at me. "Where's your head at tonight?"

I shrugged. "Sorry, I've got some shit going on."

With that, I strolled to the other end of the bar to soothe the irritated gentleman. Midforties, maybe older, dressed in a sharp navy suit that looked expensive but slightly rumpled, like he'd had a long day and a longer temper. He shoved his fingers through his slicked-back black hair, jaw tight, and his expression blazed with barely contained fury.

"I've been waiting for another drink for ten minutes," he growled.

"Sorry, man. This one is on the house." It was the best I could do to smooth over the situation. My head had been up my ass all night. It wasn't his fault.

Once I made his drink and set it in front of him, I tended to the other customers. Each time I glanced over at him, an unease snaked through me. I suspected it had nothing to do with him, but Holland. It wouldn't hurt to chat him up a little to make sure my instincts were on point, and I wasn't simply on edge about my new obsession.

"Do you need anything to eat?" I asked as I tossed the white bar towel over my shoulder. I leaned on the bar top, the snake tattoo that ran the length of my arm appeared to slither as my muscles flexed.

The tail of the snake looped through the mouth and eyes of a black skull at the top of my shoulder. A white dove perched on top of the skull, signifying life and death. My favorite tattoo, the one that sent my mother into a fucking tailspin, was the bright red devil on my upper arm. The lifelike tattoo attracted a lot of attention, but I always gave some bullshit concerning the backstory, and not the real meaning behind it.

"Another drink." He moved the empty glass toward me.

My brow arched. It would be his third, and the moment he'd sat down at the bar he'd been agitated. Adding booze to the equation never had a positive outcome. Most of the time that didn't bother me, but I had a responsibility to Riley and the other customers in here.

"Sure thing, boss." I disappeared long enough to make another whiskey and coke, but this time I added more coke than Jack Daniels. Then, I ordered a basket of fries for him.

"You need an Uber when you're ready to leave?" No way would I let someone on my watch drive drunk. Not that I gave a fuck about this guy, but my business couldn't take a hit. It may have seemed heartless, but it was my way of coping. Emotions had become a burden long ago, and I had mastered the art of putting on a facade of empathy without actually feeling anything. There were a few rare moments when I let myself care, like with my closest friends and the innocent lives we saved, but deep down I knew I was broken. As a child, I used to pray for a sign from God that I wasn't damned to an eternity of suffering for the shit I'd done. He never answered.

"I don't need some punk-ass kid telling me what to do," he muttered, staring at me as if he were itching to fight.

My brow arched as the order for his fries came up. Without a word, I collected his food and placed it in front of him. "As long as you're at my bar, you're my responsibility. We can play this two ways —you can stop being an asshole and eat something, or I can escort you outside. Your choice. I don't give a fuck what you do either way." My fingers flexed, itching for the son of a bitch to say the wrong thing.

Anger simmered to life in my gut, but I would control it until I needed to unleash it like it was a hellhound on a hunt.

The asshole shoved the basket off the bar, and the fries tumbled to the floor and on top of my boots. Our gazes connected, and I tipped my chin at him.

I approached Riley, still staring at the asshole. "I need to take this guy outside. I'll be back in a few."

"Do I need to call the cops?" she asked.

"Nah, I got it."

I slipped out from behind the bar and made my way over to him. My sore muscles from my earlier activity coiled like a spring ready to pounce. "Time's up, buddy. You're leaving now," I growled.

He turned to me with a venomous glare before launching himself off the bar stool and aiming a punch at my gut. But I was prepared for his predictable move and dodged it effortlessly. With a sly smirk, I grabbed him by the collar of his shirt and lifted him to his feet. "Bad choice, asshole."

A primal snarl escaped his lips as I dragged him toward the exit and out into the frigid night air. The cool breeze was a welcome relief against my hot and sweaty skin, fueling my adrenaline even more.

"Let me go, or I'll—"

"You'll what? I'm actually being nice since you need to sober up."

He smirked. "I'm not drunk, and you have no right to manhandle me." He struggled to free himself from my grasp.

"I'll let you go, but you have to leave. You're not welcome back here, and I better not see your ugly mug again." I released him and gave him a little shove toward the steps that led to the parking lot. "Hurry up. I don't have all night to babysit your ass, but I am going to make sure you get the hell out of here."

He huffed but descended the steps. Most of the time people didn't realize how drunk they were, and they often weaved with every step. This guy wasn't having a hard time with the stairs at all, though. Guess he was just a piece of shit with a bad attitude in search of a fight.

As we reached the dimly lit parking lot, a sudden burst of crimson sliced through the darkness. My head whipped around to catch a glimpse of what had captured my attention. My forehead creased in confusion as I looked ahead. *Holland.* What was she doing here?

She slipped her purse over her shoulder and locked the car, but it wasn't the white Mercedes I'd seen her drive yesterday. She glanced in our direction and froze.

A wicked sneer eased across the asshole's face. "My luck has just turned around."

Holland's stare rounded like a wild animal caught in the blinding glare of headlights. Without hesitation, she spun on her heel and sprinted, her purse flying off her shoulder and landing on the ground with a thud. The sound of her pounding footsteps echoed through the parking lot as she dashed toward the dense shadows of the nearby woods, fear propelling her forward. But her pursuer was hot on her trail, closing the gap with every stride, his heavy footfalls drumming mercilessly behind her.

"What the fuck is going on?" I sprinted after them as she disappeared into the dense tree line. With adrenaline coursing through my veins, I scooped up her abandoned purse and kept running, determined to catch up to them. The fear in her features was palpable—she was clearly terrified of that man. Not only did I want to find out what the hell was going on, I was itching to beat the shit out of him already. Holland was only giving me more reasons to validate my desire to punch him square in the goddamn nose.

I entered the woods, my senses alert for any sign of where they'd gone. The full, bright moon cut a path through the trees while the crisp crunching of dried leaves guided me onward, my determination growing with every step.

Out of nowhere, a bloodcurdling scream shattered the silence, causing all my muscles to tense. Ignoring any sense of self-preservation, I pushed myself even harder toward the source of the noise.

And there he was, the bastard on top of her, his weight pinning her down onto the ground.

"Did you think you could hide from me forever, you little bitch? You think changing your name to Holland would throw me off your trail?" His dark chuckle filled the air.

What? Had I been right this whole time, and she really was the girl I knew as Samantha?

"Draco, please," she begged.

Draco, huh? That name meant nothing to me—but the man had set off every alarm I had the moment he walked into Velvet Vortex. Guess my instincts still worked.

This man was a walking nightmare, but eliminating Michael at the warehouse a few days ago had summoned the savage beast inside me. My body hummed with an electrifying energy as I eagerly awaited the opportunity to confront this fucker and unleash my fury upon him.

Draco's attention was fixated on Holland, oblivious to me creeping up behind him. In a swift and calculated move, I snatched her purse strap and expertly wrapped it around his neck. With a merciless yank, I pulled him off her and tightened my grip, relishing the sight of his hands clawing at the fabric cutting off his air supply. I applied more pressure, tipping his head back. It rested against my upper thigh as his mouth opened wide with terror and he gasped, helpless against my vengeful wrath.

"Are you okay?" As I gazed at Holland, I couldn't help but wonder if she would remember me from our childhood. But as her expression remained blank, it dawned on me that she might not have recognized me at all. Our encounter had been brief ... but intense.

I was losing my fucking mind. No way could it really be Samantha. Not after I had ... This woman was probably a relative, and I owed her for what I'd done. Clearing my thoughts, I pushed those thoughts aside and focused on the present moment with Holland.

I held out my hand, not expecting her to take it. People like me didn't offer help, and people like her shouldn't trust it. But she did.

Tentatively. That small, scraped hand slipped into mine, and something twisted in my gut. I told myself it was nothing. Just control. Just leverage. But it lingered.

Her focus flitted in my direction before it locked on Draco, panic shadowing her features. "He's evil," she warned, her tone a mixture of fear and urgency. "Whatever you do, don't cross him."

I chuckled softly, unable to resist the irony. Little did she know she was giving information to the devil himself. If she understood, she might have reconsidered her choice of words.

"I've got this. Get to your car and lock the doors. I'll bring your purse to you when I'm finished here."

She nodded, apparently unwilling to argue with me. As she scurried away, I gave the leather strap another tug, then loosened it enough to allow him to breathe.

Once Holland was out of earshot, I said, "I heard what you said about her using a different name. What's her real name?" I might as well make good use of my time while I had the son of a bitch at a disadvantage.

"Fuck you," he snarled.

I leaned down closer to his ear. "Let me make this perfectly clear. If I catch you near my bar or associating with that woman again, I'll flay you to the bone, then toss you to the ravenous coyotes, all while laughing hysterically at your bad luck. I'm a sick motherfucker, and if you don't believe me, then I look forward to showing you exactly who I am."

A gentle breeze coasted through the leaves, and I waited for him to acknowledge what I'd said.

"Are you going to leave, or do I need to start the fun?" With my free hand, I reached for the cross around my neck. I slid it over my head, then tugged on the edge of the blade with my teeth.

An evil sneer tugged at the corners of my mouth as I gave in to the fierce desire to inflict pain on him. The tip of the blade grazed his cheek and down the side of his neck. "I always show up prepared for a good time."

I furrowed my brows, pretending to ponder as the grating sound of Draco's incessant whining drilled into my skull. The urge to scream and slam my fist against his head reared up inside me, but I maintained a cool facade.

I chuckled. "I'll give you one last chance to leave, but you're not going toward the parking lot. You're going to run deeper into the woods. If you even glance back at me, you can say goodbye to your eyeballs."

I removed the purse strap from around his neck and shoved him. Draco lurched forward, face-planting into the ground.

"Get up and run, you piece of shit. You've got to the count of ten." I bared my teeth and began to count, my grin curled like a serpent as I watched him scramble to his feet, panic etched on his features. With a desperate gasp, he bolted into the dark woods, the shadows swallowing him whole as the branches clawed at his fleeing form.

I had no doubt that he would foolishly try to sneak up on me, but I knew every inch of these woods.

The moon vanished behind a thick curtain of clouds, consuming every inch of the trees in darkness. All the muscles in my body tensed as my predatory instincts surged, eagerly anticipating his next move. First, I had to return to Holland and ensure he didn't show up for her again.

As soon as he was out of sight, I sprinted back to the parking lot and Holland's car.

"Open up," I demanded.

The lock clicked, and I opened the driver's side and gave Holland her purse. "Scoot over. I'm driving."

Holland scrambled over the console and into the passenger seat while I slid in behind the wheel.

"He's coming. We have to go." I pointed at him running from the tree line toward us. The stupid prick didn't behave well, but I hadn't expected him to.

Holland shook as she desperately searched for the car key in her purse. She finally managed to retrieve it, her fingers struggling to hold onto the small metal object. Without hesitation, I jammed the key into the ignition and revved the engine, tires screeching as I drove us out of the parking lot with a surge of adrenaline-fueled speed.

"He'll get the license plate." Holland's voice was thin and laced with fear. She pressed herself against the door, her shoulders rigid. She had no reason to trust me, and she was smart to be afraid.

A protective growl rumbled from my throat. No one else was allowed to fuck with her. She didn't know it yet, but she was mine. "Let him. I'll be waiting."

"Who are you?"

"I'll tell you but let me make sure he's not following us first."

She fell silent as I navigated around the club building and into the back alleyways. We didn't need to go far to find safety, and from this location I would see him coming a mile away.

Once I parked, I turned to her, searching. I hesitated, looking for any flicker of recognition, but there was nothing.

I studied her, a whirlwind of questions and thoughts consuming me like a relentless storm. If it was truly Samantha, then the way she was sitting calmly in front of me was beyond belief, and I was desperate for answers. No, I didn't simply want them—I needed them.

A simmering, deadly rage churned in my gut like sour milk on a hot day.

My mother whispered inside my head as I stared at Holland, adding salt to the open wounds. That bitch would have to wait. I shoved the thoughts back into the dark recesses of my soul and focused on finding out exactly who the woman in front of me really was.

This was the first time we'd been face-to-face, and she was even more stunning than when I'd watched her from her closet. Images of her perky tits and the curves of her toned ass while she walked to the shower flickered through my mind. She could never know that I was in her house ... or that I planned to return.

Holland's fiery red strands cascaded over her cheeks, partially hiding her features. But even through the veil of hair, her beauty was striking—porcelain skin dusted with freckles, a delicate nose, and piercing blue eyes that seemed to see right through me. As I sat there, I tried to decide if this was the same girl from my childhood. If it was, then that meant somehow, she'd survived, and I struggled to wrap my head around how. There had been so much ... blood.

I clenched my jaw, trying to suppress the urge to speak. Every fiber of my being wanted to demand answers, but I knew patience was key. Torn between pressing her for information and waiting for her to open up on her own, I fought against the onslaught of voices in my mind.

Suddenly, protectiveness for her consumed me, overshadowing any other concerns I may have had at the moment. I'd violated her space, her privacy—marked her without her knowing. But the second someone else touched her with the idea of harming her, every shred of possession in me snapped into action. She might not be mine yet, but I'd made my decision. No one else got to break her. Yet, amid this sense of duty, there lingered another issue that demanded attention. The question of who Holland really was and why she was here. Before I could even consider dealing with that shitshow, I needed to unravel another mystery.

"Who is he and what the fuck does he want with you?"

8

———

HOLLAND

The blood in my veins surged with such force that all I could hear was a deafening roar in my ears. Panic clawed at my throat, suffocating me as I frantically tried to escape the confines of the car. Each second seemed like a lifetime as I struggled to open the door and finally break free.

As I stumbled out into the night, every fiber of my being screamed for me to run, to protect myself from his potential ulterior motives. The stranger who had appeared in my driver's seat had saved me from Draco, but at what cost? In my thirty-one years of life, I'd learned that every act of kindness came with a heavy price tag. I needed to find out his intentions and rid myself of him before it was too late.

Right as I started to stand, a pair of scuffed boots appeared in my line of vision.

"I asked you a question. I can't help you if you don't talk to me."

He knelt and placed a warm palm on my waist as he took my hand in his. The heat of his touch seeped through my clothes, steadying me even as my knees trembled for reasons that had nothing to do with falling. His grip was firm but careful, as if he could break me in half or hold me together—whichever he chose. A shiver raced up my spine, betrayal from my own body, while my mind screamed that no stranger should feel this familiar. He pulled me to my feet, and I couldn't look away from him, caught between instinctive fear and something far more dangerous. A part of me thought I recognized him, but my old life was a blur—and Draco's chase had me too rattled to trust my memory.

I rubbed my arms, warding off the chill that fear brought along with it. "As I said before, he's evil. Stay away from him."

Suddenly, his presence overwhelmed my senses, searing into my brain like the fierce heat of a branding iron. His hair was meticulously styled, with a short fade on the sides seamlessly transitioning into longer, thick strands on top. The sharp lines of his chiseled jaw hinted at an untamed strength, hidden beneath the surface, lurking behind the shadows like a predator waiting to pounce.

His jeans hugged every inch of his muscular thighs and long legs, exuding an undeniable strength that was hard to ignore. My attention was drawn to the defined contours of his broad shoulders, straining against the fabric of his black T-shirt. As my gaze slid down his arm, the sinister snake tattoo seemed to whisper a warning of darkness and danger lurking inside him. But the red devil tattoo drew me in like the devil himself was summoning me.

The urge to touch him was sudden and unwelcome. I flexed my fingers, fighting the impulse to reach over and trace the edges of his tattoo with my thumb. He radiated a heat that made the air shimmer, an invisible current that grabbed me and refused to let go.

His brow arched as if I'd offered him a challenge. Completely ignoring my warning, he said, "I'm Kip, by the way. I own the Velvet Vortex."

For some reason, I had enjoyed time to myself at the restaurant. Maybe it was the warm and inviting atmosphere, but it had always made me feel safe.

"That's where I've seen you before." I licked my lips, suddenly realizing how thirsty I was.

"I'm there a lot." He placed his hands on his hips, his intense gaze assessing me as if he could easily put the puzzle pieces of who I was together. "Who is Draco?" he asked again.

I folded my arms over my chest, a clear indication that I wasn't interested in telling him about the man who had assaulted me minutes ago.

"I want to go home. Thank you for your help. I have no doubt that I wouldn't be standing in front of you if you hadn't witnessed Draco coming after me. I can handle the situation from here."

Draco's smug face flashed in my mind, and I imagined the satisfying weight of pulling the trigger. I cursed under my breath, knowing that once again he'd escaped justice. A seething rage built inside me, fueled by memories of the pain he'd caused. At that moment, I knew that a bullet to his head would be too quick, too merciful. No, he deserved to suffer just like I did ... just like ... The thought fueled my determination as I refocused on the rare gift presented to me. How many people had a second chance at life and revenge? This time, I was ready to deal with matters on my terms and make him pay for his sins.

I walked around to the driver's side of the car and climbed in. The engine purred to life, and I closed the door. Seconds later, Kip joined me and secured the passenger side.

"If you don't want my help, that's fine."

I pressed my lips into a thin line. Typically, men didn't give up so easily when they felt the need to rescue a woman in distress, but I didn't need saving.

Kip noticed me looking at him, but instead of the smugness I expected, his features held curiosity. He shifted toward me, resting his arm on the console, close enough that the heat of him bled into my skin. My pulse tripped, my body betraying me as I fought to keep my breath even.

I didn't want him to know what was happening, the way my heart thudded against my ribs as if it might jump out and fling itself at him. His scent—something clean and biting, like rain on an autumn day—

caught me off guard. I'd always considered myself immune to cliché, but here I was, melting for a man I barely knew.

The idea of asking him for help with Draco sent a shiver through me, and I found myself torn between wanting to ask and fearing the answer.

"Take me back to the club. I want to make sure that motherfucker doesn't take up space at my bar again. Something tells me he's one to push boundaries when he's told no." Kip tilted his head.

"You're not wrong." I started the car and shifted into drive. Cautiously, I eased down the alleyway. "He's mixed up with some bad people and dark shit, but something tells me you know about dark shit." I glanced at him before I focused on the road again.

He shifted forward, invading my personal space with practiced ease, and I sucked in a sharp breath with his proximity.

"I've had my share."

My brows pinched together as I imagined the possibilities. "I don't want to know. I deal with enough secrets in my profession."

He leaned back and rubbed the back of his neck. "And what's that?"

"I'm a psychiatrist."

His lips pursed into a thin line, and he remained quiet. "Tell you what, doc. I'll trade you secrets. You give me one about Draco, and I'll give you one of my own. If he comes back around, I need to be prepared. Plus, you don't know it yet, but you're going to call me if the son of a bitch shows up again."

As unattractive as it was, I full-on snorted. "I have no intention of calling you. I don't need your secrets, either." I wish it were true. There was something different about his energy. His presence was strong and commanding, which made him even more magnetic. But I'd gone down that road before with Coop, and getting involved with anyone even for a one-night stand was dangerous, especially now that Draco was back.

A prickling sensation raised the hair on my neck. Kip didn't want my secrets; he only thought he did. I was scarred and wounded beyond repair. However, I had a feeling he could be relentless, and the longer he was in the car with me, the more I wanted to know about him.

"I haven't seen Draco in seventeen years. At one time he was a friend of my family's, but he betrayed us. I crossed him, and now he's back for answers ... revenge." I'd left out the detail that Draco had known my real family, but that would fuel too many questions that I didn't want to answer.

I turned the rental car left toward the club and shot Kip a look, wondering what he was thinking. "It's your turn."

My attention bounced between him and the road while he bowed his head and removed one of his contacts before he looked at me. "I have ocular albinism, which reduces the pigmentation in the iris and retina."

My entire body flinched without my permission before I scolded myself to stay focused on the road. At least I was only driving fifteen miles an hour. Normally I was well versed in hiding my surprise, but when a large man stares at you with a white eye, it's fucking unnerving.

"Shit. I'm sorry. I shouldn't have reacted that way."

"Most people do. It's why I wear colored contacts." I caught his movement from the corner of my eye as he popped the lens back in.

I chanced a sideways look at him. "That must have been difficult growing up. Kids can be mean."

He chuckled low in his throat. "I was meaner." He pointed at another back road, then said, "Turn here. I don't want you at the front of the club in case Draco is waiting for you."

A hush fell over us as I followed his directions into the parking lot and eased to a stop in front of the employee-only entrance.

Instead of getting out of the car right away, Kip turned to me. "Give me your phone."

My forehead creased at his tone, but I rummaged through my purse until I located it. Giving it to him, I waited, scanning the area around me in case Draco was around. To my relief, I didn't see him, or anyone else for that matter.

"Call me if he shows up. That's not a polite request, either."

His phone chimed softly, breaking the mood, and I quickly realized he'd taken the liberty of texting himself from my phone to ensure he had my number. With a calm demeanor, he gave my cell back to me, his fingers brushing mine ever so slightly. I stared at the screen, my mind racing with disbelief. He had saved my life, that much was undeniable, but did that heroic act grant him the audacity to intrude into my personal space and dictate terms? As he entered my name and number into his contacts, a wave of anger surged through me like a rising tide. Who did he think he was? Yet, beneath the irritation, a flicker of something softer bloomed—gratitude. For stepping in with Draco. For his commanding presence that, for reasons I didn't want to examine too closely, made me feel … safe.

"Oh? I shouldn't argue, just do as I'm told?" I shot him a look as I flipped to my contacts and scrolled. My eyes caught the name and number he'd entered for himself, and my breath hitched. A part of me wanted to delete his information and throw my damn phone out the window in front of him, forgetting that he ever existed. He couldn't barge into my life even if he had saved me. I barked out a sarcastic laugh. "Monster? You named yourself Monster in my contacts?"

Kip's expression darkened as he leaned across the seat, his rough fingers wrapping around my throat like it belonged there, my head thumping into the back of my seat with the momentum of his actions. Whatever flicker of gratitude I'd felt vanished, burned away by the heat rolling off him and the warning in his eyes.

His handsome face was mere inches from mine, his thumb dragging slowly over the pulse point beneath my jaw, a subtle rhythm that made my breath hitch. My skin prickled under his touch, and I fought the urge to lean into it. Fought harder against the part of me that liked it.

"I am not a just or fair man, and I often decide who lives or dies. The question is, do you want me on your side, Holland?"

Goosebumps danced across my arms with his dangerous, seductive tone.

As quickly as he'd wrapped his large hand around my throat, he released me and hopped out of the car. Instead of driving off, I rubbed my neck, my skin burning from his touch, and my full attention on him as he walked away with powerful strides. I couldn't help but feel conflicted. Part of me was drawn to his dangerous and addictive energy, while another part was repelled by his unapologetic demands. What would it mean to have him on my side? Was it worth the risk?

Maybe it wouldn't hurt to have a monster on my side, but before I decided one way or another, I had to find out more about him, including what motivated him other than control.

DESPITE MY BEST EFFORTS, I couldn't shake off the racing thoughts as I drove home. My mind was caught in a never-ending match of Draco versus Kip, each taking turns hitting the ball of doubt and uncertainty back at me.

The night seemed unusually still as I pulled into my driveway, the only sound coming from the crunch of gravel beneath my tires. I sat in the car, the engine still running, mulling over my encounter with Kip. The heaviness of his proposal was overwhelming, like a dense mist that enveloped me. I didn't know how to respond. Part of me wanted to accept, to embrace the opportunity that was being presented to me. But another part was filled with doubt and fear, unsure if I was ready for such a big decision. The air inside the car was heavy and tense, clinging to me as I struggled with my warring emotions.

I stepped out of the rental, my footsteps echoing in the quiet. The moon cast an eerie glow over my surroundings, shadows dancing ominously on the walls of my house. As I reached for the doorknob, a sudden chill skated over my arms, causing me to hesitate.

Was I really considering aligning myself with a man like Kip just to protect me from Draco? A man who held the power of life and death in his hands without a second thought. Despite the danger that emanated from him, there was an undeniable allure to him, a magnetic pull I found myself drawn to. From a young age, I was forced to dance with the darkness. It was a survival instinct that had kept me alive this long. But now, with my back against the wall once again, it seemed like I would have to resort to those same desperate measures. Dread tiptoed down my spine. I couldn't help but feel torn about what I was about to do, wondering if there was any other way out of this situation.

Squaring my shoulders, I stepped inside, the familiar surroundings offering little comfort. The stillness enveloped me like an overpowering shroud, and I struggled to keep my composure.

As I made my way through the dimly lit hallway, a faint whisper echoed through the empty space, and a prickling sensation crept down the back of my neck. I froze, straining to catch any sound that would indicate I wasn't alone.

I closed and secured the door behind me, realizing that I was giving Draco too much space in my head. Still, he was cunning and evil, which meant I had to look over my shoulder with every move I made.

The sound of my Tory Burch flats echoed off the polished wood floors as I made my way to the kitchen. The warm, inviting glow of the light over the sink greeted me, but my heart froze when I saw something out of place. Cautiously, I set my purse down on the pristine white counter and turned around slowly. Fear and confusion flooded through me as I spotted an envelope with papers peeking out from the top. But I distinctly remembered leaving those documents in the living room, not the kitchen and—unopened. My pulse raced as I scrambled to think about where I'd left it in case I'd simply forgotten.

Frantically, I searched through my purse for my handgun, my breathing ragged. Doubt and fear crept into my mind as I tried to remember if I had placed the envelope near the sink or if someone had been inside my home.

I grasped the gun tightly, releasing the safety with a click, preparing to shoot at an intruder, or Draco.

With every step, my senses were on high alert as I cautiously made my way through each room, checking closets, behind doors, and even under beds. The deafening silence of my empty house only added to my growing paranoia as I desperately looked for any sign of an uninvited guest. But there was nothing, no evidence that anyone else had been there except for the misplaced documents. But that was enough, and I couldn't shake off the feeling that someone was watching me from the shadows.

I lowered the weapon and barked out a laugh. Apparently seeing Draco had stirred up all kinds of crazy emotions and fear. No one had been here, only me, which meant I'd moved the papers and simply forgotten. With a heavy work schedule, it was easy to forget where I'd put things. Hell, I'd done it a lot lately.

"Get ahold of yourself, babe. You're losing your shit, and that's not allowed." A little bit calmer, I strolled back into the kitchen and picked up the envelope. Before I stuffed the papers back inside, a lump formed in my throat as tears welled in my eyes. I swallowed as I stared at the death certificate. Today marked the anniversary. How could I have forgotten?

Desperation reared its ugly head as the unsettling truth took root deep inside me. Draco was dangerous and he would be out for revenge. Against my better judgment, I reached for my phone and messaged Kip.

Me:

I'll take you up on your offer. We can talk more Tuesday.

. . .

I CHEWED on my lower lip, waiting for his response, but I knew he was working and most likely wouldn't respond any time soon.

My phone chimed and my belly broke into flip-flops as I read the text.

MONSTER:

Good girl. I knew you'd come around. Lay low; I'll be in touch.

I STARED AT THE MESSAGE, irritated with his praise. Contrary to his belief, I wasn't a dog on command. I took a deep breath and steadied myself. The sooner I talked to Kip, the better. Even with a gun, I didn't feel safe, and that wouldn't work. I'd lived in fear most of my life, and I wasn't interested in living that way any longer. Maybe I needed a break, somewhere I was safe and could take time off from work and life, especially since Draco had found me. I could swap cars again, then drive to the cabin in the woods. I would let my parents and Autumn know I was going to take some time to recharge so they wouldn't worry about me. I could tell them about the cabin, but if I told them where I would be exactly, my mother would show up unannounced and unwelcome. It was settled. I would leave as soon as I could schedule some time off work. The sooner, the better.

Before I set my phone down, I glanced at the message to Kip once again. A little voice spoke from the corners of my mind, reminding me of a twisted promise and chilling me to the bone. "You've made your choice. But remember, when you dance with the devil, the price is always higher than you think."

9
___

KIP

I rubbed my hands against my thighs with a frenzied urgency as I watched Holland enter the building of her practice from the back door. Every fiber of my being was focused on her, the woman who had accepted my offer to deal with Draco two days ago. I'd texted her a few times, asking to meet so I could learn more about what was happening. Even though she responded, it was obvious that she was trying not to talk to me much. That had to change. What she didn't know was that not only was I following her, but while she was gone from her home yesterday, I had installed cameras with audio. Plus, I had Dope do me a solid and mess with a few of her Spotify playlists. We added some songs, deleted others, and even renamed one. When you knew a hacker as good as he was, almost nothing was impossible. It was just another subtle way to fuck with her head. Soon, she'd question her sanity like I had when I saw her again.

Watching her was hypnotizing, and I wanted to see her more and more. It wasn't about the ability to watch her dress and undress, fuck herself with a vibrator, or sing while she made dinner. There was something else about her that pulled me in her direction. It wasn't about the past. It was about the present, the future. I pushed the thoughts away because none of it mattered until I had answers.

What still bothered me was that she hadn't recognized me when I'd handled Draco, and we'd talked afterward. She looked me square in the face and had zero recollection that I was the driver of the car she almost hit when she was speeding out of the hospital garage. When I'd mentioned it to Dope, he'd reminded me that her focus had been on avoiding the crash, and brief eye contact through car windows could have been affected by a potential glare, shadows, or reflections. There was a good possibility she never saw me clearly.

I returned my attention to Holland. By the hunch of her shoulders, I suspected she could sense someone spying on her. It wasn't Draco, though. At least not that I'd seen so far—and I was actively looking for the fucking bastard.

With each glimpse of her, every subtle mannerism, my doubts about whether she was truly Samantha began to fade. But what consumed me even more were the haunting dreams that plagued me every time I shut my eyes—her beautiful appearance etched into my mind. She had become my obsession, my sole purpose, and I was rapidly losing myself to my new addiction.

The scars on my arm tingled, and I rubbed them, cursing under my breath. The heroin itch never left me, but once I had broken that dependency, I'd sworn I would never go back. If I did, it would mean they won ... and no fucking way would I let that happen.

To get my focus off the drugs, I entertained dark fantasies about wrapping my hands around my mother's neck and choking the life out of her. As much as I'd tried to talk myself into it, I needed her alive for now. When she no longer served a purpose, then I would consider taking care of her. At least she was in pain and suffering, and that gave me more peace than if she were dead. For now, anyway.

My burner phone rang, and I scooped it off the seat and answered without looking at the screen to see who it was. Only a few people had this number, so I wasn't too concerned.

"I wondered when you would give in to your calling," Death said.

I rubbed the back of my neck, not taking my attention off Holland's office building. "Yeah? Which calling is that? I have several."

Death's dark chuckle filled the phone speaker.

"Killing—and now the beautiful redhead you're tailing."

I could almost see Death's intense stare as he spoke. My forehead pinched as his words sank in. "You're following me? Why?"

"I'm not following you per se, just keeping an eye on you. I keep an eye on all of my friends."

I leaned my head back and laughed at the motherfucker. Maybe he was becoming more paranoid. He definitely had his episodes. I supposed I was on the end of his fixation this time.

"As of a week ago, we have a common enemy. From what Dope has said, he's dangerous, and now you're in his line of sight. Draco Thornfield," Death said.

I didn't think anything about him having a conversation with Dope. It was Dope's job to keep tabs on all of us, keep us out of danger, and watch our backs. He just used his hacking skills and the dark web to investigate instead of following someone.

The door opened to Holland's building, and I watched as a young man and his mother entered. Were they going to see Holland or someone else?

I cleared my throat before I spoke. "I can handle him. I did the other night. If I'd been alone with him, I would have finished the motherfucker off, but it wasn't the right time."

Death cleared his throat and paused before he said, "Do you have a plan, or do I need to help?"

Drumming my fingers on the steering wheel, I remembered what it was like to work with Death before a murder, not after.

"I'm good, but thanks for offering. You can stop tracking me now too." Honestly, I didn't want him to know that I was going to deal with Draco. This bastard was mine.

"You know how to reach me if you change your mind. And Kip ... she's already in your head, under your skin. She can make your work sloppy. I'm speaking from experience. Don't fuck up. Dope and I are around if you want to talk plans through."

My shoulders relaxed as I realized my friend was truly concerned about my safety.

"I'll reach out if I need to. I appreciate the offer." I hoped he understood to step back and let me take care of Draco my way.

"Understood. Talk later." With that, Death hung up.

I set the phone on my lap, debating whether I should be pissed that Death had been tracking me or not. He'd never given any indication that he'd watched me before, but Death didn't openly admit much unless he was concerned. Even though Dope had asked why I kept disappearing from work, I'd held him off with lame excuses ... or so I'd thought.

Over the next hour, I finally realized what I needed to do. It would take some preparation, but one thing I was clear about. I had to know who Holland really was. I had to put that piece to rest, then I'd deal with Draco. The first thing I did was slip a tracker underneath her rental car.

The dashboard clock changed to six p.m., and I started my car while I waited for Holland to leave work. Once she was on the road, and I was certain she was going home, I left her. I would have to trust that she'd be smart and stay under the radar. Plus, I could keep an eye on her anytime I wanted to.

AT ELEVEN THAT NIGHT, Holland's lights turned off except for the one over the kitchen sink. After another hour, I picked the lock on her back door and slipped inside. This time the damn hinges hadn't squeaked when I opened it, thanks to a little WD-40 that I kept in my car. I wondered if she'd noticed that or if she was too far into her head about Draco.

The lingering scent of hamburgers greeted me as I slipped inside.

I stood still for several minutes, listening for any movement. Quietly, I made my way to her bedroom and glanced in. The peach bed sheets were wrapped around her in a tangled mess. She'd clearly been tossing and turning. My attention traveled down her, my cock growing hard at the sight of her nipples pushing against the fabric of the sheet. I resisted the urge to stay with her for now. First, I needed to look for answers.

When I had visited her a few nights ago, I'd moved the manila envelope from the living room to the kitchen, not bothering to check the contents inside. However, after I'd installed the cameras, she'd fixated on the envelope with an unwavering gaze as if it held an ominous power that could unravel her world. The envelope seemed to weigh heavily on her mind, its presence looming like an unspoken threat. I suspected it might hold secrets that could shed some light on my questions.

I headed to the guest bedroom and opened the first drawer, where she'd tucked the information away. Once I'd opened it and retrieved the envelope, I sat at the end of the bed and removed the blue-and-white paper—a death certificate. Scanning the information, I searched for Samantha's name. Unfortunately, I wasn't sure if I recalled her last name. Maybe it was Blacksmith or something simi-lar. My mother had introduced her parents by their last name, but it had been so long ago that my memory was hazy. My throat tightened as I prepared myself to see her name. Who she really was, and if I had ...

My pulse pounded against my neck and sweat beaded on my forehead. Who knew a piece of paper could unnerve me so much? I scanned the name over and over again. Allison Blackwood. Frowning, I peered into the envelope and spotted several newspaper clippings. I pulled them out, scanning the first article, the obituary.

Allison Blackwood was survived by her younger sister, Samantha Blackwood, and their parents, Sam and Joy Blackwood. The celebra-tion of life would be held at Pines Baptist Church at four p.m. on October thirty-first.

A jolt of shock surged through me as I scanned the information, again and again. *Samantha!* My pulse skipped a beat, echoing my disbelief. How was she alive? What happened to her sister? It was only three days after ... after I ... I rubbed my jawline, desperately trying to fit the pieces of the puzzle together. The harder I tried to make sense of it all, the more tangled my thoughts became, leaving me with a barrage of unanswerable questions swirling in my mind like a storm.

Fury ignited like a wildfire in the pit of my stomach, burning with a relentless intensity. One way or the other, Holland would give me answers. If I was correct and she'd changed her name to Holland, that meant one thing.

This time I was more prepared than I had been the night I'd hidden in her damn closet. I reached into my back pocket and retrieved the red devil mask I had designed by the same person who had custom-made Death's masks, which meant it fit me like a second skin. I slipped it on before I left the guest room and made my way back to Holland's bedroom. I clutched the envelope in my left hand and set it down on the chair next to her dresser. Before I got answers, I wanted something else first—her.

My breath caught in my throat. Even when we'd first met, I thought she was pretty, but now ... now she was exquisite. *Mine.* And once I claimed her, she would belong to me forever. There was no turning back.

A prescription bottle on her nightstand next to a pack of birth control pills caught my attention, and I quietly picked it up. Ambien. Had she taken one? My guess was yes since I hadn't seen the bottle the other night when I'd been in her closet.

I set the pills down and waved my hand in front of her face. The rise and fall of her chest told me she was sleeping deeply. Perfect. This just made the evening more interesting. I slowly peeled the sheet from her, staring down every inch of her. Instead of her sexy little pajamas, she was naked—exposed, vulnerable. Her pink nipples hardened with the air. I continued to untangle the sheet from her body and left it in a heap at the bottom of the bed. Holland didn't even stir.

I traced a path between her breasts before I seized a nipple with a possessive grip. My tongue flicked over my lip, anticipation electrifying the air as I settled beside her on the bed. Leaning down, I captured her nipple between my teeth. Her soft cry ignited my senses, and I bit the other, savoring the intoxicating mix of pleasure and desire.

"The things I'm going to do to you, Holland," I whispered. My hand traveled with deliberate slowness down her flat stomach, a journey filled with anticipation, and slipped between her silky thighs. I spread them apart. My cock thickened as my gaze landed on her shaved pussy.

I leaned over and dragged my nose up her inner thigh, drawing in her maddening scent like a man possessed, as my cock throbbed, ready to fuck her. A wicked grin crept across my mouth as I roughly spread her pussy lips, exposing her throbbing clit. I plunged a finger into her dripping cunt, coating it in her juices before I sucked it clean, her taste driving me to the brink of insanity. Fortunately, my mask molded to my skin, allowing for the eye and mouth holes to be accessible.

Her scent invaded my senses as I worshipped her pussy. She released another soft moan, but she never stirred.

My tongue circled her clit, slow at first, then with rhythmic flicks until her thighs squeezed around my head. I pushed her legs wider. I slid two fingers inside her, crooking to find that perfect spot. She began to tense, to tremble.

I buried my face in her, grabbing her hips to keep her from writhing away, letting my teeth graze the inside of her thigh as she shivered. When I felt her tense, that quiver of orgasm approaching, I paused and looked up at her. Her expression was peaceful, dreaming, mouth half open in a silent gasp. There was a purity to it, a surrender.

I removed the cross from my neck, nearly exploding with pent-up desire. I dragged the cool metal up her inner thigh and then traced a line across her sternum, her chest heaving with the sensation. Her body was present, but her mind was lost in a haze of need and anticipation—craving the mark I was about to leave.

I pressed the end of the cross against her clit, circling it roughly before plunging it into her entrance. She gasped as I thrust it in deeper, the metal slick with her arousal. I worked it in and out, slowly at first, then faster, harder; my breath came in ragged gasps as I watched the cross disappear into her slick cunt. I was consumed, possessed, my entire being vibrating with the need to claim her, to leave her writhing and marked and mine.

She arched off the sheets, a leg thrown over my shoulder, her toes curling in the air. I let the chain fall, the cross dangling from my fist as I drove her further into the edge of her release.

Holland whimpered, a tremor passing through her as I fucked her with slow, deep strokes.

Her eyelids fluttered, the lines of sleep and waking blurring. She made a soft sound as I pressed the tip of my tongue to her clit again, flicking, then sucking, feeling her thighs clamp again around my head.

I sat up, cock aching, circled by the sweet scent of her. I took a moment to admire my work—the way her back arched for me, the way she glowed, even as she slept. While her pussy greedily took in the cross, I unbuttoned my jeans and freed my aching cock, stroking myself as the sight of her consumed me.

Shifting back, I stroked myself harder, squeezing the base. I wanted to bury myself inside her and fuck her awake, to fill her with my cum and make her beg.

But I was a patient man.

When Holland came, a soft, surprised cry escaped her lips. Her body arched like a bow, and her fingernails grazed across my shoulders, leaving a stinging sensation in their wake. I pulled the necklace free from her pussy—sliding it up her stomach, catching on the curve of one breast before laying it across her chest like a holy relic.

Holland sighed, content as her arms fell limp against the sheets. I kissed her lips, tasting the sweetness of her sleep and the last echo of her moans. With my hand tracing lazy circles over her hip, I watched the cross rise and fall on her breast as she drifted deeper into dreamless, satisfied sleep.

My cock throbbed, insistent, reminding me I wasn't done. I knelt between her trembling legs, fixated on her wet and satisfied pussy. Every nerve inside me demanded I plunge into her, but not yet. Not until she was awake and could see the monster claiming her.

Gripping my cock, I stroked with fierce, urgent tugs. Heat traveled down my spine, my balls drawing tight. Breath sawed in and out of my lungs as I licked my lips, her taste still lingering. With a guttural groan, I pressed the head of my cock to her slick entrance, her wet pussy begging to be fucked.

Teeth gritted, I tore myself away, fucking my fist instead, my focus locked onto her sprawled, vulnerable body. My hips thrust as I imagined her greedy cunt clamped around my shaft. Reaching into my jeans, I fumbled for a tissue, slapping it over my cock seconds before my orgasm exploded through me.

I paused and steadied myself before I cleaned up the mess I'd made in the tissue. Slowly, I stood and tucked myself back in my jeans and reminded myself of why I was there in the first place.

Looking around, I located a pen and a notepad on top of her dresser next to the envelope that held the death certificate. I quickly scribbled a message on the piece of paper, disguising my handwriting the best I could.

Once I was finished, I set the envelope on her bed. She would wake up tomorrow, most likely, with a sore pussy and an Ambien hangover. From what I had learned about the drug when it was prescribed for my mother, Holland wouldn't remember a thing, but when she saw the note and envelope, she would panic, thinking Draco had been in her home. It was only a matter of time before she called me for help, and I would be there for her. Little did she know, Draco had nothing on me, and I was the real monster she needed to be afraid of.

10

HOLLAND

I stretched in an attempt to ease my aching muscles. As much as I hated Ambien, I had been desperate for sleep, but even then, my nightmares followed me most of the time. Not last night, though. I dreamed of a masked man breaking into my house and fucking me with a ... My brows furrowed. A cross? I rolled my eyes at the crazy dream and slowly sat up. My pussy ached as if I'd been thoroughly fucked last night, and a flicker of panic ripped through me as I saw the envelope with the death certificate in it. I must have walked in my sleep, but then the note on top of it caught my eye. I snatched it up and read it, my pulse skyrocketing as my legs threatened to give out.

Mine.

My head snapped up and my attention traveled around the room to see if anything else was out of place. The evening was hazy after the sleeping pill, but I pieced together everything I'd done before I downed the medication. The envelope had been in my guest room. Not here. But the note was what was messing me up in the head. Who wrote it? Had someone been here again, or had I written it in my sleep? Why would I have written that note?

I stared at it, wondering if my handwriting could look that shaky and spidery.

"You're losing your fucking mind, Holland," I muttered while I tried to talk myself out of the idea that someone had been in my home. Ambien side effects could be brutal, and people had all kinds of crazy stories. That was why I hated taking it, but I also understood what happened mentally and emotionally if someone didn't sleep. I'd argued with myself about it until I gave in, but I only took half of the prescribed pill.

I stood, my thoughts spinning with the other possibility ... that Draco had broken in and touched me. My chin trembled as I fought against the tears, knowing from the way my body ached that it was a more plausible explanation. Had he left marks? I searched every inch of myself for any bruises or red marks, but I didn't find any. My pussy throbbed with the recollection of being thoroughly fucked ... and that was what messed me up most of all. Why did it feel like I'd wanted it? The ache, the arousal—it clung to me like guilt soaked in gasoline —and I didn't know whether to scream or cry.

Deep inside, I knew someone had been here. There was only one man looking for revenge, and I had to come to terms with the fact that I was no longer safe in my own home.

My attention landed on my phone as I toyed with the idea of meeting Kip and telling him more about my past with Draco. After this, I needed more protection, and I was out of options.

I picked up my phone and located his number under Monster. I tapped out a quick text message.

Me:

I need your help. Can you meet me at my office around three?

I typed out the address for him, then his response came a few minutes later.

MONSTER:

Let me check my calendar. I'll get back to you.

· · ·

AN ANNOYED HUFF slipped from my lips as I pulled up my playlist on Spotify and turned on "Killed Me" by XV Nauthiz. My chest tightened with the title, reminding me of … that was another matter for another day. I set my phone down and made my way to the shower. If Draco had touched me, I wanted to scrub every inch of my skin to remove any traces of that bastard. In the back of my mind, I realized I needed a rape kit, but if I did, they would have my DNA, and when they searched for Holland Alder, no one with that name would show up.

As I showered, I racked my brain, attempting to think of anyone else who might have been in my house, but I was coming up empty-handed. It had to be Draco or … I swallowed hard, not wanting to admit the other possibility. Seeing Draco had triggered my PTSD so badly that my hallucinations had returned, fueled by the Ambien. Was anything real from last night? If dreams were vivid enough, it was possible to feel as though I'd had sex.

"That's all it was. You were severely triggered, and your brain is playing tricks on you," I said into the running water.

Once I was clean and dried my hair, I walked to the closet and searched for the right blouse for the day at my office. I retrieved a navy one and held it up.

"What the hell is that?" I scrunched up my nose as I stared at it, trying to identify what was all over one of my favorite tops. "Dammit." I tossed it onto the floor, making a mental note to drop it off at the dry cleaners on my way to work. Maybe they could get out whatever it was. Instead, I chose a baby blue V-neck blouse and gray slacks.

Twenty minutes later, I collected my purse and laptop bag. Kip still hadn't responded, which annoyed the hell out of me. I had zero patience right now. Draco was a real threat again, and I didn't have time to play games. Maybe Kip really could help me handle that situation. *It's not like you mind seeing him again. You might not want a relationship, but he's hot as sin and a good fuck would do you some good.*

There was an undertow to the way Kip communicated, like he was always pressing for more, always testing. I hated that it worked on me. I hated more that he didn't frighten me—at least not in the way Draco did. I should have been scared of Kip. I should have told him to leave that night in my car. But all I felt was relief, as if he'd thrown a switch in my brain and every threat and every panic had drained away. His presence made even the memory of Draco seem laughable—a Chihuahua barking at a trained wolf.

I kept picturing Kip, the way the corner of his mouth twitched when he was about to say something clever, or the way he measured and nearly leveled me with his stare as if he could see the skeleton in my closet, and the shame that wrapped around it like wet sheets. The first time we'd met, he'd been so unsettlingly perceptive, pinning me down without laying a hand on me, and I'd known even then that he could be a problem. I fought it, but every cell in my body seemed to vibrate on the same wavelength as his. It was sickening and exhilarating, and I wasn't sure if I wanted to fuck him or punch him in the nose.

Irritated with the direction my thoughts had turned, I headed to my car. How could I think about him like that when I had much bigger problems to solve?

MY DAY PASSED in a blur with patients back-to-back. It was two-thirty before I had a break. At least my busy schedule had kept me focused on someone else's problems, which was a relief. I checked my phone. It was a quarter to three. I tapped the text icon and Kip's message appeared.

. . .

MONSTER:

See you at three.

MY STOMACH FLIP-FLOPPED at the idea of seeing him again—
even under shitty circumstances.

My obsession with bad boys was going to get me into trouble
again if I didn't watch it.

Needing to pee, I grabbed my purse, stepped out of my office, and
headed down the hall. The other office doors were all closed. Quiet.
Everyone must have left early.

That worked. No prying ears while I talked to Kip about my past.
I hadn't decided how much I would tell him—just enough to get his
help.

Once I relieved myself, I spent two minutes obsessively reap-
plying lip gloss and fixing my hair. I was ridiculous, but the situation
with Draco had shaken me, and some primitive part of me wanted
Kip to approve of how I kept my shit together. Or maybe I wanted
him to think I needed help. Maybe I wanted him to believe I was
breakable. I was.

I left the restroom and started toward my office.

Then everything blurred.

A flash. A man standing over my bed. His face was a smear of
shadows.

My pulse stuttered. I stumbled, pressing a hand against the wall
to steady myself.

Was it real? Or were the lingering effects of the Ambien playing
with me?

I pressed my palm to my throat and breathed through it. My body
remembered. Even if my mind didn't.

Count your steps.

I forced myself to walk, letting each step pull me out of the fear.

Back in my office, I opened the mini fridge and grabbed a yogurt
and a bottle of water—pretending everything was fine.

I was so lost in thought about the man in the mask I didn't hear the footsteps behind me.

"Well, well, well. Holland Alder, or should I call you Samantha?"

Fear clawed at my throat, the familiar voice nearly sending my adrenaline into overdrive. He shouldn't know that information.

I turned slowly, my attention meeting cold, steely blue eyes full of hate and rage.

I gulped. "What are you doing here, Cooper?" I thought I'd left the asshole behind in California. But maybe he'd never really let me go. Maybe he'd followed me all along. But if that was true ... someone must've told him where I was. There was no way he found me on his own.

He scratched his chin thoughtfully, his stare piercing through my soul. At one time, things had been good with Coop, and those were the times my brain remembered. Other times, he was downright terrifying, especially after stints of drinking and gambling. It was the main reason I moved back to Portland. I thought he might leave me alone with some distance between us. Clearly, I was wrong.

"I wanted to meet this Samantha lady. Have you seen her? She's about five foot four, red hair, gorgeous with big tits. She's a psychiatrist if I recall." He smirked. "And here I thought you were boring and stuffy. Turns out you're a dark and twisted bitch."

He closed the gap between us, his presence dominating and filling the room, suffocating me while he pressed me against the wall.

"I don't know what you're talking about." I fisted my hands in order not to shake in front of him.

He tsked and placed his fingers under my chin, roughly forcing me to look up at him.

"You need to leave. Now. I have a client on the way, and they'll be here any minute." As hard as I tried, I couldn't disguise the tremble in my command.

"Holland ... I mean Samantha, there's no need to be scared of little ol' me." He lowered his head, the tip of his nose grazing my ear. "How I've missed you."

My palms pressed against his chest, but the shove barely moved him. His laugh echoed in the small room, mocking my effort, mocking me. My pulse hammered in my throat, each beat so loud I was sure he could hear it. A cold sweat broke across the back of my neck, goosebumps rioting over my skin. My stomach clenched, threatening to betray me with a tremor, but I forced it down, locking my knees to stay steady. He wouldn't get the satisfaction of seeing me break. Not again.

I wanted to demand how he'd found me, after all the careful hiding, the new life I'd built brick by brick. But the words tangled in my throat, strangled by fear.

"You're so beautiful, Samantha." His knuckles trailed down the side of my neck, and then his thumb stroked over my throat. He pressed his hips against mine, his hard-on pushing into my stomach. At one time, I'd adored his touch, but now my stomach twisted in disgust.

"Leave. I'll scream if you don't, and my coworkers will hear and come to help. This is your final warning."

He grabbed my throat, and my skin crawled with a familiar tingle. My eyes narrowed at him as I raised my knee as hard as I could straight to his hard cock.

He grunted and dropped his hand while he stepped away and grabbed his groin. I took advantage of the space between us and moved away from him.

"You little bitch. There's no running this time."

My nostrils flared as I delivered a swift kick to his ribs. He yelped and dropped to the floor.

"Were you in my house last night?" I said through clenched teeth.

His deep chuckle raised the hair on the back of my neck.

"Wouldn't you like to know?"

I barely got the words out before his hand clamped around my ankle.

He yanked hard. My leg shot out from under me, and I hit the floor with a crack that rattled my bones. The breath whooshed from my lungs as he dragged me across the floor like I weighed nothing, and before I could scream, he was on top of me.

The weight of him was suffocating. Cold. Wrong.

I thrashed instinctively, kicking, shoving, anything to get him off, but he pinned me like it was effortless. My hands scrabbled against the floor, useless, igniting a rage in me that burned all fear to ash on my tongue.

His face hovered too close, and bile rose in the back of my throat. I couldn't look at him without my skin crawling, the need to sink my teeth into his nose overwhelming. Every inch of me recoiled, my heart pounding so hard it hurt.

This wasn't just a show of strength from Cooper. It was a threat. A reminder.

He could do whatever he wanted, and he knew it. "Listen here, Samantha." He said my name with enough venom and hate to make my plants wither.

"Fuck you." I spat in his face. Finally able to suck in some air, I screamed at the top of my lungs for help.

"Samantha," I whispered. The name sliced through me like a blade for a second time.

My blood turned to ice. Muscles locked. I peered around the corner and saw her—Holland—frozen in place. Her spine went rigid, and not even a flicker of confusion in her features. She didn't correct him. Didn't flinch. Didn't even blink. It was as if the name had struck a nerve buried so deep she forgot it existed.

"Fuck." Between her conversation and the newspaper clippings, it was all the confirmation I needed. I clenched the cross around my neck as my vision narrowed to a tunnel.

Mother lied.

The lie crashed over me in waves of heat and nausea. Everything —the obsession, the ghost, the girl in my closet—it was her.

And she didn't even remember.

I leaned against the wall and rolled up the sleeves of my navy shirt, listening as the man continued to talk. I wasn't sure how long he'd been there, and I was ready to interrupt when he called her Samantha, confirming who she was once and for all. She denied it, but between the death certificate, newspaper articles, and now this stupid fuck barging in on her—I had my answer. Unfortunately, I didn't have time to process exactly what that meant because the son of a bitch had just pinned her on the floor.

Rage burned in my chest as I squared my shoulders and stormed into her office. Before he knew what happened, I grabbed the back of his shirt and jerked him off Holland and up to his feet.

"That's no way to treat a lady, asshole." I sneered as I introduced my fist to his nose. "Besides, I think Holland ..." I paused, allowing him to wonder what I would do next. Timing was everything. "Asked you a question."

Holland scrambled to her feet, clearly shaken. "It's okay. I don't need an answer, I think I already have it." She smoothed her gray slacks and folded her arms across her chest.

"If you'll excuse me." I nodded at her as I forced Cooper out of Holland's office and down the hall. Whether he realized it or not, he helped me cover up the fact that I'd been in Holland's house last night because now she would wonder if it had been him. My cock twitched with the memory of fucking her with the cross. *Down, boy*.

Once we reached the exit door at the back of the building, I shoved him out, the bright afternoon sunshine temporarily blinding me. Cooper staggered forward until he went crashing to the unforgiving asphalt.

I knelt next to him and pulled on my necklace. The breakaway chain was strong enough to bear the weight of the weapon, but easy enough to pull away from my neck.

He barked out a laugh when he saw my crucifix. "Ohhh, are you going to pray for me now?" He held up his hands, pretending to shake with fear.

I smirked as I held the cross, then flipped out the knife blade from its hiding place. His laughter faded as he stared at the weapon.

"Nah. I don't believe in God, but I do believe in the devil." I brought the weapon to his cheek and sliced into his flesh enough to get my point across. "Stay away from Holland. I won't tell you again."

He gawked at me before he had the good sense to gulp. "Sorry, man. It was just a friendly visit. We're old ... we used to be in a relationship. You know how it goes."

I did know. Holland was mine. I would kill any motherfucker who dared to argue with me or put their hands on her. Touch her? You die.

"Do we have an understanding, or do I need to explain myself more?"

"We're good, man. Good luck though, you have no idea what you're getting yourself into. She's got a sweet pussy, but she's a real bit—"

Before he could finish his sentence, the blade slid from his cheek to the front of his throat. "Care to finish that?"

Sweat beaded across his forehead, and I stifled my laughter. I bet I could scare him so badly he'd piss his pants. I was so tempted, but I needed to return to Holland.

I stood slowly. "Get the fuck out of here. I don't want to see you again."

As he hesitated, my mind wouldn't shut up. Two different men had gone after Holland in less than a week. That wasn't coincidence. Trouble clung to her like perfume, and I needed to know why. What kind of woman drew this much danger? What the hell had she gotten herself into? My instincts screamed she was in deeper than she realized—and if I didn't keep a close watch, she'd end up broken or worse.

Cooper's attention never left me as he scrambled to his feet, then took off running down the alley.

I turned on my heel and hurried back into the building to find Holland. Even though Cooper had tucked tail and run, I wouldn't put it past him to circle back around the building and grab Holland.

My footsteps echoed through the hall as I returned to her office. The door was only cracked a few inches, and I slowly opened it. I stared at the sight in front of me as my forehead met the barrel of her gun.

"I know it was you." Her jaw clenched and her eyes widened as she glared straight through me.

Goddammit. She remembered me in her house that night. Maybe I could still play it off, use Cooper's attack to misdirect her.

I raised my hands slowly. "Holland? It's Kip. You're safe. I took care of Cooper."

She blinked several times before she gasped and lowered the gun.

"Kip. I'm sorry. I thought you were ..." She stepped back, her legs trembling beneath her.

I closed the door behind me. "Let me get you some water. Sit down." Slowly, in order not to spook her and end up with a bullet in my skull, I made my way to the mini fridge and opened it. Once I located a bottle of water, I twisted off the lid and held it out to her. "Here, drink this and take a minute. He clearly brought up some bad memories."

Her cheeks flushed as she took the water from me and placed the cold bottle against her forehead.

"Thank you." She sank onto the edge of the beige couch and took a few sips. She cleared her throat and attempted a smile. "Looks like my monster is becoming my savior."

I arched my brow, amused. "Make no mistake. I'm no savior, but I despise a man who hits women. Has he hurt you in the past?" I kept my distance and my voice low, soothing. I'd dealt with a lot of abused women in the past, and the last thing I wanted was to scare Holland.

"No. He's different. He fed on intimidation and fear, but he never ..." She frowned and shook her head. "In my line of work, I understand the patterns and lies women in an abusive situation tell themselves. It's about survival. The number of women that leave, then are hunted down and killed like animals, is staggering. Cooper has an anger problem, but his behavior today was on a new level." She tucked her hair behind her ear, looking up at me. "Honestly, he's not the one I'm scared of."

"What do you mean?" I was afraid to hope that I might finally get some answers about why she'd changed her name and how the fuck she was sitting in front of me. But I had to pace myself.

Her tongue darted across her lower lip, and I resisted the urge to entertain the idea of her mouth sliding up and down my cock. Thoughts of the previous evening returned, but I pushed them aside. This was a perfect opportunity to set Cooper up for being in her house last night. All she needed was a little encouragement to help that seed grow.

"I'm sorry. I didn't ask you over to talk about Coop." She leaned back in her seat, her body stiff and on alert. I hadn't missed that her handgun was next to her.

"I have time." I sat on the corner of her desk.

"I don't feel right about staying here. Would you be comfortable talking at my place?"

I pretended to be shocked, but the opportunity to break down her walls when I took care of Cooper had fallen into my lap.

She shook her head, grinning. "I'm sorry. That was forward. But ... why do I feel safe with you? Something about ..."

My ears pricked at her words. Did she remember me after all? Was it just taking a while to jog her memory? It had only been a fleeting moment. Glimpses of that night flashed through my mind, and I winced as the full realization began to sucker punch me in the gut. Not only was this woman Samantha, but the fact that she was sitting in front of me meant ... I hopped off the corner of her desk.

"Go home. Text me your address. I'll meet you there around six. Make sure your windows and doors are secured. I don't trust Cooper, and I sure as fuck don't trust Draco." Still, the thought of her heading out alone had my jaw locked tight, but I would have to keep an eye on the tracker under her car and the cameras in her house. She hurried down the hall as I scrambled to put the pieces together. One way or the other, I was about to find out the fucking truth, even if I had to pry it from a goddamn corpse.

12

———————

HOLLAND

On high alert for any sign of Cooper, I rushed toward my car, wobbling on my high heels. The parking lot was deserted, making it easy to spot any movement, yet an unsettling feeling gnawed at me. Maybe Kip had scared Cooper enough to keep him away, but my doubts lingered. Draco, however, was a whole different problem, one I couldn't shake off.

I reached my car as I fumbled with the keys, my mind a whirl-wind of uncertainty. As soon as I climbed in, I locked all the doors, fastened my seatbelt, and started the engine, while my thoughts still raced.

My pulse hadn't slowed since Kip had peeled out of the parking lot, leaving me alone with a head full of chaos.

Why did I feel safer with him?

The man was darkness, plain and simple. Brooding, dangerous, unreadable. His features carried a weight I recognized—maybe because I'd seen it in my own reflection too many times. A survivor's weight.

Massaging my temples, I exhaled a shuddering breath.

It should terrify me—the way he'd handled Cooper, the way he moved like violence was stitched into his bones, but instead, all I felt was ... relief.

God, what was wrong with me?

My throat tightened, a sharp sting building between my shoulder blades. Maybe it was the adrenaline. Maybe it was the loneliness catching up to me. Maybe it was the fact that when Kip stepped into that room—for the first time in years—I hadn't had to fight alone.

My fingers curled tighter around the steering wheel.

I didn't want to need him.

But right now, all I could think about was the rough gentleness in his words, the quiet way he'd sat on the edge of the desk instead of crowding me. The raw, dangerous promise in his words: that he would deal with Cooper. That he would stand between Draco and me.

A shiver rippled through me—part fear, part something else.

I squeezed my eyes shut.

This wasn't happening. I wouldn't let it.

But when I opened my eyes, my heart gave a traitorous little stutter.

Because no matter how much I tried to deny it, the feeling wasn't going away.

My phone chimed with a message, and I hesitated, my hand hovering over my purse. As much as I wanted to, I couldn't hide from the world, and I needed to check my cell. I finally fished out the phone and tapped the screen, unsure if I wanted to see whatever message awaited me.

Vivian's Dry Cleaners:
Your blouse is ready to be picked up.

I tapped out my response.

Me:
Did you figure out what the stain was?

A laughing emoji was her only response. I frowned, unsure what to make of it. Did it mean something more, or was it just a simple laugh? I would have to ask her when I got there, though part of me hesitated to know the answer.

I shifted the car into drive, easing out of the parking lot as "God's Gonna Cut You Down" by Empara Mi and dreamchild played. I couldn't understand why my playlist had taken such a twisted turn. While I appreciated a good dark playlist, it dragged me back to my past with Draco and ... the death certificate.

Ten minutes later, I arrived at the dry cleaners. I paused, looking around nervously, half expecting to catch a glimpse of something, or someone, out of place. If Cooper or Draco were tailing me, they were doing a damn good job staying out of sight.

I opened the door, the bell jingling to announce my arrival, a sound that somehow made me even more anxious.

A dark-haired, brown-eyed lady emerged from the back of the store with a mischievous smile that left me both curious and wary.

"That was fast. Are you going to wear your blouse for a hot date?" Vivian asked.

Although I'd used Vivian's dry cleaners since I'd returned to Portland, she hadn't brought up my dating or lack of one before.

"No hot date." I smiled at her.

Vivian nodded as if she knew something I didn't. She disappeared around the corner and then a minute later returned with my blouse.

"Good as new." She handed me the item.

"The stain came out?" I asked, eyeing the front of the shirt through the clear plastic bag.

"It did." Her voice held a hint of teasing. "Must've been one hell of a night."

Confused by her comment, I asked, "What was it?"

Vivian chuckled and looked around the store before she spoke. "Just making sure it's only you and me here."

Why was she acting so weird?

Vivian patted my hand as if she were congratulating me on a job well-done. "Semen."

I blanched as I felt the color drain from my cheeks. "What? No. There has to be a mistake."

"I've been doing this for fifteen years, honey. That was definitely semen."

I stood there completely dumbfounded. For seven months, I hadn't dated anyone, let alone allowed someone to invade my space so intimately. *Fuck! Fuck! Fuck!* This only confirmed my worst fears, and I couldn't blame my PTSD or Ambien any longer. Someone had been in my home last night, maybe even sooner. But who? Draco? Cooper? How long had they been in town? How long had I lived under the illusion of safety, unaware of the lurking danger? Was my house bugged? My phone? Part of me wanted to dismiss it all, but the other part couldn't shake off the paranoia.

Vivian winked and said, "At least they missed your face."

If I hadn't been in a full-blown panic, I would have laughed at Vivian's last comment.

"You know what they say, it's always the quiet ones who have the most fun." I gave her a tight-lipped grin. Or something like that. "This is my favorite blouse. Thank you so much for getting it clean."

"You bet. Have a really good evening." She laughed as I hurried out of the store.

Short, ragged breaths blasted through me as I struggled to keep calm, my mind torn between wanting to rush to my house and rip the place apart for any hint that I hadn't been alone at times and fearing what I might discover.

I barely made it out of the dry cleaners before the nausea hit.

Shit! Someone came on my top!

Vivian's words echoed in my skull. *I've been doing this for fifteen years, honey. That was definitely semen.*

My legs trembled as I put my foot on the brake and pushed the start button of the car. The blouse lay beside me on the passenger seat, like a crime scene, neatly wrapped in plastic and horror.

I don't remember what happened.

I don't remember.

A few minutes later, I was speeding down the highway as fast as the law allowed, my thoughts a chaotic jumble. I questioned everything I'd dismissed lately as stress, replaying moments I'd tortured myself with relentless doubt, obsessing over every detail, but nothing gnawed at me more than the unsettling reality of Ally's death certificate being mysteriously moved.

I gripped the wheel tighter, knuckles white, heart slamming behind my ribs like it wanted to escape me. I kept driving, but the road started to blur at the edges. Every red light pulsed like it was mocking me. Every set of headlights behind me felt like someone was following.

A chill crept up my spine as eerie music began to play in my car. "What the hell? I've never heard this song in my life." I glanced at the stereo, watching as the title scrolled across the screen: "Ring-A Ring-A Roses."

I listened, the lyrics twisting the familiar nursery rhyme into a sinister promise of finding someone, coming to get them, and stealing their last breath, leaving me questioning what was real.

Hazy memories of last night toyed with me.

A flash of metal.

The glint of a red mask.

A voice saying, *Mine*.

My thighs tensed as I remembered a mouth pressed to mine, rough touch ...

A car horn blared with a deafening wail, jolting me with a shockwave that shot through me. I veered out of the lane, gasping for air as adrenaline surged through my veins. With my heart pounding like a war drum, I skidded onto the shoulder, my hands trembling violently against the steering wheel. I swallowed over the big lump in my throat, trying to block out all the chaos.

"Jesus Christ. I'm losing my goddamn mind." Hazy images of the masked man invaded my thoughts, and my thighs clenched again. An overwhelming dark, twisted desire spread through me like wildfire. Maybe I liked being fucked and not knowing by who ... if that was what it even was. *Oh my god. What the hell is wrong with me?* Was I turned on ... by being fucked while asleep? Used? No name, no face —only rough hands and a word in the dark. I hated how my body responded to it. And I hated even more that a part of me craved it again. A part of me understood that my sexual appetite wasn't normal. Not after what I'd lived through. I thought it might settle down after healing and therapy, but apparently not. I still wanted the dark and fucked up.

"No!" I slammed my palm against the steering wheel. A part of me wanted what my mind couldn't accept. That terrified me more than anything. Dammit, I was losing my shit. My new reality was distorted ... a mess. It was only a matter of time before I slid down the slippery slope into madness after everything I'd lived through. The darkness wasn't just chasing me. It had already climbed into bed, fucked me, and whispered my name.

13

———————

HOLLAND

Flipping my turn signal on, I merged back into traffic but quickly exited to take the back roads. During rush hour, it would be faster to get home that way, but I couldn't shake the feeling that I needed to keep an eye out in case someone was tailing me.

The next twenty minutes stretched into an agonizing eternity, every second crawling by with suffocating dread, and I finally pulled into my driveway. I parked in the open, a silent plea for my neighbors to notice my presence, a precaution in case something bad was waiting for me. With my heart pounding, I chose the front entrance. It would be more likely someone would hear me if I screamed.

Once inside, I left the door open behind me. Sweat coated my palms while I removed my gun once more and took a few steps into the entryway.

I searched around the room, scanning for any signs of disturbance, but everything seemed untouched. With a quick shrug of my shoulder, I dropped my handbag, jumping as it made a loud thud on the cherry wood floor. Room by room, I conducted a search, peering under beds, into closets, and yanking back the shower curtain, my pulse racing with every unchecked corner.

"Better safe than sorry," I muttered. I lowered my arm to my side, and I flipped on the switch for the living room lights before I secured the front door. Daylight made everything look safer. But the worst kinds of evil didn't hide in the shadows—they thrived in plain sight, smiling as the world stared them in the eye.

Still on high alert, I made my way to my bedroom and set the weapon on my nightstand. I wanted to change into something more comfortable—jeans and a comfy shirt. I searched through my closet and realized I'd left the blouse in the car, but it could wait until Kip was here and could go out with me. After scouring every inch of the place, a fleeting sense of safety washed over me. But then I froze mid-motion as a chilling thought invaded my mind. I turned slowly, the hairs on the back of my neck prickling with the undeniable sensation of being watched. The soft, eerie glow of my personal computer seized my attention. I struggled to suppress the gnawing suspicion that Draco or Cooper had bugged my home with hidden cameras and tapped my phone.

My hands clenched into tight fists, a seething fury coursing through my veins like wildfire.

"Fuck you!" I yelled, sitting in front of my laptop and staring at the camera. "Funny how you were too chickenshit to visit me while I was awake and not in an Ambien-induced coma."

I closed the laptop, unsure if I was being spied on, but I was about to find out.

Over the next hour, I combed every inch from top to bottom. I unscrewed every light bulb, searched in the bottom of every lamp and behind every light switch.

I rubbed the back of my neck, seething while I stared at ten little devices that, minutes ago, had been hidden in my home—watching me. Watching me shower, dress, conduct confidential virtual sessions with some of my clients.

When the hall clock chimed, I looked away from the evidence to check the time. Shit. I'd forgotten about Kip during all the chaos. It was five-thirty, and I had to clean up before he arrived. Confident that I'd found all the cameras, I scooped them into a shoe box and shoved them in the hall closet before I hurried to my room. I shed my slacks and blouse and tossed them on the floor. I caught my reflection in the full-length mirror on the back of the door, my jaw dropping when I noticed the green and yellow bruises on the inside of my thighs.

"Shit." I moved closer and ran my fingers over the discolored marks. The bruises proved it. Even I could only wear denial as a second skin for so long.

Someone had violated me last night, but I wasn't any closer to knowing who it was. The mere thought of Draco or Cooper having taken advantage of me filled my body with revulsion. I clamped a hand over my mouth, my stomach heaving violently as I struggled to comprehend the horror of it all. I stumbled into the bathroom, barely making it in time to fling open the toilet lid before my muscles convulsed, emptying its contents with a force that left me gasping. I gripped the toilet seat, my knuckles white, fighting back the tears that threatened to spill over. My legs shook beneath me, but I forced myself to stand. I brushed my teeth and splashed cold water on my face, desperately trying to piece myself back together, but the onslaught of the last few days battered me like a relentless storm. I had to confront the truth, though which truth had tracked me down, I didn't know yet.

After several deep breaths, I dressed in jeans and a lilac top before I squared my shoulders and left the room.

I stepped into the kitchen, the chill from the tile biting at my bare feet. The sun had set without me noticing. The overhead light was off, but the moonlight filtered in through the window above the sink, pale and cold. The kind of light that made the world look haunted.

I grabbed a glass from the cabinet. My body moved, but my mind wasn't fully there—not really. I hadn't slept much lately. Not well, at least. Not since I'd woken up with a phantom touch burning into my skin.

As I turned to the sink and picked up the glass I'd left there that morning, something in the window made me go still.

My reflection stared back at me—pale, hollow-eyed, with hair tangled around my shoulders.

And behind me, a shadow.

Tall. Still.

My scream caught, strangled in my throat.

I whipped around, heart jackhammering.

Nothing.

The kitchen was empty. Quiet. Too quiet.

I waited, listening. Hoping for something—anything—that would prove I wasn't losing my damn fucking sanity. A creak. A footstep. A breath.

But there was nothing.

Except the silence pressing in.

I turned back to the window. The shadow was gone. Only my reflection remained, but something was off. My expression didn't match how I felt—my eyes were too wide, too aware, like they knew something I didn't.

I backed away from the counter, glass still in hand, my knees wobbling and threatening not to support me.

"Get it together," I whispered. "You're tired. Too damn tired."

That's when I heard it.

A whisper, so faint it barely registered.

Right behind me.

"Found you."

The words curled into the base of my spine like a cold knife. My knees buckled slightly, but I caught myself against the fridge, the glass clinking hard against its surface.

I spun around again.

Still nothing.

My lungs locked. My heart kicked into overdrive, racing so hard I thought it might explode.

I pressed my palm to my chest, forcing myself to breathe. One in. One out. One in.

Had I actually heard it?

The sound lingered in my mind, soft and male and dangerously familiar.

But there was no one here. I was alone. I'd locked every door. I always did.

Maybe it was my imagination.

Or maybe ...

Maybe it was a lingering effect of the Ambien again.

Or maybe it was the man from my dreams. The one who'd left bruises all over my body. The one I swore I left behind in the dark.

And now ... he was in my kitchen.

14

———

KIP

The house never changed. Same manicured hedges. Same pristine brick path lined with white roses, as if they could bleach the rot from the foundation.

I slammed the door to my car and stormed up the pathway, scattered dead leaves dancing across the cracked cement. Mother was always about keeping up appearances for the outside world. People saw her as a kind Christian woman who devoted her life to the greater good. I knew better. Shit had gotten even worse after my dad died. It hadn't taken me long to realize that I was born to an angel, just not the good one. And the lies she'd fed me. As much as I hated her, I'd bought them like a fish desperate for a worm on the hook.

My gaze narrowed, focused on finding answers. I sure as hell wasn't here to spend quality time with her.

Cynthia opened the front door before I could knock.

She blinked like I was a ghost, her grip tightening on the handle. "Kip. Your mother isn't—"

I didn't wait for her to finish before I slipped past her and into the kitchen. Dog wagged his tail and licked my hand. I knelt, giving him some kudos, before I stood and addressed Cynthia.

"She's in her room, right?" I said without turning around.

Cynthia hesitated. "She's not feeling well today."

"What else is new?"

My footsteps echoed through the hall like warning shots. The place was too quiet—like it was waiting for someone to die. It was.

I shoved her bedroom door open and stepped into the lion's den.

She lay propped against several king-size pillows, a silk robe the color of wine clinging to her frail body. Mother startled awake when I barged in.

"You lied to me," I said, my voice low, controlled.

She arched one perfect brow. "You'll have to be more specific."

I stalked toward her, my fingers itching to wrap around her neck and choke the life out of her.

"You lied to me," I said again, sharper this time. "Samantha." I sat on the edge of the bed and leaned over, placing an arm on each side of her, caging her in. It wasn't as if she had the strength to fight me, but I wanted to make damn sure I had her attention.

She gave a soft, disappointed sigh. "You don't scare me, Kip. Barging in here demanding answers and trying to intimidate me." She laughed. "You're playing with fire. Leave it alone."

"She's alive," I said through gritted teeth. "Why did you lie to me?"

"And?" Her gaze didn't waver. "You know what you did, Kip. Deep down, you always have."

I stepped forward, rage needling my skin. "I saw her. I touched her. She's alive and walking around fucking Portland."

"And yet here you are," she said, sneering, "still dangerous. Still spiraling. Just like you were then."

My jaw clenched as she dangled the past in front of me. I stood, my fists clenching and unclenching as I took a few steps away from her. Tingles spread through my fingers. "You fed me a bunch of fucking bullshit my entire life. Tormented me." The scars on my back pulsed with the echoes of my mother's hand, a twisted repentance for a sin I'd never committed. A mix of confusion and longing—a yearning to understand her motives and a desire to break free from the past still clung to me like a wet blanket.

"Is that what you tell yourself?" She tilted her head, the concern in her eyes so polished it almost looked real. "You think that you understand. You stupid, stupid man. I've spent my entire life trying to protect you—from yourself." She struggled to draw in a deep breath, her raspy cough filling the room. "And this is how you repay me." She leaned back on her pillows and glanced out of the window.

"She's come back to destroy you, Kip. That girl is not safe. Not for you. She's playing with you. You're nothing more than her puppet on a string. By now you're probably so obsessed with her that all you're thinking with is your dick." She stared at me, then leaned over and spat on my shoes. "Worthless."

I shoved my fingers through my hair, trying not to smother her with a fucking pillow. Would I ever be truly free from the one monster who haunted me? Even when she died, her voice was so deeply rooted in my mind, I wasn't sure.

I resisted the urge to scratch the scars on my arm. I wouldn't give the bitch the satisfaction. "She doesn't even remember me."

"That's what she wants you to believe." Mother reached for her glass of water and took a sip. "And when she twists the knife—when she finally brings it all crashing down—don't say I didn't warn you."

I narrowed my gaze at her, hate radiating off me. "You're lying again," I snarled, each word laced with venom.

"You're unstable."

The words hit harder than a slap, and my chest squeezed tight.

"You've always needed structure," she continued, trying to sit up and smoothing the silk robe across her arm. "Rules. Boundaries. Medication. You've never handled chaos well. That girl was chaos, Kip. She pulled the worst out of you and made you into a ... monster."

"She didn't—"

"She seduced you. Twisted you. She knew what she was doing. She led you to the edge and then looked surprised when you jumped."

"I never touched her like that. I—"

"You wanted her. Obsessively." Her pitch dropped lower, quieter. "Don't deny it. I read your journals. I saw the things you drew. The words you carved into your arms. You were consumed by her."

My skin turned cold. I hadn't remembered the drawings. The words. But something in her tone told me maybe she was being honest.

Or maybe she was just so convincing that I couldn't tell the difference anymore.

Was she right about Samantha? Did she remember who I was, and she was playing me? Using me to keep her safe from Draco and Cooper?

Mother reached over, grabbed her oxygen mask, and held it. "Samantha isn't up for discussion anymore. Besides, I need to talk to you about something else that's more important. I want you to meet an old friend of mine. He was close with your uncle as well."

Suspicion flowed through my veins. She rarely mentioned my uncle, Vinny, since he'd died a few years ago. He'd been my sanity in some twisted ways, taught me how to clean up after a crime scene and decimate a body. When Mother was sick of me, she would send me to help him take care of the messy aftermath.

"Why?" I bit out and crossed my arms in a futile attempt to defend myself from the damage Mother was once again causing.

"When he reached out to me, he asked if I could do him a favor. I'm on my deathbed, of course I'll grant my old friend a last wish."

"Get to the point. What's the favor he needs done?"

"You'll have to discuss it with him. He didn't give me any details. He just asked to meet you. There's no harm in that, is there?" Her eyebrow arched slightly.

Everything Mother did had an underlying reason. Out of curiosity, I asked, "What's his name and how do I get in touch with him?"

She pointed to the top of her dresser. "There's a white card with a phone number on it. Text him."

I spotted the information and picked it up. There wasn't a name, only a number. "What's his name, Mother? You need to tell me who I'm meeting, or I won't go."

She offered me a twisted smile. "You'll go, or I'll deal with Samantha myself, and you'll never get what you want."

Her words stunned me for a moment, then I marched over to her, and got in her face. "You're a fucking bitch," I growled. "You can't manipulate me with her anymore. That's over. She means nothing to me. Do with her what you want." *Now who's not telling the truth?*

She threw her head back and laughed, her petite body shaking. "Don't bother lying to me. You're obsessed with her, or you wouldn't have stomped over here demanding answers. It's starting all over again, isn't it? Are you watching her? Waiting outside her workplace? Following her?" Her smile dropped off her lips as she pinned me with a hateful glare. "You're a fucked-up mess. Nothing has changed."

"I've had enough." I tossed the card back onto her dresser. "I don't need you to find answers. See you in hell, bitch." I turned on my heel and headed to the door, then she whispered a name that made me freeze in my fucking tracks.

15

———————

HOLLAND

I wasn't sure how long I sat on the floor curled up, shaking with tears streaming down my face. My demons had finally caught up to me, and I was losing my fucking mind. I was a broken mess just pretending to lead a good life. All I wanted was to be happy … safe, but that desire had overruled my common sense. Leaving the past behind was a joke. A cruel, twisted fucking joke.

My phone chimed, and I scanned the room until I located it on my nightstand. I didn't even remember leaving it there, but I was searching for intruders and cameras when I got home. I wasn't paying attention to anything else.

I tapped the screen and frowned at the message.

Monster:
I have to cancel.

"Great," I muttered to myself. No explanation, nothing about when he could help me. Was he always this unreliable?

I pressed my palm to my forehead, struggling to steady my breath. On the brink of losing my grip on reality, there were only two people I could turn to for help—Dad and Mom. But with Cooper and Draco lurking, the fear of being tailed kept me rooted in place. Yet, if my parents were in danger, they had to be warned. Dad could protect them, and I desperately needed his help now. Torn between staying put and risking everything to reach them, I felt trapped by my indecision.

That was what phones are for. Realizing I hadn't checked my cell for any signs it was bugged, I hurried to my laptop and Googled what to look for. There weren't any indicators that I'd noticed. The battery wasn't draining faster. I wasn't hearing clicking noises or static while on calls, and the websites didn't look any different.

Satisfied my phone was safe, I sank onto the floor and leaned against my bed before I tapped the FaceTime button. Seconds later, Dad's smile lit up my screen. The soft hue of the light blue walls was a clear sign that he was in his office. When I was younger, we would spend time there, and he would let me perch on the corner of his expansive mahogany desk. The rich wood had a deep, glossy finish, and the room often smelled faintly of books and polished leather, creating a warm and inviting atmosphere.

"There she is."

"Hey, how are you and Mom doing?" I chewed on my thumbnail instead of fidgeting. I had too much pent-up fear and adrenaline to sit still for long. Especially with the upcoming conversation.

"Your mom is at book club, and I was looking through some old recipes."

"Anything good?" My mouth watered with the idea of his home-made pasta.

"Maybe some pastries? What do you think?" He looked at me over the top of his reading glasses.

"Only if I get some." I smiled at him.

His expression turned serious while he removed his glasses and set them on his desk. "Your eyes and nose are red. Have you been crying?"

I gave him a half shrug. "It was Ally's anniversary Thursday. I was so busy I almost missed it."

"I'm sorry, honey. Do you need to talk about it?"

I leaned my head back on the mattress, pausing as uncertainty washed over me before I focused on him again. "Yeah, there are some things I need to tell you. I'm torn about whether to ask you to keep them from Mom. Please, use your discretion. I trust you'll take care of her like you always do, but the weight of this is heavy." I tucked my hair behind my ear, feeling the conflict tug at my heart.

"I will. I promise. Some things your mom doesn't need to know. It doesn't serve anyone for her to work herself into a frantic, emotional mess."

I couldn't help but grin. Even when she had every justification to fall apart, she always managed to pile on extra layers of drama, turning every situation into a theatrical performance.

Clearing my throat, I started, "I love you, Dad. You've been a rock for me ever since I stumbled through the parking lot to you and Mom. I love Mom too. She took care of me, loved me even when it was difficult to put up with me. Over the years, I've considered telling you both the truth, but I was scared that since I was only thirteen you would try to find my real parents, and that couldn't happen."

Dad's expression filled with compassion. "You didn't have to say anything, Holland. When we found you and asked if we could call your parents, you were so terrified you puked ... all over your mother's shoes." His soft chuckle filled my speaker, comforting me.

"You never told me that. So many details are hazy, but others are crystal clear. I'm not even sure how I ended up at the mall. I was exhausted and most likely dehydrated, delusional at times. I just kept going until I found someone I hoped I could trust."

"The screaming nightmares were another sign that even though we were breaking the law, you were safer with us until you were ready to make a decision about your parents. We had to trust the signs and what you were able to tell us. Over time, you became like a daughter to us, and we love you as if you are our own. There wasn't a difference in our minds. I hope you know that, Holland."

Tears blurred my vision. "I do, Dad." I brought my knees up and propped the phone against my legs. "My real name is Samantha. Somehow, I had enough clarity to give you a different name, and that's how I became Holland."

He nodded. "We know. You talked in your sleep. We loved the name you chose for yourself, though, so we never brought it up."

My brows shot to my forehead with his revelation. "You never said a word to me."

"Your mom and I talked about it, and we were concerned if you realized that you were sharing information with us when you were sleeping ... well, that you would run. We didn't want to take a chance. Plus, I won't lie, it helped us understand the gravity of the situation better."

I bit down hard on my lower lip, trying to grasp the magnitude of his words. They had prioritized me, shielded me from harm. My heart pounded violently in my chest, a relentless drumbeat echoing the intensity of my emotions—gratitude, regret, grief, and a flicker of hope.

"It was my desperate attempt to stay safe while daring to carve out a new life," I confessed, inhaling a breath that trembled with my uncertainty.

"Ally, my sister, and I were just two girls. One moment we were lost in laughter and teenage chatter about boys with our friends, and the next, everything shattered—our world plunged into darkness. I only remember waking up in a cold, unforgiving cell, the bars mocking our freedom. We were either knocked out cold or drugged into submission. I can only assume it was the latter, as they forced pills down our throats daily to keep us pliant, to rob us of our will."

I didn't miss the slight wince Dad tried to hide.

"I'm not sure how much time slipped by, and for some reason our captors kept us together. Horrible things were done to us. We were sold like cattle, violated, and starved until our spirits were crushed.

We became nothing more than rag dolls, used and discarded, minute by minute in a nightmare that never seemed to end."

Dad remained silent, soaking up my words as I shared my shattered past. His eyes shimmered, wet with unshed tears, and the sight hollowed me out. Each confession seemed to carve into him, but he held the line, knuckles white against the armrest as though bracing for impact. My pain became his, and the devastation in his gaze was almost worse than reliving it. Yet he never faltered—he loved me too much to look away, too much to let me drown alone.

"I could hardly recognize Ally anymore; her once vibrant red hair had turned into lifeless strands, dull and nearly brown. Her skin sagged from her skeletal frame, and her once-bright blue eyes were now vacant and hollow. Sometimes, we didn't even realize we shared the same room, as if we were ghosts haunting one another in a dazed, drug-induced fog." I looked away, bombarded by the memories.

"But when the haze lifted, and clarity returned, Ally and I whispered our desperate plans for escape. We vowed to hide the pills in our pillows whenever we could fool them into believing we'd swallowed them. We thought that was their mistake, giving us a dirty blanket and pillow with a case on it." I paused, my heart shattering in sync with Dad's silent tears. "I'm sorry, Dad. I can stop."

He removed a tissue from the box on his desk. "No. Don't you worry about me, honey. I'll be fine. It just kills me that you and Ally lived ... Is this the first time you're telling someone what happened?"

I gasped for breath, my sobs clawing at my throat, rendering me speechless for what felt like an eternity. Even in therapy, I hadn't disclosed as much as I had to my dad. Eventually, I managed to gather my composure enough to force out the words. "Yeah. It's excruciating to talk about, but I have no choice."

"I'm here to listen as long as you need me." He nodded and encouraged me to continue.

Forcing myself to go on, I said, "There was no real way of marking time, but by our weight loss, I was thinking at least three months. Whenever I wondered if our parents were looking for us, I got sick to my stomach, like something was horribly wrong, and we were better off not seeing them again."

His head jerked back. "Do you think they were the reason you and Ally were taken?"

"Yeah," I whispered. "I don't have proof, but my gut says I don't need it. It's why I never told you about them or had you look for them."

A furious blush crept across Dad's cheeks, a sign that his blood pressure was rising. "It's a good thing I never met them, I would have made them pay for what they did to you girls." His jaw clenched with his words.

"I learned that about you really fast. You're a good man, not just when things are easy, but when it counts. Even when you have to get your hands dirty for the people you love. I needed that. Thank you." I scanned the room, grounding myself in the reality that I was at home, no longer confined within the suffocating walls of a cell. Though my body had been liberated for years, my mind remained shackled. A part of me was still imprisoned there ... haunting my dreams and occasionally manifesting as vivid hallucinations.

"Ally and I were waiting for our chance when they let both of us out of the cell at the same time. Sometimes they would sell us together to whatever man was into sisters. One guy liked us a lot and he visited often. We just had to try to get enough strength to over-power him. We hoarded what little food we were given, then tried to gauge when Mikael might visit soon. We ate as well as we could the week before, praying our plan would work and we could finally be free to start a new life together. We only dreamed of those days, and never spoke of it not happening. But the night before when we were told Mikael would be there the next day, a man that went by the name of Sal opened up our cell and drugged us. It wasn't a pill this time though, it was a needle. I remember him taking our pillows with him. Somehow, he'd learned we'd skipped pills and hid them. We'd been caught." My words trailed off, my grief consuming every part of me. "I woke up the next morning. Ally didn't. She'd died in her sleep of an overdose."

"Oh, honey. I'm so sorry. I wish I were there to hug you. We did hear you say her name, but we weren't clear on who Ally was." Dad sniffled through his tears, as mine flowed freely down my cheeks.

"I wish you were here too, but the reason I told you this is because there's a man from that place. He's found me. His name is Draco, and he's dangerous."

Dad visibly stiffened at my words. "Does he know where you are?" His tone was clipped, dangerous.

"Yes. I'm dealing with the situation, but you need to know he's out there in case he shows up at your house or if he tries to plant himself in your lives. I should have told you, but I thought he might ..."

I shook my head, furious with myself for pretending he would simply go away. "I thought he would lose interest, I guess." It wasn't the entire story, but I didn't want to tell Dad about Kip. Not yet anyway. "It's being handled, and I can't tell you any more than that."

Dad nodded slowly. "I understand. I won't ask questions about that part of it even though I want to hunt the bastard down and deal with him on my terms."

"Thank you. There's more. Cooper, my ex-boyfriend, is in town as well. He showed up at my office yesterday, and it wasn't a good visit."

"Goddammit," Dad swore. "Is he going to be a problem too? I can make some calls, Holland. I can handle *that* problem for you."

Even though Dad hadn't ever told me he had some connections, I'd put two and two together with little things he would say over the years.

"I need to take care of it, Dad. If I need you, I promise I'll let you know. For now, I want you and Mom to stay safe. I'll send you a picture of Draco. It's an older picture I found online several years ago, but he hasn't changed much."

He leaned back in his chair. "I'll need to tell your mother. I'm sorry, Holland, but she needs to be on alert."

"I understand. That's why I wanted to tell you everything now."

His shoulders tensed as he leaned forward again. "Why is Draco here? You're a grown woman with a new life. Does he want to kidnap you again?"

"I don't think so. He was always into younger ..." I couldn't finish my sentence, or I would throw up. Visions of the horrors I'd witnessed and lived through surged through me like a relentless tidal wave, clawing at the edges of my sanity, threatening to tear it apart. My palms grew slick while my chest tightened, and I gasped for air. I was torn between wanting to push through and wishing I could walk away from it all.

"I don't understand." His intense gaze never left mine.

Dad's voice tugged at me like a thread unraveling my skin. But it couldn't reach the part of me that was buried six feet under.

"I don't understand," he said again, slower this time. "Why would Draco come back after all these years?"

My body went cold. Not just fear. Recognition.

"I think ..." I struggled to speak, the words sitting on the tip of my tongue. I tried again. "He's here because of me."

Dad's spine went rigid. "What does that mean?"

I swallowed back bile.

I saw it—That night. That room. The flicker of firelight against metal. The sound of something wet hitting the floor. The way my hands wouldn't stop shaking afterward. The silence. The screaming. The silence again.

But the memory never came clean. It was a smear. A blur. A locked door in my mind that leaked blood under the frame.

"I got out," I whispered. "And I wasn't supposed to."

Dad's features blurred on the screen.

"I don't know why he waited. I don't know why he's here now. But if he's back ... it's not for forgiveness."

My fingernails dug into my palms until the skin broke.

"I think he wants to finish what they started."
Draco knew the truth—
What I did to escape.

16

KIP

The moment I slammed the car door shut and locked myself inside, I jammed the key into the ignition and revved the engine to life. Tires screeched as I tore out of Mother's driveway, leaving a haze of burning rubber in my wake. Within seconds, my fingers flew over the phone, urgently dialing Dope, who seamlessly connected me with Death.

"What's happening?" he growled.

"Yeah, dude, you never ask for a three-way convo." The sound of Dope sucking on a joint filled the car speakers.

"I can't even talk about this over the phone. We need to meet."

"Must be some serious shit, then." Death released a heavy sigh. "How about the house in the Ozarks?"

Death had secretly purchased properties nationwide under a shell corporation, and one of them was nestled deep in the heart of hillbilly country. The Ozarks had a notorious reputation for shady characters, which meant it offered a perfect refuge—isolated, rugged, and desolate. Its remoteness was a prime location for concealing illegal activities that demanded absolute secrecy.

"I'll swing by and get Dope. It's almost six here," I said.

"The plane is in Portland and ready to use. I chose to drive this trip, and I'm close enough to be there in a few hours."

My brow rose. "Hunting for deer?" The corner of my mouth curved in a smile.

"A man gets hungry." Death's chuckle filled the line.

"Dope, I'm on my way. I'll be there in thirty. Be ready." I didn't wait for them to say goodbye; I just disconnected the call. I wanted to swing by Holland's place before I grabbed Dope and headed to the airport.

For some reason, I didn't want to tip her off that I was stopping by. Since I'd canceled on her and was now headed out of town, I wanted to make sure Cooper or Draco hadn't paid her an unexpected visit before I left.

Mother's words whispered in the darkest corners of my mind, and my pulse jumped. Mother always had a way of twisting the truth. She'd give me enough to bait me, then turn the knife she'd plunged into my chest. What if it was true about Holland? What if she was lying?

I kneaded the back of my neck, feeling the tension coil and constrict my muscles like a tightening noose. My nostrils flared wide as flashbacks of Samantha assaulted me, flickering relentlessly like an old, grainy, black-and-white film reel. Mother was right—I was consumed, possessed. Samantha had been oblivious to my covert surveillance at school, unaware of the countless times I'd shadowed her every step, trailing her at a distance. Yet, that evening when she and her parents had arrived at our place ... We were young. Teens. The thoughts slammed into my chest like a freight train, leaving me gasping for air as I relived the scene.

I gripped the steering wheel with a vise-like hold as blood seemed to explode across my hands and knuckles, painting them crimson.

"Fuck. No." My nostrils flared as I attempted to dismiss the sensation. It couldn't be real. Anger started to simmer deep within me. If my mother wasn't lying, and the nightmares and hallucinations were true, then how was it possible Holland didn't remember me?

She had touched and kissed me, and then ... Beads of sweat formed on my forehead as her ghostly image swirled in my mind.

As I drove down her street, I vowed that I would get the answers I needed from her. I was fed up with being manipulated. If she thought I was messed up, I was ready to reveal exactly how fucked up I really was. I'd give her tons to unravel in her counseling sessions.

I parked in her driveway and noticed her car wasn't in the garage, which was unusual since she always parked there.

Hurrying up the walkway, I rang the doorbell.

A few seconds later, the door cracked open, the chain stretching tight against the frame. The light glinted off the handgun she pressed to her side, her eyes wide.

"Kip, I wasn't expecting you." She disappeared for a minute, then the sound of the chain sliding against the door caught my attention. Seconds later she stood in front of me.

My pulse faltered and I found myself tongue-tied like a nervous teenager at a loss for words. Her red hair cascaded down her shoulders, and she wore a loose-fitting white Whitmore College sweatshirt paired with matching shorts. Just one glance at her made me question everything I'd been mulling over during the drive. Extracting secrets, confronting her betrayal and lies, seeking vengeance—it all seemed to dissolve as soon as I saw her. *Get it together—she's playing you, manipulating you like your mother did.* With that thought, a fire burned inside me to make her pay.

She gave me a tired smile. "Hey." Holland opened the door and motioned for me to come in.

Her red swollen eyes told me she'd been crying.

"What's wrong? Did Cooper come after you again?" The hair on the back of my neck bristled as the thought of him laying a hand on her a second time pissed me the fuck off. *Get a grip, man.*

I was a man possessed. One minute, I wanted to bury myself in Holland and fuck her until the sun came up, the next, I wanted to kill anyone who touched her. *Mine.*

"I wasn't expecting you after the text." She folded her arms across her chest, pushing her gorgeous tits up. My cock sprang to life as I recalled seeing her naked and on display for me the other night as I fucked her with my cross. I stopped myself from reaching for the necklace. If she had any recollection of what I'd done to her with it, she would know it had been me the moment she saw it. Eventually, Holland would come to understand that her monster was her savior, but she could never run from me.

"Answer me." I stepped closer to her, backing her against the wall. Instead of seeing fear in her expression, I saw hunger, pain, and desperation. I reached up and dragged my knuckles down her cheek.

My fingers wrapped around her throat.

Not hard. Just enough for her to feel it. To know she was mine.

Her brow quirked but not in alarm. There was something else behind that look. Trust?

Suddenly, the room blurred, air thinned, and my ears buzzed like a hive of bees. The memory slammed into me before I could stop it.

Blood on the carpet. Her father screaming.

She was crying. A girl. Red hair soaked in redder blood.

"Why don't you remember?" I whispered.

She blinked. "What?"

She kissed me in the dark once. Or did I imagine it? I tasted copper. Her lips. A sob that wasn't mine.

I pressed closer, my body shaking. "You know who I am."

"Kip, I—"

She begged me not to let go. She screamed. I screamed louder.

"You said you'd never forget," I gritted out.

I was on my knees, my hands covered in blood, shaking—

Holland's lips parted. Her breath hitched, but she didn't pull away.

"You were there that night." I blinked hard, lost in the fog. "You saw what they did to me. To you."

Gunshots. Fire. Her mother slumped over the table. My uncle saying something I couldn't hear.

"Kip," she whispered, her voice soft, strained. "You're scaring me."

Her words snapped me out of the flashback. My hand recoiled like I'd touched fire, and I stepped away, putting distance between us.

"Fuck—Holland—"

She didn't move. Just stared at me like she finally saw the ghost inside of me.

"I can't stay. I'll have to touch base with you tomorrow. I wanted to check on you."

"Oh. Okay." She rubbed her arms as if warding off a chill. "Well, I'm fine. I haven't seen Cooper or Draco."

Her nose sounded stuffy as she talked.

"Keep your door locked," I ordered.

She didn't know it, but I would check on her through the cameras in her house while Dope and I were flying to Arkansas. If I saw anything go down, I would reach out to Riley. She'd done me a solid before when I was out of town. That was one thing about her: she'd proved herself over and over again while working at Velvet Vortex and the society. When we were risking lives and breaking laws, we had to be able to trust the other person working with us. Riley definitely had our backs.

"I will. Thanks for checking on me." Her words were full of gratitude, and I pushed down the overwhelming urge to hold her, but then Mother's words whispered at me again.

"When we have time, we need to talk."

Curiosity flickered across her pretty features. "It sounds serious."

Her soft tone went straight to my cock. "Yeah." I took a step back before I did something stupid like pin her to the wall and kiss her. I was losing my goddamn mind riding the roller coaster. I needed to jump off before I completely lost my shit. Just because she was beautiful didn't mean she wasn't dangerous.

Before I made a reckless move, I spun on my heel and stormed out the door. Dope was waiting for me at his place, and the chaos waiting for me loomed like a storm on the horizon. I had to stay laser-focused on the impending shitshow that threatened to consume everything in its path.

I PACED THE CREAKING FLOORBOARDS, my boots thudding like war drums in the cabin's silence. The place was remote —meant to keep secrets buried.

But mine were rotting through the floor.

Dope settled into the old navy recliner, its fabric faded and frayed with time. The cabin was modest, a compact sanctuary. Despite its size, it was everything we needed—hidden away from prying eyes, a safe haven that provided shelter from the world's chaos.

Death, a silent presence, leaned against the dark-paneled wall, his silhouette blending into the shadows. His arms were folded over his chest, and he watched me intently, as I wrestled with the words that hovered beyond my grasp.

Finally, I said, "Mother."

"You want us to take care of her finally?" Death asked, a hint of excitement in his tone. As far as I knew, Death had never killed a woman, but my mother wasn't human, so there was that.

I cracked a grin. "As much as I would love to be rid of her ..." I coughed into my hand as I said, "I need her alive."

Death tilted his head, eyeing me. "Do you want to fill us in? I have another bastard to fillet, so let's get on with it."

Dope snickered at Death's comment.

"I visited Mother," I said, wiping my sweat-slickened palms on my dark wash jeans.

I hesitated.

"She gave me a number. Said an old friend wanted to meet me. She didn't say who until I was halfway out the door."

I looked at the ceiling. Maybe if I didn't say it out loud, it wouldn't become real.

"She's friends with the Pied Piper."

The room dropped into silence so heavy I could feel it clawing down my throat.

Then—crack.

Death's fist slammed into the wooden wall beside him, splinters flying.

"Say that again."

I stared at him, stunned.

Death rarely lost control. He was calm. Calculated. Deadly.

Dope sat up straight. "No fucking way, man."

"She gave me his number. Told me not to keep him waiting." I swallowed. "Like he was some goddamn dentist appointment."

Death crossed the room in three strides, grabbed the collar of my shirt, and slammed me against the wall so hard the cabin shuddered. Pain shot through my spine as I swore through clenched teeth.

"Do you have any idea what you just stepped into?" he snarled.

"I didn't fucking choose this," I snapped. "He came to her. He's been in her life. In mine. Maybe for years. And I didn't even know."

Death's jaw was clenched so tight I thought his teeth might break. His gray eyes looked hollow. Haunted.

"He doesn't visit, Kip. He infects. He poisons everything he touches," he gritted out and let me go.

Dope stood, crossing over to us. "What do you think he wants?"

"To finish what he started," Death muttered. "He's not done with us. With any of us."

I couldn't breathe. My skin itched. Like I was being watched even now.

"He's already in my head," I whispered. "Isn't he?"

Death didn't answer. He didn't have to.

"Ella hasn't been the same since she met him," Dope said softly, his usual sarcasm stripped from his words. He returned to his chair and grabbed his computer. "Neither has Sebastian. The Pied Piper gets into people and spreads like a festering wound. Makes them think they're making their own choices when he's pulling the damn strings."

"But they're not," Death added. "They're dancing to his fucking song."

Dope's fingers flew across the keyboard, and we waited while he worked his magic. A few minutes later, he turned the laptop toward us, screen glowing with a grainy photo. A group of smiling faces. Faded. Chilling.

"Recognize anyone?" he asked.

I leaned in, and the blood drained from my cheeks.

"That's him," Death said, pointing. "That's definitely him."

"And that's—" I froze. "That's my *mother*."

Her arm was slung around the Pied Piper's waist like they were old friends. Like he hadn't ruined entire lives.

And beside them—

"Uncle Vinny," I whispered.

He was grinning. Alive. Happy. Standing next to a woman I didn't recognize.

"I thought he died in a car crash," Dope said.

"That's what I was told. I don't think this picture is that old, but it could have been right before he died."

I stared at the screen.

And then my stomach dropped.

"No." I shook my head in dismay.

"What?" Dope asked.

"Back row. Left." I pointed. "That's Pastor Elias Pendleton. He baptized me. I went to school with his son."

"He's part of it too?" Death growled.

"He's in every photo I've seen at my house," I said numbly. "Every family album. School functions. Sunday mass. Birthdays. Fucking everywhere. I thought it was because I was friends with his son, but this ..."

My knees nearly gave out. I braced myself against the edge of the table.

"It was all fake. All of it. My family pretended to be something that they're not."

Death stepped back as if the image physically burned him. "The Pied Piper doesn't only kill people, Kip. He builds nests. Cultivates monsters."

I focused on my mother's smile in the photo.

My voice cracked as a new reality crushed my chest. "What if I was one of them?"

No one answered.

Because no one could.

17

HOLLAND

I smoothed my gray pencil skirt before I sat in my office chair and looked out the window. My emotions had been on a crazy, unpredictable spiral and in a lame attempt to cheer myself up, I'd worn a soft pink blouse with my skirt. It hadn't worked. I was constantly looking over my shoulder for either Draco or Cooper, questioning every sound along with every person I saw walk through the parking lot. Clinically speaking, I wasn't sure I hadn't mentally split beyond repair. The PTSD and hallucinations were playing hell with me, and no matter what I did, I couldn't shake them. I shouldn't have been working, but listening to other people's problems made me feel a little better about mine.

It had been days since I'd last seen Kip. He'd texted to check if Draco or Cooper had shown up again, but he hadn't asked to meet. Still, his words looped in my head—*you know who I am.*

Did I?

The way he'd said it ... like a confession, or a threat. Like he knew something about me I didn't know about myself. For a moment, his eyes had gone distant, almost fractured, as if he were standing in two places at once.

I shifted in my chair, promising myself I'd ask him when the opportunity was right. But the waiting gnawed at me. One minute, I was furious he wasn't here like he said he would be. The next, I was replaying the press of his body, the wall at my back, the raw hunger in his voice.

When he'd pinned me against the wall, for the first time in years, I'd felt alive.

Desire pulsed through me, dark and addictive as my thoughts returned to the masked man. Was Kip into role play? Would he act out a fantasy with me? I was used to dark, rough sex. I thrived on it. Wanted it. That much I understood after what I'd lived through. It was no use trying to deny it anymore. Cooper had also fed that part of me, but he was gone, or so I hoped since I hadn't heard anything from him since Kip had tossed him out of my office the other day.

I touched my throat where Kip had wrapped his fingers around it, my pussy clenching. A flash of his scent hit me like a drug. Burnt amber. Spiced cedar. Clean and masculine—but underneath, something darker. Sinful. Familiar. But I couldn't place where I'd smelled it before. He must have used the same soap when he'd met me at the office, then dealt with Cooper.

My phone pinged and I reached over and picked it up from the side table.

Unknown:
You look so beautiful today.

My pulse skipped a few beats, and I held my breath as I stared at the screen.

Me:
Who is this?

The little gray dots danced across my screen as I waited for a reply. Since Kip was in my phone as Monster, it wasn't him.

Unknown:
How you forget me so easily, Samantha. I'll have to remind you.

Goosebumps peppered my arms. It had to be Draco or Cooper.

Me:
Who is this?

The response was almost immediate.

Unknown:
How did you do it? You were skinny, disgusting, and pathetic. Not to mention weak from nearly starving.

It was Draco!

Me:
Stop texting me and rot in hell. If you come near me again, I'll call the cops.

A laughing emoji filled my screen.

Unknown:
You do that because if I go down, you're going down with me.

The hair on the back of my neck rose, my skin prickling with the threat. He had nothing on me, and he knew it. He was just trying to scare me. It wasn't working.

Me:
You have nothing.

Unknown:

I don't need anything on you. I have other ways. Btw, your mother doesn't look anything like you. Oh, wait. She's not your real mom.

Despite my best efforts, my entire body shook with the knowledge that he was watching my parents. I needed to get them out of here and to safety. Now.

I refused to give him the satisfaction of an answer. Draco was deranged and twisted. It wouldn't matter what I said, he would laugh it off.

I brought up my contacts, and instead of messaging, I tapped the call button. Gripping the phone so tightly my fingers turned white, I raised the cell to my ear as it began to ring. Four rings later, I was greeted with a generic voicemail. I disconnected the call and slapped my hand over my mouth, muffling my scream. Why the fuck had Kip offered to help when he wasn't available?

"Fine, I'll deal with matters on my own." When had I started depending on others to take care of my messes anyway? I was an adult, a grown-ass woman. I'd dealt with Draco and Cooper before. I could handle it.

Scrolling through my phone contacts, I located the information for the luxury getaway I'd visited a few times. Celebrities visited often, so the security was tight, and the place was private. No one ever used their real name, and although they had group activities, it was also a retreat with pools, drinks, amazing food, massages, facials, and so on. It was a slice of heaven.

I made a quick call to see if they had availability for my parents, then booked their stay for a few weeks. The next step was to figure out how to get them there without Draco realizing what we were up to. Maybe Dad could help with that.

With a quick tap of the screen, I pulled up FaceTime and called Dad. Seconds later, he answered, all smiles as he moved around the kitchen.

"Hi, hon."

"Hey. Are you alone?"

His forehead creased as he glanced around the room. "Let me get my AirPods before you continue. Your mom is home."

I waited as he located the white case, then popped one earbud in. "I'm ready."

"You and Mom are going to a private resort and spa for two weeks. Someone has eyes on you. Do you understand what I'm saying?"

Dad's forehead creased. "Yes. I'm assuming from what you're saying it's not the ex."

"Yeah. Worse. I'm so sorry. The least I can do is keep you two safe and relaxed. You'll probably see some celebs there, so that might be fun. Your food, room, massages, and everything you can think of is available and paid for. Think of it as my apology."

Dad gave me a pointed look. "You're not responsible for what he's doing. I appreciate the effort and that you're on top of it."

"I figured Mom wouldn't really need to know why you were going, either. Only that you were surprising her."

Dad pondered that for a moment. "I can work with that without raising suspicion."

That was a relief. I wanted Mom to have fun, not be terrified the entire time she was there. After giving Dad the information and Draco's picture, he agreed to not let his guard down.

I chewed my thumbnail until Dad gave me a disapproving look. He must have realized it was down to the nub. "There's one detail I don't have figured out. I was hoping you could help."

"Hang on, Holland. I hear your mom coming."

Seconds later, Mom appeared on the screen. "Take your earbud out, so I can say hi."

Dad did as Mom requested.

"Hi, Mom. How are you doing?" I gave her a thousand-watt smile, doing my best to hide the real reason I'd called.

"Good. I didn't know you were calling, or I would have put my book down."

"It's okay. Dad and I were just talking about you, actually. Dad. Wanna tell her?"

"Tell me what? What's going on?" she asked, her gaze bouncing between us.

"It's good, Mom." I wanted to diminish any drama before she worked herself into a full-blown panic.

Dad cleared his throat. "It was a surprise but go pack, Evelyn. I'm taking you to a fancy resort for a few weeks. Holland helped me pick it out. She's been there before. Celebrities stay all the time. We'll lounge by the pool, eat amazing food, and get massages every day if you want."

Mom's expression lit up like a kid with a bucket of candy on Halloween. "Are you serious?"

"Yeah, go have fun and relax, Mom. Dad was asking me to take care of the plants while you're gone. Since he hadn't told you yet, he wanted to make sure everything was taken care of. Go pack!"

"Oh! Oh! This is so exciting. Thank you!" She turned to my dad and kissed his mouth.

My heartfelt laugh filled the line. At least there was something positive in a dark situation.

"Have fun, Mom. I'll talk to you when you get back." I blew her a kiss, loving seeing her so happy.

"Love you, hon. Thanks for taking care of the house while we're gone." With that, she hurried off.

Dad replaced his earbud. "That went well. Now, what's the other issue?"

"I need to figure out how to get you there safely since there's an ... obstacle."

His brows knitted together, and I could almost see the wheels in his head turning. "I have a friend that might be able to help us. They could be a decoy, allowing us to leave undetected."

I sucked in a breath. "What if they got hurt?" My voice wobbled with my question. I couldn't handle being responsible for anyone else. It was bad enough that my parents were caught in the middle.

Dad chuckled. "Don't worry about that. They can take care of themselves." He winked. "Let me make a call, then I'll message that your mom and I are going shopping this afternoon and ask if you want to meet for lunch. Politely decline. Then you'll know we're on the way out the door once the decoy has left. I'll let you know when we're at the resort safe and sound."

Shit. I hoped like hell the plan would work. It had to. I couldn't stand the thought of anything bad happening to my parents.

"Okay. I love you. Have a good time, Dad."

"We will, but I want you to be diligent, Holland. Stay alert and keep Homer close by at all times."

Homer was the name I'd given my gun, but I rarely called it that unless I had to in order not to scare people or if there was a possibility someone might be listening in.

"By the way, Holland, I won't let you pay for the resort. I love and appreciate it, but that's a lot of money. I'll take care of it. You invest or save ... or hell, book some time there for yourself."

I raised a brow at him. "We'll discuss it when all of this is over and you're home. Be safe."

"You too. I'll keep you updated."

"Okay. Bye." I blew him a kiss, then disconnected the call.

I glanced at the clock. It was almost one, which gave everyone plenty of daylight. I didn't think Draco would strike until it was dark.

After I checked my calendar for additional appointments, I tried to focus on notes for my next client. An hour later, Dad's message came in inviting me to lunch. I breathed a sigh of relief and politely declined. Once they checked into the resort in Idaho, I would feel a little better ... maybe. The drive was a few hours long, but mostly on the interstate, so plenty of people would be around if something happened.

Now? I had to wait to see if Draco realized what was happening or if my parents would be safe from the son of a bitch.

18

———

KIP

"I have to go. I have an ... appointment," Death said. "But you two keep digging into Kip's mother and uncle and how they're associated with the Pied Piper. I'll talk to Ella and see if I can get her to fucking talk."

"She's scared, Death. Whatever the Pied Piper said to her grabbed her by the fucking throat," I said, remembering how pale she'd been after the conversation with him a few months ago. We had someone who the Pied Piper wanted and demanded him back. In exchange, he allowed us all to live. Not many people rattled any of us, but the Pied Piper was in a league of his own. Powerful. Smart. Deadly.

"And right, there's the problem. I'm the only man allowed to grab her by the throat. When I find out what he said to her, the mother-fucker will never see me coming. Soon, we'll be rid of him once and for all."

Death never made promises he couldn't keep. Not intentionally anyway, and I worried that this might be one of them.

"I'll be in touch." He tipped his chin at us before he turned around and left the cabin, the door slamming closed behind him.

Dope blew out a huge breath. "Fuck. Me." He removed the rolled-up joint from behind his ear and flipped it between his fingers, but he didn't light up.

"No shit. How the hell are my mother and uncle involved with the Pied Piper?"

"Shit, dude. Even the pastor? That's some fucked-up shit, right?"

I shrugged. "Look at the people who protect Death; I shouldn't be surprised by the pastor of the church."

Dope stretched his legs out in front of him. "You never mentioned your pastor when we were kids. I mean, as you got older, you wore your cross, but I know it's a blade, so it's not like it's for religious reasons."

I snorted. "I don't believe in God. Never have."

"Why? I mean, after today, I have questions. You shared some shit about your childhood, but you've been secretive over the years. Now we learn your family is associated with PP. You need to start telling Death and me what's going on, so we know how to play the motherfucker's game."

I bowed my head, the weight of the past clawing at the scars on my back and arms. "You guys know Mother and I aren't close."

"I remember that because you were gone a lot, even during school. She always had you helping her with a new church somewhere or Bible camp."

A low, angry chuckle escaped me. Over the years, whenever my friends had asked about my family and why I never spoke of them, I had rehearsed what I would say when the time came—when I could no longer keep the truth buried, when it became dangerous for them not to know. But even then, I couldn't give them everything. Maybe one day. But not that day. For the time being, I gave them enough to keep us one step ahead of the Pied Piper.

"You guys know Uncle Vinny taught me how to clean. When Mother got sick of seeing my face, she'd send me out on jobs with him. That's part of why I was gone. Between that and all her church trips, we spent a lot of time at one of our houses outside Portland. A lot of shit went down there."

Dope's eyes narrowed while he pursed his lips together in a tight line. "Those skills are invaluable, but I have to admit that learning that trade as a teenager is pretty fucked up. I mean, those years shape us. Look at you now. You're cleaning and covering up shit for a serial killer."

The muscles in my jaw jumped. "It does something to your brain ... breaking down bodies and cleaning blood and bone. Not much fazes me. For years, I was afraid I couldn't feel anything like a normal person. Hell, I didn't want to." My voice was low, haunted.

"The heroin? Is that how it started?" Dope's tone was free of judgment, and if we had to have this particular conversation, I appreciated his support.

"Yeah. I don't even remember the first time. I lived in a haze, wondering what was real or not."

"Is that another reason you'd disappear when we were in school?"

I rubbed the back of my neck, the phantom pain in my arm toying with me. "At first, it was here and there at night or on the weekend when I didn't have to be around people, then it got worse. Honestly, there's not a lot that I remember during those days." *Except her.*

"Death and I wondered why you always wore long-sleeved shirts and never went shirtless even when it was a hundred fucking degrees."

"Just hiding the scars." My skin jumped with anxiety. There were a few other things I could finally tell Dope. "Mother is a religious fanatic. There were times that she forced me to repent for whatever sin she thought I committed. Other times, I disappeared it was to recover from ... repenting."

Dope grimaced. "Okay. That's weird shit."

"Her idea of that wasn't getting on your knees and praying for forgiveness. I mean, part of it was, but she pushed the boundaries of everything she ever did." I prepared for Dope's reaction and then I tugged on the black long-sleeved T-shirt and pulled it over my head.

"This is what I mean." I stared at Dope for a moment before I slowly turned around and showed him my back.

"Jesus. Fucking. Christ. No pun intended, but what the fuck?"

I winced. At times Dope had no good way with words and blurted shit out. And here we were.

Irritated I'd shared that with him, I tugged my shirt back on. "The only reason you know about this is because of who she's friends with. Are we clear? We never talk about it again," I growled.

Dope raised his hands in surrender. "Fine, but I have questions first. Give me that, man. Your back is scarred like you were in a fire, but not as raised. Did she burn you?" Dope swallowed hard and sank back into his seat.

"Nope. She carved me up with a knife. At one time, the cuts were angel wings, like she thought she could redeem my soul after sending me out to clean crime scenes."

"That's some warped shit," he muttered. "We had no idea you were going through that. Why didn't you say anything? We could have helped. Death could have taken care of her back then. Fuck! No wonder you hate her so much. How do you take care of her now? I'm surprised you haven't fucking killed her. She's dying anyway. You wouldn't even have to feel guilty."

I glanced away from him, shame ripping through my chest. "Because she was how I scored. At first, she gave me opiates for the pain after she carved me up, then when I was addicted to them, she used them to control me. It was her way to ensure I never told anyone what she was doing."

Dope's jaw hit the floor. "Fucking hell, this keeps getting worse. Your own mother got you hooked on heroin?" He slapped his hands over his face and shook his head.

"She's evil. There's no other way to say it. She manipulated me, controlled me, made sure I helped my uncle and kept silent about the work."

"And what did your uncle have to say about her carving you up?

He knew, right? Those summers you were gone as soon as school was out ...” His expression twisted with pain.

“He never stopped her. Now you know.” *Just not everything.*

Dope stood and walked over to me. Before I realized what he was doing, he threw his arms around me in a big hug. “I’m sorry for letting you down, Kip. We were kids so we didn’t know to look for signs of abuse and shit. That’s no excuse. I’ll do better by you. You’re my brother. You know I’ll kill for you ... even give my life to save yours.”

His words sank in, and I gave him a brotherly hug back. “Same for you, man. You couldn’t have known. We were young, and she was a master at covering it up. So was I.”

Dope released me and stepped back. “Okay.” He rolled his shoulders and then popped his neck. “I need to think in order to figure out how I’m going to look for the connection between the Pied Piper and your mother and uncle ... fuckin’ A, man, even the pastor. That doesn’t make any damn sense.”

“I’ll try to think of anything I can remember, but those years are pretty hazy.”

“I need to get back home with all my equipment. I have a feeling this shit is going to be the challenge of my life.” Dope grinned. “I’m ready to take that bitch down. Should we make her suffer more or?”

I gave him a lopsided grin. “She’s dying and struggling to breathe. If we kill her now, we’ll be doing her a favor.”

“Yeah. No. Not fucking helping her.”

Dope collected his computer and shoved it into the laptop bag, and we headed back to the airport where the plane was waiting for us. Since Dope was deep in research, I turned the stereo on and “my truth’s a lie” by Psylosia played while my brain spun out like a tornado with thoughts of Mother, Uncle Vinny, the Pied Piper, and Holland. *Holland.*

My dick sprang to life with the recollection of pinning her to the wall, but the goddamn flashbacks had taken over, and for a moment, I hadn’t been able to distinguish between the past and present. How could she not remember me? Maybe she was the same, her past hazy due to the hell we'd lived through.

Mother's words stirred inside my gut, followed by a rush of rage. Anger at Mother and uncle, but even I knew that Mother's words were always laced with truth and lies. The problem was which ones? I was finished letting her play me like a goddamn fiddle. I was going to make sure this shit was going to end ... tonight.

19

———

KIP

By the time we touched down, I was caught in a whirlwind of emotions, teetering on the edge of anger and uncertainty. Lies seemed to weave through every facet of my life—my family, Holland, and perhaps even the pastor of the church. Was there more to the story? How much did he really know about me, and was there a past connection with my family that had faded over time, or was he still very much a part of it? And where exactly did Holland factor into all of this? I was desperate for answers but unsure if I was ready to confront them.

After stepping off the plane, I climbed into my car and grabbed my cell from my back pocket. Even though I wanted to check the cameras at Holland's place on the flight back, I couldn't risk Dope being nosy and learning that I was watching her. Hell, I hadn't even mentioned her to the guys. Until I had answers, there was no reason to. With a few taps on my screen, I opened the app for the live video. Nothing.

"What the fuck?" I muttered, opening and closing the app again. Frustrated, I deleted the app and reloaded it again, but still nothing. "Goddammit." I slumped against the car seat while I realized that she'd most likely discovered the cameras I'd planted. There was a small possibility that Draco had bugged her place and removed them too. However it played out, it wasn't good. First, I couldn't see her anytime I wanted to. Second, I had no damn clue if Cooper or Draco showed up and hurt her.

A fierce blaze ignited within me as I jammed the key into the ignition and roared toward her house. It wasn't late enough for her to be asleep, so unless she wasn't there, I had to devise a way to slip into her place undetected.

And when I did, there would be hell to pay.

An idea formed in my thoughts.

"Hey, Siri, call Ryan Steele." Seconds later, his phone rang through the speakers.

"Hey, man," Ryan answered. "What's up?"

Ryan and I had worked together in the past and had become good friends. He was a Portland cop, but he played both sides of the fence at times when it was needed.

"I need a diversion."

"Yeah? What's up?"

I could almost hear him smile through the phone.

"I need to sneak inside a house, but she might be there. Are you able to help me with a diversion to draw her outside? She's got some bad company following her, so I don't want her alone."

"Lady Luck is on your side. I'm off work tonight, but it wouldn't be a problem to knock on her door and report suspicious activity in the area. Does she have an alley or anything behind her home?"

"Yeah. I'll need to come through that way, so have her walk outside in front. I only need five minutes or so. Probably less, but just to be safe."

"I'll tell her we're looking into a break-in and ask if she saw anything, ask her to stay vigilant and keep an eye out for potential witnesses," he said.

A wicked grin eased across my features. "I appreciate it. I owe you one."

The line grew silent, and I wasn't surprised when he asked, "How's Cami? Have you seen her?"

"No, not lately. From what Ella has said, she's doing good, but still struggling to get past your breakup." Ella and Cami were best friends and discussed everything. There were no secrets between them, including Cami's feelings about Ryan. But he'd fucked up, and some lines you couldn't cross without doing irreparable damage. I was starting to think this was one of those times.

"Good," he muttered. "I want her to hurt as much as I am."

"We all wish you two would work things out. You're miserable without each other." I flipped on my turn signal and then turned onto Holland's street. She wouldn't recognize my Mustang since she'd only seen me drive my BMW. Having a few different cars came in handy when trying to stay under the radar with the cops.

"Okay, I'm in her neighborhood. Her car is in the driveway, so let me know your ETA to show up." I rattled off the address, and Ryan said he'd be there in half an hour. We hung up, and I drove around to the back of her place and parked at the end of the alley, watching to see if there was any activity from Draco or Cooper. As far as I could tell, it was quiet.

After I parked the car a few streets over, I ran through the alleyway until I approached Holland's place again. The sun dipped lower in the sky, casting long shadows that stretched across the pavement, and by the time Ryan arrived, the sky had deepened into a dusky blue, cloaking everything in a soft, muted light. This twilight provided the cover I needed.

From my vantage point, I could observe both the front and side of her house with ease, the warm glow from the windows contrasting against the growing darkness.

I chuckled as Ryan rang her doorbell and she cautiously answered. In less than a minute, she was hurrying outside with him as he pointed down the street. With her back to me, I made my move. A few other neighbors opened their front doors, which gave me even more protection from being seen as I hauled ass across her backyard. Ryan was a fucking pro, and I owed him a solid in return.

I reached her back patio and jiggled the knob. "Good girl," I whispered as I carefully maneuvered the lock pick, feeling for the subtle clicks that signaled success. At least she was wise enough to secure the place, a small gesture toward safety. Little did she realize, however, that this barrier was no match for my skills, and it wouldn't keep me out for long.

As soon as I triggered the lock, I slipped inside and quietly closed the door behind me, the soft click resonating in the silent hallway. Time was slipping through my fingers, and I quickly navigated the dimly lit rooms, searching for the perfect hiding spot. Not that I would be concealed for long, but I needed her to fall asleep before I could make my move.

The hall closet seemed promising for the moment. From there, I had a clear view of her in both the living room and the kitchen. The bedroom closet wasn't a good option since she might open it when she went to bed. The hall closet, however, was ideal, allowing me to hear any whispers of conversation she might have over the phone.

The front door opened, and I made out the soft murmur of Ryan and Holland exchanging goodbyes. I slid into my hiding spot, tucking myself behind a curtain of coats and a fortress of luggage, and settled in to wait for the right moment.

MOST OF THE TIME, I was patient. Methodical. But nearly three hours crammed into this fucking closet was peeling back every last shred of my restraint.

Too much time to think.

Too much time to rot.

I should've been calm. Focused. But instead, I kept replaying the same loop—Holland's voice, her laugh, the smell of her shampoo lingering on the clothes beside me—and *Mother's* voice ... dripping like venom into every memory.

Mother was in here with me. Not physically, but inside my fucking skull. Whispering how Holland had used me. Lied to me. Twisted me around her pretty little finger like she was no better than the woman who gave birth to me.

What if they were working together?

What if all of this—every smile, every soft look, every inch of her skin that I'd worshipped—was just a ploy to gut me from the inside out?

A slow burn was crawling up my spine.

Mother always said love was weakness dressed in prettier clothes. And maybe she was right. Maybe Holland had never been mine to begin with. Maybe she was *Mother's*—another one of her fucking puppets.

I bit the inside of my cheek until I tasted blood.

She'd never told me Samantha was alive. She'd let me believe I'd killed her. Let me die in that guilt, beg for forgiveness, *break* for it. And now that I'd finally found her again—alive, and still so fucking beautiful—I didn't know if I wanted to protect her ... Or rip her fucking soul from her body for lying and trying to destroy me.

I couldn't breathe in this fucking closet anymore. All I could think of was to end this misery. Take care of each player in the game, but what was a game to them was my goddamn life. I was about to take it all back once and for all.

Focus. Bide your time. Don't let them win.

It was nearly midnight when my ears perked up at a sound near the back entrance. Peering through the almost nonexistent crack I'd made for myself, I watched as she slipped on her robe over her pajamas and rushed to the back of the house.

"Don't open it, Holland," I mumbled. There was nothing good about a late-night visitor like this unless ... she was seeing someone. Jealousy sparked to life inside my chest, flaring up at the thought of her being with someone else. The image of him kissing her, his lips brushing against hers ... the bastard touching every part of her that belonged to *me* filled me with a turmoil that added fuel to the fire already burning inside of me.

She discreetly peeked through the small window shade, then froze. Her expression twisted as fear registered on her face. Before she could call for help, the back door swung open, and Cooper rushed inside. He grabbed her, slapped a palm over her mouth, and closed the door behind him. His arrival was an unexpected surprise, but as far as I was concerned, a damn good one. I rubbed my hands together, pulse steady, smile sharp as anticipation lit my veins on fire. This shit just got fun.

I pulled the devil mask with the voice disguiser from my back pocket, slipped it over my head, and now I had two targets.

"Welcome to hell, motherfucker."

20

HOLLAND

Terror beat through my veins as Cooper forced me away from the door and into the living room. I tried to bite his hand that was forcefully over my mouth, but he shoved me onto the couch, releasing me. I jumped up before he could pin me to the furniture.

"I dare you to fucking scream, bitch," he seethed as he stood over me.

"What do you want, Cooper? We have nothing else to say to each other. We're over. We've been over."

His wicked chuckle filled the room, and the hair on my arms stood on end.

"We're far from over, Holland. In fact, I wanted to discuss something with you."

"What's that?" I crossed my arms tightly in front of me, as if forming a protective barrier against the waves of hate rolling off him. The tension in the air was almost tangible, and I hoped I could reach him with reason. It was evident that something in him had changed. The man I once knew wasn't this aggressive. A sense of foreboding settled over me, and I had an inkling that I was on the verge of discovering what had caused his turnaround. "Do you need money?"

He threw his head back and laughed, a lock of his blond hair falling onto his forehead. I used to love it when that happened, and I'd gently brush it out of his brown eyes. The idea of touching him made my skin crawl.

"No. I have more than I'd hoped for. As soon as I helped find you ... well, Draco paid off all my gambling debts and then some. Apparently, you're worth a lot of fucking money."

Against my will, my brows shot up to my forehead. "Draco? How do you know him?"

"I didn't have a damn clue who the hell he was until about three months ago. He approached me at a casino. Said he was looking for a woman named Samantha, and that you had an old debt to pay." Cooper shifted his weight from one foot to the other. "Imagine my surprise when he showed me a recent picture of you. I have no idea where he got it, but it was clearly ... well, Holland Alder. *My* Holland."

"I knew it," I whispered, more to myself than to him.

"Back at the clinic, when you showed up—I told myself it was a coincidence." I swallowed hard, the memory punching me in the gut. "But it never sat right. You knew my name. You knew where to find me. I thought maybe I was simply being paranoid ... but *Draco* sent you. You were watching me before I even knew Draco was in town."

"Bravo." He clapped.

I gritted my teeth. "I'm not your possession, Cooper."

"You're right. You're not. You belong to Draco. I have orders to deliver you alive."

My fear was so tangible I could taste it on my tongue, but this time it was laced with determination. There was no way in hell I would let Cooper take me to Draco. I'd escaped him once, and I refused to be his prisoner again.

Cooper's mouth curled into a sick grin. "If it helps, I get to bring you in with a few bumps and bruises, as long as you're breathing." He looked down at his hands, turning them over, as if considering how far he could push the instructions. "Draco wants you scared. Desperate. So, when he gets you, you'll be more compliant."

It sounded exactly like Draco. He'd want to savor my fear, burn it slowly into my bones. Every instinct screamed at me to run, but Cooper blocked the only path to the back or front door.

He took a measured step closer, a practiced calm in his gait. "You should have stuck with me, you know. I would've kept you safe." His gaze steadied on mine, and I realized how fragile his self-delusion was. I'd become the pint glass he'd once hurled at a wall—something he'd break just to hear the sound, then curse because he had to clean up the mess.

"I'm not going," I said, my tone clear, almost formal as if resigning from a job. "I don't care what he's paying you. I survived him once. I'll survive him again."

He grinned, and the silver necklace around his neck caught the living room light, glinting. "You think you survived him? Sweetheart, that's not what he said. He says you still owe him, and you know damn well he always collects."

Images crashed through me—a locked door, bruises blooming like violets, a man with hands soft as cake icing and what they could do when pressed against a windpipe. Old debts. I forced myself not to shake.

"Do it, then." I stood. My knees turned to rubber while I flexed my fingers. "If you're going to break me, get it over with."

For a second, Cooper flinched, and the shadow dropped from his expression. I remembered the man who had once spent an hour tracking down my favorite Korean pastry in a storm, just so he could watch me smile. But that was a different version of Cooper.

He lunged, and I sidestepped, grabbing the lamp instead of the pepper spray on the side table. He snatched the lamp from my hand and slammed it onto the floor. It shattered, the bulb popping with a loud sound.

I managed to scream, secretly hoping the cop from earlier was near and would hear me. Someone please hear me.

"Shut the fuck up!" Cooper shouted, but I screamed again, louder, a shrill bloodcurdling sound. He slapped me, and the room tilted. I clawed at his cheeks and drew blood, and he jerked back with a curse.

"That's the spirit," he spat, wiping at his face. He reached behind him, and for half a second his balance shifted. I seized the moment, launching myself at his back and driving us both into the glass-topped coffee table. Cooper slammed into it chest first. The surface shattered beneath us with a vicious crack, glass exploding outward as we crashed through. Tiny shards embedded in his hair and clothes, slicing his arms and cheek, and trickles of blood smeared everywhere. The sharp impact jolted the breath from my lungs, but I clung to him as he tried to yank free. I wrapped an arm around his throat—awkward, desperate, but fueled by a panic so pure it felt like electricity.

Cooper thrashed, bucking to throw me off. My chin smashed into his bony shoulder. The taste of blood filled my mouth, slick and metallic, as his elbow connected with my temple. Stars burst behind my eyes, but I didn't let go. I dug my nails into his neck and squeezed, shrieking until my voice broke. We rolled off the table, scattering shards across the floor, until he managed to pin me. His knee ground into my ribs and all the air left my body.

"You're making this a lot harder than it needs to be." He wheezed, his features flashing with rage. He pressed a fist on my windpipe, just hard enough to make the edges of my vision flicker. Tears spilled down into my hair, but the despair that should have come never did. Instead, I spat blood into his face.

He recoiled, wiping away my saliva, and in that split second, I twisted free.

I didn't stop to think before I crawled across the ruined lamp, the jag of the broken bulb slicing the heel of my hand, and fumbled for anything with weight. My fingers closed on a clear, heavy ashtray—mine, from another life—and I swung.

The thick glass object caught Cooper square above the eyebrow.

There was a sick, wet sound, and his head snapped sideways. He collapsed, covering his head, his cursing blurry and indistinct. Blood ran over his mouth and onto my floor.

I staggered up, struggling to regain my balance. My phone was on the side table, five feet away. As I lunged for it, Cooper's hand caught my ankle, sending me sprawling across the floor. He rolled onto his knees, swaying. I kicked at his chin but caught him on the cheekbone, his teeth clacking shut. He didn't yell this time—just crawled after me.

On the third try, I reached the phone, but Cooper's weight came crashing down on my back. The cell skittered under the couch. He locked my arms behind me, bearing down so hard that the breath in my chest dwindled to nothing.

"I told you Draco didn't care what shape you were in," he gasped into my ear. "Might as well make this worth my while." His hand slid up the back of my shirt. I shrieked again and bucked against him. We tumbled sideways and he jerked my pajama shorts down over my hips. He easily pinned my arms over my head.

"You were always a good fuck. This one's for old time's sake." He scrambled with his pants and flipped open the button.

My pulse thundered in my ears, drowning out everything but the frantic rasp of my breath. Tears burned, hot and useless, blurring my vision as panic clawed up my throat. His weight pinned me, my ribs straining, the same helpless pressure I'd felt in that filthy cell years ago. The stink of sweat, the rasp of a stranger's laugh—it all bled together, past and present twisting into one nightmare.

I kicked, writhed, fought like a cornered animal, but the harder I thrashed, the deeper he pressed me to the floor. Terror surged, colliding with white-hot rage. I wasn't that broken girl anymore. I would not let him take this from me again. I'd tear his eyes out with my bare hands before I'd let him break me.

An odd sound stilled me as my hallway closet opened and the man in the devil mask appeared behind Cooper.

"You don't get to touch what's mine, motherfucker." He growled, edged with danger. He leaned down and wrapped an arm around Cooper's neck and hauled him to his feet.

I yanked my shorts up and pushed to my feet, every muscle screaming in protest. My knees buckled, trembling beneath me, and my body shook so violently I had to slam a hand against the wall to stay upright. My vision swam, blood seeping into my eye and stinging as I swiped it away with a shaky hand. My chest heaved, lungs burning for air, and still I forced myself to focus—because the devil was standing in my living room.

Cooper fought against the devil's hold, but there was no use. A chilling laugh filled my house, and in one swift cut, the glinting blade sliced across Cooper's neck, leaving a scarlet trail in its wake. Blood gushed from the ragged wound in his throat, pooling fast across my floor, snaking into the cracks of the wood in a macabre river. His eyes stared wide and empty, his lips parted as if frozen mid-curse. The torn flesh along his neck flapped grotesquely, peeling open like the skin of a split grape.

I couldn't look away. Horror rooted me to the spot, but beneath it —God help me—something else flickered. A dark, morbid fascination. I'd seen this before. The way life bled out in a hot, endless spill. The way death took its time. My stomach heaved, but still my gaze clung to the scene, riveted, as if my body remembered something my mind refused to name.

I gasped in horror, watching as his lifeless body crumpled to the floor like a lead ball.

"Shit. You killed him!" I sputtered, not realizing I was speaking out loud. Even though I was disoriented from the attack, I was still clearheaded enough to understand that Cooper had been murdered in my living room ... *Jesus!*

The devil stalked toward me still holding the knife, his moves cold and calculated.

"What do you want? I know you were here the other night. I remember the mask." I stepped back, but only managed to bump into the wall. I quickly turned to the side, giving myself enough room to run.

The man in the devil mask cocked his head, a slow, judicious movement, as though studying a new exhibit. "Good. You're smarter than you look." His gloved hand was still slick from Cooper's blood, and a single drop of blood poised on his thumb like a garnet. "It's better if you don't scream. There's only you and me left now, so don't waste your energy. You'll need it."

The light glinted off his blade, and my legs threatened to collapse, but I forced them to work, to slide against the wall to move further from him and away from Cooper. The devil kept coming, relentless and silent, until we were at the mouth of the hallway.

How the hell had I landed in this situation? I knew the answer though. My fucking heart was a damn fisherman's net—tattered and always catching the wrong thing.

He knelt and assessed the pool of blood forming under Cooper's corpse. The devil ran his fingers through the dark substance before he stood and laughed.

Every cell inside me fucking froze as the top quarter of a silver cross peeked out of his shirt.

"I want answers," he demanded.

"It was you and ..." I pointed at the piece of jewelry hanging from his neck. "You fucked me with your cross," I stammered. "I'm not crazy. It really happened."

A cruel smile eased into place. "You were so beautiful the other night. Waiting for me to touch you... taste you. Your tight cunt wrapped around my cross like a good girl, letting me fuck you. I can't wait for more, and the way you were moaning and how hard you came for me, you wanted it."

I gawked at his words as my thighs clenched with the memory, along with his dark and sultry voice. I shook my head, realizing I'd lost my damn mind.

He lunged for me, and I sidestepped him, edging toward the

kitchen. Bottles, knives, boiling water, the back door—despite all the horror, I scrolled through options, a sick game of survival. I'd played it before and won. I could do it again. But he was close now, dangerously close, and the bright overhead light revealed the mask's features.

I grabbed the nearest thing—a loaf of bread, ridiculous—and threw it at his head. It bounced off harmlessly, and he laughed as he closed the gap. I grabbed the butcher knife next, swung hard, but he caught my wrist and twisted until the blade clattered to the wood floor. In the same motion, he yanked me up by the hair and pressed my face into the fridge.

He chuckled at my feeble attempts to escape him. The devil released my hair and slid his weapon to the front of my neck, his warm breath grazing the shell of my ear. "I'm impressed that you held your own with Cooper."

That scent again. Burnt amber and sin. My brain screamed at me to run. My body begged to stay. As hard as I tried, I couldn't pinpoint his voice. He was using a disguiser, which made it nearly impossible. There was something that nudged me, though. Something familiar about him.

"I tried. I would have managed it on my own. You didn't have to kill him," I snapped.

"Oh, I definitely did." He trailed his free hand down my back and over the right cheek of my ass, lingering there for a moment.

"I like a woman that puts up a good fight. It makes my cock so fucking hard." He pressed his hips into my back, and I gulped at his size. I should have been alarmed that he was holding a weapon to my throat, but strangely, I didn't care. If he killed me, I would finally be free—free from Draco and the relentless shadows of the past that haunted me both in my nightmares and in my waking hours. Each memory was torment, a never-ending torture, and I was already spiraling out of control. It would only be a matter of time before my parents would be forced to seek help for me, perhaps committing me to find some relief. In a twisted sense, the devil would be doing me a favor.

"Good for you." My tone was snarky as hell, but for some stupid reason the level of smartass I was capable of when scared was crazy.

He jerked me away from the refrigerator and marched me over to the back door. "If you scream, you die. If you run like a good girl and I don't catch you, I'll leave you alone." His hand slid over my breast and cupped it, tugging on my hard nipple through my thin pajama tank.

My breath hitched, a traitorous gasp slipping past my lips. Heat pulsed low in my belly, sharp and wrong, colliding with the terror clawing at my throat. I hated the way my body responded to him—hated that the devil's touch could make my knees weak even as my mind screamed to fight.

"Open the door," he instructed.

I did as he said, staring through the darkness at the exit into the alley. On the other side was a protected wetland. It was mostly wooded with thick, tall grass.

"Head for those woods, and if you make even a small cry, I'll cut you down in your backyard. Do you understand me?"

I nodded, my heart pounding like a wild drum in my chest, each beat echoing the fear that coursed through my veins. Over the years, I'd learned several skills to stay alive. I'd simply hoped that I would never need them again.

"Run, Holland, or should I call you ... Samantha? When I catch you, I will rip the truth from you."

I should have been praying for a head start. But some sick part of me wanted to be caught.

I bolted into the night, adrenaline surging, and my lungs burning. With every step, one question chased me harder than he did.

Why did it feel like I wanted it?

21

———

KIP

Holland's bare feet barely touched the grass, her movements swift and fluid as she darted away like a startled deer caught in the headlights. Her speed was surprising, a burst of energy I hadn't expected, but I towered over her at six foot three, while she was barely five four. I could have easily overtaken her, yet watching her sprint away in fear stoked the fire of rage burning inside me. The deceit, the tangled web of corruption she'd woven, all boiled down to one simple act of betrayal. She could have let me know she was alive.

Her red hair streamed behind her as she dashed through the open gate and sprinted across the dim, narrow back alley. I could only imagine the soreness that lingered in her muscles from her fight with Cooper. I'd toyed with the idea of taking care of the bastard sooner than I had, but I'd been waiting to see what other information and answers she'd provide. More than that, I'd needed to gauge what kind of a challenge she might be. She was smart and fast. I'd give her that. But not even those traits would save her from hell.

At one point, I'd thought Holland had seen the door crack open, and I had been caught. I slowly closed it and waited, listening to that fucker come after her. The moment I decided to take care of the situation, the fucking door stuck and trapped me inside. It was too dark for me to see what had wedged it closed, but with the amount of shit she had in there, my guess was something caught when I secured myself in the hiding place.

Every second it refused to budge, my temper boiled hotter, until the only thing I wanted more than breaking down that door was tearing Cooper apart piece by piece for laying his filthy hands on Holland. And yet, beneath it all, my rage circled back to her—Holland, the girl who kept running, the girl Mother swore had destroyed me. Mother's voice still echoed in my head, whispering her lies, painting Holland as the enemy until I couldn't tell which fury burned hotter: the one for the men who'd touched her, or the one for her betrayal.

I lingered in the shadows, watching as she reached the edge of the dense woods. A chuckle escaped my lips as I observed her clumsy attempt to navigate the thicket, her arms flailing in a desperate attempt to maintain her balance. My thoughts ran rampant with what I planned to do to her when I caught her. Make her pay for what she'd done to me and then fuck her raw and make her beg for more would be a nice start.

With several long, purposeful strides, I crossed her backyard. The moonlight cast a silvery glow on the grass, and I could hear the soft crunch beneath my boots as I moved. Carefully, I slipped my extra knife into the sleek, leather calf harness that Death had given me years ago for Christmas. He'd given Dope one as well—a practical keepsake that spoke volumes about our shared life both inside and outside the society.

As I entered the woods, the towering trees loomed above, their branches weaving a dense canopy that blocked out most of the light, leaving only a few scattered beams to pierce the darkness. Each step I took pressed the dewy grass beneath my feet, leaving a trail that quickly vanished in the shadows. I had come prepared, every detail of my plan carefully considered.

Once hidden by the thick cover, I slowed my pace. My senses

heightened as I strained to catch any sound that might reveal her whereabouts. The air was cool and carried the faint scent of earth and pine. A slight rustle to my right caught my attention, prompting me to peer intently through the night, searching for any sign of movement.

"Samantha. Why the name change?" I asked.

She didn't respond.

I softly whistled "Me and the Devil" by Gil Scott-Heron as I stalked in her direction. After her fight with Cooper, she wouldn't last out here long, especially with no shoes on.

"I have so many questions, little ghost. All of which I intend to get answers one way or the other. It's up to you how that plays out."

A rabbit shot out of the grass and ran to the left of me, which told me Holland was nearby.

I remained still, watching and listening. The sound of ragged breathing caught my ear. To anyone else it might have been undetectable, but I'd had years to perfect the skill of listening. Really listening.

Slowly, I took soft steps in her direction and counted each one as I grinned. How many times had I mentally played this out—chasing, stalking, and then fucking her—claiming every part of her mind, body, and soul.

I stepped up to the side of a tree, my movements as quiet as a whisper in the night. The moonlight cast intricate shadows across the clearing, but her white and pink pajama set stood out, glowing like a beacon in the darkness. Her chest rose and fell rhythmically, creating a soft, mesmerizing pattern. I licked my lips, anticipation building inside me. With deliberate steps, I emerged from my hiding place, my focus fixed on her. It took only a heartbeat before she sensed my presence, a subtle shift in the air alerting her that I was there.

"No god will save you now, Samantha."

She launched off the side of the tree she'd been leaning against and ran like her life depended on it. It did.

I hurried after her but paced myself. A part of me wanted to continue the chase, the other wanted to grab her right then. I'd waited long enough.

I increased my speed, weaving through the dense forest, my attention locked on her as she darted between the trees. As I closed the gap, I lunged forward, my fingers entwining in her hair, and with a swift, forceful tug, I yanked her backward.

"You gave it a good try, little ghost. Just not good enough."

She stilled against me. "What do you want?"

"Answers but first ..."

I threw her onto the ground, savoring the sight of her crawling away from me as fast as she could. Survival instinct was an interesting thing. She knew without a doubt she couldn't escape me, yet she tried regardless.

With a swift move, I grabbed Holland and rolled her onto her back before I pinned her arms over her head.

"Why did you change your name?" I asked.

She swallowed hard before she answered. "I was running from someone. Apparently, I didn't do a very good job though."

"Why were you running?"

"He's a dangerous man. Evil. He made Cooper look like an angel."

I tugged on my cross, the breakaway chain giving way. I forced my knee between her legs, forcing them apart and allowing me the access my dick was begging for.

Her eyes followed my movements as I placed the crucifix against her pussy.

"Do you remember?" I was curious how much she thought was the Ambien.

"Yes," she said, her voice shaky but filled with need. "I thought it was a dream until I saw the bruises on my thighs the next day."

I placed my hand on her chest and held her down, my fingers digging into her flesh as I rubbed the cross against her pussy through the thin fabric of her shorts. My cock was rock hard, almost painfully so, but the ache would be worth it once I claimed her.

"Take off your shorts and panties. Now." My tone was clipped and authoritative with no room for arguing. I flicked open the blade of my knife, the cold metal glinting in the dim light, a silent threat if she dared to resist.

Her chin quivered as she stared at the weapon, fear dilating her pupils. But when she lifted her hips, it wasn't just terror guiding her —it was need. A shiver rippled through her as she slid off her clothes, her thighs parting in invitation even as her eyes screamed conflict.

I dragged the cold silver over her slit, watching her breath stutter, her juices slicking the metal. My pulse thundered. She wasn't only scared. She was turned on—wet, desperate, and trying to hide it.

The realization lit me up from the inside out. She might fight me, but part of her wanted this. Wanted *me*. Holland had a darkness in her that matched my own, a desire to dance with the devil. And fuck, that made me harder than ever.

I roughly spread her lips and thrust the handle into her wet pussy, fucking her with slow, deliberate strokes. Her mouth parted in a silent gasp, and her hungry cunt drew the metal deeper inside.

"You're such a dirty whore, fucking a cross. You like it. You like breaking the rules, don't you?"

"Yes," she panted as I picked up the pace.

"What did this man do to you? The one you changed your name to avoid?" My thumb rubbed over her clit as I waited for her to answer.

"I can't tell you." Her hips lifted off the ground as she moved in sync with the crucifix. "It's too dangerous."

I smirked. "More dangerous than the devil breaking into your house, killing a man, and then chasing you through the woods?"

She nodded, a soft moan escaping her.

I wrapped my hand around her throat, her pulse quickening against my palm. Her scent was intoxicating, a potent mix of fear and arousal that sent my senses reeling. I flicked her clit with my tongue, a light tease that made her hips jerk as she clawed at me, nails biting into my flesh as she struggled for breath. I glanced up, seeing shiny tears form in her eyes, which glistened under the dim light.

As I pressed my palm harder against her throat, a flicker of clarity cut through the haze. The fury I felt for Holland wasn't hers to carry —it was Mother's. Her voice had been whispering in my head for years, twisting memory into knives, painting Holland as the enemy until I couldn't tell truth from lies. For a breath, I saw it. I knew it.

And still, I couldn't stop. The bile rising in my chest wasn't just desire or rage. It was the sick realization that every thrust, every choke, was me trying to exorcise my mother's poison from my dark soul, to silence the lies she'd carved into my flesh and mind. My grip shook, my vision swam, and the brief clarity splintered into static. I was slipping again, dragged back into the madness, the edges of reality fraying until all I could taste was Holland's fear and my need to break her. If I couldn't silence the ghosts in my head, then I'd silence her cries instead. I bent lower, drawn to her like a starving man, needing to devour, to consume.

I licked her pussy, a long, languid stroke, savoring the taste of her on my tongue. She would rethink who the real monster was. Draco was nothing but a shadow, a weak and pathetic excuse for a man.

I loosened my grip just enough for Holland to drag in a breath, her chest heaving, but I didn't let her go. Couldn't. The feel of her trembling under me lit a fire I'd spent years trying to smother. With one hand, I removed the cross from her and set it beside us in the dirt. With my other hand, I worked my jeans open, buttons snapping, my cock straining for her.

When I lined myself up and shoved inside, the heat of her clamped down around me so tight my jaw locked. A guttural growl ripped from my throat as her body pulled me deeper, every inch of me swallowed in her wet, hot pussy. I'd imagined this, dreamed it, but reality was brutal and addictive, like being torn open and remade all at once.

For a heartbeat, something cracked open in me—raw, dangerous.

The thought that maybe this wasn't just about punishing her, but about needing her in a way I didn't dare name. That flicker of weakness seared through me, terrifying in its intensity.

I crushed it. Buried it. I wasn't here to feel. I was here to claim.

Her nails raked my shoulders, clawing, and the sting drove me harder. She wasn't just taking me—she was marking me, claiming me in her own way. My fingers tightened on her throat again, her face flushing red as she gasped beneath me, and still she met me thrust for thrust, her body trembling but greedy, hungry.

Pleasure and rage collided, a storm I couldn't control. Every clench of her cunt around me made it worse, made me want to drown in her and destroy her in the same breath. My vision blurred with the force of it, my body burning with years of anger, hate, and desperate fucking need.

Her back arched, her cry spilling into the night as I drove into her, relentless. Each thrust was punishment. A claim. A vow that she was *mine*. Dark. Twisted. Forever.

Her vision unfocused as I squeezed harder, nails bruising her delicate skin. The music of her choked moans echoed in the hush between dying pine trees. I brought her up to the very edge of consciousness, watched her skin pale. What if I finished her for real? What if I never let go, just kept thrusting and crushing until every ounce of rebellion drained from her cheeks and all that was left was the silence I craved?

The thought pulsed through me, thick and electric. My chest heaved, my mind frayed, fury and desire warring with each other and ripping me apart from the inside.

I fucked her harder, grinding her back and ass against the ground until her thighs streaked with dirt. She raked my arms and chest with her nails, desperate like a wounded animal. The sting pushed me further, fed the chaos unraveling in me. She convulsed, spasming, and I barely registered that she was coming until her juices leaked around my cock.

I slowed, gasping, trying to gather myself, but sanity was already slipping. I was unraveling in her grip, every thrust a punishment and a prayer, a plea for her to take the madness from me. Then the fury surged back, raw and uncontrollable. I slammed her into the earth until her sobs shook the night.

"Tell me," I spat, twisting my hand so she couldn't try to pry it off. "Tell me what he did, or you won't breathe again." My cock drove deep each time I punctuated the words.

She tried to pry herself loose as I held her by the throat and pumped into her, harder, deeper, punishing. She gurgled, a pink flush riding high on her cheekbones. Her arms dropped to her sides, and for a second I wondered if she'd pass out before I finished. My cock hardened with the thought, with the power—she was utterly at my mercy, helpless, like every other pathetic piece of trash suffocating this world.

I leaned closer to her, my lips finding her ear. "You want to live?" I whispered. My voice was thick, almost unfamiliar. "Beg for it."

She clawed at my hand, but when she tried to speak the words came out as a rasp. I loosened my grip a little, and she gasped, "Please, please—"

"Please what?" I drove into her again, slamming her hips to the earth, making her feel every inch of me. "Don't kill you?" My hand caught her jaw, forcing her eyes to mine. "Beg. Plead. Fucking whimper."

Her lips trembled, tears streaking her face. "Please," she whispered again, *"kill me."*

The words cracked something deep inside me. For a heartbeat, the fury faltered. She wasn't asking me to spare her—she was begging me to end it. To release her from her past, her pain. And the worst part? I saw it in her eyes. She meant it. She'd already made her peace with death.

My chest tightened, a pain I couldn't breathe through. God help me, I wanted to gather her close; to tell her no one would ever touch her again. That she was safe now. Instead, I buried it, forcing it down beneath the storm in my blood. I couldn't be soft, not with her looking at me like that, not when I was this close to losing my fucking sanity.

Her words tumbled out, raw and shaking. "He ... he was going to sell me for good. I heard him on the phone. Said I was worth more if I was scared. Said I was a purebred and some monsters like the taste of new meat. I ran. I ran so fucking far. I thought I was safe. I thought ..."

The fury that tore through me wasn't for her—it was for him. For Draco. For every bastard like him. My hands trembled against her throat, not from hate this time, but from the violence I wanted to unleash on them all.

"You're never safe," I ground out, but the words shook, more promise than threat. I rolled her over and drove into her from behind, my fist in her hair. "Not with men like that alive. But you'll never belong to them again. You're *mine*."

Her body convulsed around me, sobs breaking into moans, her fight bleeding into surrender. She arched back against me, her cunt gripping me so tight it made my vision blur. I leaned close, my lips brushing her ear. "Good girl. My good, stubborn girl. You tell me the truth, you give me everything, and I'll make you come for me."

Her body clenched, trembling in release, and I let go with her, pouring every ounce of rage and need into her until I was empty.

When I pulled out, I smeared my cum across her stomach and thighs, marking her. My hands shook as I did it—not with fury, but with something I refused to name.

"Tell me again," I rasped, needing to hear it, needing her to anchor me. "Who's the most dangerous man you know?"

Her glassy eyes met mine. "You are," she whispered, voice trembling between awe and horror. "You're a monster."

And God help me, hearing it from her lips nearly undid me.

Seconds later, she was clawing at my arms as I tried to restrain her. I'd let my guard down after I'd come inside her. Before I realized it, she grabbed at my face and jerked the devil mask off. She gaped as she blinked at me, dumbstruck.

Reaching into my back pocket, I removed the syringe, pulled off the cap, and stabbed her in the neck.

"You shouldn't have done that, Holland."

22

KIP

Once I collected myself in the woods, I tossed Holland's limp body over my shoulder and carried her back to her place.

After placing her on the bed where I could watch her in case she woke up sooner than expected, I searched the room and mentally noted what I would need. I gathered some of her clothes, toothbrush, computer, phone, chargers, and other belongings. If anyone snooped while she was gone, I needed it to look like she had taken time off for a much-needed vacation.

As I packed her bag, I recalled the name of the place she worked and the information I'd found after she'd nearly hit me with her car. I located her phone on the nightstand and used her finger to unlock it. I shook my head with how easy it was. I scrolled through her contacts until I located Howard Blaine, one of her bosses.

Even though it was late, I fired off a text that a family emergency had come up and she'd be taking time off work but would be in touch soon. I pocketed her cell and looked around one last time for anything else she might need on her extended stay away from home. Little did she know, she wouldn't be coming back anytime soon.

She knew who I was now. And with everyone else thinking she was handling an emergency, I had exactly what I needed—time.

Time to get my answers.

Time to make sure she didn't turn me in.

Because that? That could never happen.

After I meticulously cleaned up Cooper and the bloody chaos he'd left on the living room floor, I retrieved a body bag from my car and crammed him inside like a sardine in a tin can.

"Good riddance, you stupid fuck."

The first light of dawn was creeping over the horizon, casting a pale glow across the landscape as I hurried to conceal his corpse in the trunk of my car. Once we reached our destination, I would make sure he vanished without a trace, leaving no clues behind for anyone to follow.

But there was still one more problem to resolve—Draco. Before dealing with him, it was crucial to uncover the reason behind his obsession with Holland.

HOURS LATER, Holland was naked on the cot and chained to the wall of one of Death's warehouses in Idaho. This one had a remodeled bathroom and kitchenette, which meant Holland and I could stay as long as we needed.

Her eyelids fluttered open, lids heavy with exhaustion, and a soft moan escaped her lips as she tried to shift her position. The chain around her neck clinked and scraped across the rough cement floor.

I stood leaning against the wall, my attention fixed on the woman who had once shattered my world. My anger simmered beneath my skin, begging to be unleashed, but my cock had other ideas.

Her gaze followed the chain's length to where I stood, and I waited for the gravity of her situation to sink in.

"You fucking kidnapped me, Kip?" she seethed.

Her body shook. I suspected it wasn't from fear but from a rage that fueled my desire to crush her defiance underfoot, and to grind my heel against her pride.

I shrugged. "You left me no other option."

She looked around the room, at the cinder block fortress I'd chosen for us, at the bottle of water and granola bar on the floor beside her. "I'm not going to help you. And I'm not going to talk." The chain clinked as she sat up. "Are you going to kill me here?"

"I haven't decided." I liked the way the chain made her voice vibrate with every movement, liked the smallness of her in this cold, dark place. Her skin was patchworked with red marks where Cooper had hit her as well as dents from my hands on her neck, which were starting to turn purple. My jaw clenched so hard it hurt. Cooper's marks didn't belong on her. No one's did. The thought of him laying a hand on her made my blood boil, made me want to dig him out of the ground just so I could kill him again, slower this time. She might be chained here because of me, but she was still mine to break, mine to worship, mine to protect. Even from bastards like him.

"You have to let me go," she said, but it was so hollow it was almost funny. "If you kill me, they'll find you."

I smiled, and maybe it was the first time I actually meant it. "Who's 'they'? You think anyone's looking for you, Holland? I've been in your place. I know how little you matter to the world."

She made a sound, a dry laugh, and then spat on the floor. "Then why the fuck do you care so much?"

I crouched down, closer to her level, and waited for her to recoil, but she didn't. "I want to know why Draco wants you."

She said nothing.

"You're going to talk, Holland," I said, "even if I have to take you apart piece by piece." I brushed her thigh, slow and deliberate. "You're not getting out," I said, and she shrugged.

We stayed like that, silent, and the only sound was the tremor of her chain and our breathing. "You killed Cooper," she said finally, not a question.

"He wasn't useful anymore."

"Is that what you do? Decide when someone isn't useful anymore and then you slit their throat?"

I stood and walked to the table before I pulled the kitchen chair across the floor, the legs scraping across the cement. I sank into the seat and leaned forward. She glowered at me.

"That night in the car, I tried to tell you that I wasn't a fair man and that I often decided if someone lived or died. I wasn't bullshitting you."

I stared at her, searching her for any hint of her remembering me. "You're not here because of Draco. He just did me a favor and helped me plant myself in your life. The situation has taken a turn, though, and I need to know if I should deal with him or not."

"You're going to turn me over to him?" She narrowed her gaze at me, attempting to hide the fear.

I placed a finger under her chin and forced her to look at me. "You might be in chains and naked, but let's get one thing clear. You're mine. He won't touch you again."

A flash of relief crossed her face. Was I to interpret that being chained and naked on a bed with me was better than being with him? What kind of monster was he? I was well aware of what kind I was.

"If you don't like where you're at, you have no one to blame except yourself." I leaned back in my chair again.

"What the hell is that supposed to mean?" she asked. "You have no idea what I've lived through. What I've survived. How can you even say something like that?"

I rubbed my jaw as I pondered if I should get to the point, but I couldn't rush things. I had to savor the words when they left her lips, and she admitted that she betrayed me.

"We have all the time in the world. Your bosses aren't expecting you at work for at least a few weeks, if not more. Your parents are on vacation, and I have your phone, so I can easily convince them that you're safe and sound."

Her shoulders rolled forward in defeat, but I knew it was too easy. I hadn't won, we were just starting the war.

"What did Draco do?"

She rubbed her arms, goosebumps dotting her flesh. "He stole my sister and me when we were barely teenagers. No, not steal us. He bought us from our own family—like meat. And every night, he made sure we remembered what we were worth."

He touched her? Sold her? The only reason he was still alive was because I hadn't known. But I know now. My brow rose with her confession. "And?"

"He sold us for sex. We were raped, drugged, and starved to keep us under his control."

My stomach lurched, bile scorching my throat. The chain around her neck suddenly felt like my own hands had put her back into that nightmare.

Shame dug in deep, colliding with a rage so sharp it rattled my bones. I wanted to hunt Draco down and kill him slowly, make every bastard who'd touched her bleed.

Understanding dawned on me. It made sense why she wasn't begging and pleading for me to let her go—to let her live. She'd had this life before, and this time she was determined to walk away with her dignity and life intact.

"How old were you?" My words were laced with eagerness. Her next words would fucking flip my world and everything I knew inside out. I thought the Pied Piper had fucked with me, but this?

For the first time since I'd taken her, Holland choked back a sob. She looked away, shame and guilt dancing across her expression. But what would she have to feel guilty about?

"It was my thirteenth birthday." She lowered her head, her red hair hiding her pain from me.

The words shattered me. Thirteen. My chest seized, lungs refusing to work as the number echoed in my skull. She hadn't even been a woman yet—just a child. The same age as some of them I helped save. The same age my world changed forever.

My vision blurred, my heart a fist of fury. Every memory I thought was mine to bear suddenly seemed smaller than the hell she'd survived. And I'd chained her here, naked, like I was no different from them.

The room blurred in and out as the flashback took me away from reality once again.

"Get out! Now!" a voice said.

Dazed, I searched the room, but all I heard were shouting and screams. My uncle jerked my arm so hard I thought it popped out of the socket, but none of that mattered.

"Stop! Let me go!"

Two men grabbed the redheaded girl, and her big blue eyes landed on me for a moment.

"What are you doing to her?" I yelled as I broke free from my uncle and ran toward her.

"You know what to do, Kip. You know," my mother ordered from behind me. She dug her fingers into my biceps as she pulled me toward the girl. "We're out of time. Do it."

Black dots clouded my vision as I tried to resist the drive inside me. I gritted my teeth against the pain inside my chest. The girl's screams were devoured by even more. I struggled to breathe against the crushing weight on my chest and then ...

When I came to, my hands were covered in blood and the redheaded girl was lying on the floor. I stumbled toward her, shaking so hard my legs could barely carry me. The chaos had calmed down, but the body count had risen.

"Kip!" Holland screamed.

My head jerked to the side, and my neck popped with the sudden movement, nearly knocking my chair backward.

"Kip? Look at me. Don't you dare fucking die and leave me chained up like this."

She couldn't hide the fear in her voice. Holland should be afraid. Very afraid.

I rubbed my neck, realizing I'd had another blackout, but how had she known? I'd been able to hide them from Death and Dope, but not her.

"What happened? You were gone all of a sudden, and your eyes rolled back in your head. You were shaking. Are you epileptic?"

I ignored all her questions.

Maybe it was the flashback.

Maybe it was the rage.

It didn't matter.

All I needed now was the answer.

23

———

HOLLAND

The irony of the situation hadn't escaped me. I was this man's prisoner, chained and naked, but I wasn't scared of him anymore. Once I'd removed his mask and seen it was Kip, a switch had flipped in my brain. He'd fucked me with his cross, touched me, claimed me, and protected me. I refused to die in this hellhole. But there was something about him. Something dark that I was drawn to even in my predicament. However, what I'd just seen scared the shit out of me. When he'd started to convulse, I'd wanted to take care of him. There was no denying it. I was as fucked up as they came. I was attracted to Kip on an emotional and physical level. It was as if I knew him, but that didn't make a damn bit of sense.

The other thing that became clear when I'd thought he was going to die was that I could tell him the truth. If I had any hope of escaping, I had to let him think I trusted him. Oddly enough, I did. I had a feeling if he knew more about Draco, Kip would finish him off like he had Cooper. It was simply a matter of how I framed the story. Kip had already proven he wanted to protect me on some level even when he was furious with me. That part I still didn't understand, but my guess is that I would find out soon.

I cleared my throat. "I'm alive because ..." I looked at the ceiling, trying to talk past the lump in my throat. "There was a guy that loved fucking sisters. He asked for Ally and me any time he was in town. Normally, Draco would drug us with pills, but they stopped checking our mouths to see if we'd swallowed them after a while. Ally and I spit them out and hid them in our pillowcases instead so we could be clearheaded enough to plan an escape. But the night before we were supposed to meet the client again, Draco's brother, Dominic, visited us in our cell and drugged us ... with a needle in our neck. We weren't strong enough to fight him off, and the drugs hit hard and fast." I glanced at Kip, his jaw so tight the muscle jumped. Was he angry at me or Draco?

"Ally didn't wake up the next day," I said, my voice cracking with grief. "He'd overdosed her." I ground my teeth, fighting the tears that threatened to spill down my cheeks. I wiped my eyes and blew out a heavy sigh. Then I slowly looked at Kip. My stare was cold, hard. "Before we were delivered to clients, we were fed an extra sandwich. I suppose it was to keep up our energy or something, I'm not sure. Maybe it was more psychological torture. When his brother returned with a tray of food, he brought a glass of orange juice. We were never allowed anything other than plastic cups and spoons. Nothing sharp. Ever."

My nostrils flared with the memory. "Before he realized he'd fucked up, I grabbed the glass and threw it against the wall. It shattered all over the floor, and I snatched up the biggest piece that had landed near my feet. He lunged at me, and I tripped him. When he fell on the floor face down, I climbed on his back, jerked his head up by his hair, and slit his fucking throat. I'll never forget the blood that poured out of his jugular. The son of a bitch was helpless and dead within a few minutes. I grabbed the cell keys, unlocked the other girl's cages, and ran for my fucking life." Our gazes were locked on each other, the silence in the room was music to my ears.

A corner of his mouth twitched, and I realized he was fighting off a smile.

"He's not after me because I ran," I whispered. "He's after me because I killed his brother."

The words hung in the air between us, sharp and brutal. I expected him to call me a liar. A murderer. But instead ... I wasn't sure if I'd pushed him too far—or if I'd just won him over for good.

"You slit Draco's brother's throat to survive. No wonder he wants you back—no wonder he'd pay through the teeth to drag you home." His jaw clenched. "Fuck no. Over my dead body."

All the psychology textbooks in the world couldn't explain what I felt when he looked at me like that—like I was his, like I always had been.

"Why? Why do you give a shit? I'm chained to a wall and your prisoner," I said. "What makes you any different than he is?"

"Because I hunt men like him. I kill men like him who hurt women and children. Even a monster has lines."

I wanted to know more, craved more of who Kip was. What made him into the man and monster I'd seen. I suspected he wouldn't share with me yet. Time would only tell, and from the looks of it, I had plenty.

He shifted in his chair, his attention trained on me, assessing. "You liked it, didn't you? The blood on your hands, watching the life drain from his eyes. Has little Samantha grown up fighting the compulsion to kill others? Is that what drove you to become a psychiatrist? Bloodlust?"

I refused to answer him. The only way that he would recognize what I felt and fought against was if he dealt with it himself.

"You don't need to answer. I already know. But here's the thing."

I pulled my knees to my chest, fighting the cold that made me shiver.

"That's not what I was asking you earlier," he growled.

"What? You asked me how I was alive. I told you." Maybe his seizure had affected his brain cells, because I was well aware of what he'd asked me.

He placed his elbows on his knees, his stare stabbing at my soul.

"That night. It was the night before your birthday. Your family came over. It was the first time I saw you. We didn't talk because I was hanging out with some friends, and you and Ally stuck close together. Later that evening, I heard a scream, so I ran into the house, but no one was there. I heard another one and ran to the outbuilding on the property. When I opened the door, I saw you and your sister along with my uncle and Mother. You were fighting your parents. I rushed in, trying to help you, but then ..."

He shot out of his seat and paced the room. "There was blood everywhere. All over me, all over the floor. Your father was slumped over a table with a bullet in his forehead. I don't know what happened to your mother or your sister. But you ..." He massaged the crook of his arm as if soothing an old wound. "You ..." He barked out a laugh and spun on his heel, facing me. "I ... I. Killed. You. I fucking killed you with my bare hands. You were dead on the damn floor."

My pulse hammered in my ears, drowning out his words even as they carved into me.

He was talking about *me*—about a night I had locked away so deep it only lived in broken flashes.

The night before my birthday? I clawed at the memory, desperate, but his face wasn't there. His voice wasn't there. Nothing about him was familiar. What I did remember was my father's heavy hand on my arm, Ally's fingernails digging into my palm as we hid behind her, and my mother's frantic whisper—*Run.*

And then ... the echo of a gunshot. The metallic tang in the air. Someone slumped forward.

A bullet in their forehead.

I didn't know if I had seen it or if my mind had painted it after the fact, but the weight of it crushed the air from my chest.

I pursed my lips. "That's not what I remember. I barely remember a guy my age being in that room. I had no idea it was you. It was a blur. I was trying to get away when I realized what was happening, and so was Ally. When we were fighting back, my father knocked me out. The next thing I knew, Ally and I were locked up in a dirty cell. You didn't kill me. In fact, you never touched me, Kip."

He placed his palms on the side of his head and yelled, "I know what I saw. There was blood all over my hands. *Your* blood."

"It had to have been someone else. It wasn't me," I said softly, my compassion and training kicking in. How had he carried something like that his entire life? I'd seen it in my clients, and I'd lived it myself. Someone's past didn't just haunt them. It *built* them.

It was all making sense now. His need to insert himself into my life, protect me, and why he kept demanding answers and asking if I remembered him.

"Our minds are powerful, Kip. My guess is that you couldn't stop them from taking Ally and me, and so your memories became something you could make sense of. You put a puzzle piece into that spot that didn't fit, so you made it fit. We do it all the time. Denial, PTSD, the brain protects us. You didn't kill me."

He scratched his arm as a storm of emotions twisted his features. "She ..." he bit out. "As punishment, she forced me to relive it over and over and over. She never let me forget what I'd done."

"Who is she?" I kept my tone soft and accepting of everything he was telling me.

He shook his head. "If it wasn't you, then who the fuck did I kill?"

I wished I had an answer for him. "I can't imagine what that's been like, especially if you were trying to help whoever that poor girl was. But Kip, if Ally and I were taken from your property, then there's a good possibility I wasn't the only one. Maybe you saw it happen a few times and snapped."

Kip walked toward me, his body language angry and overwhelming. "I get it. You think you can fix me now? You feel sorry for the poor kid that killed an innocent girl with his bare hands." He leaned down, his face mere inches from mine. "It shaped me all right. I became a highly skilled cleaner. Do you know what that is or are you so busy pretending that bad things don't exist in the world when you sit behind your little desk and take notes about your patients? Maybe it gives you power over other people to know their secrets."

The muscle in my jaw ticked as I willed myself not to throat punch him. "I don't know what a cleaner is."

"My uncle taught me how to dissolve a body, bone, blood, hair into nothing. I can make anyone disappear without a trace left on this fucking earth. Along with that came an overwhelming urge to kill, so I do. I choose men to feed to a serial killer to be tortured and murdered. Men like Draco. Lately, I've done some killing myself. All the bodies and blood get into your head, and there's something addictive about having the power to give or take a life." He straightened. "You know that though. You feel it too.

We.

Are.

The.

Same."

To my surprise, he walked to the kitchen, opened a cabinet, and then gave me a blanket.

"Cover up. You're clearly cold."

I grabbed the blanket and wrapped myself in it, shivering from the chill in the room. Humanity is a strange thing. We will do anything to survive, even kill, but the secrets behind those actions make us who we are. I'd seen it over and over in my profession. I knew what Kip was. The things he'd done. The way he watched me from the shadows like I already belonged to him.

"I'm going to go shower," he mumbled before he disappeared from the room. Once I made sure that he was gone, I reached into my hair and located the four sharp bobby pins I'd tucked in. After being locked up by Draco, I swore I would never be a prisoner again. It was one of the skills I'd learned. Not only to survive but to pick any lock.

Over the next five minutes, I worked on the lock on my collar. The soft click told me I'd finally been successful. Quietly and without moving the chain much, I set the collar on the bed. Next, I had to locate my clothes. I hurried off the cot and then searched the kitchen cabinets, but I didn't find anything.

I rushed down the hall, hearing the shower still running, and poked my head into one of the rooms. There was a queen-size bed, but nothing else. In the next room, I found my duffel bag on the bed. I ran to it and opened it. He'd certainly packed enough for me to be gone a long time. I just wasn't sure if he intended on letting me live or not.

Within seconds, I was dressed and had slid my feet into my tennis shoes. At least now I had a better chance of outrunning him if he realized I was gone.

His confession of killing a girl echoed through my mind, my chest tightening. From the moment I'd met him I knew there was something different. Something that pulled me to him. When he'd pinned me against the wall at my house, all I wanted to do was kiss him. Feel his mouth on mine, but I'd wanted him to make the first move.

I tiptoed down the hall and stopped at the bathroom. The door was cracked open, and I peeked inside. I covered my mouth before I gasped as I saw him through the shower glass. Jesus, he was gorgeous. The water ran down his broad shoulders and streamed down his chest and abs all the way to his glorious, hard cock. He fisted it and slid his hand up and down, stroking his length. My pussy clenched, weeping at the idea of him inside me again. I should leave while I had a chance to escape, but I stood rooted in place, watching as he pleasured himself. He turned his back to me, and a small cry escaped me. Scars covered his entire back. I stepped closer to make sure I wasn't imagining what I saw. They weren't. Some scars were still thick even though it was clear they were older. What the fuck had happened to him?

My heart shattered in a million pieces, and I was pretty sure he'd taken it and would never give it back. There was so much more to this man than what he'd shown me. I should run from him. But I needed him like air. Even if he was poison.

If I was smart, I would slip out, into the night, and never look back.

But I was frozen, breath caught in my throat as I watched him through the small opening.

Water streamed down his scarred back, each line carved into his skin like a road map of pain. His head hung low under the spray, one of his palms braced against the tile, muscles taut—and when a shudder racked his body, I realized it wasn't just from the water.

I pressed a trembling hand to my mouth. My stomach squeezed so hard it hurt.

I wanted to run.

But God help me, I wanted him more.

My fingers hovered at the hem of my shirt, torn between escape and surrender.

I backed away—one step, two—throat constricting with panic. I could still do it. I could still get out.

But then.

His head lifted. Slowly. Deliberately.

His eyes—twin shards of something wild and broken—locked on mine through the glass. Stripped of his contacts, they were unnaturally pale, the color bleached out like old photographs left in the sun. There was something unsettling about their lightness, almost ghostly, as if I was staring into the eyes of a predator who'd learned to wear human skin.

And he smiled.

"Going somewhere, little ghost?"

24

———

KIP

The water slammed down on my back, scalding, but it was nothing compared to the fists pounding inside my skull.

Her words echoed like a gunshot through bone. *You didn't kill me.*

For years, I saw her face in every nightmare—her body limp, her throat crushed under my hands. I carried her death like a brand burned into my skin, letting it shape me into the thing the Horizon Society wanted: a cleaner, a weapon, a man who only killed the monsters worse than himself.

But now, she was here. Alive. Breathing.

Standing at the edge of the bathroom, trembling. Not because of what I'd done to her, but because of what the world had done.

My chest cracked open, a raw, splintering sound in my head. Relief twisted sharp through my gut, tangled with guilt so thick it tasted like iron on my tongue.

I didn't kill her. God help me, I didn't destroy her. And now? Fuck, now I would tear the sun from the sky to keep anyone else from touching her.

I felt her before I saw her, the soft shift of energy, the faintest tremor in the air.

I turned. Slowly. Deliberately. Water streamed down my scars, those old maps of pain, and I met her wide gaze.

"Going somewhere, little ghost?" I rasped, voice gruff.

Her breath hitched. Her fingers clenched at the hem of her shirt. And for one brutal second, I wanted her to run.

Run—so I could catch her. Run—so I could take her apart, piece by piece. Run—so I didn't have to confront the fucking truth rattling inside me that she ruined me in the best way just by standing there.

But she didn't run.

She peeled her shirt over her head slowly, shaky, defiant. She flipped open the button on her jeans and revealed her bare skin, marked by bruises from hands that weren't mine. Fuck, how I wished they were, though.

She reached for the shower door, and I opened it, catching her wrist.

"Why?" I asked, yanking her close enough to feel the heat of her skin. "Why aren't you running?"

Holland's gaze dropped to the bathroom floor, then returned to me. Her lips parted, and she licked her lips. "I ... I just can't."

My chest tightened with her words, the cage around my heart breaking enough to allow a flicker of light into the darkness. She was mine. But God help me. I was hers too.

I hauled her into the shower and pressed her back against the tile, pinning her with my body. Her hands braced on my chest, soft and small and shaking.

I buried my face in her hair, inhaling her scent like I was a starving man. "You've been haunting me for so fucking long," I rasped against her ear. "Little ghost, you don't get to leave now."

Her fingers slid up, tangled in my hair, pulling me closer instead of pushing me away.

And right then—right fucking then—I knew. She was the only

thing that made me feel alive. And I was the only thing that could ruin her completely.

My mouth crashed down on hers, demanding, taking, possessing. I gripped her thighs, hauling her up, and she responded by wrapping her legs around my waist. No one else would ever have her, touch her, or scar her again.

Her breath caught, a wrecked sound against my lips, and I swallowed it whole.

"Say it," I growled, mouth at her throat, teeth grazing skin that tasted like heat and sin and something dangerously close to hope. "Say you're mine, little ghost."

Her nails dug into my shoulders, desperate, as her head fell back.

"I'm yours," she said, her voice breaking like it cost her everything. "I'm yours, Kip."

Fuck. Fuck.

Every brutal, bloodstained piece of me lit up at once. I lined my cock up with her wet entrance, pushing in slightly, just enough to tease her and make her beg for more. Her pussy clenched as she ran her nails down the scars on my back. Without warning, I thrust into her tight cunt.

"Kip," she whimpered as I rocked against her. I lifted her and then she slid down my cock over and over, and I fucked her until she was gasping. When her cunt clenched around me, it wasn't just possession. It was survival. It was home. Every dark, feral thing inside me was unveiled, raw and exposed, in the embrace of the one girl I believed had been lost to the grave.

"Ride my cock, little ghost. Remember who you belong to. Your monster has claimed you. Show me you want to stay."

She grabbed handfuls of my short hair as I slid her nipple into my mouth and bit hard enough to make her cry out, then I soothed the pain with my tongue. I sucked a line between her breasts, open-mouthed and possessive, leaving marks she'd see tomorrow and remember me with.

"Kip," she gasped in a choked whimper.

I moved with her, and her nails dug into my skin with each roll of my hips. I gripped her ass, lifting her, and she slid down my cock, over and over, her tight cunt enveloping every inch of me. Her thighs, slick with sweat, locked around my hips, her heels digging into my lower back. Her lips found my ear, her breath ragged and hungry, like she wanted to consume me.

I let go of control, fucking her hard and fast, my hips snapping against hers, making her gasp with each thrust. Her head fell back against the wall, mouth open, hair sticking to her cheeks in damp arcs. I leaned in, biting into the curve of her neck, tasting the droplets of water. She shuddered, her nails clawing at my ass, pulling me deeper. My cock throbbed, impossibly hard, and I could feel her clit, swollen and slick, grinding against me.

Her moans grew louder, frantic, echoing off the tiles, louder than the groan of the old pipes. I pressed her harder against the wall, my hand snaking between her legs, fingers circling her swollen clit. She writhed, desperate, her hips bucking against me, fucking my cock like her life depended on it.

"Oh, fuck, fuck, please don't stop—" Her voice was hoarse, pleading, a sound I wanted to hear more of. Her pussy was soaked, clenching tightly around me, pulsing through my entire body.

"Oh god," she whispered, her words barely audible over the pounding water. And then, more desperately, "Don't you dare stop."

She rode out every thrust, her head thrown back, gasping, until the tremors took her, and her pussy squeezed me hard.

I pulled out, then turned her around to face the shower wall. Dropping to my knees, I parted her legs and pressed my mouth to her pussy, tasting her, licking her, making her gasp and writhe as my tongue slid into her. I lapped at her, feeling her shake, hearing her beg, before standing and lining up behind her. I pushed in, deeper than before, all the way until my hips pressed against hers. She turned her head, her cheek flat to the wall, and moaned.

She came with a violent spasm, pussy clenching my cock, nails puncturing the skin on the side of my leg. I fucked her through it, chasing my own release.

I followed, unable not to, emptying inside her in a few, short, sharp thrusts. She milked me for every last drop, wringing me dry.

She turned her head and bit my bottom lip, hard enough to draw blood, then soothed away the sting with a slide of her tongue—and that, more than anything, undid me. Somewhere deep inside I started shaking, a low-grade tremor building behind my ribcage, radiating out until it hit the tips of my fingers. Holland touched parts of me no one had ever dared to reach. She held the broken pieces of my heart like they were worth saving. And for the first time in my life, I wondered if I might be worth saving after all.

25

____

HOLLAND

I had the opportunity to escape, yet I hesitated. It seemed irrational, but part of me didn't want to go. I could see the shattered pieces in Kip, and his darkness was both unsettling and compelling at the same time. I felt drawn to it, even as I questioned my own sanity. He didn't need to restrain me or prevent my departure because I was caught in a web of my own conflicting desires.

I held his cheeks gently, gazing into his colorless eyes as the water cascaded around us. Uncertainty clouded my thoughts about what the future held, yet a part of me was eager to discover it. It wasn't about seeking protection; even on the days when Draco frightened me, I had defeated him once and believed I could do so again. But now, I wasn't alone. Kip stood by my side, and while that should have brought comfort, it also stirred my anxiety, as I questioned whether I was ready to rely on someone else. Over the years, I'd held everyone at arm's length, and now I was willing to let someone in. I hoped like hell I wasn't making a mistake.

He nipped at my ear. "I'm glad I didn't kill you years ago."

I threw my head back and laughed. "Me too."

Kip reached behind him, and the sound of the rushing water

abruptly stopped as he turned off the shower. Steam swirled around us, misting the bathroom mirrors and carrying a warm, humid scent. He opened the glass door and reached for the towel he had neatly placed on the edge of the sink. The fabric was soft and plush, still carrying the faint aroma of fresh detergent.

With a gentle gesture, he extended his hand toward me, helping me step out of the shower and onto the plush bathmat, which felt warm and comforting beneath my feet. He carefully began to dry my hair, the towel absorbing the droplets that clung to each strand. His touch was tender as he moved from my hair to my shoulders, and then to every inch of my body, his actions deliberate and filled with care. His gentleness was both soothing and unsettling, more intimidating than his possessive nature, yet it marked a shift in the dynamics between us—a silent promise to look after one another.

As I dressed, he dried himself off, each movement accentuating the powerful lines of his tattooed and muscled physique. My attention was drawn to him. I was unable to look away, my breath catching in my throat. A stirring heat rose inside me, a tangible reaction to his presence, as every fiber of my being responded to the sight of him. He stood before me, a masterpiece of strength and artistry. He was a tattooed, muscled god. I nearly dropped to my knees and worshipped him, but I would have to save that for later.

"Kip?" I asked. "No more chains. If you want to tie me up and fuck me with your cross, I'll do that willingly. You need to believe me when I say I want to be here. Are we clear?"

He gave me a lopsided grin. "You'd let me fuck you with my cross?"

I rolled my eyes. "Is that what you took away from that?"

He wrapped the towel around his waist and took my hand as he led us out of the bathroom and to one of the bedrooms. For an old warehouse, it had everything someone would need to hide for a while, and I wondered why.

"I heard you." He reached beneath the bed, removed a duffel bag, and tossed it onto the mattress. My attention remained glued to him as he dressed in jeans that hung low on his hips and hugged his ass and thighs. His expression turned solemn. "I killed someone, Holland. Maybe it wasn't you, but it was a redheaded girl. I snapped that day, something inside me isn't right. I'm not like other people who have normal feelings. I *like* to kill. I love the power to end someone and then remove every trace of their existence from the fucking earth." He sighed before he pulled his navy T-shirt over his head.

I stopped myself from throwing my arms around him and soothing the ugly demons that were clearly tormenting him. The urge to comfort him was overwhelming, but I couldn't become Holland the psychiatrist. I had to stand firm as Holland, the woman who was falling for him. His equal.

"The difference now is that I can channel it to men like Draco. If there's a thing such as redemption, then that's how I try to earn mine. Help innocent women and children."

"Will you tell me more?"

A hush fell over the room followed by the loud growl of my stomach. I grinned, embarrassed. "It's been a while since I've eaten."

"Shit." He glanced at his watch. "How about almost twenty-four hours?" He took my hand again and led me to the living room and tiny kitchen. "Sit and I'll make us something to eat."

I sank onto the chair he'd been sitting on earlier and stared at the chain resting on the floor. "You cook?"

He half shrugged. "If I don't cook, I don't eat. It's that simple."

Once he grabbed steaks from the refrigerator, he opened the cabinet and located a few potatoes. He seasoned the food, then popped the potatoes into the air fryer on the countertop. He opened another cabinet and removed two glasses along with a bottle of bourbon. "Drink?"

"Please."

After he poured us the amber liquid, he sat at the small table and placed my glass in front of me. "I want to trust you, Holland. I want to be able to share things with you about my life, but it has to go both ways. I understand now about Draco and Cooper, but if we're doing this, then no fucking bullshit. No lies, no half-truths between us. Not only that, but I'm also going to share things with you in the greatest confidence, so if you need to be psychiatrist Holland with me when we have these conversations, I'll sign a confidentiality form. I'm not kidding about any of this. It's not only me who's involved, and I can't risk their safety if you go AWOL."

I traced small circles against my thigh, lost in the puzzle he'd given me.

"What do you need to feel safe?"

He smirked at me. "Not any psychobabble. Just be real. You don't have to analyze me or fix me. I don't want to be fixed, but I do want to understand who I killed." He stood and tapped an impatient rhythm on his arm. "For now—"

A loud bang had me sliding onto the floor and under the table without realizing it.

"What the fuck?" Kip motioned for me to stay there as he reached into a kitchen drawer and removed his gun.

Female laughter echoed through the hall as footsteps approached.

What the hell? I crawled out from under the table as a beautiful dark-haired woman with blood spattered all over her clothes and pretty face. She entered the room followed by a dark-haired guy with a man slung over his shoulder. We all froze, staring at each other.

"What the fuck are you doing here, Kip?" the man growled.

Kip rubbed his jaw, then folded his arms over his chest. "Ella, Death, meet Holland." He motioned to me.

I gave them a little wave and managed to speak, my voice high-pitched and foreign to my ears. "Hi. We're about to have dinner." I cringed at my choice of words. What the fuck had I gotten myself into? If there was a time to run, it was as soon as I could manage to get around these people and out the door. Clearly, I'd made a huge fucking mistake.

"She wants to run," Ella said, her body language rigid as she assessed me. "But that can't happen so you might as well have a seat."

I thought I had been in danger before. But now the real madness had come for me. Even though I tried not to assume these people had killed someone, the evidence supported my fear. And Kip knew them?!

Kip nodded. There was no use in resisting. I would have to plan my escape when I had time to assess the situation. I would only have one chance. I could easily identify the woman. The man wore a grim reaper mask similar to Kip's devil one, so I couldn't identify him, but I was fucked and not in a fun way.

Death, as Kip referred to him, tossed the person on the floor, and I folded in on myself. The face was mutilated—eyes carved out, mouth twisted into a Joker's smile. This wasn't Kip's world I was stepping into. It was hell, and I'd just been welcomed as a guest.

"It's date night," Ella said without even cracking a smile as she joined me at the table. "I find it interesting that Kip brought you here for starters. Kip hasn't said anything about a girlfriend, but it would explain some of his disappearances lately. However, my point is that this isn't a normal place to hang out and have dinner. So why are you here?"

I fidgeted in my chair, staring at the dead body. I couldn't tell her that Kip had kidnapped me and brought me here against my will and then I decided to stay. It also wasn't my place to share he'd killed a girl when he was younger, and it was haunting him.

Ella reached out and patted my hand. "It's okay. The first time someone figures out what this place is used for is always the worst."

Kip tried to warn me, but as usual I didn't listen. I would be lucky if I walked out of this alive, right? If shit went south, Draco wouldn't have a target to hunt because I would be buried next to the corpse on the floor. Inwardly, I shuddered and willed myself not to show my fear.

"Uh, yeah, we were taking a weekend away and getting to know each other better." I tucked my hair behind my ear. Not taking my attention off Death. His gray eyes were cold, unfeeling, but when he looked at Ella, I caught a glimpse of humanity.

"I was debating telling Holland more about the Horizon Society. She knows a little bit, but not who I work with," Kip explained.

Death motioned for Kip to follow him, and they left the room.

"They're going to try to figure out what to do with you." Ella raised a dark brow at me. "We had no idea Kip was here, which puts us in an awkward position."

I turned in my seat and looked at her, no longer wanting to see the dead man. For a moment, I weighed the pros and cons of opening up to Ella. At this point, I had nothing to lose, and everything to gain. Offering her leverage against me, the same as I had on her, might level up the playing field in my favor. I hoped anyway.

"I suspect we're more alike than you think. First, I'm a psychiatrist, so the things I've heard are under strict confidentiality. I know how to keep a secret. Second, I've killed someone with my own hands, slit his throat open like he was a turkey on Thanksgiving Day," I said, shaking only on the inside.

I savored the look that flashed over her expression—hunger tinged with calculation. Was she surprised that I'd shared my darkest secret with her in an attempt to bond? A moment passed. Her gaze dropped to the unmoving guy at our feet, then lifted again, met mine as if weighing me, as if measuring my soul for leverage.

"So," she said, lips barely moving, "you understand."

Wind rattled the dirty, gold-flecked glass of the door behind her. The light had shifted now, to the color of faded peaches and sticky kitchen floors. She stood, crossed over to the body, and knelt—quick, clinical, like muscle memory. It was a ritual I knew well: catalog the evidence, decide what to hide, what to leave for the next person to see or not.

Only then did I notice the gloves. She'd been wearing them the whole time, but I hadn't even paid attention.

The lifeless corpse at her knees was leaking a slow, syrupy trail of red into the cracks between tiles. It struck me that neither of us had called the dead man by name.

"Why did you kill someone?" She returned to her chair and sank into it.

"When I was young, my sister and I were kidnapped and woke up in a cell."

To my surprise, Ella flinched and her back stiffened. Had she lived through something similar?

I continued, trying to mask the amount of pain I was feeling as I shared with her, "We were sold for sex, starved, and beaten. My sister died there, but I killed someone and ran for my life. That man's brother is hunting me. He found me at Velvet Vortex one night, and Kip helped me out of a bad situation."

Ella tilted her head. "Is he still in town or did Kip handle the situation?" She added air quotes to the word handle.

I understood what she meant. "I'm not sure if he's still in town or not, but my guess is yes." *Unless he followed my parents.*

"Have you shared all of this with Kip? You're not just kissing my ass in order to live?" She gave me a soft smile. "I can read people really well too. I worked for a defense attorney that represented some of the biggest mastermind criminals in the US. For some reason, not only do I believe you, but I already like you." She stood and pushed her chair under the little table. "I'd better check on the guys. They're awfully quiet." She began to walk away, then looked over her shoulder at me. "I highly recommend that you don't run, Holland. It won't go well for you. With me on your side, I might be able to talk Death off the ledge. Maybe."

The second she left the room, my gaze snapped to the front door.

And for the first time, I let myself wonder.

Could I make it out before one of them decided I was next?

26

——

KIP

"Why the fuck didn't you tell me?" Death asked, pacing the small bedroom.

I checked my watch for the fifth time, wondering if Holland was still alive, or if Death had given Ella a signal to kill her. I'm not sure my timing had ever been so shitty. When I'd kidnapped Holland, I had no idea that Death and Ella were hunting in the area. Holland had been my dirty secret. One I had zero intention of sharing until we'd figured some shit out.

"I have a life outside of what we do."

Death's low, dark chuckle echoed through the space. "You mean kill people and clean the scenes?"

"Yeah." I shifted my weight from one foot to the other.

"She saw Ella's face and the body we brought with us. My first thought is to let Ella deal with it."

I closed the gap between us and got in his space, my chest heaving. "No. That's not an option. I'll vouch for her, but no one is laying a hand on her." I stood my ground. It was rare that I ever went toe-to-toe with him, but this situation called for a no bullshit stance. "No one will hurt her now or ever."

A wicked smile pulled at the corners of Death's mouth. "Interesting. You're in love with her."

That wasn't what this was. Love alone didn't claw at your insides until you couldn't breathe without her scent in the air. I lay awake at night, fists clenched, body shaking with the need to own, to consume, to cage just to keep her safe from the world.

What I felt for Holland was more. Darker. Addiction. Obsession. A hunger that had lived in me since the first time I thought she'd died in my arms. She wasn't a woman to me anymore—she was a need. My need. My possession. My ruin. But I'd never admit that to Death. He wouldn't understand. He would see it as weakness. So I gave him the easy answer.

I stepped away. "Something like that. It's a long story. I met her briefly when we were kids."

Soft footsteps approached and then Ella appeared, leaning on the door frame. "You knew her before she was kidnapped?"

Surprised that Ella had that information, I shot her a pointed look. "How do you know?"

Ella gave me a gentle smile as she walked in and sat on the edge of the bed. "Holland shared some things with me. Who she killed, how she knew you. Ya know, chit-chat between new friends." Her attention turned to Death. "If Kip vouches for Holland, I'd like to give her a chance. I just gave her an opportunity to run, so if she's still here in another sixty seconds, she's either too terrified to take off, or she wants to be here for Kip. She might make a good addition to the group. Something inside me says she's safe."

I exhaled. I wanted to hug Ella, but Death had to get on board before I could feel any real peace.

Death approached Ella, slid his arm around her shoulders, and asked, "Do you trust her?"

"I do," I interjected. "Aren't I the one you should be asking?"

"I agree. This conversation is with Kip, but I do support him at this point. And so, what if she says anything about the dead dude? When Kip is done, there won't be any evidence left. It's her word against ours. All of ours." She paused and looked at me. "Right? Even yours?"

"If you're questioning my loyalty to you and Death, don't. I won't ever betray you. Not for anyone."

"He loves her," Death added.

"So? You loved me, and it didn't jeopardize your friendships. It all turned out well." She reached up and touched the back of his hand. "Kip, why don't you see if Holland is still here. If not, then the chase is on."

"Better fucking not be." I walked out of the room and down the hall, my throat dry, wondering if she'd bolted out the door as soon as Ella's back was turned. My body vibrated with tension, trying not to play out the worst scenario in my mind.

I rounded the corner, and to my relief, Holland was cracking open the air fryer and checking on dinner.

"Will Death and Ella be joining us? If so, I need to pop in a few extra potatoes."

My legs devoured the distance between us, and I pressed her firmly against the countertop. Grasping her chin, I tilted her face upward and claimed her lips with a fervent kiss. She didn't fucking run. She was checking the damn potatoes.

"You didn't leave when you had a chance," I murmured, my words thick.

Her warm palm found its way to my chest, resting over the pounding rhythm of my heart.

"No. I decided you were worth the risk," she replied, her voice steady and resolute.

A raw, primal growl tore from my throat as I lowered my head, whispering with a fierce intensity, "Your loyalty will be rewarded."

With a deliberate touch, I trailed my hand down her thigh, pressing against her pussy through the fabric of her jeans.

"Oh, good. You're still here. Can I help with dinner?" Ella asked from the edge of the hall.

I kissed Holland again, then turned my attention to Death.

"We should talk ... outside."

Death walked around the body as if it weren't crumpled and bleeding on the floor.

Once outside, the soft chirps of crickets filled the evening air.

I crossed my arms and stared into the darkness. "I need your word that Holland is safe." My tone was clipped. I wasn't fucking around about her. I needed to focus on other things, like learning who I killed and Mother.

"As long as she doesn't turn on us, you have my word."

Death was a lot of things, but he was brutally honest, and his word was ironclad. It was one reason we'd been friends for so many years. We trusted each other.

"That's fair. I won't jeopardize any of us."

"I know that. It's why Holland is still alive. Between us, Ella could use another friend."

My brow arched. Death wasn't the sentimental type except when it came to Ella, and then, it was only brief moments like this.

"She has Cami."

"Yeah, but she can't share her ... as Ella calls them, our dates."

I chuckled. "I get that. It's not like she can call her and say hey, guess what sick fuck I killed today."

"Exactly. If Holland has the same darkness, which I suspect she does or you wouldn't have brought her here, then they might be good for each other."

I rubbed my jaw, the new stubble scratching my fingers. "She didn't come by choice."

Death didn't miss a beat with my confession. "And now?"

"She's here by her own free will."

"Good."

Silence, thick and heavy, weighed between us.

"Have you talked to Dope? Has he learned anything new about the Pied Piper?" I wasn't interested in discussing Holland anymore.

"Not yet. I know he's digging. Have you reached out to him yet?"

"No. I've been a little busy. Plus, I was hoping Dope would have some information before I did. Help me walk into the situation more aware of what the Pied Piper is up to. I don't trust the motherfucker any farther than I can piss."

Death crossed his arms over his chest and looked out into the tree line. "I wish Ella would tell us what he said to her, but any time I say his name she walks away. I'm not making any headway."

"Whatever it is, it has to be big, or she would have told us. She's protecting someone."

"Or someones. Hell, it might be all of us." Death walked toward the overgrown path.

I followed him, inhaling the clean country air. It was quiet and calm, not something we got in the city very often.

"That would be a heavy weight to carry all by herself."

Death stopped and looked at me. "Exactly, which is the kind of game the sick son of a bitch would play."

I let out a breath, but it rattled on the way out. My hand drifted, almost absently, to the cross hanging at my neck—fingers curling around the metal, the hidden edge biting into my palm. I squeezed. Harder. Harder. Until I felt the skin split.

Blessed are the meek, for they shall inherit the earth. The words slid through my mind like a knife through water. My mother's voice. Sweet, soft, slicing me open from the inside out.

Pain sparked up my arm, bright and jagged, grounding and weightless all at once. I didn't remember pulling the cross free. Didn't remember dragging the blade across the inside of my forearm, just shallow enough to sting. Just deep enough to feel.

"... Kip."

Death's firm tone snapped the air like a whip. I blinked. My vision cleared, the world shuddering back into focus. Blood welled in a thin, trembling line on my skin.

His stare locked on the cut, then flicked up to my face. "Kip?" Death asked softly, "What the fuck are you doing?"

I swallowed but my throat was dry and raw. "I'm fine."

A lie. We both knew it. But Death only gave a slow, measured nod. Filing it away. Watching. Waiting.

"Get some rest, man." He turned, disappearing down the path back to the warehouse, but not before I saw it—that flicker of something rare in his features.

Worry.

27

HOLLAND

The remainder of the evening unfolded in a much more relaxed manner as we gathered around the table for dinner. The aroma of the meal mingled with the soft glow of candlelight, creating a cozy atmosphere that contrasted with the tense undercurrents of the earlier conversation. I had no idea what Death and Kip had discussed during their time outside, but a nagging suspicion lingered in my mind. It was likely about me and the decision of whether I would be allowed to live or not. If I were in Death and Ella's shoes, I would have made my decision hours ago—and it would've ended with me zipped in a body bag. I seemed to have struck a chord with Ella on a deeper, more primal level. It was fascinating how swiftly people forged connections with others when bound by shared dark secrets. It felt like an unspoken form of insurance, a pact.

After dinner, Death picked up the rigid corpse from the floor with a practiced ease and then he and Kip left for a while.

Ella and I slipped on our safety masks and gloves Kip had provided and set to work scrubbing the bloodstains from the floor with a potent chemical solution that was left in the abandoned building. It hadn't taken me long to realize what this building was used for: a remote place to kill and clean victims.

This wasn't quite how I'd imagined the evening playing out, but in the process, I picked up a few useful tricks regarding Kip's cleaning techniques.

Once the men returned, Death and Ella said goodbye, and Kip and I slipped into bed, exhausted. I curled against him, my head resting on his chest, the steady thrum of his heartbeat beneath my ear. His arms banded around me, strong and unyielding, yet tender in a way that made me feel safe for the first time in years. I spread my hand over his heart, claiming proof he was real, that he was here.

He shifted just enough to pull me closer, his thumb brushing lazy circles across the sliver of skin exposed where my top had ridden up. His touch was soft, almost absentminded, but it sank deep, quieting the chaos in my mind. I let my body mold to his, every breath syncing with the rise and fall of his chest, until the tension bled out of me.

Sleep came quickly—peaceful, unbroken. For the first time in years, I didn't dream of my sister or Draco.

Sometime past midnight, a sharp shift in the air jolted me awake. Snapping out of a deep sleep, I patted the bed next to me searching for Kip, but it was empty. The sound of running water reached my ears, and I rubbed my sleep-filled eyes. Was Kip taking a shower at this time of night?

I crept down the hall, bare feet soundless on the wood floor while my heart thudded in a tight, uneasy rhythm. The door was cracked open just enough for the light to spill into the dark.

"Kip?"

No answer.

I pushed it open. And froze.

Kip sat on the closed toilet lid, head bowed, forearms resting on his knees. His fingers were white-knuckled around the cross at his neck, the blade edge pulled free, his hand moving in slow, precise strokes—dragging the sharp tip across the inside of his forearm.

Thin lines. Shallow, careful, precise. Like he'd done this a hundred times before.

His lips moved, breathless, soundless, but I caught the shape of the words.

"... though your sins be as scarlet, they shall be white as snow ..."

My stomach flip-flopped. Not at the blood, but at the way his body rocked, small, rhythmic, like a boy being scolded.

"Kip," I said again, soft but firm.

His shoulders flinched. His head jerked up, his stare wild—and empty. The Kip I knew wasn't behind his eyes right now.

Fear prickled my skin. This wasn't the man I had slept next to. For a second time, I wondered if I'd made the biggest mistake of my life staying here.

I crossed the room anyway. This wasn't the first time I'd dealt with a fragile situation, and it was important that I help bring him back to the present slowly. I knelt in front of him, then reached up and wrapped my fingers around his.

"It's Holland. I'm here in the bathroom with you. You cooked for me, and it was the best steak I've ever eaten. Death and Ella seemed nice under the circumstances," I whispered, waiting to see if any of the words about our evening would snap him out of his trance. "Come back."

His mouth opened on a ragged exhale. His eyes darted to mine, confused, desperate.

"I—I wasn't—"

"It's okay," I murmured, even though it wasn't. Even though none of this was okay. But I was here, and so was he, and somehow, that had to count for something.

I pried the cross from his hand and set it gently on the counter. I slid my palm up his scarred arm, feeling the tremor still shivering under his skin.

Confusion and fear twisted his expression. "I don't ... what am I doing here?"

"Stay with me," I whispered.

He stood, sweat beading his forehead. He grabbed the cross and slipped it around his neck again.

"Where did you go?"

He shook his head, extending a hand to help me up. Even as I posed my question, I noticed the unmistakable signs. PTSD, undoubtedly severe, but there was something else, something elusive. I'd only encountered it twice before, and I needed more insight from him before reaching any conclusions.

I took his arm and guided him to the living room. He collapsed onto the couch, visibly shaken, his eyes lost in a distant world. As I rummaged through the refrigerator for some milk, I hesitated. Should I give him time to gather himself, or should I press for answers right away? I was also eager to examine the marks on his arm, but uncertainty gnawed at me.

I joined him, offering the milk. He accepted it, drinking it all, though I couldn't tell if it was out of thirst or the need for distraction.

"Kip? Can I see your arm?" I asked tentatively.

He frowned, a flicker of reluctance in his features, but eventually extended his left arm. The thin line of dried blood told a story of its own. The cut wasn't deep enough for stitches, only surface cuts, but its presence raised more questions than answers, leaving me torn between concern and the urge to uncover the truth.

"What are the scars from?"

A shadow of shame crossed his face. "Heroin."

"You have an addiction problem?" I asked, trying to keep my tone free of judgment, though internally, I was torn.

"Not anymore. It's been years."

Thank god. At the same time, I knew how powerful addiction was. "How did it start?"

He leaned back in his seat, stretching his legs out in front of him, as if trying to physically distance himself from the memories. "Mother. The scars on my back are from her. She gave me opiates for the pain after she spiritually cleansed me and carved up my skin. The addiction was fast and hard, but she kept feeding me the drugs. She used them to control me. It was her way to ensure I never told anyone what she was doing."

Spiritual cleansing. Jesus. "Shit. Kip, that's ..." Words failed me. I was caught between disbelief and anger, but he seemed detached, his voice steady and emotionless as if he were recounting someone else's story.

"She's evil. There's no other way to say it. She manipulated me, controlled me, kept me helping my uncle and silent about the work. I cut all ties with her and my uncle until she got sick. Now she's back in my life." I didn't miss Kip's expression.

"She lives close?" All the color drained from my cheeks with my question. The woman who sold me and ruined Kip's life. The woman who was ultimately responsible for my sister's death.

"An hour away. It's the same place that you and your sister ... since we saw each other last."

A heavy silence filled the space between us. It was there that our lives changed, turned inside out for the worst. Something clicked inside me, turning off my humanity as I realized that the bitch lived close. Revenge was finally at my fingertips. *Soon.*

I placed my palm on his thigh, unsure if it was to comfort him or myself. "What was your mother up to? Cleaning the bodies?"

"That was part of it. I don't remember what else. I didn't realize shit was as fucked up as it was until a year or so ago. My friends kept saying I would disappear, and I had no goddamn idea what they were talking about."

Dissociative gaps that long? It wasn't just trauma. Someone had broken his mind deliberately. I reached up and rubbed the back of his neck as I continued. "That had to be alarming."

"Something like that. At first, I thought I was using again, but that didn't make any sense." He tilted his head so I could reach his neck better.

"Do you remember anything from that time at all? Do you remember tonight?" I asked, a bit anxious myself.

He exhaled heavily and shook his head. "I only remember

hearing you at some point." He rubbed his hands together, glancing at me with uncertainty. "I'm fucked up, Holland."

I smiled at him, trying to reassure him that I wasn't going anywhere. "Lucky you, I like fucked up."

"With your background, do you know what's happening to me? Am I losing my goddamn mind? For some reason, I thought Mother would crack first, but I'm not so sure anymore."

Without warning, Kip turned on me and grabbed me by the throat. "Don't tell. Don't you say a word," he snarled at me.

My nails dug into his wrist. I couldn't breathe. And maybe it wasn't just the air being stolen from my lungs—maybe it was the realization that I was trapped, and he wasn't letting go.

28

———

KIP

The room shifted, and a loud buzzing rattled my skull. Samantha blurred in and out and then everything went black. When I came to, everything was hazy. I tried to focus, but my brain was foggy, and the people were unclear.

"What are we going to do with him?"

From the far corner of the room, I looked around, trying to identify who spoke. My arms burned from being restrained behind me.

"I can make him disappear," my uncle responded.

Several people sat around the table, but it was so dim it was difficult to make out faces. However, I knew some of the voices.

The man who had spoken earlier folded his hands on top of the table.

"His friends will miss him," Mother added. "The school will notice and then they'll start snooping. That can't happen."

The mumbled conversation faded in and out as they discussed someone's fate. My fate.

"He can serve a purpose."

Pastor? I scrambled to piece the conversation together. Why were they all together in one room? Who was the leader of the group?

"I've been waiting for the perfect time to introduce this idea, and it seems as though your son will be the key, Lily."

I knew who that was, but …

"I want to bring someone else to join us."

"Are you sure that's smart? We've already gained five additional members. There's such a thing as too many," Pastor Pendleton said with an edge to his words.

"What purpose would this person serve?" Mother asked, her tone curious.

I strained to hear what he said, but I couldn't make out the words. Maybe the drugs were messing with my mind too much.

"The person I want to bring into the group has a rare specialty. Before I bring him in, I need to discuss some matters with him. I'll keep you posted. In the meantime, lay low and watch that one." His pudgy finger pointed in my direction.

Why was I a threat? I was tied up and drugged. It didn't make sense.

The screech of the chair dragging across the floor made me wince, and I looked to the leader of the group. Our gazes connected, and a wicked grin eased across his blurry face. I squinted, trying to make out his features, but the fucking drugs clouded my vision. My heart raced and sweat trickled down the sides of my forehead.

"Your eyes are fascinating." He strolled over to me and knelt, assessing me as if I were a caged animal under scientific study.

"I think you'll do quite well, Kip."

I licked my dry lips, trembling from his proximity, his power, the true evil that radiated off him. This wasn't the same as the evil that Mother carved out of me.

"What's your name?" I managed to ask.

He chuckled as he stood. "In due time."

A strange and unsettling noise abruptly drew my attention, coinciding with the sudden cessation of the buzzing in my head. The area around me wavered, flickering in and out of focus like a poorly tuned television.

I saw myself from the outside: fingers tight around Holland's throat, her feet scraping the floor, her lips turning blue. She wasn't fighting me, not really. She'd only stared at me, mouth open and appalled, and then, with a clarity that pierced the fog, I remembered where I was.

Holland's eyes, usually so bright and clear, were now wide with terror, her pupils dilated as she pulled at my hands, which were wrapped around her neck. A wave of horror washed over me as I realized what I'd done, and I jerked back, releasing my grip. She gasped for air while tears cascaded down her cheeks.

"Fuck, what did I do?" *This is how you killed the other girl, remember?*

Holland coughed, gasped for air, and turned away from me.

I jumped to my feet and scooped her into my arms, carrying her to the bathroom. "Little ghost, are you okay? I'm sorry." My voice shook as I struggled to stay in reality. "Something is pulling me back. I'm not sure I can stay present," I choked out, struggling to reach the bathroom. I grabbed the shower door and flung it open, quickly turning on the cold water like the times when I'd almost overdosed on heroin. I sank to the floor with her in my arms. She curled into me, sobbing.

"Little ghost ..." I rocked her back and forth, the cold spray soaking our clothes, but helping me not slip away again. "I don't understand what's happening."

She reached up and trailed her fingertips across my jawline. As we huddled together, she trembled, her lips grazing the shell of my ear.

"It's okay," she said, though her throat showed a faint bruising outline of my desperation, darkening with each beat of her pulse. "You're back. You're here."

"I'm not," I rasped. "I'm not—I keep leaving."

The world twisted again, like a camera shutter refusing to close, and all I could see was the memory: my grip on her pale neck, the whites of her eyes, but it wasn't Holland.

She shifted in my arms. "You're here. You're holding on. You didn't let go, Kip."

The world wanted to drag me back under, to where I was a weapon and nothing more, but Holland's tiny, cold hands on my face kept me tethered. I pressed my brow to hers, fighting the urge to run, to be somewhere else, someone else.

After a long time, she spoke. "You could kill me, Kip. But you won't. You didn't the first time, and you won't now."

I wanted to protest, to deny it, but my voice was gone. I only nodded, the gesture sharp and final. The implication sickened me. Holland was right. She was never safe, not with me, not with a man who could forget her name in a single moment and become a stranger.

I kissed her forehead. "How do you know? I can't even trust myself."

I shifted so Holland could rest against my shoulder. Her breathing evened. I watched her throat move, fascinated and appalled that I had the power to stop it forever. I had always thought, in my damnable arrogance, that I was the one in control—the lever in the machine, not the worn rope fraying at the edge. Now I saw the truth. I was the weakness. Holland was my strength.

She started humming, the kind of song sung to children. Her chin rested in the crook of my neck. "Tell me what you saw," she said quietly. "Tell me so I can help you back if you leave again."

I answered with silence as I tried to recall what I'd seen.

"My father had hands like yours," she whispered. Her words barely made it through the roar of my pulse. She coughed. A ragged, raw sound. "Large, powerful."

I understood she was talking to calm me. She shivered, and I realized the cold water was still running.

"Let's get you warmed up." I cupped her cheeks and looked at her. "But I think you should leave. I'm too dangerous. I would never forgive myself if I killed you. It fucking broke me once. I can't live through that again."

The indecision on her beautiful expression was like a dagger, plunging into my chest and ripping my heart out.

29

HOLLAND

I stood in front of my bedroom's full-length mirror and stared at the fading bruises on my neck. Three days had passed since Kip had attacked me. When he'd offered me the chance to leave, I had to go. Not to punish him, but he'd terrified me. I needed to wrap my head around what had happened, because I knew damn well Kip wouldn't hurt me like that. Rough sex, breaking into my house, stalking me, killing men? Sure. But not hurting women. It went against what he did with the society. It went against his moral compass.

That was the moment everything snapped into place. The signs. The blackouts. The look on his face when he didn't know me. I couldn't say it out loud—not yet. Not until I had proof. But I knew. And if I was right ... It changed *everything*.

Thanks to Kip, my bosses thought I was dealing with a family emergency, so I didn't need to report to work yet. I located my cell on my nightstand and pulled up Monster in my contacts.

Me:
I miss you.

Even with the scare, I messaged him several times a day. I didn't want him to think I'd disappeared. I wouldn't abandon him, but I had to have some space to dig into my suspicions.

My phone chimed.

Monster:
You too. I'm working tonight to keep myself busy, and not to break into your home and watch you sleep.

I couldn't resist a smile. He was doing everything he could to keep it together, and I had more respect for him than ever before. He'd been abused, used, and broken. But what I'd seen was on a new level, and I couldn't turn off my training at this point. I had to find the answers, and I knew exactly who was going to give them to me even if they didn't want to. A surge of dark anger rushed through me. It was the same feeling that fueled me when I'd killed Dom. I took a deep breath, allowing that fury to drive me. After all, the best revenge was waiting so long they never saw me coming.

I chose a scarf from my closet along with pressed dark-wash jeans and a comfortable baby blue top. I needed to be able to move quickly, so I slipped on my Nikes. My pulse stammered against my wrist. I'd dreamed about this day for a long damn time, but it never occurred to me it could become reality.

Flipping my hair over my shoulder, I tipped up my chin in the mirror.

"Do this for you, Holland. Do this for Ally. Do this for the man that you're falling in love with. Set you all free."

THE HOUR DRIVE seemed like an eternity as I turned the conversation in my mind over and over. No matter what, I had to stay in my psychiatrist head and not spiral into the chaos clawing at my insides.

The house was pristine as I parked my car in the driveway and assessed my location. I sat in my car and noted the front and back entrances. No matter where I was, I always marked the exits. Some habits never died after captivity. Know your surroundings, be aware, be ready to kill at a moment's notice.

I climbed out of the car and snatched my purse from the passenger seat. Slinging the strap over my shoulder, I steeled myself and felt the reassuring weight of the gun through the bag. Each step I took echoed sharply against the pavement, slicing through the quiet morning air. The birds chirped innocently, creating an illusion of tranquility. But I knew the reality beneath that facade.

The front door cracked open before I reached it, and a woman with kind eyes smiled at me.

"I'm Cynthia," she said, motioning for me to come in.

"Hi, I'm Holland. The fibrosis clinic sent me to do a quick evaluation on Lily." I gave her a warm smile, inviting her to trust me. "The insurance has threatened to stop paying her bills unless we get this done."

"Damn insurance. She's dying—what else do they want? They're getting their money. Can't they let her die in peace?"

"It's frustrating for sure. I would just hate for her family to have large medical bills to pay after she ..."

Cynthia frowned, and her lips pressed together. "You're right. And her son. He's a great guy. Kind, protective, always checking on her." She closed the door behind me, and I stepped inside, glancing toward the kitchen.

The sleek granite countertops were white-veined with soft gray in contrast to the matte-black cabinets with gold handles, polished to a mirror shine. A farmhouse sink gleamed under the window, framed by sheer linen curtains that floated with the light breeze from the air conditioning. The backsplash glittered with tiny white and black mosaic tiles.

For a heartbeat, I almost forgot where I was. Almost.

But then the details sharpened. The granite—cracked at the corner, a hairline fracture creeping across it like a scar. The brass handles were rubbed raw in places from obsessive polishing. The air smelled faintly of roses, but underneath, there was something sharp, chemical—like bleach clinging to the grout.

A crucifix hung above the stove, the edges worn smooth where it had been traced over and over. I suspected not in devotion, though, in penance. My stomach twisted. I remembered those hands. I remembered how they offered cookies one moment and gave me away the next.

The refrigerator rattled softly, its surface covered in pastel magnets and yellowing scraps of paper with Bible verses in delicate, looping script. My fingers drifted to the butcher block, tracing the deep scars etched into the wood. For a second, I was young again— feet swinging from a tall chair, a glass of milk sweating on the table. I had no idea what was waiting.

Outside the window, white roses bloomed like they were trying too hard. Too white. Too perfect. But just past them, I saw the weeds, black and gnarled, climbing up the trellis, fighting their way in. Add a little glitter to anything and it hides the ugly.

My thoughts returned to why I was here, and I curled my hands into balls. I wasn't a little girl anymore. And this time, I wasn't the one who would be begging.

I left the kitchen on shaking legs while my heart thudded hard in my throat, a brutal, punishing drumbeat as I crossed the house.

The hallway was silent—too silent. No creaks in the floorboards, no low murmur of a TV, no trace of life.

The door to Kip's mother's bedroom was cracked open. For a second, I simply stood there, staring at it. My fists clenched at my sides, nails biting into my palms.

I pushed it open.

The room was dim, heavy with the scent of lavender and sickness. Soft white curtains filtered the late light, and an oxygen machine hissed quietly in the corner. She lay in a massive four-poster bed, wrapped in a pale blue blanket, her silver hair spread neatly over the pillow like someone had combed it just so.

She looked smaller than I remembered; much frailer. Her skin had thinned to near translucence, and her bones were prominent under her papered flesh. Her hands were folded loosely on her chest. For a horrible second, I thought she was already gone.

Then her eyes opened. The same eyes. Pale blue, sharp as a scalpel. Her lips pulled into the faintest, knowing smile.

"I was wondering," she rasped, voice thin but laced with something that still cut deep, "when you would visit."

Something inside me cracked. I wanted to run. I wanted to scream. Instead, I stepped forward, my jaw tight with tension.

"I'm not here to wish you well," I whispered. "I'm here to watch you die."

Something I couldn't identify flickered across her expression as I stepped closer. For a moment, I wondered if she even recognized me. But then her lips curled into that same knowing smile.

"I always knew you'd come back," she whispered.

I let out a shaky breath. "Stop."

Her smile didn't falter.

"You think you broke me," I said, my tone carrying a steel edge. "You think what you and my father did—selling me, handing me off like a piece of property—made me small. Weak." A bitter laugh caught in my throat. "You didn't break me. You made me dangerous."

Her jaw set and her fingers twitched against the blanket. I stepped closer, close enough to see the faint tremble in her jaw.

"You made me smart. You taught me how to survive in the dark. You made sure I learned to cut before anyone could cut me." My voice cracked, rage and grief coiled tight in my chest. "You made me into everything you were too much of a coward to face."

For the first time, the smile slipped a fraction.

My heart hammered against my ribs as flashes of the past played in my mind. "But here's the thing."

Her eyes snapped to mine with a hint of anticipation.

"I know what you did to Kip."

30

———

KIP

"I'm sorry, you did what?" Dope asked, his brows furrowing as he reached for a rolled joint resting on the edge of his desk. He smoothed his burgundy shirt and shook his head.

"Choked her." The words tumbled out before I could stop them, and I instantly wished I could take them back. But I needed their help. I needed to know what the hell was wrong with me.

Death leaned against the wall in Dope's downstairs gaming and work room, arms folded, watching me. His black shirt and pants gave him an even more ominous appearance. Lethal. His gaze was sharp, focused, as if he was seeing me for the first time. Different.

I was different. I was falling in love with a girl I thought I'd killed. And years later, I was confiding in my friends in a way I never had before.

"She's okay. I'm not." I shoved both hands through my hair, gripping my skull like I could hold myself together. "Killing evil bastards is one thing. But hurting a woman?" I shook my head. "Fuck no. That's not me. That's never been me." I toyed with the hem of my blue T-shirt.

"It's not you," Death finally said. "It's against who you are. And nothing you tell me would change my mind. Something is fucking with you. What did Holland say?"

His tone was calm, calculated, but warmed slightly when he said Holland's name. Maybe he was getting used to the idea of her being in my life.

"She said she needed to do some research. I told her about the heroin and my disappearing for days, how I had no idea what the hell you guys were talking about when you kept asking where I was when I disappeared."

Dope leaned back in his computer chair. "Interesting. No wonder you were defensive as shit about it. You don't remember anything at all?"

"No. But sometimes I'd suddenly find myself in an old, abandoned church or the basements of old buildings."

"Here in Portland?" Death tilted his head with curiosity.

"Sometimes, but other times I was in Washington or Idaho." I cleared my throat. "Holland asked if there was a particular feeling with the time loss. It's hard to explain, but I wasn't in control."

"Like choking Holland. I mean, dude, save that shit for the bedroom." Dope pressed the button of his lighter and fired up his joint.

My brow arched at him as Death chuckled.

"I'll be curious what Holland finds out. Give her my number so I can help if she's okay with that." Dope started to type something on his computer, but I couldn't make out the words on the screen.

I quickly relayed the rest of the events and what I'd seen and heard while in the so-called flashback. Shit, I wasn't even sure what they were anymore.

"So, you couldn't see any faces, but you recognized the voices?" Death pushed off the wall and joined me on the couch.

I didn't know if they were flashbacks, dreams, or memories resurfacing through a fog of heroin and trauma. All I knew was they felt real. Too fucking real.

I pressed my lips together, the conversation lingering in my mind.

"Yeah. Mother, Uncle, Pastor Pendleton. There were some others at the table too, but I wasn't sure who they were."

"For some reason, I don't recall your mother's first name. What is it again?" Death waited for me to answer.

Hell, I knew why he didn't remember, but I didn't want to get into that conversation right now.

"Her first name is Lily."

For a fleeting second, Death's entire body stiffened. "How did I not know that? The pictures of her with the Pied Piper ... when I met with him and talked before, he mentioned a woman named Lily." Death swallowed and his spine snapped to attention. "That he'd dated."

The room fell into an unsettling silence as I struggled to come to terms with what he'd revealed. Shock slammed into me like a tidal wave.

"What the hell? My mother *dated* that fucker?"

"Yeah," he growled.

Just the mention of the Pied Piper's name set us all on edge. He was dangerous, manipulative. We were simply pawns in his elaborate game.

I leaned my head back and groaned. "Fuck. My. Life." I looked over at Dope, his gaze narrowing, deep in thought. "Jesus. He's been in your life since the beginning, and you had no idea."

I shot off the couch, my anger rising to the surface. "Which also means that he might know Holland. As in he was there that night I killed someone. A young girl my age. With red hair and blue eyes."

Dope swung around in his chair, his mouth gaping open and closed like a fish out of water. "Okay, this shit is getting more insane. You thought you killed a girl when we were teenagers and never said a fucking thing about it?"

"Mother kept me supplied with drugs to ensure I kept my mouth shut, remember?"

"Fuck. That woman has to go. Like I get that we don't hurt

females, but she's a fucking monster, so in my book the bitch doesn't count."

She's a monster, but so am I.

Dope returned to his computer, his fingers flying over the keys on the keyboard.

"Lily Lytton aka Lily Clemmons aka Lily Harrison." He grew silent again and leaned closer to his screen. "It's interesting what pictures people put on the dark web." He glanced at me sideways. "Oh. Fucking. Hell."

Death and I crowded around our friend, peering over his shoulder.

Dope smirked while he typed. "Old chat logs about girl after girl for sale. I can't believe they thought this shit was safe. But guess what? Some dumbass admin kept nightly backups, and they're still sitting on an unsecured network attached storage. It's referred to as NAS for short. It only took me five minutes to find."

A chat log flickered on the screen with dozens of usernames. Threads about "new shipments." And one photo.

My attention landed on the words and image from years ago, and my heart skidded to a fucking stop.

Her.

"They didn't post her like they did the other girls—like a product," Dope muttered, his focus on the screen. "They kept her hidden, passed around like some twisted secret." He continued to scroll, his jaw tight.

Death leaned over his shoulder, reading aloud, "Love a sweet little redhead? Contact the Pied Piper." He pinned me with a sharp look. "That's Holland. Only younger. What the fuck is this, Kip?"

My vision blurred, pulse pounding in my ears as I stared at the image. Trying to convince myself what I was seeing wasn't real, I blinked hard, but the screen stayed the same.

"It's Holland," I rasped. "We met once, but she was introduced as Samantha. That was the night I thought I killed her. I killed someone, but it wasn't her."

Dope let out a low whistle, leaning back in his chair, still zoned in on the chat logs.

"The Pied Piper was trafficking? Should've figured. But I'm shocked he didn't cover his damn tracks."

"Me too," Death said. "But it's in our favor."

Dope frowned, his forehead creasing as if he was deep in thought. "Wait. Let me get this straight. Lily, your mother, dated the Pied Piper? And they ran in the same college circle with those other psychos."

"Yeah." I wasn't sure what he was getting at.

Dope froze. His mouth opened and closed before he finally spoke. "Shit. Kip ... you're sleeping with Holland?"

A sour, burning knot twisted in my gut.

"She's gorgeous," I said, piecing together what he was getting at. "Wouldn't you?"

Death's hand dropped heavily on my shoulder, his words sharp as they landed. "Let's hope she's not blood, man."

I stiffened, my goddamn heart stopped before it stuttered to life again. Dope sat forward again, tension crackling in the room.

"Think about it. If Lily and PP were swapping more than favors back then ... then Holland could be more than just some girl caught in your mother's shit. Dude, what if Lily is her mom too?"

The air felt thin, suffocating. I yanked my phone from my back pocket, thumbs fumbling across the screen. I didn't even know what I was typing, just that I had to reach her.

Me:

I need to see you. Now.

I dragged a hand down my face, fingers digging into the back of my neck like I could claw the panic out. Please, God—or devil, or whoever the fuck is running this show—don't let this be true. Don't let the girl I'm obsessed with be my fucking blood relation. That was a brand of fucked-up I wasn't sure I could survive. Not with the way I wanted her, the way I needed her.

Dope let out a shaky laugh, rolling his shoulders and popping his neck.

"Dude, you're in love with her, aren't you?"

I swallowed hard, my chest squeezing tight.

"Yeah. I haven't told her yet, but yeah. For a while."

Death exhaled, the sound like a damn funeral bell. "You might want to hold off on that confession, at least until you're sure how she's connected to you."

31

HOLLAND

Her eyelids fluttered.

For a moment, I wondered if she'd drifted off—or died. I hoped for option two.

But then her mouth twitched, curling into something sharp, evil.

"Oh, darling ..." The rasp scraped out, but it was as sharp as a blade. "You have no idea what I did."

I tried to speak, a strangled sound catching in my chest. "You—" My voice broke. I slid my hand into my purse and dug my fingers into the gun, pressing hard, desperate to ground myself. "You broke him. Your *own* son."

Her brows lifted slightly. "Kip was already cracked. We simply shaped the pieces."

"Liar." My breath tore out of me, ragged and raw. "You didn't just ruin me. You ruined him too."

Her brows lifted slightly.

"You twisted everything. You carved up his soul and called it love, so he would never know what you did."

"And look what he became," she murmured, gaze distant now, as if reliving those times. "My goddamn masterpiece."

The machine beside her hissed. The slow, mechanical drag of air keeping her alive, when she should've suffocated under the weight of her sins years ago.

"He was a wild dog," she whispered. "Snarling. Biting. Bloody. We made him ... useful."

A tremble rippled through me, rage crawling up my spine like a second skin. "You turned him into a killer."

She smiled—sickly sweet, gentle. "He was always meant to serve."

I took a shaky step forward, the gun in my purse heavy against my hip. I couldn't hear past the static in my mind as her words spun so fast in my brain, I struggled with what to say next. I understood that you couldn't reason with sanity, but I needed to try anyway.

"You *sold* me."

She bared her teeth, more animal than human, and I saw a flash of yellowed teeth. "You were a pretty little thing. So easy to give away."

My vision blurred.

Suddenly, I was young again, knees scraped, hands shaking, hiding in the closet, praying to a God I didn't believe in. I was strapped to a table. I was dragging a piece of glass across a man's throat.

And now? I wasn't small anymore.

The cold metal of my weapon pressed against my palm.

Her gaze dropped to my handbag, and her expression flickered—something unspoken bleeding through. "You'll never outrun it, Holland. You carry it in your blood."

"I'm not you," I snapped.

Her chin jutted up with a knowing. "No, hon. You're worse."

For a second, I swayed, her words slapping me in the face, and then I smiled. How could I be worse than the woman in front of me?

"Then I'll use it to my advantage." The gun came up, and I held it steady.

An unsteady exhale escaped her, more sigh than sound, as if the idea of me putting a bullet in her head amused her.

The weapon felt heavier than it should have. Heavier than it had in my hands during all the nights I practiced. Heavier than when I'd killed Dom. Heavier than the rage simmering in my chest.

I leveled it at her. My muscles jittered for a fleeting moment and then stilled again.

"Say it," I whispered.

Kip's mother's lips curved, thin and papery. "Say what, hon?"

"Tell me why you did it." I gritted my teeth.

The oxygen machine hissed between us. The room felt too small, too closed up, and the air was thick with lavender and bleach. My heartbeat thundered in my ears.

Her pale eyes glittered. "You think you're here for justice?"

I took a step closer, my weapon steady but my lungs locked, and I struggled to breathe.

"I'm here for the truth about why you hurt your son. Why you sold me and my sister."

She sighed, almost tender—like a mother recalling a bedtime story. "Oh, little girl—"

"Don't call me that."

Her hands twitched on the blanket, the same hands that had once held a child down and carved his skin and drugged him.

"We shaped Kip." Her voice softened, reverent. "We tamed him. Without us, he would've been nothing but teeth and blood. We made him a weapon."

My throat burned. "You turned him into a monster."

Her gaze sharpened, cutting through me. "And you love him anyway."

For a second, the room spun. The gun shook with the weight, and my grip tightened on the weapon. "You're going to die alone in this bed."

Her lips curled like shriveled, rotten fruit. "We all die alone."

I chewed on my bottom lip, and my arms dropped a fraction. "Tell me how it happened," I hissed.

Her expression hardened, sharp as ice chipping away at bone. "Tell you what, hon?"

My jaw clenched so tight it ached. "Say what you did to me. To my sister."

A flicker of amusement ghosted over her features. "Oh, Samantha."

The sound of my name in her mouth was a blade dragged over old scars.

"You were just ... so easy."

My chest caved inward. I fought the wave, that crashing undertow of memories, the dark, loneliness, the locked doors, but it surged up anyway.

"Two redheaded angels, dropped right in our laps," she said, almost fondly. "So pretty. So perfect. So easy to pass along."

A cold sweat broke out down my spine. "You sold us."

Her pale lips twitched. "We saved you."

"Saved me?!" My voice cracked sharp, ripping through the silence. "You handed us over to monsters."

She whispered it like a prayer, "And you survived."

The walls closed in, and my vision blurred at the edges.

"I survived because Ally died!" I choked, tears I didn't want, didn't mean, burning hot down my cheeks. "I survived because I slit Dom's throat and ran until my feet bled."

Her attention didn't waver. "A girl like you was never meant for softness."

My palm pressed against the weight of my weapon. A reminder and a promise that I was safe. Yet, the hate inside of me nearly doubled me over, the scream caught behind my teeth so violent it burned. I wanted to pull the trigger. God, I wanted to. But I couldn't. Not yet. Not like this.

Her smile slipped slightly, something old and brittle showing underneath. "You were Samantha back then," she added, with a cold, idle cruelty, like she was recalling the name of a doll she'd discarded. "Your sister never let go of her real name, but you? You slipped into the new one like it belonged to you."

Then, the final blow, soft as a whisper on the air:

"You don't know who you are, do you?"

32

KIP

My stomach twisted into knots as I paced the small room, staring at my phone and willing Holland to message me back.

"Where are you?" I muttered.

A sudden unease coasted over me as images of Draco getting his hands on her entered my mind. We hadn't heard from him in a week, but I knew he was watching her, planning. She was armed and could certainly defend herself. I saw it myself when Cooper was attacking her. She was smart. Calculated. Even so, I needed to know that she was safe. See it for myself.

"I need to go check on Holland. She hasn't messaged me back, which is weird." I took a minute to fill them in on Holland's captivity, Draco, and Dominic.

"I'm surprised you left her at all with this asshole Draco after her," Death said, frowning.

"She needed some time after I attacked her. Hell, I don't trust myself at the moment, so I agreed." I second-guessed myself for allowing her space when that sick fuck was still on the loose. I needed to take care of him once and for all. Holland didn't deserve to be hunted by the motherfucker.

The phone screen glowed in my palm, the faint buzz of the call going to voicemail for the fifth time. Why wasn't she answering? She knew how important it was to stay in touch with Draco still running loose. We'd been messaging over the last few days even though she was taking a break. It hadn't been long enough since I'd tried to contact her to dive into a full-blown panic, but I had a gut feeling that something was off. Anxiety twisted in my stomach as I tried to process the information we had. Was I trying to save the girl I'd fallen in love with or ... my sister?

I clenched my jaw, lowering my cell slowly, trying not to crush the thing.

Dope leaned back in his gaming chair, legs splayed out, lazily spinning a flash drive between his fingers. "Maybe she just needs a minute, man."

Death, on the other hand, didn't look so convinced. He stood against the wall, arms folded, his sharp eyes on me like he was watching a grenade without the pin.

"She's smart," Death said carefully. "But she's alone. You sure you want to give her space right now?"

Shaking, I paced the edge of the room. The monitors behind Dope flickered, code scrolling, the dark web threads still half-lit on one screen. Holland's picture was frozen on another of her younger, thinner, her hair tangled, expression wild.

"I shouldn't have left her," I ground out. "Fuck, I shouldn't have—"

"She asked for it," Dope cut in gently. "You said she needed time."

"Yeah, well, maybe she shouldn't have fucking trusted me with that choice."

I stopped, pressing a fist hard against the wall, teeth bared, trying to breathe through the white-hot panic blistering in my chest. The room was suddenly too small, too loud, and too quiet all at once.

"She's just ..." I blew out a heavy sigh and rubbed my aching forehead. She's the only thing holding me together.

"Where would she go?" Death asked. His tone was careful now, grounding, like he was trying to keep me tethered to the floor. "You know her better than anyone. Where could she be?"

I blinked hard, a pulse of heat flashing through my head. And just like that, the wrong memory slammed through me. Not now. Not now. But it came anyway.

Flash —

A red-haired girl, crying in the dark.

Hands holding me down.

Words as soft as a hymn: "Some sins are born in the blood."

I staggered, my palm dragging down the wall, and my throat tight.

Death was in front of me in a blink, gripping my shoulder. "Kip."

"I'm fine," I said between gritted teeth.

"You're not," he said calmly. "And if she's out there, we need you sharp, not spiraling."

The faintest thread of vanilla drifted through the air—soap, clean skin, sunlight on bare shoulders—Holland, or the memory of her, or maybe I was fucking losing it.

Dope stood slowly, clicking his tongue. "Man, you're half in love and half in a psychotic break. We need to lock this shit down."

I pushed off the wall, dragging a shaking hand over my mouth.

"I need to find her," I said hoarsely. "Before this gets worse."

Dope focused on his keyboard. "Sit down, asshole. Let's figure out where she went before you break your own goddamn skull."

Death squeezed my shoulder once before letting go.

And for a moment, just a moment, I thought I heard her voice inside my head, soft, trembling: "You're not a monster."

Dope's fingers flew over the keyboard, the dim light from the monitors throwing green and gold across his face. His jaw worked from side to side, tongue poking his cheek in concentration.

"Hold up," he muttered. "I'm scraping the old directories on this computer while I'm looking for the location of Holland's phone."

Death dropped onto the couch beside me, elbows on his knees, watching me from the corner of his vision. "Take a minute," he said quietly.

I dragged in a sharp inhale, chest tight, fists clenched on my knees. My whole body itched to move—to run, to drive, to hunt—but the rational part of me, the part that still gave a shit, stayed rooted. For now.

Dope let out a low whistle, his attention traveling across the screen. "Holy shit. You remember those old chat logs we pulled from the threads a few minutes ago?"

I looked up sharply. "Yeah. Why?"

"Guess whose IP is stamped all over the admin files?" Dope smirked, sharp and humorless. "Dear old Lily."

A crack split down the center of my skull, or maybe it was inside. "My mother?"

"She wasn't just playing sidekick, man. She was fucking running the whole goddamn thing. I've got timestamps, login credentials, payments—she built the damn house."

He turned the monitor toward me, his jaw tight, his expression dark. "And I've got archived message threads. Look."

My gaze snapped to the screen. I froze.

There, pixelated, timestamped, and undeniable was a photo. Red hair. A kid's face, wide and terrified, tied to a chair. Shadows loomed behind her. A man's hand on her shoulder. My mother negotiated Holland's sale in the thread. The Pied Piper's signature approved the sale.

"Jesus Christ," Death muttered, rising beside me. His features were carved in stone. "Your mother didn't only take Holland—she was running the fucking show."

I stumbled back, hitting the wall, my breath ripping out of me. My fingers dug into the drywall, scraping like I could peel the world open and find a version that didn't end with this.

"All of the flashbacks, I knew my mother was involved, but I wasn't sure how much. I thought she tried to save Holland, but I'm all fucked up. I—" My shoulders slumped in defeat. "How could I ever come back from that? She'll never forgive my family for the part they played. She's the only woman I've ever loved, and I'm going to lose her either way because of what my family did, or worse, she's my fucking sister."

Death rocked back on his heels. "But do you love her enough to survive this?"

My head whipped up, vision burning. "What the fuck does that mean?"

"It means," Death said softly, "you better know whether you're saving her ... or saving yourself."

The room blurred.

Dope's voice was a low hum, Death's a sharp echo, the computer screens a pulsing glow I couldn't focus on.

Blood. Family. Holland.

The words cracked through my skull, sharp as a bone splinter. My fists slammed into the wall, once, twice, three times, the pain a jagged thread barely holding me together.

"Goddammit," I choked out. "She can't be—"

Dope spun in his chair, exasperated. "Kip, man, slow the fuck down."

"I'm past slowing down," I snarled.

Death stepped forward, gripping my shoulders hard enough to make my teeth clack. "Focus. Where would she go now?"

I staggered back, chest heaving, head swimming.

Dope frowned at the screen. "Her phone last pinged over near Cottage Grove."

My gut twisted as bile scorched my throat.

"She wanted answers. I know her. She wanted to confront this."

Death's gaze landed on mine, sharp, assessing. "And she went to Lily."

Tension snaked through my shoulders and neck. "Fuck."

Dope clicked again and he released a low whistle. "Hold up. Her car's moving, man. She's on the highway. Looks like she's headed back to Portland."

For a heartbeat, I stood there, pulse pounding, air slicing in and out of my lungs like a knife.

Relief hit me hard.

But tangled in it was something darker, sharper—panic.

She went to my mother. She went alone.

And now she was coming home, raw and rattled, and I wasn't there to hold her, to steady her, to explain all the things I didn't even understand myself.

My jaw clenched, my chest heaving now that she was okay.

I needed to be at her place when she got there. I needed to see her. I needed to make this right before it all slipped through my fucking hands. Even if she was my sister, she deserved to have support through this.

"I'm going," I said, already shoving my arms into my jacket and then grabbing my car keys out of the front pocket of my jeans.

Dope rose halfway from his chair. "Kip, man, wait."

"I can't wait."

"And Kip?" Death's words caught me, quiet, steel-edged.

I turned, breathless, wired, raw.

"Keep it fucking together."

A hollow laugh punched out of me. "No promises."

The cool air hit like a slap as I stumbled into the night, the street-lights gleaming off wet pavement. My fingers trembled as I unlocked the car, jaw clenched so tight it felt like my teeth might break.

She can't be mine. She's mine. She's the love of my life … fucking hell, what if we're related?

The thoughts tore me apart, again and again, as I slammed the door and twisted the ignition.

The engine roared to life, and I wrapped my hand around my necklace, the cross biting into my palm.

If she's breaking, I'll hold her. If she's running, I'll catch her. If I lose her, I'll burn this world to the ground.

Tires screeched as I tore out of the driveway, the city lights smearing past in a blur of red and gold. My heart was a war drum in my chest.

And under it all, a whisper I couldn't shake, an old, rotted voice I would never outrun telling me this was all my fault.

"You're not a monster." Desperation clung to the words I spoke out loud.

But God help me, I was.

And I was coming home to her.

33

HOLLAND

The words slithered under my skin, cold and sharp, cutting places I didn't know were still vulnerable.

In an instant, my mouth went dry. "Shut up. You know nothing about me."

Her laugh was a wheeze, a death rattle laced with triumph.

"I'm sick of being nice, you little bitch," she spat. "You have no idea whose blood runs in your veins."

The world tilted, and the floor shifted. I staggered back, my gun lowering as bile rushed up my throat.

Her glare sliced through me with a glowing cruelty.

The room faded in and out: a boy in the dark, whispering my name.

I shook it off as my knees almost gave out. I caught myself on the doorframe, the weapon slipping to my side.

Kip's mother's fingers twitched under the blanket, but her smile stayed sharp.

"You want the truth? Isn't that what you came here for?" she rasped. "You were never just some trafficked child." A wheeze scraped from her throat. "You were *his*."

My stomach twisted. "Whose?"

Her pale eyes blazed with a chilling intensity, mocking me with every glance. "The leader of us all," she sneered, her words dripping with venom. "The one they all feared. The man who claimed ownership of you before you even took your first steps. The most merciless and infamous serial killer alive today."

I stumbled back, the breath knocked out of me while my head refused to believe her lies. "We call him the Pied Piper."

The name hit me cold, but it was unfamiliar, meaningless. But the way she said it, like a hymn, like a curse, like she was tasting it on her tongue. It made my fucking skin crawl.

"I don't—" My brow arched. "I don't know who that is."

"No, you wouldn't, would you? You were small the last time you saw him." She shifted slightly, making a faint sound from the oxygen machine.

"The Pied Piper isn't a man most people meet. He's a shadow. A whisper in your nightmare. A cruel promise in the dark." Her gaze flicked up to mine, slicing straight through me. "He plays his music, and we all follow."

A shudder ran down my spine, something black curling under my skin.

Kip's mother's voice dropped to a reverent whisper.

"Your mother was one of them. And you—you were his little accident."

My knees locked. My hands shook around my weapon.

"When she betrayed him, he took you," she revealed. "Because he could. Because it proved he was untouchable. Because it proved to the rest of us that blood meant nothing to him."

The room blurred, my vision splintering at the edges. "No ..."

"Oh, yes," she murmured. "He gave you up like a tithe, a little red-haired offering. And Ally ... oh, poor Ally. She was simply collateral, in the wrong place at the wrong time."

My chest squeezed tight, threatening to cut off my air supply.

"Who is my mother? Is she alive?" The words tasted bitter on my tongue, but I had to know.

Kip's mother tilted her head, assessing me. "You look like her. Or you did. She's gone. You don't betray the Pied Piper and live to talk about it."

A whisper of sadness passed through me, but I would digest that information later when I had time to wrap my head around it.

Kip's mother tilted her head. "Did you ever wonder why you're so angry? Why you fight so hard? Why you survived when you should've died?" Her smile curled. "It's in your cells, your DNA." She pointed to the front of the house. "It's time for you to go, Samantha," she whispered, her words fading like the last thread of a hymn. "You have so much to learn."

My brain rejected the idea that a killer was my father, shoved it away, but it scraped at the walls inside my skull. Bile scorched my throat as my vision blurred, black stars crowding the edges.

I'm his.

I wanted to rip the blood from my body. I wanted to cut his legacy out of my skin. I wanted to burn everything and everyone down.

But mostly—I wanted to never, ever have been born. A serial killer!

Running from the room, I rushed outside. I stumbled down the steps, heart jackhammering in my chest, skin crawling like something was slithering right under the surface. The afternoon light cut at my vision, hot and sharp and too bright.

She's lying. She always lies.

My feet hit the gravel. My hands fumbled for the car door but missed the handle once, twice. A strangled cry tore from my throat.

She's a manipulator. She's poison. She's Kip's mother, and she wants to hurt me, hurt him.

I yanked the car door open, collapsed into the driver's seat, and yanked the belt across my lap.

She's lying. She's lying, she's lying.

Under my ribs, something old and buried was screaming.

The engine purred to life, but I didn't drive. I sat there, fists clenched on the wheel, forehead pressed hard against it, while I stopped myself from marching back in there and killing the fucking bitch. But I couldn't. Not yet. I needed more from her before she met her maker—the devil himself.

And the reality was ... I knew.

I felt it deep in my bones, like the chilling shiver that raced down my spine when a sinister shadow slid across my skin. I sensed it with the same unnerving certainty as when my name was whispered in the pitch black when in captivity, and instinct told me exactly who it was without the need to turn around.

Some part of me had always known. The nameless hands, and the faceless voices. Not the men who bought me. The man who made it possible. My father. Pied Piper.

"No," I whispered, pressing my shaking fingers to my mouth. "She's lying. She's twisting it. She's angry I lived and afraid I'll report everything I know to the cops. She wants to break me by telling me I'm the daughter of a cold-hearted monster."

But even as I said it, even as I forced the words out like a chant, like a dangerous spell—my pulse was pounding out a brutal beat: *It's true. It's true. It's true.*

And in the back of my skull, a song I didn't remember ever learning hummed softly, and I wanted to gouge it out.

Memories I didn't know I carried ripped open inside me—images, voices, the sting of rope on my wrists, the sour stench of sweat and fear. They surged like a tidal wave, too much, too fast, crashing through the cracks in my mind until I couldn't breathe. Truth. Lies. All tangled together, clawing at me, dragging me under.

34

———

KIP

Twenty minutes later, I navigated my car through the narrow alley that ran behind Holland's house, my attention darting from fence to fence, scanning for any signs of neighbors or Draco. The sun was still high, casting long shadows across the neighborhood, which made sneaking around feel extra risky. I parked my car beneath the thick branches of a massive oak tree—the leaves overhead forming a patchwork shield that hid most of my car from view.

Before I got out, I leaned over and pushed the button that popped the trunk. Inside, a messy pile of clothes greeted me, and I dug through it until I found what I needed—a pest control shirt, faded blue, with a stitched patch that read "Mitchell." I changed quickly, the cool air brushing my skin as I tossed my old shirt back into the car. Then I locked up with a soft click. If anyone noticed me, I would just say I was there for a routine bug inspection. The disguise would hold up—I looked the part.

To my relief, no one saw me as I entered Holland's place through the back door. Silence welcomed me, and I swore under my breath. Where was she? I located my cell in my pocket and messaged her again. This time I let her know I was in there in case she returned.

Another hour ticked by as I wrestled with the idea that Holland might be my ... shit. I couldn't even think the word. Every time I thought of her naked and under me, my cock got so hard it hurt. Entertaining the idea of watching her fuck herself with my cross wasn't going to help when I had to break things off with her. How the hell had this happened?

I knew though. The Pied Piper had planted himself in our lives without our knowledge for years, playing all of us like a puppet master. Every time we turned around, we learned a new secret about him, and how he'd orchestrated so many events in our lives.

Finally, my phone pinged with a text message. I hurried to grab it out of my pocket, my heart in my throat.

Holland:
I'm on my way home. I'll see you in an hour.

Me:
Okay.

Gray dots jumped on the screen, indicating that she was messaging.

Holland:
We need to talk.

Me:
Yeah, we do.

I seriously doubted we were going to bring up the same topic that we needed to discuss. She had no idea what Dope had found or even who the Pied Piper was. My shoulders slumped forward with the weight of the needed conversation. I couldn't kiss her the second I saw her or even hold her. I would lose my shit and not stop. My cock begged for her tight cunt, and then a little voice inside my head whispered, "Sister, dude." My dick had never deflated so damn fast.

The anticipation gnawed at me like a relentless itch I couldn't scratch, and the waiting was driving me to the brink of madness. I doubted my sanity would hold out until she arrived. Desperate for distraction, I rummaged through her refrigerator, scanning the contents until they landed on a package of ground beef. Inspiration struck, and I resolved to prepare her spaghetti—a dish that held a sentimental place in my heart. My uncle, despite his flaws, had a knack for cooking, and he'd passed his recipe down to me when I was older. The thought of the rich, savory sauce bubbling on the stove filled me with a sense of purpose as I gathered the ingredients.

I searched for a pot and pan and began cooking. I timed the food to finish around the time she should be at the house.

It seemed like an eternity later when the front door opened and Holland walked in. It fucking sucked that I had to keep my distance, but I held myself back and waited for her in the kitchen.

"Hey," she said, her tone soft.

I leaned on the kitchen counter and crossed my ankles. "Hey. Are you okay? Draco didn't come after you or anything, did he?"

She slipped her purse off her shoulder and set it on the kitchen table. Holland looked amazing in her dark wash blue jeans that hugged her ass and legs. I wanted to part those legs and lick her pussy until her juices were dripping down my chin. *Stop!* I pinched the bridge of my nose in a vain attempt to stay focused on the conversation that we needed to have.

"I haven't seen him, which makes me nervous." She reached up and removed the scarf from her neck and tossed it on the table.

Guilt swallowed me whole as the outline of my fingers on her throat glared at me. I reminded myself that I'd hurt her, and it was another reason to keep my distance. I couldn't trust myself not to black out again. I just didn't understand why it had happened or how to stop it from happening again.

"Something smells good." She sniffed the air as she walked to the stove. "You cooked me dinner?"

"Yeah. I needed something to keep me busy."

She turned to me and placed her palm on my chest. "I need to talk to you."

Her eyes lifted, soft and searching, and she rose onto her toes, closing the space between us. For a split second, I thought she might kiss me—and God help me, I wanted it. Needed it.

But Lily's face slammed into my mind, her name on Holland's lips, the puzzle pieces twisting into something I couldn't untangle. What if I was right? What if Lily wasn't just my mother but hers too?

The bruises on her throat. My fingerprints. Her red hair glinting the same way Lily's once had. My gut knotted, nausea and need warring inside me.

At the last second, I pulled back, turning to the stove and stirring the food as if it mattered more than the fire burning between us.

I didn't dare look at her. I couldn't. If I did, she'd see everything I was hiding—the guilt, the hunger, and the fear that she might be my sister.

"Same, but you go first."

She wiped her palms on the thighs of her jeans as if they were sweaty. She was nervous. She should be, I'd tried to kill her, and she had zero reason to trust me.

"I ... I visited Lily today."

Oh. Shit. I already knew she was at my mother's, but that didn't mean she'd seen and talked to her.

"When you told me she lived nearby, I had to see the woman who —." Her words trailed off. "Sold me."

I stirred the noodles before I drained them over the sink, waiting for her to continue.

"I thought ... I wasn't sure what I was thinking really. I needed to see her, to see her dying. I needed to stand in front of her and prove that she didn't destroy me."

I set the pot back on the stove and turned off the heat.

"How did it feel?" Funny how Holland and I had swapped places. That was typically her question to ask patients, not mine. As calm as I appeared, I was barely holding my shit together.

"Good. Bad." She paused and her gaze dropped to the floor, then returned to me. "I wanted to kill her for what she did to Ally and me, and there's no telling how many other innocent lives she ruined. Is it wrong that I wanted to kill her? Actually, I showed up with the intention of doing just that. I even aimed my gun at her."

A thousand voices in my head cheered for Holland. "I wish you had pulled the trigger."

Holland shifted from one foot to the other while playing with the diamond pendant on her necklace.

"Have you thought about killing her after what she did to you? It would make sense if you had. No judgment over here."

I chuckled. "So many times. I can't ... even after all the fucked-up shit she's done, I can't cross that line. Plus, it would put her out of her misery, and I would rather see her suffer until the day she dies and rots in hell."

"What stops you? Is it because she's a woman, or because she's your mother?"

I chewed on her question for a moment. I hadn't given much thought to it other than I couldn't have her blood on my hands.

"Both. A part of me doesn't even connect with what happened all those years ago when I killed that girl. Whatever really happened, it was driven from a different place inside me. A shadow self that I don't know any more. Killing monsters is my gig. Not women."

Holland closed the gap between us, the light scent of her flowery perfume teasing my senses and shooting straight to my cock. I wanted to wrap her in my arms and kiss her, but I couldn't.

"She's a monster, Kip. There wouldn't be any shame in ending her. You even know how to destroy the evidence." Her tone was soft but sincere, as if she was giving me permission to do the one thing that I'd wrestled with for years. Killing my own mother.

Holland pursed her lips into a thin line. "When I talked to her, she admitted hurting you. She has no remorse for what she did to either of us. I don't think she's capable of feelings, honestly. I actually went to see her for another reason, to find out what else she did to you."

I frowned as I crossed my arms over my chest, putting a physical boundary between us so I wouldn't grab her and carry her to the bedroom.

"What do you mean?"

"Let's sit down. First, I need a glass of wine. Would you like a drink?"

She walked to the cabinet and opened it, revealing a few bottles of red wine, a bottle of vodka, and two bottles of whiskey.

"I think some whiskey would be good. Something tells me this is going to be a helluva night," I said. She had no idea.

After we settled on the couch with our drinks and turned to each other, I waited for the bomb to drop—that we were blood, that I'd fallen in love with my sister, that every kiss was another scar waiting to happen. Beads of sweat broke out on my forehead, and anxiety caught in my throat.

"I'm not sure how to say this." She shifted on the cushion, clearly nervous.

"Just say it, Holland. I think I know what you're going to say. There's no easy way, so put us out of our misery."

She tilted her head, a gentle expression softening her features. "Oh, you think I don't want to see you anymore?"

"Something like that."

She scooted closer to me and placed her hand on my thigh as she kissed me softly.

I should've stopped her. My body begged me to let her. But my soul? It was already hers.

"That's not what this is about. Not at all," she said against my mouth.

I wrapped my fingers gently around the back of her neck, inhaling her scent as our lips met with a desperate intensity that felt like my very existence hinged on her. It did, and yet, I had to convince myself to let go. Her soft moan vibrated through our kiss, our tongues entwining as I sought more of her taste, teasing and yearning.

But then, she pulled back, a smile on her lips. "I want you too, but we really need to talk. This can't be put off any longer." Her words hung between us, leaving me torn between desire and the gravity of what lay ahead.

Little did she know that would be the last time I kissed her in that way. It felt wrong to want her, yet I couldn't deny that I did, which meant I was forced to deal with the inevitable—saying goodbye for good.

"Listen, when you blacked out and choked me, there was something strange about it all."

Her words made me flinch internally, torn between shame and curiosity.

"I'm not telling you this to make you feel guilty, Kip. In fact, I think I know what happened."

I was both intrigued and apprehensive. "You do?"

"I had a client years ago who had been abused and tortured, but it went further than that." There was a hint of excitement in her tone, and it unnerved me.

"What do you mean?" I asked, needing to understand but fearing the truth.

"Kip, not only were you drugged over and over, but ..."

35

KIP

The air pressed in, thick and heavy, making it almost impossible to breathe as I waited for her to speak.

"Not only were you drugged, but, Kip also ... you were conditioned. Reprogrammed. And I think I know who did it," she said, her voice calm but somehow more chilling for it. "And what's worse, however your mother and uncle did it, I think they still have some kind of hold on you."

Doubt and denial swirled inside me—a storm I couldn't escape—leaving me caught between wanting to dismiss her words yet feeling the uneasy sense that maybe she was right.

"Why do you think this?" I needed more puzzle pieces than she was giving me.

"Your lapses in time and not knowing what happened, the drug use, the manipulation. I think it was more than the heroin."

She set her wineglass down on the little table next to the couch, then stood and paced in front of me, wringing her hands.

"I don't think you remember what actually happened, Kip," Holland said. "I think they—your family—made you believe you hurt me or another girl."

My jaw clenched so hard it ached. "Don't."

"They drugged you, didn't they?" She stepped closer, her expression shimmering with something between terror and heartbreak. "You have marks on your arms, Kip. I've seen them. Old track scars. That's not ..." She swallowed hard. "That's not recreational. That's forced use."

My pulse slammed against my throat as I jumped off the couch, unable to sit still. My fingers twitched at my side. *Don't let her see you break. Don't let her see—*

"You blacked out," she whispered. "You disappeared, you lost time, you woke up in places you didn't remember. That's not just trauma. That's programming."

"I killed you," I rasped, the words tearing out of me raw, wrong, rotting on my tongue.

I remembered her. Blood. Screaming. I remembered the needle. I remembered the lies. But none of it ever fit. It never felt like mine. And maybe that's because ... it wasn't.

"No, Kip." Her expression softened. "You thought you did. But I was there. I remember now. You weren't the one holding me down. You were ..." Her breath hitched. "You were the guy who was screaming."

The room tilted. Flashes slammed into me—her face, tear-streaked, younger, reaching for me. My mother's fingers digging into my shoulders. Uncle's laugh in the dark. A needle. The sick-sweet rot of heroin. No. No.

"I think they made you believe it," Holland said softly now, like she was talking to a wounded animal. "So you wouldn't go to the cops. So you would stay quiet."

My knees nearly gave out. My vision tunneled.

I remembered—a small hand in mine, blood on the floor, her screaming, me screaming, and then—the cold flood in my veins, the snap of the belt, the smell of incense and bleach, my mother's whispered prayers in the dark.

A rough, cracked laugh tore from my chest. "So what, I'm your charity case now?"

Her shoulders tensed. She crossed the last few feet between us and curled her fingers into the front of my shirt. "You are not the monster they made you believe you were."

Monster. Killer. Broken. It thudded under my skin like a second pulse, fast and loud and vicious.

But I focused on her warm touch.

"You're ..." She hesitated, like she was barely holding herself together. "You're the boy who tried to save me."

Something split open inside me. Not clean. Not sharp. A jagged, wrenching crack right down the center. I sucked in a breath like I'd been buried for years. Holy fuck. She was wrong. She had to be wrong. But—but what if she was right?

I was shaking, but it wasn't rage. It was from something I didn't have a name for.

Her hands stayed fisted in my shirt, pulling me in to keep me from losing my shit.

"Kip," she whispered, like it hurt to say my name. "You felt it too, didn't you?"

I clenched my jaw until I felt the crack in the joint. "Felt what, Holland?"

"That something was wrong," she said gently, her stare pinned on mine like she could dig the truth out of me. "That it had always been wrong."

Something in my chest twisted so hard I thought it would split me wide fucking open.

"I—" My tongue burned as the word rasped out. "I remembered blood. I remembered her crying. I remembered my mother." My throat ached with the words that scraped my throat as I spoke them aloud. "Her saying, 'look what you did.'"

Holland's grip tightened. "I don't think that was your memory, Kip. That was what they made you believe by reconditioning your mind."

My legs buckled, and I crashed down onto the edge of the couch, head sinking into my hands, lungs pulling air like I'd been underwater too long.

I saw it:

My mother cinching the belt around my arm. My uncle whispering in the dark, telling me I was brave, telling me it would help me forget. Me fumbling to untie a girl while someone laughed behind me. The rush, the warmth, the blackout.

"I tried," I whispered, not even sure if I was talking to her or myself. "I tried to help you."

"You did," she said, her voice breaking as she dropped to her knees in front of me. She cupped my face as if I were fragile. "You were only a kid, Kip. You tried to stop it, but they were bigger. They were crueler."

A choked sound ripped out of me, something between a laugh and a sob.

She touched under my eyes, thumbs brushing away something wet I hadn't realized was there. "You didn't kill me. You never did."

I grabbed her wrists, hard. She didn't pull away. She stayed, solid and soft, holding like she was trying to stitch me back together with her bare hands.

"I don't know who the fuck I am," I rasped.

She sank her teeth into her lower lip, but she didn't look away. "You were the one who tried to save me," she whispered. "And you are not your mother's monster."

And right then, it split—the cold, hollow place inside me, the one I'd locked up tight for years. Not clean. Not sharp. A slow, deep crack, like ice breaking under old weight.

Because deep down, where I'd buried everything, I had always known the truth was different from what I'd been told. I just wasn't sure how different.

"I need proof, but I'm not sure we'll ever find it. All I can tell you is that I've worked with people who have survived this, and they got through it." She rubbed my back. "We'll get through this one way or another, if you want me by your side."

Fuck. With everything she'd said, I'd forgotten about the possible blood relation. "It depends. There's something else we need to talk about."

Concern flickered across her features. "Okay. You can tell me anything, Kip. I think you know that by now."

Except this. This would fuck her up for the rest of her life when she learned she'd slept with her brother.

I licked my dry lips and swallowed.

"Holland. I—I—" I leaned my head back and stared at the ceiling, trying to form the words that refused to leave my mouth. There was no other choice, though. I had to. I looked at her, our gazes locking.

"There's more, Holland." I swallowed, throat raw. "I think ... we're." I paused. "I think you might be my sister."

36

HOLLAND

The world tilted. Not because I believed him—but because some part of me had feared this exact moment. And still, even now, with that word hanging in the air like a guillotine, all I could think about was how he'd held me when I was shaking, how he'd looked at me like I was worth saving. Was that love? Or was it just the kind of devotion trauma breeds when two people bleed beside each other for too long?

I didn't know.

But I wanted to know.

I wanted to choose him. Not because he'd saved me, but because he saw me. And right now, that was more terrifying than any bloodline.

I stared at him like he'd grown two heads. "What?" I backed away and covered my face with my hands, the weight of his words slamming into me like a bolt of lightning. "Why would you say something like that?"

Kip's shoulders sagged, every sharp line in his expression etched with defeat. "Because my mother ... Lily ... she was involved with some dangerous people, Holland. One of them helped her orchestrate your kidnapping."

The pain on his face cracked something open in my chest. "About a year ago, that man came back into our lives. We don't know what he wants yet. We're trying to figure it out."

"Can I ask who?" I wrapped my arms around myself, chasing away an invisible chill.

His gaze locked onto mine, his jaw tight. "You can't repeat this to anyone. Pretend I'm your patient, and this is protected under confidentiality. If you breathe a word, it'll put you in real danger. This man makes Draco look like a fucking saint."

"You have my word," I whispered.

Kip stood, running his palms down the front of his jeans like he needed to ground himself. "He goes by the name 'the Pied Piper'."

The air shifted.

My head dropped as the name echoed through my chest like a curse. I looked up, butterflies tearing through my stomach like shrapnel. "Why would you think we're related?"

He swallowed hard. "Because my mother used to date him."

A sharp, broken laugh escaped me, brittle and unhinged. It felt like my sanity was hanging by a single, frayed thread. "I'm sorry," I muttered, stepping closer. "That's just ... no. We're not related, babe. We're not brother and sister."

His brows pulled together, confusion darkening his features. "How do you know?"

"Lily told me today that the Pied Piper is my biological father." I blinked, swallowing down bile. All this time, I thought Ally and I were bound by blood—sisters in every sense. But we weren't. We had different fathers. The man who destroyed my life had created me. "But my mother—my real mother—she's dead. Apparently, she betrayed him and he had her killed. Then he and Lily sold me."

Silence stretched between us, thick and suffocating.

Kip's arm snaked around my waist, his fingers digging into my side like he needed to anchor himself to the truth. "Are you sure she's dead? That Lily's not your mother too?"

I shook my head. "We look nothing alike. And as much as I hate her, I believe her. She twisted the knife too well for it to be a lie. She enjoyed it too much."

I hesitated. "But are you sure your dad isn't the Pied Piper?"

Kip's forehead creased. "No hesitation. No doubt. My dad died in a car accident when I was five. I remember him. He wasn't a monster—he was quiet, kind. Not long after he was gone, my uncle showed up and forced his way into our lives. Years later, I found a paternity test hidden in one of my mom's locked drawers. It proved my dad was my biological father. The Pied Piper isn't related to me."

Relief hit like the first second of air after a fist to the ribs—violent, messy, and clawing at my insides.

"Then we're okay," I whispered. "We're not related."

His mouth crashed down on mine, possessive and raw, and I melted into him like gravity had chosen him as my center.

"You're mine, Holland. I don't just want you. I need you. I need you wrecked and raw, your pussy juices dripping down my cock, my name the only word you can remember. I'll devour you, mind, body, and soul, until there's nothing left for anyone else. Only you, shattered, stitched into my soul. Look at another man, and I'll burn his goddamn world down. Then I'll fuck you in the ashes."

My pulse skipped, heat tearing through my veins. I leaned into him, feeling the hard press of his cock through his jeans.

"Then make me forget there ever was a world before you," I whispered. "Use me. Break me. Just never stop needing me."

A low growl escaped his throat as he kissed me again, possessing me with an urgency. He slid his hand up my back and to the nape of my neck. His fingers dug into my skin before he wrapped my hair around them and pulled my head back. His lust-filled expression turned my entire body to liquid heat. Kip leaned down, scooped me into his arms, and carried me to the bedroom. He sat me down.

"Do you remember the night you took the Ambien?" His words were low, raw, and filled with need.

"Some."

"You nearly came for me as I called you my little whore. Your cunt was dripping wet as it greedily fucked my cross."

I sank my teeth into my lower lip, my thighs clenching.

"Little ghost, you're a dirty little slut for me, aren't you?"

"Yes." My tongue darted over my lips, still feeling his mouth crashing on mine.

"Take off your clothes, little ghost."

I stood and slowly removed my top and jeans. His attention raked over me as I stood in front of him in my bra and thong. Sliding my bra straps off my shoulders, I undid the clasp and let it drop to the floor.

"Fuck," he whispered. "I can't wait to fuck those gorgeous tits."

As far as I was concerned, this man could fuck me any way he wanted to. I was his to do with as he pleased. I slipped my thong over my hips and down my legs before I stepped out of it.

"On your knees."

I walked over to him, then knelt before him, waiting for his next command. He leaned forward and grabbed my chin hard enough to make me gasp from the pain.

"I put you on your knees, not to beg—but to belong. There's no god here but the one who makes you come."

Unable to speak, I nodded. Kip leaned back and unbuttoned his jeans before he lowered his zipper and freed his large cock. I stifled my moan, ready to suck him until he came in my mouth.

"You're not safe with me, little ghost, but you're seen. And I would rather die than let anyone take that from you again." He stroked the back of my hair, his words penetrating deep inside me. Kip was the only man who truly saw me for what I was. The darkness that consumed me, the thirst for more, the desire to get blood on my hands and stand by his side.

"Open." He stood and rubbed the head of his cock against my lips.

I did as he said and he grabbed the back of my head, holding me still as he shoved his entire length into my mouth, choking me.

"That's it, Holland. Don't pretend you're okay for me. Don't filter the rage, the scars, the nightmares. I want it all. The pain. The darkness. The wreckage. Because those are the pieces that make you mine."

My eyes glistened, but I didn't cry. Not yet. I just welcomed him like a confession.

He slid his cock in and out of my mouth until my jaw ached from the size of him. My fingernails dug into his thigh, leaving red marks on his skin. I might be his, but he was also mine, and I would mark him too.

"Your hot mouth feels so good. Such a good girl taking it all."

He smoothed my hair, his dark gaze trained on me as I ran my tongue along his shaft. I wrapped my fingers around him and stroked as I sucked and licked.

"Jesus," he said quietly. Kip stepped away and pulled out of my mouth. I wiped the trail of saliva from my chin and waited for his next command. He continued to watch me as he reached up and tugged his necklace, freeing the cross.

"Get on the bed and spread your legs."

I swallowed, my throat suddenly dry with the idea of what he was about to do to me. From what he'd said, I'd loved it when he'd fucked me with his cross, but I'd been asleep and didn't remember much, only the feeling after the fact. But the woods ... my belly flip-flopped as I crawled onto the mattress and parted my legs for him.

"You're wet just thinking about what I'm about to do to you, aren't you? Your tight cunt is dripping wet, ready for me to do with as I please." He knelt in front of me and then took the cross and ran it up the inside of my thigh. Kip leaned in, his breath grazing my center. With his free hand, he gently spread me apart, then ran his tongue over my swollen clit.

A soft whimper escaped me as he dragged the crucifix up my leg until he reached my pussy. He pressed it against my entrance, the cool metal causing me to jump.

"Are you nervous, little ghost?"

"A little."

With a wicked gleam in his eye, he pushed the cross inside me, slowly. My gaze widened as he slid it in and out. The ridges of the metal sent pleasure rippling through me, and I gasped.

"Oh, god."

Kip chuckled. "He's not here, but your monster is." He released the cross and stepped back. "Fuck yourself with my cross. Let me watch your tight cunt take it all in."

He sat back down as I took control and pushed it inside me, then pulled it out again. My body trembled as it reached new places inside me. My lips parted as I allowed myself to fully give in to the pleasure. I pumped it faster while the whole world fell away. The only thing that existed was the sharp, searing edge of the crucifix, the hungry pulse of my cunt, and the way Kip's eyes set me ablaze with each thrust.

He looked at me, unmoving for a moment, cock in hand. He stroked himself slowly, deliberate—never breaking that dark, devouring eye contact. I fucked myself shamelessly with his cross, whimpering as it hit a spot inside me that made my toes curl. The metal was slick with my arousal. Each time I pulled it out, another string of wetness clung to it, and when I pushed it back in, my hips rose off the bed like I was begging to be filled even deeper.

"Look at you," he rasped. "Sainted. Desecrated."

The deep, hard pressure of the cold steel worked me into a quivering mess. My hips bucked off the bed, straining for more of it, more of him, because all I'd ever done was reach for the next damn thing I was told I couldn't have.

Through the haze of sensation, I watched Kip. He stroked his cock slowly, torturing himself as much as me. The cross was slick, and it slid in more easily every time. I wanted to be ruined like this. I wanted to know what it was like to be split open and worshipped at the same time.

"Harder," he ordered, his command low and mean. "If you can't fuck yourself properly, I'll do it for you."

I shuddered and obeyed, pushing the cross in deep, as far as it would go, feeling my cunt flutter and clamp around it, greedy, insatiable. My clit throbbed so hard it was almost painful, and I moaned, louder than before.

He leaned in, his voice a growl against my ear. "You look so fucking pretty like this. So broken and so hungry." He yanked the cross from my hand and left it inside me, then bent over and sucked my clit between his lips, tongue flicking mercilessly as he fucked me with the cross, punishing and relentless.

I jerked, grabbing his hair, dragging him closer. I rode his tongue, the ozone scent of holy things turned sacrilegious.

"Say it," he commanded, never letting up, each thrust of the cross synchronized with each suck on my clit. The pleasure built and built until I thought I'd die from it.

"I want you." My confession was raw and desperate. "I want you to fucking break me."

"That's my girl," he praised. "You're not allowed to break unless it's for me. You hear that? I own the pieces of you."

Without warning, Kip grabbed my thighs, yanking me to the edge of the mattress. The cross slipped out and landed on the bedspread. He lined himself up and shoved his cock inside, so hard I cried out. Pain and ecstasy braided together, almost too much, almost perfect.

His hands locked on my hips, and he thrust into me so hard I nearly screamed.

I barely adjusted to the size of him, the stretch and fullness, before he was pounding into me, chasing his own darkness, pushing me into the mattress. I wanted it all. The pain. The bruises tomorrow. The way he'd leave his mark on me from the inside out.

He fucked me punishingly, each thrust relentless, owning every inch of me. He grabbed my throat, squeezing until my vision blurred, and I clawed at his wrist, desperate for more, not less. My hand flew to my clit, two fingers rubbing fast and frantic as he drove into me.

"That's it. Take it," he growled. "You're mine. Say it."

"I'm yours," I cried, and he squeezed tighter, forcing the words from me like a confession wrung out in a church confessional. "I'm yours, Kip. Fuck. Please."

"Good girl."

"You want to come, little ghost?" He found my hair, twisted it tight, and bent my head back so I looked up at him, helpless and pinned and desperate.

"Please," I whispered.

With a grin, he pulled out and slapped my pussy with his cock, hard enough to make a wet sound. "Earn it," he said. "Beg better."

I let go of all remaining pride. "Please, Kip. I need you. Fill me up, ruin me."

He shoved back inside and fucked me even harder, his rhythm brutal. At the last moment, he pulled out and pressed the crucifix against my clit. The cold metal made me scream, my whole body locking up, and my release so intense black dots danced before my vision.

"Look at me," he demanded, and I did, meeting the wildness in him.

He kissed me hard, teeth clashing, and when he bit my lip, I tasted blood, and the world spun. I was a live wire, burning through every nerve ending.

He let go of my throat and snaked his hand between us, rubbing my clit with two rough fingers, forcing another orgasm out of me. I broke against him, tremors racking through me as I came again, my vision turning white at the edges. He fucked me through it, cruel and perfect.

Kip watched me shudder and writhe, then pushed deeper into my spent, spasming cunt and finished with a guttural moan, flooding me until I felt full to the brim. He stayed there, forehead pressed to mine, breathing shallow and ragged.

After a long minute, he withdrew. His warm and sticky cum leaked out of me, and he smiled with proprietary pleasure as it smeared down my thigh.

"You're so much better awake," he said softly, almost kindly. "Stay with me, Holland."

I didn't know if he meant the moment or forever.

37

KIP

I'd had a lot of sex in my life, but nothing like that ever. I pulled out of Holland, then climbed off the bed and headed to the bathroom. Once I located a washcloth in the cabinet under the sink, I turned on the hot water. Once it was the perfect temperature, I saturated the cloth and returned to her. Gently, I cleaned her off as I kissed the inside of her thigh.

Her eyes glistened as she watched. "I've never had anyone do that before." Her voice was soft as if she was trying not to fall apart.

I returned to the bathroom and placed the cloth in the sink.

"I plan on you having a lot of firsts." I climbed in next to her and kissed her mouth, savoring the taste of her pussy on her tongue.

She placed her hand on my cheek, a blur of emotions flashing in her expression.

I pressed my forehead against hers and whispered, "I love you, little ghost." I looked away, unwilling to see her reaction as my throat constricted. I hadn't ever said those words to a woman before. I hadn't ever loved anyone like I did Holland—an all-consuming obsession and devotion.

"Look at me." Her words were gentle yet commanding, and I did as she asked, my heart pounding with a mixture of anticipation and fear, bracing for the impact of her next words.

"I love you too, Kip." Her confession was a beacon, piercing through the murky shadows of doubt and despair that had clouded my mind, illuminating everything with a single, brilliant light.

A silly, broad smile slipped into place as I was unable to contain the joy her words brought. "Yeah?"

"Definitely." Her laughter filled the room like a warm, comforting embrace, wrapping around us and lifting the atmosphere. "In fact, I'd like to show you just how much."

Her next words were like a tidal wave, sweeping over me and leaving me reeling with disbelief and wonder. Never in a million years had I imagined Holland would do something so unexpected.

THE SUN WAS ALREADY high in the bright blue sky by the time we reached the driveway. I hadn't slept much, but I didn't need rest. I needed closure. I parked in front of the house and then turned off the engine. Holland shifted in her seat and turned to me.

"Are you sure?" She reached for my hand, and I gave it a gentle squeeze.

"Are you?" I pinned her with a stare and searched her for any uncertainty, but I didn't even see her flinch when she told me her plan.

"Yeah. I'm ready."

I leaned over the console and kissed her. "Let's go. The sooner this is over, the better, and we can hopefully move on."

"You have help. You're not alone in this anymore, babe." She pressed her soft lips to my knuckles.

We climbed out of the car, and I took her hand in mine as we walked up the sidewalk and to the house. I reached for the handle and turned it, then opened the door for Holland.

Dog barked as we entered Mother's place. "It's just us," I said, petting him as he licked my arm. "Did Cynthia feed you before she left?" His tail wagged as he sniffed at Holland, and then he trotted off to the kitchen where his food bowl and water were.

"He's smart." Holland's smile widened as she watched him. "What will happen to him when your mother is gone?"

"I'll see if Cynthia wants him, but if I recall, she's a cat person."

"Will he go to a shelter?" Her eyes pleaded with me. "Kip, you can't do that to him."

"I couldn't do that. Dog has some good years left. If she doesn't want him, I'll take him. Hopefully, my girlfriend will help when I have to go out of town." I winked at her.

"Then don't. Don't ask Cynthia; let's take him. I can even take him to my office for patients that need a pet during the session." Her face lit up with her idea. "Dog?"

Surprisingly, he came to her when she called. Holland knelt and rubbed behind his ears. "Do you want to live with Kip and me? Would you be happy, buddy?"

Dog barked once, then licked her chin. Holland's laughter filled the room, and I wondered how she could feel so happy at the moment, but Dog had that effect on people.

She stood. "It's settled, then."

"Good. I was having a tough time with the idea of not seeing him anymore." I gave her a crooked smile. "Are you ready?"

"Yes." She turned on her heel and headed toward Mother's room.

The door was nearly closed, and I knocked before I pushed it open. "Mother," I said, my voice sharp.

She jerked awake at the sound of me entering the room. The oxygen machine whirred in the background as Holland and I walked into her room.

A sharp laugh slipped through her thin lips. "If it isn't the devil and his bride."

"I'll cut to the chase. I know you need your rest," I said, walking to the edge of the bed. Holland walked around to the other side and sat down.

"You're not looking too well." Holland took Mother's hand in hers and patted it as if she loved my mother with undying devotion.

I had to give it to Holland; she had fucking balls walking in here and confronting the woman who'd sold her and Ally. Not to mention visiting her a second time.

"I'm dying, you little brat. What do you both want?"

"Information." I sank onto the mattress and pinned Mother with a glare. "Before I meet the Pied Piper, I want to know what I'm walking into. Why does he want to meet with me?"

Mother wheezed, "He doesn't tell me his plans, Kip. Just get in touch with him. It will be worth your time."

My brow arched, and I wondered what in the hell could possibly be worth my time with the Pied Piper.

"How so?"

"The information you're looking for. I was sworn to silence. I saw what the Pied Piper did if you crossed him." Her attention cut to Holland. "Don't cross him, Kip. You need to meet with him and see what he has to say."

"Let me see if I understand correctly. You can't tell us anything about the Pied Piper, the pastor, and why ..." I choked back my words. I couldn't trust her with what I'd done.

"I've told Holland too much already, but I'm dying, so it wasn't enough information for the Pied Piper to come after me."

"Hmm," Holland said. "I'm guessing anything else you might share would be a death sentence?"

"If I'm dying, it's going to be on my goddamn terms, and I'll take my secrets with me." She swallowed and then broke into a coughing fit.

"I just wanted to make sure we understood that you're not going to answer any questions we have." I reached out and smoothed a strand of her thin hair from her forehead. "I sent Cynthia home, by the way. I gave her the week off."

Mother glared at me. "You can't do that. I can't take care of myself. I'll starve to death."

"No, you'll probably die of dehydration before you starve to death." Holland's tone was gentle as if she were talking to a small child.

"Nobody asked you, Samantha." Spittle flew from Mother's mouth as I watched the fear twist her expression.

"Instead of being a bitch, maybe you should beg for forgiveness. I mean, you're in a really bad place to be so rude." Holland tilted her head as she pinned Mother with a deadly stare.

I held back my chuckle as Holland played mind games with Mother. It served her right. It was too bad the moment couldn't last longer, though.

"Get her out of my house, Kip. Right now. Don't you dare let her come back."

Holland stood. "It's okay, you don't need to kick me out. I'm almost done here." With powerful strides, she walked to my side of the bed and flipped a few switches on Mother's oxygen machine.

I removed the oxygen mask from Mother's face as tears welled in her eyes. "I thought about killing you and ending your misery. Ending mine and Holland's, but then Holland had this brilliant idea. It would allow you to sit with everything you've done in your lifetime as you struggle to breathe on your own. No water. No food. Completely and utterly alone."

I paused, allowing what I'd said to sink in before I continued.

"A lot like what you did to me and Holland. It was dark and lonely, Mother, but it shaped us into who we are. And crazy enough, fate threw us a plot twist and we're together. Funny, isn't it? The girl you told me I'd killed and tortured me over? Carved up my skin while you cast demons out of me. For what? A sin I never committed." I took her hand in mine. "At least not *that* sin. I've committed a lot of others, including murder. Just not any women."

I leaned down close to her ear. "You'll be my first."

Her body trembled and her fingers wrapped around my wrist, but her hold was weak. "See you in hell, Mother."

Holland rolled the machines and other medical devices out of the room. Mother was smart even now, and I didn't trust her to not figure out how to get out of the bed and crawl to her oxygen machine. Before we left, we removed any help from her. No phone, no food, and I would turn off the water from outside. Plus, we would install cameras so we could enjoy watching her die, struggling to breathe and calling for help. The same as Holland and I had done for too long.

I stood and flashed Mother an unapologetic smile. "We're taking Dog, too. He'll be happy with us."

Tears streamed down her cheeks while she reached for me, but I moved out of the way.

"Don't do this. You don't want to do this," she pleaded.

"Or what? You're going to miraculously get out of this bed and carve me up some more? Goodbye, Mother." The sound of the door closing behind me echoed with a finality that cut straight through me.

It was almost over.

But monsters don't die quietly. They beg. They claw. And they curse you with their final words.

And just like she always had, she sucker-punched me one last time.

38

—

KIP

The road cut through the woods like a scar, black and winding, hemmed in by silence.

Dog sprawled across the backseat, tongue out, content after pacing the halls of hell. Holland sat next to me, her knees pulled up to her chest, her expression unreadable in the glow of the dash.

I hadn't said a word since we'd left. I didn't trust my voice not to crack. I didn't trust myself not to scream. Not after what that fucking bitch told me. Not after that.

My phone sat in the cup holder, and it blinked with movement.

Holland shifted. "Is that her?" she asked, nodding to my cell.

I nodded at the screen and watched Mother struggle to breathe, alone.

"Yeah. She's still reaching for the mask," I muttered.

"Good." She glanced away, and I hit the button and put it on sleep mode. That was enough. "What did she say to you before we left? You're clearly in your head about something. What happened?"

I gripped the wheel tighter. My knuckles burned. "You sure you want to know?"

She looked at me—not scared, not soft. Just ready.

I swallowed over the tightness in my throat. "She said my uncle's still alive."

Holland blinked, confusion creasing her brow. "But... I thought—"

"I thought he was dead too." My fists clenched. "Hell, I fucking buried him myself. Closed the casket. Said the words. Lowered the fucking box."

Silence pulsed between us. Then I added, "I never told anyone this before, but a few months ago ... I dug up his grave."

Her eyes snapped to me. "What?"

"Yeah." I smirked. "It was the middle of the night. I was in a bad place. Hallucinating. Dreaming about blood and chains and him whispering in my ear. I kept seeing his face, hearing his voice in my mind, and I couldn't make it stop. So I went to the grave."

"What did you find?" Holland asked in a whisper.

I flicked my blinker, took a sharp turn toward the main road, the tires crunching the gravel. "Nothing. The coffin was empty. Only a damn locket sitting inside." I glanced at her. "Yours."

She gasped. "Mine?"

I nodded. "The one you had when you were a kid. I didn't understand it. I figured I'd stolen it when I was drugged. Or maybe Mother or Vinny put it there, fucking with my head as usual. One more twist of the knife."

"But Kip..." Her hand found mine on the gearshift. "Why didn't you say anything?"

"Because I didn't trust myself." I let out a jagged laugh. "I thought I'd imagined it. That I'd hallucinated the whole damn thing. I'd been seeing ghosts for years. Why not one more?"

She didn't speak. Just looked at me, her fingers tightening on mine.

"But now," I said, "now I know I didn't imagine shit."

Her silence was permission, and I pulled over to the side of the road.

The forest breathed around us. Dog yawned as he sat up, his ears alert.

I reached into the glove box, removed a small velvet pouch, and opened it.

Turning it upside down, I dropped the locket into Holland's outstretched hand.

She stared at it. Her forehead pinched.

"I lost this," she said softly. "The night Ally and I were taken. It was ripped off my neck when they grabbed me."

My jaw clenched and my pulse thundered in my ears.

"I think he was there that night," I said. "Uncle Vinny. I think he's the one who dragged you off. And I think he kept that locket as a trophy."

She clutched it as though it might dissolve. "If he's alive ..."

"He's not hiding." My words were low. Cold. "He's hunting again."

She didn't move or even blink. Holland stared at the locket as if it had started whispering secrets in her sister's voice. Then her fingers closed around it so tight her knuckles went white.

She didn't put it on. Instead, she stared at the thing like it might bite her; the chain was made of barbed wire and the charm held a scream.

"Are you going to wear it?" I asked.

She shook her head, barely breathing. "No. That girl wore it. The one who never came home."

She slipped it into her coat pocket, burying it as if it were something sacred and venomous all at once.

I didn't push. Some things weren't meant to be worn. Some things only needed to be survived.

"You're sure about Vinny?" she asked, her tone quiet. Controlled. Too controlled.

I nodded. "Yeah. She wouldn't have told me unless it served her. She didn't want to die alone, struggling for air. She even admitted she was going to die on her terms, but we took that choice away from her."

Holland looked out the windshield as the sun set and the darkness pressed in.

And then—she fucking laughed, but it wasn't a soft or sweet laugh.

It was the kind of laugh people made right before they lit a match and set shit on fire.

"She said it like a final confession," Holland whispered. "Like it was holy. Like her last sermon before starving to death in a house she turned into a tomb."

Her chest rose. Just once. Then, "Good."

She turned to me, lifted her chin, and squared her shoulders.

"I hope she dies trying to scream," she said. "I hope she calls for help and no one comes. I hope she feels the same helplessness she sold us into."

I didn't say a word. I didn't have to because she was right.

"But Vinny ..." The muscle in her jaw tightened. She removed the locket from her pocket and stared at it. "He was worse than her. She convinced herself all her work was for God and good intentions. He didn't need either. He liked it."

She glanced at me. And I saw it then—the unraveling. The girl trying to hold herself together with a skeleton made of rage.

"I used to dream about him," she said. "Not my father, who was also a part of it. *Him—the Pied Piper*. His breath in my ear. His hand on my shoulder. The way he smelled like peppermint and bleach."

My fingers flexed against the wheel while Holland kept talking.

"He used to quote scripture. While he watched. While he bid on girls like they were cattle." Her voice dropped to a hiss. "He told me I was lucky. That my red hair made me worth more."

She stopped and looked down at the locket again. Then she did something I didn't expect.

She opened the car door and got out. Rain was misting and she stepped into it like a baptism with her head tilted back and eyes closed.

Dog barked once, but he stayed put.

I got out and came around to her, but I didn't touch her. Not yet.

She spoke without looking at me. "Do you believe in fate, Kip?"

"I used to," I said. "Before I learned monsters get to write their own destinies."

She stared straight at me as storm clouds danced across her features.

"Well, I believe in revenge," she said. "And if your uncle is alive?"

She reached for my hand. "I'll help you find him. But I want to help kill him."

The rain kissed her skin in tiny droplets.

And I watched each one like it was a holy thing, like the sky itself was paying tribute to her. To this moment.

She stood at the side of the gravel road, red hair soaked, fists clenched, trembling—but not from fear. From purpose. From fury. From the weight of everything she hadn't said until now.

She was fire made flesh. Not fragile but forged. Every breath she took was a refusal to be silenced. And I loved her for it. I *ached* for it. I wanted to fall to my knees before it.

I stepped closer, slow. Careful. Like I was approaching a wild thing that hadn't decided whether to run or rip out my throat.

There was power in her, something brutal and sacred, and I didn't flinch from it. I *worshipped* it.

Let the world fear her. Let them look away.

I never would.

I was hers, and she didn't even have to ask.

"Okay. And for the record, I would've killed her," I said softly. "If you hadn't come with me. I would've put a pillow over her face and watched the life drain from her."

She looked at me, something fragile flickering beneath her gaze.

"But your way was better," I added. "Quieter. Colder. You gave her exactly what she gave us."

A slow, bitter smile curved her lips. "No blood. No bruises. Just time and silence—and her own sins. That's fucking justice."

I wrapped my arms around Holland and pulled her to me. We stood there, two devils pretending to be human under the weight of too many ghosts.

Then she asked, barely a whisper, "Do you ever wish you could forget it all?"

I didn't answer right away. I focused on the trees instead. The mist curled between the branches and I thought about the road we still had to walk.

"I used to," I said. "But if I forgot it, I wouldn't remember who to kill."

Her laugh was a broken thing. "You really are fucked up."

I kissed the top of her head. "So are you, but you're perfectly mine."

She looked up at me, and for the first time, I saw it. Not just pain. Not just rage. Understanding. Not the kind you speak. The kind that lives in your bones, under your skin, behind your eyes.

"I'm tired, Kip," she said. "Of being hunted. Of waking up with ghosts in my chest and bruises I didn't earn."

I brushed my knuckles across her damp cheek. "I won't let anyone touch you again," I said. "Not him. Not anyone."

She nodded once. "And I won't let anyone hurt you either."

She reached up, brushing a raindrop from my temple. Then she whispered, "If we burn, we burn together."

I held her tighter, and for the first time since I was a kid, I didn't feel alone. I felt ... seen.

We weren't healed. We weren't whole. But we were ours.

And that was enough to start the war.

39

HOLLAND

"I'm going to drop by Velvet Vortex, then I'll see you later." Kip leaned over the car console and kissed me.

"Sounds good." I kissed him one more time before I climbed out of his car. Truthfully, we both had a lot to process, and I needed a minute to myself. I suspected he did, too.

His car idled in my driveway as I walked to the front entrance, unlocked it, then gave him a little wave before I stepped inside. Kip had insisted that he walk me inside, but I refused to lean on him for everything. I had my gun. I knew how to use it if I had to. So far, I'd been lucky. The thought of hurting another human being hurt my heart. At the same time, if my life depended on it, I'd already proved what I was capable of.

Thoughts of Dom invaded my mind, the sticky blood all over my hands as I sliced his neck with the piece of glass. Maybe those memories should terrify me, but they give me peace to know that he would never get up and hunt me ... but Draco.

I clutched my purse to my side as I scanned the living room and kitchen before I closed the door behind me. I wasn't stupid enough to think Draco was our only problem left, and once Kip and I dealt with him, I would be free for good.

I barked out a laugh as I drew my weapon and walked toward the kitchen. I swept the living room again, a shiver crawling up my spine. The last time I stood here, there'd been a smashed coffee table, an ashtray in pieces, Cooper's body bleeding out across the rug, and pools of blood soaking into the floorboards. Now ... nothing. Not a single trace. Everything was spotless, scrubbed clean like it had never happened. Kip's handiwork. The kind of "cleaner" job I hadn't been conscious to witness.

Everything was normal. All that was left was the bedroom, closet, and bathroom.

Feeling more confident, I looked under my bed and in the closet. It was all clear. Normally I would have chided myself for being so cautious, but I should have been this careful all along. If I had, maybe Draco wouldn't have found me. I blew out a sigh of relief as I realized I needed to pee. I set my handbag and gun on the nightstand and hurried to the primary bathroom. Pushing the door the rest of the way open, I stepped inside and flipped on the light. A scream ripped through me, piercing the air as I struggled to wrap my head around what I was seeing.

Draco.

In my bathtub.

Dead.

But moving? I stared at his stomach, my mouth forming another scream.

"Fuck going pee." I glanced down at the floor to make sure I hadn't pissed my pants, then ran out of the room to find my phone and grab my gun. Once I had them, I bolted to the living room, trembling as I brought up Kip's number.

He answered on the first ring.

"Miss me already?" he asked, a smirk in his tone.

"Yes. Please come over now."

"Holland? What's wrong? Are you safe?" Fear clung to his words.

"Yes, but I don't want to tell you over the phone other than ..." I gulped. "I'm not alone."

"Fuck!"

Tires squealed, and I imagined he pulled an illegal U-turn back toward my place.

"I'm only five minutes away. Stay on the phone with me."

"I will. Hurry. I—" I stammered. "I don't understand. It doesn't make sense." My voice was a whisper.

"Did you call the cops? I'm three minutes away."

"No. Oh god, as much shit is going on? No. The idea didn't even cross my mind." I leaned against the wall for support, counting in my head to distract myself from the sight of Draco in my tub. *How is he moving if he's dead?*

"Good girl."

Those two words made my thighs clench. Kip's praise was low, possessive, and for a minute my body forgot there was a man in my bathtub and just focused on how I wanted Kip to bend me over, pull my hair, and fuck all the darkness away.

"I'm here. Open the front door."

Seconds later, he barreled into my house. He grabbed my shoulders. "You're okay? You're not hurt?"

I glanced around. "Where's Dog?"

"In the car with the window down. He'll stay put until I call him."

"Follow me." There was no way to explain what happened, because I wasn't even sure.

We reached my bedroom, and I pointed to the bathroom. "The tub."

I followed him and waited for him to assess the situation.

"What the fuck?" Kip shot me a look. "Well, Draco looks dead, but why is his stomach moving?"

"I didn't stick around long enough to find out. I tucked my tail between my legs and called you."

Kip crouched beside the tub, his face grim. He didn't flinch. Didn't gag. Just stared like he'd seen this kind of thing before.

His fingers brushed along the seam of Draco's abdomen. "Stitched."

"What?" I choked, still frozen near the doorway.

"Stitched shut. Clean. Surgical."

Draco's torso twitched again—his stomach bulged, skin rippling like something was crawling beneath it. I slapped a hand over my mouth, bile burning the back of my throat.

"What is that?" My voice cracked. "Why is he still moving?"

Kip exhaled hard through his nose. "Snakes."

My knees buckled. I clutched the doorframe like it could anchor me to reality. "You're not serious."

"They're alive." Kip didn't look away from the horror in front of us. "He sedated them. Probably kept them chilled to slow their heartbeat. Then sewed them inside while they were unconscious and before they woke up inside him."

I staggered back, bile burning its way up my throat. "That's not— how is that even possible?"

"It doesn't need to be possible," Kip said flatly. "It needs to be theatrical. Symbolic."

My gaze shifted to the small white slip of paper pinned to Draco's shirt. Neat handwriting. Precise. Stained with a single drop of blood.

I forced myself to look.

You're welcome. —Dad.

The words hit me harder than the corpse.

My stomach clenched. "He did this for me."

Kip stood, his expression unreadable. "He did this for himself."

"He killed Draco because he hurt me."

"He killed him because Draco touched what the Pied Piper thinks he owns."

My chest rose and fell too fast. "But he sold me. He gave me to those monsters."

Kip turned to look at me fully. "And in his mind? That made you."

I blinked at him, stunned. `

Kip's tone darkened. "That's how narcissists work. They don't see betrayal. They see creation. He doesn't regret what he did to you—he thinks it forged you. That your pain was part of some divine design."

"He sold his daughter," I whispered, "and now he thinks he's my father again?"

"He never stopped," Kip said. "Not in his head. Are you surviving? That just confirmed his god complex. He thinks you became strong because of him."

I looked at Draco's bloated corpse, the snakes writhing beneath his skin.

"He thinks this makes us even."

"No." Kip stepped closer; his stare locked on mine. "He thinks this makes him worthy of your forgiveness. Of your loyalty. Of your fucking love."

I couldn't speak. Couldn't blink. Inside that rotting shell, slithery, gross things thrashed—trapped, waking, coiled in hell.

Just like I had been once.

My jaw trembled. "He turned Draco into a sermon."

"He turned Draco into a sacrifice," Kip said. "The snakes, the body, the message—it's biblical. He thinks he's cleaning house. Ridding you of your abuser. Like a father should."

"But only now that I've survived," I whispered. "Only now that I'm something he can claim."

"Yes," Kip said. "Because now you're the monster he designed. And monsters belong to him."

I gulped as the snakes squirmed beneath Draco's ruined skin, and I didn't scream again. I didn't cry. I stopped feeling altogether.

A buzzing silence filled my ears, as if my brain was trying to shield me from what I wasn't supposed to survive.

But I had.

Again.

Always.

I bent down, plucked the bloodstained note from Draco's shirt, and held it between two fingers.

You're welcome. —Dad.

A tremor passed through me. Not from fear. Not this time.

Something colder. Something sharper.

Kip watched me cautiously. "Holland?"

"I'm fine," I said. And I was. In that strange, terrifying way that meant I wasn't.

I turned and walked out of the bathroom.

The world could explode behind me, and I wouldn't flinch.

Not anymore.

Kip didn't say anything as he wrapped Draco's body in plastic sheeting. Efficient. Silent. His movements were clinical, practiced, and detached. Like this wasn't the first time. Like it wouldn't be the last.

"I'll be back for the blood," he said, dragging the corpse down the hallway toward the back door.

I nodded, but I was already walking toward my bedroom. I didn't know what I was looking for. Maybe bleach. Maybe something to scrub the walls clean.

What if the Pied Piper sat on your bed or, worse, put Draco there?

Frantic, I tugged the sheets off the bed and peeled the comforter back.

That's when I saw it.

A small square, face down on my pillow.

It wasn't there earlier.

My breath caught in my throat as I reached for it. Flipped it over.

A picture.

Me.

Asleep. Turned toward the wall. One arm curled under my pillow. Hair tangled. Neck exposed.

The timestamp in the bottom corner: 12:13 a.m. Two nights ago.

I hadn't been with Kip. I'd been alone. And yet, in the photo ... a shadow hovered near the foot of the bed. Barely visible in the corner of the frame.

Watching.

I dropped the photo. Stumbled back. My skin went cold, but I didn't scream.

I picked it up again. Folded it slowly. Carefully. Slipped it into the pocket of my hoodie.

No panic.

No tears.

Only the sharp, clean edge of rage.

"You don't get to haunt me anymore," I whispered into the empty room. "Next time, I'll see you coming."

The next three days passed without another message from the Pied Piper. I'd insisted on staying with Holland because even though she said she was okay, I knew she was upset. Her moods tipped from *what the fuck is happening* to *I'll hunt the motherfucker down*. What she didn't understand yet was that the Pied Piper was smarter, darker, and a lot more cunning than she realized. Maybe since she was his daughter, she could outmaneuver him.

After I'd explained more to her about the Pied Piper and the ties to Death and Ella, I'd told her I needed to bring them and Dope into the loop. At first, she'd said no, but then she'd agreed that we were stronger in numbers.

"Hey," she said, approaching me from behind and sliding her small hands down my chest. She kissed the top of my head.

I leaned back in the kitchen chair, but didn't take my attention off my phone screen. "Hey yourself." I nodded to my cell, watching. "She hasn't moved since yesterday."

"Is that normal or do you think she's gone?"

"I think she's gone, but I need to go make sure. Cynthia will be back from vacation in a few days, so I need to make sure everything is in its rightful place, including evidence that we were there."

"That shouldn't be a problem." Holland straightened. "I was there without you, then we both set the scene for her to die."

"I wanted it to look like we were there with her, and she wasn't alone." I patted Holland's arm. "I should go." I stood, the kitchen chair sliding back, and she moved away.

Dark circles framed her blue eyes, and her red hair was piled on top of her head in a messy bun that begged me to pull it down. Even in her baggy sweatshirt and black yoga pants, she was beautiful. *Mine.* Every fiber in my being refused to leave her, but I had to make sure Mother was dead. I considered taking Holland with me, but I needed to do this on my own. I would ask if Ella might be able to keep her company while I was gone. Ella along with Holland could handle any shitshow. Ella was as lethal as Death when she needed to be.

"I'll see if Ella can swing by and keep you company." I retrieved my phone from the table and tapped the screen, not waiting for Holland's response. It wasn't an option for her to say no anyway.

The phone rang, and on the third ring, Ella answered.

"Hey, how are you?" she asked, her voice chipper.

"Good. I need a favor, though. Are you around today?"

"For you? Of course. What do you need?" she asked.

"Would you be interested in hanging out with Holland at her place? I can explain when you're here, but it would help me deal with some things today and not be so distracted." I rubbed the back of my neck, my thoughts returning to Mother. She hadn't moved, but I wouldn't believe the evil bitch was really gone until I touched her cold, lifeless body.

"Give me half an hour."

"Perfect. Thanks, Ella. I'll text you the address." I winked at Holland as I disconnected the call and messaged Ella the details she needed. "You two have the ability to get into a lot of trouble together." I reached out and placed my fingers under her chin, forcing her to look at me. "Promise me, little ghost—promise me that you won't take any matters into your own hands. Be a good girl for me while I'm gone."

She smirked. "I promise."

I arched a brow at her. "What I mean is *you and Ella* stay out of trouble."

Her lower lip jutted out in a playful manner. "You're no fun, baby. I thought we could help Death and Dope find the next victim, or something to pass the time while you're gone."

I chuckled. "That's not a call I can make. That's up to Death. Once you earn his trust, which will take a while, he might let you help. Build that friendship with Ella first. That's your best bet if you want in on the action."

"Yes, sir." She grabbed my sides, bunching up the fabric of my gray T-shirt.

I gripped the sides of her jaw and squeezed, my cock springing to life with her words. Yes, sir was exactly what I liked to hear.

"You'll be my good girl?"

"Of course." She fluttered her eyes at me.

I quickly leaned down, scooped her into my arms, and carried her to the kitchen counter. She yelped as I tugged her yoga pants and thong down her legs, discarding them on the floor.

"Kip, Ella will be here soon."

Her words cut off as I parted her legs and buried my face in her pussy, licking and sucking. Her lips parted as I feasted on her wet cunt, her gasps and moans of pleasure driving me to continue.

She threaded her fingers through my hair and tugged. I reached up and pulled on my necklace, the cross breaking free.

I dragged the cold silver cross across her skin as I kissed up her stomach, up her ribs, her sternum. Fuck, I wanted to mark her. I wanted to fuse the memory of me into the marrow of her bones so that when I was gone, she'd never be able to exorcise it.

Straightening enough to wipe my mouth, I then pressed the

crucifix to her entrance and then slid it in and out. Holland squirmed and lifted her hips off the counter.

"Who do you worship, little ghost?"

"My monster." Her words were breathy as I continued. I leaned down and ran my tongue over her clit, sucking and nipping as she fucked my cross. In the back of my mind, I realized that Ella would arrive soon, but I didn't care. I needed my little ghost before I left her. I needed to fill her with my cum, mark her skin with my teeth, and leave my scent all over her.

Removing the cross, I placed it on the counter next to Holland. I lifted her and set her feet on the floor, then flipped her around and bent her over, pinning her cheek to the counter. Her legs parted, her wet cunt begging for me to bury myself in her.

I ran my fingers over her soaked slit, then eased two inside her before I curled them, hitting her sweet spot.

"Fuck me."

"Say it," I demanded.

"Fuck me, please."

"Who owns you? Who owns every piece of you?" I slowed my pace, waiting for her to respond.

"My monster. I will always belong to you. Every part of my soul is for you to ruin."

"That's it, Holland." I removed my hand and ran my knuckles from her pussy to her asshole, spreading her juices. Lining my cock up at her cunt, I shoved inside her and then eased a finger into her ass. Her gasps filled the room as I fucked her, claiming her. All of her.

She took every inch like she was born for it, her hair in a tangled curtain across her face. I watched the curve of her back, the twist of her shoulder blades, and felt the animal inside me claw for more. Every thrust was punishment and worship, absolution and sin.

Her cunt and tight asshole clamped around me, hot, greedy, defiant. I bent over her, teeth to her neck, biting down as I pumped my hips, reckless and unrestrained. Holland keened, the sound muffled by her arm, and I knew she was close. I reached around and pressed tight circles on her clit. She bucked, nearly unseating me, but I pinned her harder.

"You're mine," I growled, and it came out rough. "No one else will ever touch you again."

She nodded, trembled, "Yours. Always yours, Kip."

She spasmed, walls fluttering, and her legs shook. I rode her through it and didn't let up even as she cried my name and slumped into the countertop. I couldn't stop, not when I was so close to falling into the same abyss. I fucked her like she was the only thing anchoring me to the earth. I cursed and shuddered as the tension built, and I trembled uncontrollably. The release was overwhelming, a wave that crashed over me and left me feeling hollowed out and struggling to catch my breath. My chest rose and fell rapidly as I lay there, spent and panting.

I collapsed over her, kissing the sweat-slickened curve of her spine. We stayed fused together, chest to back, the aftershocks rippling through us both.

I stood and eased out of Holland, and she turned toward me. She kissed me—desperate, hungry, tasting herself on my tongue. She bit my bottom lip, hard enough to draw blood, and I laughed into her mouth. Pain meant she was real and not a fucking hallucination. I loved her so fucking much it scared me. I wanted to burrow inside her again, take up residency in her body, never let the world outside touch us again.

Her hand crept down to my cock, half-hard and sticky, and she stroked me back to life with lazy pulls. I moaned as she hopped onto the edge of the counter and guided me back into her. We moved together, slow now, a dance instead of a battle. She wrapped her arms around my neck, pressed her forehead to mine. She was trembling, still coming down, but her eyes never left mine.

"My monster," she whispered.

I nodded. "Always."

There was a sound in the hallway—the front door opening, then Ella called into the house. "Holland? Kip?"

Holland smiled, unfazed, and kept riding me, never looking away. We finished together, silent and secret, a truce in the ruins of the kitchen. When she climbed off me, she pulled up her pants but left the cross on the counter, smeared with both of us. She looked back, tossed her hair, and smirked.

"Hey, Ella. We'll be out in a minute."

"Take your time," Ella responded, a hint of laughter in her voice.

We hurried to the bathroom to clean up before we saw our friend.

"You'll be in good hands," I said before brushing my teeth with the extra toothbrush I'd found in one of the drawers.

"Let me know about your mother."

After we freshened up, I kissed her. We headed to the living room, where Ella had made herself comfortable on the couch.

"I need to run. Holland can fill you in." I kissed Holland one more time. "Thanks, Ella. I owe you one."

"No, you don't. We're family. Go take care of business." She smiled at me.

I nodded once before I turned to leave.

Holland grounded me. Calmed the monster. And now I was walking away with blood on my hands and fire in my chest—because we all knew the Pied Piper was out there. Watching. Waiting. And if he made his move while I was gone? I'd sacrifice every last piece of myself if it meant she'd come home again.

I returned to the kitchen and picked up the cross. I debated washing Holland's mark off it, but I didn't. Instead, I reattached the necklace, the heavy metal kissing my chest—still warm from her, like a brand. A warning. A prayer.

Let the next monster come. I was fucking ready.

41

———

KIP

As I pulled into Mother's driveway, an uneasy knot twisted in my stomach, churning like sour milk left out too long. The air felt heavy, and the once pristine paint on the house seemed to sag under the weight of years of memories. If she wasn't already gone, I would turn my back and walk away once more, but the need for closure anchored me here, urging me to deal with what had been left unresolved.

The hinge on my car door squeaked as I opened it, breaking the eerie silence as I climbed out. My tennis shoe crunched into the gravel while I locked up. Slowly, I made my way up the sidewalk and to the front entrance. I unlocked it, then let myself in. The place was hot, suffocating. Not only had Holland and I moved all the life-supporting machines, but I'd also turned off the air conditioning before I'd left.

The floorboard creaked beneath my weight as I walked down the hall to Mother's room. My pulse stammered against my neck as I pushed open her door, my attention sweeping the room before it landed on her.

Mother's face twisted in a silent scream; her mouth still open like she'd called for help that never arrived. The room smelled of rot, urine, death, and karma.

I stood at the side of her bed, staring at her frail, stiff body. Everything inside me said she was dead, but I had to make sure. My brow arched as I searched the room and spotted a handheld mirror on her dresser. I retrieved it before I held it under her nose for a long minute. Nothing. I raised my hand and placed it on her neck, feeling for a pulse for another minute. Nothing. Her skin was cold to the touch. Finally, I was convinced she was gone. For good. No false alarms like what I'd heard of before.

My heart rate calmed as I allowed reality to sink in. For the first time in my life, the house was silent. No prayers. No screams. No chains.

Leaving the room, I wandered through the rooms and finally opened the door to the basement. Years ago, I'd sworn I would never revisit hell, but here I was for no other reason than to claim the room that had stolen my soul and shaped me into a cold-blooded killer. But I'd won. I was still alive and rebuilding the shattered pieces of myself.

I flipped the light switch at the top of the stairs, then descended them one by one. The musty air curled in my nostrils, a scent so thick I could taste it. Iron, mildew, and the faintest note of the bleach she'd used to scrub out the blood. It must have been years since anyone had swept the steps; every tread was cushioned in a blanket of dust that muffled my footsteps. When I reached the bottom, I stood before the same door she used to lock me behind. The gouges from my fingernails, desperate and childish, still flared in the trim like tree rings counting out the years of my captivity.

I stepped inside and pulled the chain dangling from the bulb, flooding the concrete tomb in yellow light. The cot had collapsed, its mattress slumped and caved where my body had once lain. In the far corner, a plastic bucket—the first and only friend I was permitted—still waited, cracked and discolored. I ran my fingers along the initials I'd carved into the cinderblock wall with the end of a spoon. KIP.

I let out a laugh that sounded nothing like my voice. The air was so still it felt preserved, like a crime scene, which in a way, it was. I could feel her here, not as a ghost, but as a residue. The aftertaste of her cruelty. I wondered if she would haunt me, and I realized I didn't care. She could never be as real in death as she had been in life, and in life, I had already beaten her.

I walked the perimeter, pausing at the spot where she had once chained my ankle to a pipe for three days. I bent down, examining the rusted loop like a museum piece. My arms and legs remembered the exact diameter of the chain, the rhythmic ache when I'd shifted each night to keep from freezing. I imagined cutting the pipe loose, taking it with me, but I left it there. Someone else could marvel at her methods.

The darkness closed in on me, stealing my breath as I spotted the collar next to the cot. The cross. The blood stains on the concrete floor. The hymns she used to sing while carving up my skin.

"You can leave now. You can walk out a free man. Don't let her chain you anymore." My words rumbled through the space. I should've felt free. But freedom, when you've never tasted it, feels a lot like grief.

The basement was smaller than I remembered. My body was bigger, a different geometry, and the ceiling seemed lower. I stood up straight and stretched, filling the space she'd tried for so long to smother out of me. The only thing left to do was to say goodbye, but goodbye was not a word she'd programmed into me.

Instead, I climbed back upstairs, leaving the light on as an act of defiance. In the kitchen, I opened every cabinet and let the silence fill the rooms she had once dominated. I found her address book next to the sink, its leather cracked and swollen. I thumbed through entries for friends who'd long ago stopped answering her calls. I thought of burning it, but even that felt too sentimental.

Over the next hour, I returned all the medical machines back to her room. For the last time, I slipped the oxygen mask over her nose and mouth, turning the machine on. With everything back in its rightful place, I flipped the switch on the two window units to cool the place off before I called 9-1-1 and reported Mother's corpse.

At the front door, I looked back into the living room, half expecting her to sit up on the sofa, laugh her staccato laugh, and order me to bring her a sandwich. But she was as silent as the house now, and both belonged to the past. I stepped over the threshold, shut the door, and walked down the path, the sunlight blurring my vision. I sucked in the fresh air, clinging to the life surrounding me. Clinging to thoughts of Holland's kiss, her love. It was time to return to her. Our work together had accomplished what we needed it to. Vengeance. Power.

No longer able to stay in the house with the memories and her corpse, I walked outside. I knew that Mother was gone. But the rot she'd planted? That would live on forever.

Once back in my car, I tapped out a message to Holland that Mother was dead. Then, I made the other calls to report her death and to tell Cynthia that Mother was gone and to let me know if she needed a recommendation. I also told her that Holland and I had Dog.

After the cops arrived, and I was free to go, I started the engine and drove down the driveway. Maybe I should have felt something like remorse, but I was past that. Regardless of if I had to look at her in person or not, she would haunt my dreams for the rest of my life. My only regret? I hadn't thought of Holland's plan years ago. But Holland also needed revenge. To stand up to the woman who'd destroyed her and killed her sister. She'd reclaimed her power the moment she rolled the oxygen machine down the hall and away from Mother. I was proud of her.

Forcing my muscles to relax, my thoughts returned to Holland. She didn't know it yet, but she was about to move in with me. I refused to take no for an answer. If she wanted, we would get our own house together instead of moving into each other's space. The more I thought about it, a new place together sounded better. It fit.

We were closing the door on the past and moving forward. Together. I loved her. I owned her, but she owned me too. Every goddamn part of me. Monster and all.

I glanced in the rearview mirror, spotting a black SUV behind me. There wasn't a lot of traffic on the back road I was on, but something felt off. It had appeared out of nowhere, not helping with my suspicions.

The vehicle surged forward, then slammed into the back of my car.

Metal screamed. Tires shrieked. The wheel jerked violently in my hands.

My car spun.

Once.

Twice.

The world tilted and blurred as I fought for control, heart hammering, hands slick on the wheel. But it was too late. The trees were coming fast. A wall of trunks, dark and unyielding. I yanked the wheel, hard. The big ones rushed past in a blur of bark and shadow.

Then I dropped.

Down the slope.

No road. No traction. Just speed.

Branches whipped at the windshield as the car plowed into a grove of young pine trees, the front of my car smashing headfirst into the tall trunks, the crunch of metal deafening. The seatbelt jerked me back as the airbag deployed, slamming me backward. Somehow, I managed to remain conscious.

My body felt heavy, every muscle stiff from the impact. My head swam, thoughts sluggish, and when I tried to move, pain ricocheted down my side like broken glass. I was too slow, too dazed to react when the shadow fell over me.

My door opened, and my seatbelt was cut off.

"What the fuck?" I came out swinging, trying to see who the hell was dragging me out of my car, but a black hood was shoved over my head before I could see their faces.

"Nighty-night, motherfucker," one of them said.

A sharp pain shot through my skull, then the edges of my vision turned to black before I slipped into oblivion.

42

HOLLAND

"What are your intentions with Kip?" Ella asked without even a smile.

My forehead creased. "You don't waste any time, do you?" I settled into the chair opposite the couch, sinking into the soft leather.

Ella gave me a pointed look. "He's family. Even though you met Death and me when we dropped by unexpectedly on you and Kip, it doesn't mean we're friends."

"That's fair. It was a very compromising situation, for sure."

Ella arched a brow at me. "Is that a threat?"

I held up my hand to stop her. "Not at all. We exchanged information. You know I've killed someone as well. I shared that in order to try to connect with you, and for you to trust me. If I went to the cops, you could turn on me, too. I have no intention of doing that. Kip trusts me, but I know it will take time for you and Death to trust me as well. I understand how all of this works." I rubbed my sweaty palm on my jeans, hoping this conversation would take a turn for the better.

"I'm very protective of my family. Kip, Dope, Death ... we live a life that no one would ever want. When we found out about you, well, it was a bit of a surprise." Ella shifted in her chair, her green eyes pinning me with an intense stare. I knew she wasn't someone to fuck with, but I also knew if we could become friends, I would have a friend for life.

"When you guys showed up that night, we were just starting to figure things out. We met when we were kids and reconnected recently."

"How?"

I bit the inside of my cheek and wondered how much, if anything, Kip had shared with his friends. I didn't want to overstep, but I had a feeling this was my one chance with Ella, and I couldn't fuck it up.

"His mother."

Ella scrunched up her nose as if the word alone had a horrible smell. She was right.

"That woman is a monster."

"I would agree with that. She and another man sold me and my sister. We lived in captivity for months. I was able to escape, but Ally never saw the outside world again. They overdosed her."

Ella's expression hardened, compassion edged with fury. "They should've burned for what they did," she said, voice low. "I'm sorry, Holland."

"When one of the men I escaped from came after me recently, Kip was there to help me out of a bad situation. That's how we reconnected. Hell, I had no idea who he was. I saw his face for only a minute before I was taken, and everything was a blur."

"I'm sorry that happened to you and your sister. I can't imagine how horrible that was."

I tucked my hair behind my ear, memories playing on repeat.

"I'm not sure how I'm sitting in front of you, actually. But I am."

"What's the name of the man who came after you?"

"Draco. But he's gone now. He won't be bothering me ever again." I stared at her, hoping she would understand what I meant without me having to come right out and say it.

Images of Draco with snakes in his stomach flashed through my mind, and I closed my eyes briefly. It wasn't the dead body that grossed me out, it was the movement and being able to see things slither beneath his skin.

"Good. I assume Kip helped with that?"

"Kind of. More the cleanup." I didn't volunteer anything else, and to my surprise she didn't ask more. I'm sure she would talk to Kip later.

"What else should I know about you?" Ella asked. The corner of her mouth twitched, and I suspected she might know more about me than I did her.

"Well, I'm a psychiatrist now. I've rebuilt my life, and I'm in love with Kip." *If I still have a job since Kip called in without notice to the office and hospital.* Maybe that would help her understand that I wasn't going anywhere.

"I know. I saw how the two of you looked at each other before he left. Plus, Kip has never been with just one woman. His work is demanding, so he kept it to a no-strings-attached policy. Clearly that's changed."

I couldn't help but smile. "What about you?" I wasn't sure she would open up to me much, but I wanted to try.

"I used to work for an attorney before I met Death, Kip, and Dope. I mentioned that when we met. Have you heard about the Horizon Society?" She stretched her arm over the back of the couch.

"Kip has told me about it. I think it's amazing work. Maybe someday I can help."

"It definitely serves multiple purposes. Has he told you the other purpose?"

"I'm not sure."

Ella grew silent as if she were debating whether to tell me or not. "The men we help families escape from are dangerous and evil. When families are chosen, the men are turned over to Death who then has someone to ... eliminate."

Holy shit. I couldn't believe she trusted me with that. We were gaining ground.

"Oh, Kip said he gave a serial killer some men to kill, but he didn't mention it was from the society or who killed them." I should have been at least a little bit surprised, but it all made sense. Not much seemed to rattle me anymore, either. Not after what I'd lived through years ago and recently. Maybe the fact that I was a serial killer's daughter had something to do with it. A lack of emotions, but not about everything, only the monsters. "It's actually brilliant if you ask me. At least they can't come back after the women and kids to hurt them again."

"You seem pretty calm about it."

I laughed. "Ella, if you knew who my father was, it might make more sense. It seems I'm comfortable killing someone when I need to. What Kip does hasn't ever bothered me. I love and respect him for having the guts to take care of the families and children."

Ella tilted her head, her dark hair flowing over her shoulder. "Who's your father?"

Suddenly uncomfortable, I squirmed in my seat like a little kid.

"I don't remember him, but Lily, Kip's mother, told me who he was."

Ella grinned. "And you believe her? She's known for taking a strand of truth and weaving a new story around it to manipulate people."

"I haven't had time to verify it yet, but something in my gut tells me she wasn't lying to me." It would be nice to have verification, though.

Ella reached for her back pocket and produced her phone. "I can have Dope look into it for you. What exactly did Lily tell you?"

I watched Ella's expression for any changes as I spoke. "Apparently he's a notorious serial killer."

Ella didn't even blink as she waited for me to continue. When I didn't, she said, "There are a lot of killers out there. What's his name?"

I swallowed, my throat suddenly dry and tight. "No one else

knows except Kip, and we've been dealing with his mother and not had time to verify all the details yet."

Ella motioned for me to continue.

Suddenly, my phone buzzed. I reached for it on the coffee table, thumbed the screen, and read Kip's message.

She's dead.

Two words. That was it. No name. No need.

But I knew exactly who he meant.

A slow smile curved my lips. I looked up at Ella, met her stare, and whispered like it was a prayer laced in gasoline.

"Lily's dead."

Let the bitch rot in hell.

43

———

KIP

Groggy, I rubbed the back of my head and winced. Slowly, I peered through the haze and tried to figure out where the hell I was. I sat in the middle of a room in an uncomfortable chair. I rubbed my arms, attempting to help the blood flow through my body again.

The cabin seemed small with a kitchen, living room, and fireplace. The worn couch and two chairs were the only furniture other than four kitchen table chairs that looked like they belonged in my grandmother's house.

Footsteps approached, and I turned my attention in that direction.

"Good, you're awake."

I blinked several times and hoped I would snap out of my dream, but I remembered that voice, and with the pain in my skull, I knew I wasn't fucking dreaming either.

My gaze landed on his black dress shoes and slowly traveled up his black slacks and white dress shirt. His short dark hair was peppered with gray, and it matched his well-trimmed beard. He rolled up his sleeves, smiling.

"What am I doing here?"

"You're fucking my daughter. I thought it was time we had a chat —caught up on life."

I should have known the Pied Piper was behind this.

"Also, I'm sorry to hear of your mother's passing." He crossed his legs, placing his ankle on the opposite knee, calm, composed.

"I'm not," I growled. How did he know? She just fucking died ... unless he stopped by, and I wasn't watching the cameras. *Shit.* I would have to unravel that if I survived our meeting.

"But it doesn't explain why you ran me off the road and knocked me out. What do you want? I have shit I need to do." I hesitated, then grinned. "Like bury your ex-girlfriend. How long did that last, anyway?"

"A few years. We were off and on. She found out about Samantha and Ally's mother, Julianne, and broke things off with me." He shrugged. "I never did well with commitment."

Mentally, I sifted through the images Dope had dug up. "How do my uncle and Pastor Pendleton fit into your group?"

The Pied Piper smiled. "I know you've been looking for answers, and it's best that you get them from me."

"Because you'll be honest with me?" I snorted. "You're as bad as my mother. A nugget of truth and a hell of a lot of lies."

"You can believe me or not, but I think most of it will make sense to you." He smoothed his white dress shirt. "There is a group of us. We met in college. I'm not sure what you already know, so be patient with me as I explain."

"Sure, because I have nowhere else to be right now." I stared out the window at the thick line of trees in front of the cabin. I assumed we were in the middle of nowhere, and even if I ran, I wouldn't get far.

He continued as if I hadn't smarted off to him. "We were a close group, and small at first. As time went by, we picked up a few additional people. Pastor Pendleton and a man named Jameson Stanford to name a few."

I wanted to tell him to hurry up and get to the point of why I was really here, but I kept my mouth shut.

"Lily met the good pastor right as he was starting his first church. She was interested in a relationship with him, but he didn't return her feelings. Honestly, I don't think she actually cared about him at all. It was a stab at me, to get me back for cheating on her." He chuckled. "I didn't give a shit who she fucked, but she was angry at me, especially when she found out about Samantha. What I didn't expect was what Lily did after that."

"And that was?" I pretended to be bored, but I wanted answers. Lily was gone, and it dawned on me this might be my only chance to learn what had happened, and who I'd really killed that night.

"When Pendleton rejected her, she went after Julianne. Simply put, Lily killed Samantha's mother."

My stomach dropped to my toes. Lily was a lot of things, but a cold-blooded murderer?

"How?"

"Poisoned her over a few weeks. Invited her for dinner and drinks almost every night, then she administered the final dose in Julianne's drink one evening."

"Did she just want her out of the way, or did she want your undivided attention? What was her endgame? She had a reason for every fucking thing she did. Every lie that left her mouth." I folded my hands in my lap, pretending to be calm.

"Both. She thought it would hurt me. It did, but I never gave her the reaction she wanted. Eventually, she gave up and used her time and energy to do what she did best."

"Use people?"

"Actually, yes. She had been dabbling in sex trafficking and knew she could make a lot of money if she had the right cover. She approached me with her idea. It was solid, but we had to deal with some loose ends first."

"Samantha and Ally?" I knew the answer before I even asked.

"Ally was just caught in the hurricane, if you will. But Samantha, my daughter, had a purpose. She was tested, and well, she passed." His smile lit up his face as if he was having a proud father moment.

I gritted my teeth, planning how I could kill the motherfucker here and now for selling his own kid. "You're a sick fuck."

"Think what you want, but look at who she is today. Smart, a survivor, and she even took after me ... a killer."

"It's not the same. Hers was self-defense," I gritted out, my hands fisting in my lap.

"And Lily? It was her idea to leave her alone to die—just like she'd done to both of you."

I could feel the color drain from my cheeks. If he knew how it went down, it also meant that he had something to blackmail us with. *Fuck!* My heart skipped a beat. But how would he know that?

"I have no idea what you're talking about." I lifted my chin in defiance.

He chuckled. "Kip, I know exactly how it played out, but we'll get to that later. First, I'm sure you have so many questions about that night and what really happened afterward."

I did.

But I didn't ask them.

Because whatever came next—it wasn't a conversation.

It was a reckoning.

And somehow, I knew ... the answer to who I killed was going to destroy me more than the body ever did.

44

———

HOLLAND

Ella's shoulders sagged with relief. "That's great news. I didn't know her, only of her, but from what Dope and Kip have told me, she was straight up evil."

"I suspect even more evil than we know." I hopped out of my chair, antsy that Ella was staring at me as if I single-handedly killed Kip's mother. Or maybe I'd allowed someone to see a glimpse of guilt that left as quickly as it appeared.

"Would you like something to drink?" I made my way to the kitchen and opened the cabinet. "I have some wine!" I called to her.

"That sounds great, thank you," Ella said from behind me.

Startled, I jumped, nearly dropping the wineglasses as I pulled them off the top shelf.

"You seem stressed. What can I do to help?" Ella held out her hand for a glass.

I gave it to her, retrieved the bottle of wine, and poured us both a healthy glass.

"Five ounces is underrated." I attempted a laugh, but I suspected Ella saw right through me. I recorked the wine and put it back in the cabinet.

It was then that a little white box with a pink bow caught my attention. *What the hell?*

It sat there delicate, out of place. Too perfect. Too intentional.

I hadn't ever seen it before. I *knew* I hadn't.

A cold chill skated down my spine. Not the shiver kind. The kind that roots you. That makes the air too thick to breathe.

I took a step closer, pulse thudding in my ears. That box hadn't been here this morning, which meant he'd been here. *Again.* In my fucking house. Touching my things. Watching me, maybe. The picture in my pocket burned a hole through my jeans.

My fingers hovered over the lid. I didn't even need to open it. I knew who it was from.

My father.

And suddenly the walls didn't feel like walls. They felt like eyes. A cage. The air didn't feel like air, it felt like his breath on the back of my neck.

My throat tightened. My skin crawled. I wanted to scream—to throw the box, to burn it, to run—but I didn't move because this was the game, wasn't it? It was all mind games with him.

Placing the box on the counter, I glanced at Ella, who took a sip of her wine. Carefully, I lifted the lid and stared at a stack of pictures. I removed them one by one, staring in disbelief.

"Holland?" Ella asked.

I hadn't noticed the tears that had slipped down my cheeks and landed on the countertop.

"Sorry." I wiped my face and sniffled. "It's pictures of Ally and me, my sister."

Ella approached and put a gentle hand on my shoulder. "What the hell?"

She grabbed the next picture from the stack, a small gasp escaping her. "Do you know that man?" Her voice rose in pitch, and for the first time I saw fear twist her facial features.

"He's ... he's my father," I managed.

Ella turned ghostly pale. "Your father?" She threw her head back and laughed as if she'd lost her mind. "Does Kip know who your father is, Holland?"

I took a gulp of my wine. I shouldn't have opened the damn box, but I felt safer doing it with someone here. Besides, Kip was close to his friends, and I suspected he would confide in them now that they knew about me.

"He does, but only today. I just found out from Lily, and I wanted to verify the information before Kip said anything to you and Death."

"Fucking hell." Her head dropped and her shoulders sagged with the weight of the world. "The most evil, vile, intelligent monster I've ever met ... his blood is running through your goddamn veins."

"Yeah, I thought about that too." I blew out a heavy sigh as I put the lid on the box and tucked it into a drawer. I would deal with it later. From what I'd seen so far, it was to let me know that my father had always been around even if he hadn't been in my life. A reminder that he was always watching.

Ella nodded toward the living room. "Let's at least sit down. Tell me more."

We settled in again, and I filled in the gaps and brought her fully up to speed about the first time I'd seen Kip, what had happened to Ally and me, how Draco and Cooper had tracked me down and that they were now dead, and the rest of the details that had led up to Lily's death. I thought Ella would have left by now with the crazy shit I was telling her, but not once did she look at me with an ounce of judgment. I liked her. A lot.

"That makes sense about you killing Dom, but Draco and the note your father left take it up a new level of fucked up."

"Yeah, but I don't understand why now. After all this time, why are Kip and I learning the truth about him? What's his goal?"

Ella tapped her fingernails against the wineglass and stared at me. "If I had my guess, he's bringing his family home."

"He has more than one daughter?" For some reason, the thought hadn't crossed my mind.

"I have no idea, but he has his eye on Death and me too." Her voice dropped. "Not because we're related—because he still sees us as his property." She leaned up and removed her phone from her back pocket. "Can I ask Dope for help? Better yet, maybe we should pay him a visit and tell him everything. He should be able to find some answers for us."

"I need answers. I'm confused and honestly scared. But Ella, whatever else we learn ..." My jaw clenched so tight it ached. "The Pied Piper has to be brought down. He sold me. My sister died in captivity. I owe the motherfucker."

Ella stood, her wine forgotten. Her eyes—once filled with suspicion—burned now with something darker.

"No," she said. That one word full of a deadly promise. "We all do. He's been playing god for far too long. But this time?"

She extended her hand. "He has no idea what kind of monsters he just brought home."

45
———

KIP

I leaned back in my chair and shifted, trying to find a more comfortable spot. "If you know so much, then who the hell did I kill because I thought it was Samantha? I fucking deserve to know."

The Pied Piper stood and walked to the little kitchen and opened the fridge. He retrieved two bottles of water and brought one to me. "I get so parched during these kinds of conversations." He unscrewed the cap and took several sips before he returned to his seat.

I twisted my lid, breaking the seal, and drank some myself.

"Tell me what you know, and then I'll fill in the gaps." He set his drink on the floor next to the couch.

"From what I can remember, my uncle, Mother, and who I thought was Samantha's father were all in a room. Samantha was crying and her father was pulling her across the room. It was clear he was hurting her. Samantha was screaming for help, and I was trying to get to her, but Mother and Uncle Vinny blocked me. After that, it was all a blur. I remember blood on my hands and Holland's body was crumpled on the floor next to me. There was so much blood. Fuck, I'm not even sure how I killed whoever the girl was or why."

One bushy eyebrow rose. "Interesting. And what if I told you none of that happened. You in fact never killed anyone until you were older."

I struggled to breathe. Mother had said the same, but everything that came out of that bitch's mouth was a twisted lie. I had no reason to believe her until the Pied Piper confirmed the information. "All the days and nights Mother made me repent and carved up my back, screaming at me that I'd killed her..." The memories slammed into me so hard it knocked the wind out of me. "It was all to control me."

"Jameson is better than I ever thought he would be." He smiled, a faraway look on his face as if he were reeled back in time. "Kip, you never killed that girl. Other than Samantha and Ally, there were no other girls that night. We weren't even at your house when they were taken. We were in the basement of Pendleton's church."

I blinked at him as if he was the one with the memory problems.

"No, you're wrong. It was at my place. Well, the outbuilding. Holland remembers it too."

"Holland's memory of that night is shaky at best. Yours ..." He steepled his fingers tighter, staring at me over the top of them.

"What?" The bite to my tone carried a warning.

"Yours were planted. Nothing you remember is true. It never happened."

The words dropped like a match into gasoline.

I shot out of my chair so fast it scraped across the floor, wood screaming. My pulse thundered in my skull.

No.

I knew this theory. I'd heard it before. Holland had said something similar—her voice steady, her eyes wide with that unbearable concern I couldn't face. I'd brushed her off then. I had to. Because the alternative? It meant my memories—my whole self—might be a lie.

But hearing it now from him, from the abomination who had ruined everything, made it real. Undeniable.

The floor tilted under me. The air thickened like smoke in my lungs.

I paced too fast, like I could outrun it, outshout it.

"What the fuck do you mean?" My voice cracked, and I didn't care. "You better explain fast before I tear you and this whole goddamn place apart."

And I meant every word.

My skin vibrated with rage, panic, betrayal. Because if he was telling the truth, then everything I'd believed about myself, everything I'd done was built on rot. What was worse? To be a killer in truth, or to discover my entire life had been molded and twisted from lies?

I didn't know if I wanted the answer ... or if I just wanted to rip his throat out before he could say another word.

The Pied Piper never even blinked at my threat.

"At one time, Jameson worked for the military, and he specialized in mind control and embedding memories that never happened. At first, he was used to helping soldiers who suffered after being in wars or trauma. He basically reprogrammed their trauma with good experiences that helped them move on. Live a good life again."

I folded my arms over my chest, a chill creeping up my spine.

"Then, I met him one evening at a bar. What he didn't know was that his skills were already on my radar, and I felt they might be very useful. I was right. It's actually amazing that all of these years you thought you killed a girl. And even I know that goes against everything you are at your core. Yes, you're a killer, but you protect women and children at all costs."

"Yeah, so what? You know that about me. What the fuck actually happened to me?"

"I know this is a lot to take in, but I think it will be worth your time. Sit." He pointed to the chair.

"I don't want to."

"Sit, or I won't give you the answers you want." He stared at me patiently, waiting.

Reluctantly, I sat down again.

"Lily and your uncle learned of an opportunity to dive deep into the underworld and have a part of the sex trafficking business. It was a huge moneymaker, and it funded a lot of my 'missions', if you will."

"Your kills? Paying off people to not turn you in?"

"Exactly. We all met and discussed the possibilities of the business and what that meant for our futures."

Bile swam up my throat as he referred to selling girls as a goddamn business. Everything inside me wanted to slit his throat. My hand instinctively went to my cross, but it was gone. My anger boiled over into a full-on rage that I was barely able to contain. That weapon was everything to me. It was marked with Holland's arousal, the knife I used to protect myself and kill when I wanted to.

"Where's my cross?" I glared at him.

"It's safe for now. You'll get it back when you leave. You have my word." He motioned to the kitchen counter, and I saw my necklace near the sink.

"Like your word is something to be trusted." My nostrils flared.

"I'm many things, Kip, but I do keep my word. You'll see." He reached for his water and took another sip. "Now, where was I? Oh yes. After much discussion, we all agreed that the best place to run a sex trafficking ring would be right out of the church. Summer camps, youth groups, Halloween carnivals that were *safe*."

What the fuck?

"Pendleton offered his place; your mother attended religiously." He chuckled. "Pardon the pun."

I didn't laugh.

"It was the perfect front. Everyone loved Pendleton and his sermons were very good. He was quite impressive. They didn't put me to sleep like other pastors did. He was fun and engaged the congregation."

I couldn't believe the shit coming out of this man's mouth. He sat in church, pretending to be someone good while he, my mother, and the pastor stole girls and sold them. Would he be happy to be reunited in hell with my mother? Regardless of how I felt, I had to play along. I was finally getting answers.

"I remember the church, I think. I was there with the pastor's son a lot since Mother always dragged me there."

"Yes, you did spend a significant amount of time there. Until you walked in on us selling Samantha and Ally. That's when everything changed and measures were taken."

46

HOLLAND

I followed Ella down the stairs to what she called Dope's dungeon, the smell of weed making me scrunch up my nose.

"He loves his pot," Ella said, fanning her hand in front of her nose. "I have no idea how he's so fucking smart the way he smokes, but he's a fucking genius." She laughed.

"He probably uses it to slow down his brain. Often people self-medicate with whatever helps instead of medication with serious side effects. Has he ever mentioned OCD or ADHD?"

"Not outright, but he says the weed helps him focus. All it does is make me sleepy, and I struggle to string a sentence together." She shook her head, her soft laugh bouncing off the walls.

I grinned as we entered the dark room where a redheaded, good-looking man sat at a desk with two computers whirring in the background and three large screens spanning his desk.

"Ladies." He nodded at us as we joined him.

"Dope, this is Holland." She sat on the loveseat as I reached out to shake his hand.

"Awww, the woman who brought Kip to his knees. You're a badass just for that accomplishment." He grinned at me.

My cheeks burned with his compliment.

"Don't mind him. He literally has no filter. He's not super good at reading the room, either." Ella gave him a pointed look.

"It's the weed. I'm slow to react at times." Dope laughed, then sank into his computer chair. "It's good to meet you, Holland. Kip has ... well, he's said some things." Dope cleared his throat. "That came out wrong, but we're all connected it seems, so no reason to beat around the bush. He told us about Draco and what you went through. When he couldn't get in touch with you the other day, I saw my man unravel like never before. He's in deep." He rolled his chair up to his desk again.

"I didn't mean to worry him. I was visiting his mother."

"Bet you were," Dope said. "Hope that went well for you."

Ella nudged me in the side with her elbow. She knew how it went already.

"Kip's mother died today," Ella said to Dope.

"Holy hell. Really?" His voice held a note of excitement.

"Really," I added.

"It's about damn time she returned to the pits of hell from whence she came." Dope cackled, imitating a demon.

I couldn't help but laugh. He was entertaining as hell.

Dope scrolled, the screen flying by. I wasn't sure how he could see what he was looking for at that rate.

"What can I do for you, ladies?"

"Do you want to tell him, or do you want me to?" Ella asked gently.

Even though we were getting to know each other, I had a feeling Ella and I would become good friends. Deep friendships were developed over dark secrets just as much as the good times.

I sat up straight and squared my shoulders. "When I was visiting Lily the other day, she said that I ... that I ... was the Pied Piper's biological daughter," I blurted.

Dope's hazel eyes popped open wide, and he stared at me with his mouth hanging open. It took him a moment before he closed it.

"Shit. That was rude. I'm sorry. I don't know why anything surprises me anymore. Fuck, I've seen it all. Done it all."

"We need to verify that information, Dope. Lily lied and twisted the truth, so before we dive into the deep end of those shark-infested waters, we need proof. We figured you could help."

Dope popped his knuckles. "Oh, hell yeah. I'm on it. But—" He held up a finger. "Would anyone like a beverage? Tea? Soda? A joint to chill you out while we see if your father is the most evil being ever born?"

"Dope," Ella chided. "Really?"

Guilt flashed across his expression. "I'm on it." He returned his attention to his computer, typing with a determined focus, the clicking was the only sound in the room for several minutes.

"Hmm." He continued typing. "Hmm." More typing.

I shot a glance at Ella, a little exasperated with his nonverbal comments.

She gave me a sheepish smile and mouthed "sorry".

"Interesting," he said.

Dope tapped the spacebar, leaned back in his chair, and scratched his chin.

"Almost in. If there's a blood record buried in here, I'll find it."

My stomach twisted. I hadn't slept. The skin under my eyes was so sensitive, I wondered if it was bruised.

"And you're sure it's here?" I asked.

He shot me a look, half stoned, half razor-sharp.

"These people kept records on everything. And I mean everything. If the Pied Piper sneezed, someone logged it."

The screen flickered. A black window blinked to life—lines of code dancing like static on a broken TV.

"We're in," he muttered.

Folder after folder populated. Latin names. Redacted reports. Dozens of birth records tagged with code names and obscure religious phrases. One caught my eye: "Offerings: Book of Daughters."

"Open that," I said.

Dope clicked.

Inside: dozens of entries, each tied to a different child. Dates. Notes. Some redacted. Some were marked with symbols I didn't understand.

Then—

"Here," he said, his shoulders suddenly tight. "Entry 27. 'Project Lilith.'"

The screen filled with text. My pulse skipped several beats.

Subject: S.A. (Samantha Alder) DOB: [redacted] Paternal: 'Acquired via D.C. Initiative.' Maternal: J.M. Disposition: Reserved. Trauma resistant. Ideal for conditioning.

Dope exhaled. "Shit ..."

I leaned forward, reading it again.

"They cataloged me like livestock," I whispered. "Conditioning?"

Dope didn't respond. Just scrolled lower.

A faded handwritten entry bled through the screen like rot beneath wallpaper. A transfer log.

'Transferred to Primary Parent (Codename: Pied Piper). Status: Claimed.'

The words blurred. My vision pulsed. The floor tilted.

Dope scrolled lower.

My stomach twisted, and I tasted iron.

"He claimed me," I said. "Like a ... like a fucking possession."

Dope sat back, silent.

"So it's true," I said. My voice didn't sound like mine. "He's my father."

Dope hesitated, like he didn't want to be the one to say it.

"It's not DNA," he offered. "Not proof-proof. But yeah. It reads like a ... possession record."

I stepped back, heart jackhammering in my ribs.

"They planned this. From the beginning. He saw me, as a child, and saw something he could manipulate ... control."

The screen blurred. My body pulsed with heat—shame, confusion, fury.

I stumbled back, my hand gripping the back of Dope's chair.

"I was never supposed to survive him," I whispered. "I was supposed to *become* him."

My nails dug into my palms until my skin burned with the pain. Pain I welcomed.

And then something in me cracked wide open.

Not panic. Not grief.

Rage.

Cold, coiled.

"He wants someone as twisted as him?" I hissed. "Fine. Let him see what his daughter grew into."

Dope looked at me, startled.

"I'll find him," I said, teeth clenched. "And when I do—I'll bury him in the shadows he fucking built."

And that's when he clicked open another folder. One buried at the bottom.

"What the hell?" he said. "I got something weird."

47

———

KIP

"What do you mean?" I asked, craving more answers as he continued.

"You were never meant to know what was going on, but your mother caught you listening in on us meeting with the buyer. Samantha and Ally were in the room next to where we were all talking. You were supposed to have been with Pendleton's son, but for whatever reason, you found your way to the basement and the extra rooms we had there to hold girls and conduct our business without prying ears." He sipped his water before he continued.

"By the time we realized how much you'd heard, you were barging in and trying to help Samantha. Vinny took his gun and knocked you out."

My forehead creased. "No, there has to be more to it."

"There's not. You were knocked out. But you heard enough to put us all away for several lifetimes. We couldn't have that. Your mother was beside herself, desperate not to lose the entire operation. That's when I called Jameson. I not only trusted him, but he had also helped me deal with other risky situations."

"What did he do to me?"

The Pied Piper stretched his legs out in front of him. "He worked with your mother and uncle to brainwash you, and then he planted new fragments. As I said, you never killed a girl, but Jameson made you think you did."

My insides shook with rage and confusion. How had I believed I'd killed Samantha for years, but those images were a fraud? What else was a lie? Did I have any moments that were my own? That were real?

I choked on my words before I finally asked, "Are *all* my memories fake?"

He waved me off as if it was the silliest question he'd ever heard. "Oh no. I wouldn't let Jameson mess with anything else except that night."

"What part did my mother play?"

"Her job was to get you addicted to heroin. She shot you up often, then Jameson would put you in front of a movie projector and play a scene where a young man murdered a girl. It was messy and bloody, and straight out of a horror movie. But as you watched, his voice told you that it was you. You'd killed her."

I rolled my shoulders in a poor attempt to gather my thoughts. "My mother carved my back up, locked me in the basement, chained and sometimes naked. She did it for weeks at a time. If I never killed anyone, then why ... why did she do that?"

"To control you and ensure that you never told a soul what happened that night. If Jameson's plan didn't work, we had to control you another way. It was insurance, if you will."

My body trembled at the confession. I'd never killed anyone. I'd lived my entire life in hell, scarred, and in darkness because I'd caught them trying to sell Samantha and Ally that night. My hands fisted and un-fisted.

"We had big plans for you. Everything that you endured was for the bigger picture, Kip. It shaped you. I did that. I created you. I forged you into the man you are today. Your bloodlust was planted years ago. Your desire to help Death kill and clean was embedded even then. I orchestrated this from the beginning, and over time, I've enjoyed seeing my plans unfold."

"How do I know this meeting with you is real if my mind was tampered with?"

"It's real, Kip. I promise you that."

"Fine." Spittle flew from my mouth. "I have another question."

"Let me have it." Pied Piper motioned for me to continue.

"I have blackouts. I don't remember shit, but I wake up in old churches, basements of abandoned buildings. Is that from the brainwashing?"

The Pied Piper stared at me, not saying anything for a minute. "Some of that is residual from the brainwashing." He shifted in his seat. "But before we dive into that, are you sure you don't have any other questions about Jameson?"

I did. I had a ton of them, and the more answers he gave me, the more questions I had. My first one was how would I kill the twisted motherfucker in front of me? Then, it dawned on me.

"Mother told me Uncle Vinny died but—"

"When you dug up his grave, it was empty," he finished for me.

My gaze narrowed on him. "How the fuck did you know?"

He ignored my question. "Your uncle pissed off the wrong people, including your mother, and he went into hiding. He dug his own grave in case anyone suspected he was still alive. Vinny recently retired from working with me. He's a close friend, and I was saddened when he was diagnosed with dementia. His mind is gone, or I would have brought him with me to see you. He always thought you were a good kid with a bright future."

Stunned, I massaged the back of my neck, remembering Samantha's locket I'd found. Vinny must have dropped it while he was digging. Did I even want to see Vinny after everything he'd done to me? Done to all the girls he'd sold? No. I had nothing to say to him. As far as I was concerned, he got off lucky not remembering the shit he'd done. I wished he did remember, that it was seared into his brain like Mother's knife had seared my skin.

"I don't know why I dug it up in the first damn place," I said.

"I was in control that night. You needed to question what Lily was telling you about so many things, so I guided you to the breadcrumbs. If I'd told you everything right then, you most likely would have broken beyond repair. I couldn't take that chance, so I guided you to what you needed to know, bits and pieces at a time, including my daughter." He smirked.

"As for her, I approve of you two together. It has turned out better than I could have hoped." He paused, as if waiting to see if I had anything else to say or maybe to let our meeting sink in. I wasn't sure anymore.

"Anything else?" he asked as if he were checking off a to-do list. Maybe in his mind he was.

I sat there, silent.

"All right. Then I'll loop back around and answer how I know so much about you and why I brought you here."

48

HOLLAND

A grainy scanned document filled the screen. Handwritten therapist notes and doodles in the margins. At the bottom: a child's drawing. Sloppy but vivid.

A cage. A small boy inside. A taller figure just outside—red hair, messy. Glasses drawn in jagged lines. And on the boy's arm, barely visible—a tattoo of a rabbit with its neck snapped.

I froze. The child in the cage slammed me with horrible memories of my own capture.

Ella leaned in. Her eyes narrowed. Then she turned toward Dope. "That tattoo …" she said. "You have that on your arm."

Dope glanced down, then slowly pushed up his sleeve. Exact same design. Exact same place. "Huh," he said with a half-laugh. "Yeah. Forgot about that."

"Why a broken rabbit?" I asked.

He scratched his jaw, suddenly restless. "It was a crazy night when I was seventeen. Got high, blacked out, woke up with it. Didn't even remember doing it." He chuckled like it was no big deal.

Ella didn't push. Neither did I. But something in me shifted. No child would've drawn that by accident. And Dope's tone? Too casual. Too smooth. Like he was playing dumb ... or terrified to remember.

Ella glanced at the floor, and I watched her retreat into something unspoken. Then Dope rolled his sleeve back down—too fast. Like he couldn't bear to look at it.

His hand went to the mouse, but he didn't close the file.

Instead, he right-clicked the image and dragged it into a folder hidden deep inside his desktop—one I never would've seen if I hadn't been watching. But I was watching.

The folder name flashed for a blink: "Oblivion_Temp"

My spine straightened. My stomach turned. He clicked away like it had never happened. Face blank. Knuckles white.

And just like that, the moment passed.

Except it didn't.

It lodged itself in the back of my throat like a secret trying to claw its way out. He didn't know I saw. And I didn't say a word.

The ripple it left behind stretched through the room, tightening the air like a noose. Dope leaned back in his chair like the world hadn't just shifted under our feet. Ella remained quiet, lost in whatever haunted her. And I sat frozen—body rigid, pulse skimming the surface of my skin.

That image wouldn't let me go. The cage. The child. The tattoo that shouldn't exist.

It made me want to scream, but instead, I swallowed it. Screaming never helped. I'd learned that long ago.

I pushed to my feet, walked toward the wall behind the office desk, and stared out the tiny window. The glow of streetlamps bent in the puddles, stretching like broken halos across the asphalt. It was nearly four in the morning, and the world was quiet—too quiet.

Behind me, Dope cracked his knuckles and pulled up another script. He was already moving on.

"There's more," he said. "Whatever P.P. left buried, I'm gonna find it."

"Be careful what you wake." Ella didn't look up, but her voice was steady.

Dope snorted. "What, like he's watching us from his villain lair? Don't be dramatic."

I didn't respond. But my fingers twitched while I removed my phone from my jeans pocket.

Kip hadn't texted. Not even a check-in. Not that I expected him to. Not after what he was doing. Where he'd gone. Who he'd gone to see.

Still ... silence had a way of unraveling things in me. I sat again, just to feel the weight of the couch beneath me. Solid and real.

"Anything?" I asked.

Dope squinted at the screen. "A lot of encrypted crap. But this ..." He clicked open a folder with no name. "... looks like a ghost drive. No metadata. No owner stamp." He leaned forward. "Could be a live link."

Ella looked up. "Meaning what?"

He didn't answer. Instead, he pulled up a black terminal window. Empty. No files. Only a blinking cursor at the top. Waiting.

He leaned in. Typed a command. Nothing. Then—

The cursor jumped, flickered, and letters began to form.

WHY ARE YOU STILL LOOKING

The words weren't typed by Dope. They weren't part of the code. They simply ... appeared. One letter at a time. Like someone else was in the system.

"Uh—" Dope stiffened. "You guys seeing this?"

Ella shot to her feet.

I leaned forward. My throat burned.

Another line followed.

SOME DOORS SHOULD STAY CLOSED

Dope scrambled to disconnect the Wi-Fi, but the mouse froze on the screen.

"I'm locked out," he muttered.

I SEE YOU

My blood turned to ice.

"Shut it down," Ella snapped. "Now."

Dope slammed the laptop closed. The other large screens cut to black.

Silence thundered, and no one said a word. The only sound was my heart hammering in my ears.

We sat that way for what seemed like forever.

Then Dope exhaled before he reopened the laptop.

"It's offline now," he said. "Whatever that was, it's severed."

Ella crossed her arms. "Not if they already got what they wanted."

I stared at the black screen. The image of those words burned into my brain.

Something vile had reached through the digital void and touched us.

My body went cold. But my mind? My mind fractured. Not all at once—but in delicate, hairline cracks.

He was still out there. Still orchestrating. Still watching.

And for the first time in years, I felt like prey again.

I clenched my fists until my nails bit deep. My breath stuttered in my chest. Every cell inside me wanted to scream—but I didn't. I couldn't.

Screaming never saved anyone.

I swallowed it down.

The rage. The terror. The instinct to run.

And somewhere in that storm of silence, something in me twisted.

I wasn't the same girl he'd marked.

I'd grown teeth in the dark.

Let him come.

I would tear the music from his goddamn throat and bury the fucking flute in his chest.

The silence after felt surgical—like it had cut something out of me.

"There was no IP return. No traceable link," Dope said. But he didn't sound convinced.

They weren't threats. They were warnings. But they didn't make me want to run.

They made me want to fight.

"He's still watching," I said quietly, saying out loud what we were all thinking.

Ella looked at me. "You think it was him?"

"I think it was someone close. Someone with access."

Dope leaned forward again. His mask was slipping now. No grin and no jokes.

"That wasn't a script. That wasn't in the file system. Someone typed that. In real time."

I glanced at him. "Then they knew we were inside."

He nodded slowly.

I stared out the window in the basement.

Something about the shadows seemed different now. Not just dark, but hungry.

Thirty minutes passed. Dope stayed quiet. He hadn't spoken for a while. I watched him out of the corner of my eye, his gaze unfocused, flicking occasionally to his forearm where the tattoo lived. Where the boy in the drawing had worn it first.

Dope didn't say he was scared. He didn't need to. And I didn't need to tell him I'd seen him save and hide that file.

Some truths weren't meant to be dragged into the light—not yet.

But I knew this much:

The Pied Piper wasn't only a memory. He wasn't a relic of our pasts. He was still here. Still playing. And we had just stepped a little farther onto his stage.

49

———

KIP

"I have eyes and ears everywhere, cops and politicians are on my payroll, I own more property and land than you could ever imagine. So, what makes you think that I don't know about you? What you did for your uncle with cleaning the bodies, the kills you've not shared with your friends, the bloodlust, and what you all do in the Horizon Society. I do think it's brilliant to feed Death his victims so he can stay under the radar. Dope had a good idea with that one. Death is very creative in how he kills and tortures as well. And Ella." The Pied Piper clapped his hands together several times, the sound echoing through the small cabin. "I just adore her. Death did very well with her."

My chest squeezed tight as he rattled off more details about my life, including when I'd left on trips with Uncle Vinny, and when Mother had put the belt around my arm and shot heroin into my veins.

"Lily was reporting to you," I muttered.

"They all are, but some of those details my people weren't around to see. Think, Kip. How would I know where Death killed his latest victims to make sure there wasn't a trace of evidence? You came in to clean as well, but I was there before you almost every time."

I frowned, trying to understand how he knew. Who was his informant? My nostrils flared as Dope came to mind. He had the tools and skills to cover his tracks and conversations. Maybe all the information he'd found on the Pied Piper was fed to him to keep us off the Pied Piper's trail. It would explain how he knew where we were all the time.

I leaned forward. "How?"

The words that tumbled out of his mouth next sent ice through my goddamn veins.

"Didn't you ever wonder how you were able to get your cross?" he asked.

I shrugged. "I was older and stronger than Mother. It was the knife she carved my skin with, and I swore she'd never fucking do it again. I overpowered her and ripped the chain off her neck one day."

"Did she wear it all the time?"

I shook my head. "Hardly ever; that's why I took advantage of the opportunity."

"Don't you think Lily was smarter than that?"

My jaw clenched. "What are you getting at?"

"You were supposed to have the necklace, Kip. I wanted you to have it. It was a gift from me."

I gawked at him. "Why the fuck would you give me a gift?"

Silence.

The air around us crackled with a dark, foreboding energy that threatened to turn me inside out.

"Before you took it from Lily, I had a tracker and a camera put into one end of the cross. It's not visible to anyone. You thought you chose to wear it out of rebellion, but you've hardly taken the necklace off for years. It also served as a symbolic collar. It marked you as mine. No one was to touch you or Death. Even—well, we'll save that for a conversation for another day."

Jesus Christ, I'd fucked Holland with that cross!

"From the look on your face, you're remembering all the ways you've used that crucifix."

He waited, letting his words soak in as the color drained from my cheeks.

"Don't worry." His laugh sounded hollow to my ears. "I turned off the camera and sound several times. Those private times were for you. I had no interest in your twisted sexual appetite."

I had no other choice but to believe him because I couldn't fathom the other option. "Why? Why did you want *me* to have the necklace?"

An evil smile twisted his features. "Because you were always meant to be the perfect weapon, Kip. And I have to say, you've done an exceptional job."

Cold sweat broke out on my skin, fear creeping down my spine.

"With what?" My voice shook with my question.

"Do you remember the first time you met Death? Because I do."

My world tilted on its axis as all the puzzle pieces snapped together at once.

"You used me," I said, the words like glass in my throat. "You planted me beside him. Like a fucking watchdog."

"You were planted, used by me to keep track of him and everything he did. When he killed, you were there, when he disappeared, you and Dope looked for him. I knew the plan for the society, when he met Ella ... every single moment of your lives, I've been able to keep up with."

"That doesn't explain why I would black out and find myself in a basement and not remember shit."

The Pied Piper rubbed his jawline, his cold eyes flat and void of any emotion. "We met and you updated me on what I needed to know. Sometimes the camera wasn't enough."

My heart fucking sputtered in my chest, skipping several beats and struggling to start again.

"I met with you face-to-face?"

"Yes."

I nearly doubled over, my ribs splintering beneath the weight of it. My betrayal wasn't a crack—it was a rupture. A goddamn implosion. I had wanted to know the truth for so long, but now it would destroy my entire world and everyone I loved, including my best friends.

"Why are you telling me all this now? If you were using my cross to keep up with everyone, why tell me about it?"

The Pied Piper flashed me a wicked smile. "Because I don't need you to keep me posted anymore."

"Which means you have someone else."

His smile widened. "Kip, you and Death were created by me. For me. Your entire lives have been orchestrated by me. You *both* are my sons, so to speak. I want you both to come home and work for me. You're a team. You trust each other, and whether you like it or not, you both have been working for me anyway. It's time to reunite my family, including my daughter."

The world shrank to the size of a pin, a single point of pain lodged directly into my head. "You're not fucking serious."

He patted his leg as if to emphasize his words. "But I am. Haven't you wondered why you always find your way back to me? Why your crew has never been torn apart by law or blood? Why, no matter what, I always come up aces and you always survive?"

His right hand twitched, as if he was smothering a smile or a scream. "You are in my family. Granted, not blood related but you know that means nothing. You are mine."

Mental images glitched through my mind: flashes of chrome and blood, secret basements, me gasping awake and not knowing how I'd gotten blood under my nails. And behind it all, the thin old man in the tailored suit, whistling a children's song as he watched us burn down the world.

The curtain ripped away, and I saw it. All this time, when we'd thought we were the ghosts in the pipeline, the ones above and outside the game, we were just running along lines he'd drawn for us in invisible ink.

I could run. I could kill him. My fingers itched for my knife—but even as my impulse surged, another part of me, foreign and icy, stitched my palms to my lap.

"You never had a say in this," he said, circling me. "You were made to be a weapon. The necklace is simply a reminder, a keepsake, in case you got sentimental and started thinking you had choices."

Bile rose in my throat, and I struggled to stand. "No," I said. "I'm not helping you anymore."

"You are," the Pied Piper said, but his voice had lost all pretense of warmth. "I have always known what you were, even when you tried not to know it yourself. There is no leaving this family. The sooner you accept it, the sooner we can begin the next movement."

The word "movement" hung in the air, festering. The Pied Piper walked to the window and parted the living room curtains with a single, spidery hand. The daylight had faded, but the forest outside appeared washed out and brittle, as if something evil waited just beyond the glass.

The Pied Piper stepped past me, and for a moment, I caught his scent—a mix of expensive cigars and leather. He paused, glancing over his shoulder, gaze sharp enough to pin me in place, lips curled into a semblance of a smile so fucking creepy my skin crawled.

"Xavier says hello, and he's doing well. I'm quite proud of the progress he's made."

His words—that name—dropped like a blade. Not a message but a warning.

Without another glance, he opened the door and snapped it shut behind him.

My breath caught, and my hands shook as I lowered myself to the floor, the cracked hardwood biting at my palms.

"I have a message for Xavier too," I whispered to the empty room. "Fucking die."

We never talked about Xavier. Not about who he is. Not after what happened. Not after Death let him go.

Breath sawed in and out of me, every inhale stinging like a dry cough. All the other betrayals in my life—my mother, Uncle Vinny—they paled in comparison to what I'd done to Death. Fury flared to life inside my chest at the Pied Piper. At the same time, I admired the scope of his cruelty. It was genius in its comprehensiveness, an elegant calculus that accounted for every possible outcome before it ever began.

I thought of Holland—her frantic, generous mouth, her hands on either side of my face, the way she'd always looked at me like I was about to perform some miracle. She deserved someone better. But she was one of the few people who understood my darkness, which made sense since her father was beyond a monster. He was pure evil.

When I looked down, the cross caught a ray of light filtering in from the window. The camera. The tracker. The gift that wasn't a gift. I wondered if Dope could remove what the Pied Piper had planted in it. It wouldn't matter if I went to Dope's and the Pied Piper tracked me; he already knew where Dope lived and all our conversations. I would give him this last one. I stood, grabbed my cross from the kitchen counter, and walked out the door. I pulled out my cell and laughed when I saw there was no signal. It would be a long fucking walk before I got any, but it would give me time to figure out what the fuck I was going to tell my best friends ... and the love of my life. How would I tell someone I helped destroy them? That I was the weapon they never saw coming?

50

———

KIP

After almost three hours of walking, my phone was finally in range. The only person I wanted to see was Holland. I couldn't handle facing Death and Dope yet. Even with the long walk, my mind was spinning out. Guilt, anger, then depression cycled through me like a hurricane, dragging me out to sea after every horrible cycle. I needed my little ghost. I needed to hold her, feel her warmth against me as I searched for any good in my dark, fucked-up world.

When I tracked her car, the map showed she was almost there, and I looked around my surroundings. I was in the middle of fucking nowhere with open fields and no landmarks. I added a pin to the map to find the cross later. I tugged on my necklace, releasing the catch, then found a safe place about ten steps off the road. I kicked at the dirt until I'd dug a shallow hole with my shoe. I placed the cross in the ground, then covered it back up. Hopefully, it would be safe until I could return and have Dope help me remove any tracking and video equipment.

It was another ten minutes before she pulled up on the country road next to me. Exhausted, I climbed into the car.

"Kip." She grabbed me and kissed my mouth. "Are you okay? What happened?" She rubbed my arm, her gaze scanning me from head to toe, worry clouding her expression.

"It's a long story, but your father said hello." I rubbed my face, my hands and body covered in dirt from walking through the woods.

"Shit. You were with him?" The muscles in her shoulders visibly tensed as she shifted into drive and made a U-turn.

"Yeah. I would love a shower and some food before we talk. I'm okay. You're safe. I'm safe, so please don't worry." I reached out and stroked the back of her head, red strands feeling like silk beneath my fingertips. "I love you, Holland. And if it matters to you, we have your father's blessing."

Her jaw clenched for a second. "He found you because of me?"

"No, babe. He found you because of *me*." I leaned back in the seat, sinking into the soft leather of her rental car. Did she realize she could return it now that Cooper and Draco were dead? At least those fuckers wouldn't mess with her again. Her father and I had made sure of that. My stomach rolled with the looming conversation.

"I know it's a big favor to ask you to wait, but I need to wrap my head around what happened. It was only a conversation, but it was a big one."

"Okay. But you promise you're okay? He didn't hurt you?"

"No. He didn't touch me. His goons did, but ... fuck. They ran me off the road and I'm pretty sure my car is totaled. Not to mention they knocked me out, so I have a killer headache."

"Kip! You could have died." She dared a quick glance at me, tears welling in her eyes.

"I love that my little ghost worries about me, but baby, I've lived through a helluva lot worse. I'm fine."

She nodded and followed with a little sniffle.

"Here's what I'm super clear on. I love you. I hope like hell you can say the same after I tell you everything."

"Why would that change? You know I love you. We've walked

through hell and back, and we're still here for each other. Don't doubt me now. I love my monster." She flashed me a sweet smile, and my heart melted in my chest.

Holland had no idea how much good was in her. The darkness too, but she genuinely cared about most people. She wanted to help. She was a much better person than I was. Reaching for her hand, I leaned my head against the seat, willing the cold reality to stop fucking with me for just a little bit.

FINALLY, clean and fed, I sank into Holland's couch, and she settled in next to me. I turned to look at her and trailed my fingertips down her cheek.

"Thanks for feeding me. I feel a bit better after eating."

"Of course. How's your head feeling? Do you need some Advil?" She kissed my knuckles.

"I'll get some later. I want your help, Holland."

Her expression softened. "Whatever you need."

"The Pied Piper has been in our lives for a long time without us even realizing it. I learned just how much today." I swallowed the lump of betrayal down, willing my food to stop churning in my gut.

"I got answers. You were right. I was brainwashed, programmed. When Mother shot me up with heroin, the Pied Piper brought in a man to reprogram my mind. I saw myself kill a young redhead and a man take a bullet to the forehead. Lies. All of it. They kept me drugged and played movies, convincing me I'd done horrible things. Then Mother would keep me in the basement, chained, alone, and hungry. But that was better than her carving up my skin, forcing me to repent for sins I never committed."

"Her depravity continues to shock me. She was sick and straight up evil. I'm so glad she's gone. I don't regret any of what I did."

I leaned over and gave her a gentle kiss. "Me too. I thought we made a good team." I attempted a cocky grin, but it faltered.

I grew silent, preparing myself to tell her the worst part. "I buried my cross where you picked me up. I'll have to get it later."

She shook her head, confused. "Why?"

"Because the Pied Piper has used it to track and spy on me for years. I've had that cross since I took it from Mother when I was a teenager."

Her cheeks paled, and I assumed she was thinking what I had.

"He swore he didn't watch when I used the cross on you."

She swallowed hard. "Do you believe him?"

I rubbed the back of my head where the throbbing distracted me.

"Yeah. I don't think he lied to me. He said he'd planted me to keep an eye on Death."

Her hand flew to her mouth and she gasped. "Oh, Kip. I'm so sorry."

"Not nearly as sorry as I am. I betrayed the only family that ever fucking mattered. The ones who saw me—really saw me—and stayed anyway. I brought the Pied Piper into our lives ..." My words were heavy with guilt and grief.

"No. No, that's not true. He was with us all along. You said it yourself. Death will understand."

I barked out a laugh. "Not so sure about that. He'll probably beat my ass. He might not kill me, but I don't know."

"Don't say that, babe. You're brothers. I'm sure Ella and Dope can help manage the situation."

"I'll need to talk to them first and let them know. I'll need Dope to help me with my cross anyway. I asked the Pied Piper why he was telling me about how he used me and the crucifix, and he just said he didn't need me anymore at least not the way he used to. He also said it was time to come home and work for him, both Death and me. You too."

Her hands fisted and a flush crept up her neck. "Fuck him. Fuck him for all the pain he's caused. Fuck him for selling me and hurting you. It's a twisted game to him. If he breaks us down, he can rebuild us how he wants. It's Psych 101. He's a master manipulator, but I'm his daughter, and I will figure a way to bring him down."

I grabbed her face and kissed her, hard. "I love you, Holland. I love your mind. Your body. Your soul. He's right about one thing. We belong together."

She kissed me back, her lips warm and inviting against mine. "I love you too, baby. We will figure this out," she said against my mouth.

I released Holland and settled back against the couch, placing my palm on her thigh.

"What else did he say?" she asked.

"Just filled in the gaps of my blackouts. I was meeting him and telling him what Death was up to, reporting on him." A lead ball formed in my stomach, and I felt ill all over again.

"Jesus. I thought you were still being controlled. What about now? Did he say?"

A flicker of unease coiled in my chest. If the Pied Piper still had hooks in me ... what else had I done?

"No. I'm not sure how to break that connection, honestly. Do you?" Hope flickered to life in my chest. "Do you think I can break free from him, Holland?" I was so busy spinning out over betraying my friends, it hadn't occurred to me that he could still control me. The cross meant nothing if I was still under his power.

"I can help. I don't know if it will work, but I had a similar experience with a patient. He broke free. I trust you can too."

"Okay. What do I have to do?"

She took my hand in hers. "First, I wanted to tell you that I was with Ella and Dope at his house. We verified that the Pied Piper is my biological father. Well, as Dope said, it's not a DNA test, but he found old chat threads where the Pied Piper had claimed me as his ... then sold me." She closed her eyes, and I squeezed her hand, wishing I could erase all the pain. Holland looked at me. "So, there's that. But." Her voice trailed off. "Something else happened." Worry flickered through her expression. "There was an image of a boy, and he had a tattoo on his arm. A tattoo of a rabbit with its neck snapped."

I stared at her, hard. My thoughts whipped around inside my head. "I know that tattoo."

"I do too, now. Dope said he got the tattoo when he was drunk one night, but he didn't remember anything. It was somehow there the next day."

"Fuck." I jumped off the couch. "This was in the thread with the information about the Pied Piper?"

"Yeah."

"Fuck!" I grabbed the back of the couch, shaking with anger. "Dope is mixed up in all of this somehow?"

"That's my best guess. When Dope thought Ella and I weren't looking, he saved the file. He pretended it was no big deal, but something happened. That rabbit tied him to the Pied Piper. So even if you did spy on them for that motherfucker, Death and Dope were already connected, Kip."

I resisted the overwhelming urge to send my fist into the wall. Instead, I paced the living room with my arms glued to my sides so I wouldn't hit something.

"What time is it?" I asked, more to myself, as I looked at my watch. It was almost nine at night. Even though I was exhausted, I was too wired to sleep.

"I can't sit by while the Pied Piper is ruining everyone I care about. I need to talk to Dope and Death and face the consequences."

"I know that won't be easy, babe. What do you think about seeing if we can break the connection first and then you'll have something positive to bring to the table? The betrayal won't sting so bad that way."

"Is it wrong to say that your brain is as sexy as your body?"

Holland laughed. "I love that you said that. Thank you. And I promise after this is over..." She stood and walked over to me, slipping her arms around my waist. "That I'll reward you." Pushing up on her tiptoes, she kissed me. "I think nighttime will work best to see if we can break the hold over you. Basically, we have to take you back to the night it happened."

I gritted my teeth, all the years of thinking I'd killed Samantha, all the horrible things I'd done were about to end. A part of me knew the truth, and I hoped it was enough to set me free from the Pied Piper's control. There was only one way to find out.

"Do it," I said. "Let's rip the monster out by the root."

51

KIP

We stood in front of the door and stared at it like it was a mouth waiting to devour us.

Holland didn't say a word. She turned and looked at me. Her eyes shimmered, not from fear—but from the weight of knowing what we were about to walk into.

Mother's house hadn't been touched since her body had been removed. When we stepped inside, the stench of mildew and dust smothered us; it seemed the walls themselves had started to rot now that she was gone. The silence felt unnatural. As if the home knew it had been abandoned by its master and left to die too.

The basement door creaked louder than I remembered as Holland opened it. She flipped on the light switch at the top of the stairs. This would be the first time she saw where I was hidden like a shameful secret. Tortured.

"Are you ready?" Her voice was steady, confident.

I wish I felt the same. What if this didn't work? I hesitated while my fingers clenched the old wooden railing. The bulb at the top of the stairs flickered and buzzed like it knew my name. It did.

"She can't hurt you anymore," Holland said softly behind me.

I wished I believed her. The scars on my back burned with each step, the descent into hell gripping me by the throat and refusing to let go.

We reached the bottom, and my boots hit the concrete with dull thuds as I walked to the middle of the room. The air grew colder the deeper we went.

The light from above barely reached the bottom of the staircase. Just enough to show the old chains on the wall. The drain in the center of the floor. The shelf of rusted tools still lined up like trophies.

My mouth went dry.

I felt Holland behind me—her presence like a tether. But I couldn't move.

"You don't have to do this," she whispered.

"No. I do. He can't control me anymore. He can't use me to hurt the people I love. If we don't break the bond, I'll never be free. Neither will you."

My chest ached as my lungs forgot how to breathe.

It hit me all at once.

Flash.

Leather.

Flash.

Scripture.

Flash.

Mother—her words dripped with venom: "Repent, and the Lord shall forgive you."

My knees buckled. I collapsed hard on the concrete, pain shooting through my legs.

"Kip!" Holland's voice cut through, but I couldn't find her. I was falling deeper.

My skin crawled. My ears rang, and my fingers twitched as if I could find something to hold onto and stop my descent to hell.

I wasn't present. Not really.

"Hey." Her hands cupped my cheeks. Her touch was gentle, but her next words were firm and calculated.

"Look at me. Kip. I need you to listen. I need you to trust me."

My lips moved without sound.

"I'm going to hypnotize you and take you under. Exactly like I've done for patients before. You're safe with me. Do you understand?"

I nodded—barely.

"Okay," she said softly, brushing my hair off my forehead before she set her purse on the floor next to us. "Focus on the sound of me speaking to you. Nothing else matters. Not the cold. Not the chains. Not the pain. Just me."

Her words slipped under my skin like warmth. My heartbeat pounded against my ribs and my gaze lost focus.

"You're safe. You're safe. You're safe," she repeated, like a spell. "Now close your eyes."

Darkness met me like an old friend.

"Tell me where you are," she asked.

I was breathing shallowly. "Basement. Pipe on the wall. Cold. It's cold."

"What do you see?"

"Rusted tools. A worn Bible. Leather strap."

Her hands found mine, and I grabbed hers as if they were my only lifeline.

"Go deeper, Kip. What's the first thing you remember when they took her?"

The flood came before I could brace for it.

Flash.

Screams.

Flash.

A cage.

Flash.

Red hair. Blue eyes. A child.

Flash.

"You'll forget this, Kip. The Lord demands obedience."

I started shaking.

"I saw her," I choked out. "They tossed her in a cage like she was a rag doll. She was only a kid. Red hair. She screamed—and I—I tried—"

"You did," Holland said, trembling slightly. "You tried to save me."

"They dragged me away. Injected me, and said I killed her. They put her necklace in my pocket, told me it was my fault."

Tears escaped down my face.

"I believed them. I thought I was the monster. I never fought it because I thought I deserved it."

"You didn't," she whispered. "You were just a kid."

"They made me forget."

"But you remember now. You remember the truth."

My fingers dug into the floor. The air turned sharp in my lungs.

"They said God would never forgive me. That pain was proof of devotion. My mother—she carved the sins into my back. Told me if I bled enough, maybe I would be saved, but she didn't know what I'd become. A monster."

"You survived," Holland said, anchoring me with every word. "And now you're taking it back. It's okay to open your eyes."

Holland reached into her bag and pulled out something wrapped in cloth. She didn't say a word—just placed it in my hands.

A photo. Old, grainy, and torn at the edges.

A room. Gray concrete walls. A metal cage in the center. A figure in the background.

Her.

Me.

My breath left me in a single, violent shudder.

It was a still from a surveillance tape. Dated years ago.

The girl inside the cage was maybe thirteen. Red hair tangled around her face. Her lip was split. She clutched the bars.

And outside the cage, barely visible in the corner of the frame, standing by the door—

A boy.

Slumped. Drugged. Head down. Hands covered in blood.

Me.

My knees buckled.

"I—I was there," I whispered. "I didn't dream it."

"No," Holland said softly. "Your brain buried it. But your heart never let it go."

"I wasn't hurting her," I muttered, panicked. "I didn't—God, I didn't hurt you—"

"You didn't," she said. "You saw me. You came in. I remember now. You told them to stop."

I stared at the photo. My younger self looked lost, distant, barely conscious.

"They punished me after," I said. "Stripped me down. Injected me. Told me I killed you. Made me forget."

"But you didn't forget."

And I hadn't. That was the worst part. It had always been there. Locked behind chains. Drowned in heroin and scripture. But now—

Now the lock had rusted through.

I dropped the photo and let it fall.

The scream ripped from my throat—raw, guttural. Years of silence, agony, and rot clawing their way free. I curled into myself, rocking and trembling. Holland's arms wrapped around me as I fell apart.

"I was never the monster," I whispered.

"No," Holland said, wrapping her arms around me. "You were the boy they broke."

But there was more. God, there was always more.

My voice came out wrecked. "There's something I never told anyone. Not Death. Not Dope. Not even myself."

She didn't speak. Just held me. Let me unravel.

"They used to leave me down here," I said. "Days at a time. No food. No light. Locked in the chains."

She was silent. Still. Letting the weight of it fall.

"I was fourteen. It was winter. The pipes froze, and the cold started getting in my bones. I thought I was going to die. I wanted to die. But then I heard something. Singing."

Her forehead pinched. "What song?"

My throat clenched. "Come, little children, I'll take thee away ..."

A shiver racked through her.

"I thought I imagined it," I said. "But it wasn't in my head. It was him. The Pied Piper. Upstairs. Singing like it was a lullaby. My mother ... she was humming along."

I swallowed hard, hands clenched.

"And then she came down and—" I stopped. My jaw locked.

"Kip."

"She kissed me on the forehead," I said. "Told me God had chosen me. That pain was how I'd prove I was His favorite. Then she made me kneel on rice until my knees bled. She stood there, humming hymns, saying every drop of blood was proof He loved me."

I couldn't meet Holland's gaze.

"I did it," I whispered. "I bled for a God I didn't believe in. Because I thought maybe ... if I did it right ... I could be clean again."

I waited for her to recoil. To pull away. To break. But her grip tightened.

"That wasn't faith. That was abuse wrapped in holy lies. You weren't worshipping. You were surviving."

Her words cracked the last shard in me. Tears blurred everything, and I shut my eyes again.

"I'm not clean, Holland."

"You're not supposed to be," she whispered. "You're real. That's why I love you. Here and now you're free. Lily is dead. The Pied Piper is losing his control."

"I didn't hurt you. I didn't hurt you," I chanted, still living in the flashback. Blood on my hands, high, and curled up in the corner half naked.

"I'm right here, baby. Do you see us in this room together now? Can you see us?"

"No. But I hear you as if you're somewhere in the distance. I want to find you."

"Good. Listen to my voice. Do you still see me when we were younger? In the cage?"

"Yeah."

"What do you want to do?"

Flash.

I stood and crawled to the girl in the cage. Shaking, weak, and so high I struggled to see, I pulled myself up. "It's okay. Don't be afraid."

The corner of her mouth twitched, and she nodded as I searched around on the floor for a tool. Anything to pick the lock. Mother had no idea I'd practiced, swearing that one day I would break free and fucking kill her.

"There." I squinted at the small hairpin with a butterfly on it.

"That's mine," she whispered. "My father gave it to me for my birthday." She wrapped her small hands around the cage bars and watched, hopeful.

I knelt, picked up the hairpin, and busied myself with picking the lock. It popped open with a small click.

"Got it." I removed the lock and swung the door open. "You don't have much time, so listen carefully. There's a tunnel that will take you under the house and outside. Wait until it's dark to run."

She stepped out of the cage and threw her arms around me. "We will make it out of here, right?"

I patted her back, my vision blurry from the drugs. "You go. You can't get lost but stay to the right. You'll see the grate. Wait until it's dark, then kick it open and run for your fucking life."

"Come with me. You can't stay here. They'll kill you for helping me."

I grabbed the cage bar behind me, steadying myself as she let me go.

"I'm already dead."

Tears blurred her eyes.

"But give me one thing to hold onto."

"Anything," she whispered.

"What's your name?"

A sweet smile slipped into place. "Samantha. My name is Samantha." She kissed my cheek, then disappeared into the darkness.

I blinked, the room fading in and out as the shadows started to slowly peel away as I came out of the hypnosis. I saw her again—clearly. Holland. Her red hair. Her loving gaze. Her hand on my heart.

"You're not my sin," I said. "You're my proof."

She leaned forward and kissed my forehead.

And I shattered.

"I wore the cross," I said, reaching for it but found nothing. "I thought it protected me. It was Mother's. It was fucking hers. I need to destroy it."

Holland nodded, tears still falling. She wrapped her arms around me, held me while I crumbled.

"I love you," she said. "Even in the dark. Especially in the dark."

I buried my face in her shoulder.

"There's something else I've never told anyone before but lived with it for years." I squeezed my eyes closed against the memories. These, I knew, were facts and not fiction built on lies. I wasn't high those times. I was aware of every word I said, every smile I gave, and every hand I held. A weight of a thousand bricks crushed my chest as I spoke.

"They made me into a weapon. Used me to hurt people. I don't even know how many times they had me make friends with the girls my age and a little older. Mother said I was good looking, and all the girls would fall for me ... little did they know I was leading them into captivity to be raped and tortured."

"We'll make it right," she whispered. "Together."

She helped me to my feet.

"How will we know if it worked—the hypnosis and the connection with the Pied Piper."

"I think it did. Kip, you were never theirs. A part of you always knew what they did to you. But only time will tell. If it didn't work, then I'm with you, so I won't let you go see the Pied Piper. I'll take you under again and we'll repeat the process until you're okay."

I turned back to her.

"I need to tell Dope and Death everything. Help take the whole thing down. No more hiding. No more fucking silence."

Holland smiled through her tears.

"It will take time to make sure you're free," she whispered, brushing a tear from my cheek. "But you're not in that cage anymore either."

I stared at her. At the girl I once tried to save, and the woman who'd just saved me back.

"That's enough," I said. "For now." But deep down, I knew—we were only beginning.

52

KIP

I couldn't recall the last time my palms were drenched in sweat, not even during the most intense hunts alongside Death. In those moments, adrenaline surged through my veins, eliminating any trace of fear or hesitation. But this was entirely different. This was a gut-twisting dread as I prepared to confess to my family the unforgivable reality. I had betrayed them.

I reached Dope's uncle's cabin, and the smell of the light rain still lingered on the tree leaves. I took a deep breath, trying to calm my pounding heart, but there was only one thing for me to do: walk into the living room and tell my friends what I'd done. How it played out was what I was afraid of. What would I do without the only people in my life who had supported me for years? They had never questioned my sanity or my loyalty. That was all about to change.

As much as I wanted Holland with me for support, it wasn't her battle to fight. I had to take responsibility for what I'd done on my own. Not only that, but I was also concerned my friends would think I'd brought her along to take my side and defend me against them. That wasn't the case at all. This was mine to face—my sins, my burden.

I knocked on the door and pushed it open, the hinges squeaking and announcing my arrival.

Dope, Death, and Ella all looked in my direction.

"Hey," I said, closing the door behind me, the loud click echoing finality. "Thanks for meeting me."

If they'd been playing cards or telling jokes, it all stopped. Every eye landed on me, and to my surprise, I didn't flinch. I never called a meeting, so the moment I fired off the group text they knew some serious shit was going down. They were right.

"You're late," Death said, like it was a crime as big as murder. He spoke with a casual indifference that made people forget he meant every word literally.

Dope appeared exhausted as he clenched a can of off-brand energy drink. Ella watched me like a hawk, a half-chewed pen cap dangling from her mouth.

No one moved. Four heartbeats in a vacuum. I studied the grain of the wood floor, counting cracks where stories might live, then looked up at them.

I wiped my palms on my jeans, felt the sweat clinging like guilt. Then I said it.

"I fucked up."

Maybe if I'd shouted it, it would have sounded more heroic. Instead, I felt the walls compressing in.

Death pinned me with a deadly stare.

"Fucked up how?" Ella asked, her question was soft but guarded.

I dragged my hand through my hair and tried to name the feeling twisting my insides. Guilt, plus another thing—horror, maybe, or inevitability.

I stood in front of the empty fireplace, my fists clenched at my sides, and for a second, I didn't know how to start. How could I admit I'd been the weapon all along?

"It was the cross," I said, voice low.

Dope blinked. "What was?"

I looked at my shoes, stalling. There was no other way to do this than blurt it out. "The one I wore every fucking day. I thought it was hers, and I wore it as a reminder—a scar." My throat tightened. "Turns out it was ... the Pied Piper's."

Ella sat up straighter. "What are you talking about?"

I turned to look at them. My family. The only people I had left.

"I was his camera." The words cut like glass.

Dope's hand froze halfway to his mouth. Ella's mouth parted. Even Death blinked. That's when it landed: what I'd said.

"Everywhere I went, every kill I helped with, every time I walked into a room—he saw it. Heard it. Through me. Through the goddamn cross."

Death's chair scraped across the hardwood floor as he stood. "You're fucking joking."

I met his glare. "You think I would make this shit up?"

"You let him spy on us," he growled.

"I didn't let anything happen," I snapped. "I didn't know. He had that tech on me before I even knew what the hell I was."

Dope leaned forward slowly, his expression turning grave. "The tech's real. My guess is that he used audio nodes, micro transmitters, signal-activated triggers. Most of it is undetectable unless you break it apart. Honestly, I wouldn't know for sure until I saw it. But it's possible. More than possible."

He looked at me, eyes sharper than I'd ever seen them. "He embedded you."

"Guess I was born prepped to bleed," I muttered.

Death stepped toward me, rage rolling off him in waves. "You could've told us sooner."

"I didn't know sooner."

He scoffed. "You expect me to believe that? That for years—"

"Death," Ella said, quiet but firm.

He didn't look at her. His attention was locked on me like I was the kill he couldn't end fast enough.

"He's not the enemy," she added.

"He handed us to the enemy," Death snapped.

"I was a kid," I said. My voice wobbled, but I didn't care. "A teenager when they started drugging me, chaining me in the basement, and carving shit into my back. You think I chose this?"

The silence hit like a punch. Even the walls seemed to hold their breath.

Dope swore. "Jesus Christ ..."

I laughed, the sound bitter and humorless. "Yeah. That's who they prayed to while they destroyed me."

Ella stood, slow and measured. "You were a weapon, Kip. A pawn."

"Not anymore."

Death crossed his arms. "So what now? You just walk back in and say sorry? Sorry I fed your whole goddamn life to a psychopath?"

My jaw locked. "I didn't know. I don't know how to make this shit right. You have no idea how fucking twisted up I am about this. I'm sorry. I'm so fucking sorry."

I turned toward Ella, and something in her expression reminded me of the night the Pied Piper had a discussion with her. She'd never told us what he'd said. I suspected she couldn't. That he was holding something big over her head.

Before the words even fully left my mouth, Death moved.

One second, he was across the room. The next—his hand was at my collarbone, shoving me hard against the stone wall behind me. My shoulder cracked into it with a thud that echoed through the cabin.

"You don't get to be sorry," he growled. "You don't get to come back from this."

His breath was hot against my face, full of rage, betrayal, grief. The kind of fury that came from someone who'd buried too many people and wasn't willing to lose one more.

I didn't fight him. I deserved it.

"I didn't know," I said again, quieter this time. "I swear to god, I didn't know."

"You were in our house." His voice broke, as if it physically hurt to say the words. "Around Ella. The kids. You were wired, Kip. Wired."

"I didn't fucking know!" My words sounded raw, hollow. "I would've ripped it off the second I—"

"Enough!" Ella stepped between us, one palm on my chest, the other flat against Death's. Her presence sliced through the tension like a blade.

Her forehead creased. "Death, stop. We're all a pawn in the Pied Piper's chess game. Each one of us is being used whether we're aware of it or not."

He didn't move. His jaw was clenched so tight I thought his teeth might shatter. His eyes never left mine. "I trusted you," he said. "You were supposed to protect us."

The words hit hard.

Ella pushed against him gently. "He still is."

Death stared at me for a beat longer. He took a step back. Two.

Without another word, he turned and walked out the front door, slamming it behind him so hard the walls rattled.

The silence that followed was suffocating. I inhaled deeply, trying to steady my overactive nerves.

Ella's palm was still on my chest. She didn't move it. "Give him time," she said softly. "He's not angry because he hates you. He's angry because you matter."

I didn't answer. Couldn't. Because her words gutted me more than Death's hands ever could.

Her words made sense. "Ella?" I swallowed over the lump in my throat. "What you said, I don't think Death caught it. He's using you too. That night he talked to you privately. The Pied Piper is using you, isn't he?"

Her mouth clamped so hard her teeth clacked. She folded her arms across her chest. "That's not what I meant. All I'm saying is that the more we learn, the more secrets come to light."

"Not in a good way," Dope muttered behind us.

"I need to go after Death. I'll work on him, Kip. This isn't goodbye." Sadness twisted her expression and then she threw her arms around me and hugged me tightly. "Holland is lucky to have you." She released me. "And so are we. We'll figure all this shit out." She gave me a wistful smile before she hurried out the door and after Death.

I slumped against the wall, exhausted and gutted.

"When you texted us, that's not what I was expecting, man. Not at all."

"Sorry to disappoint you."

"Kip, man, you've been through fucking hell and back. The idea that the Pied Piper used your cross, it's not on you if you ask me. But no one did, so." Dope tapped his fingers against the can. "It's fucking genius." He rubbed his jaw, appearing deep in thought.

"Lucky us. I mean, some killers are dangerous because they don't have a conscience. This motherfucker is even more deadly because he's a goddamn genius. He's next level."

"I'm not sure I can keep up with him, but I'll try. We have to figure out how to bring him down."

The room filled with silence before Dope said, "You're not wearing the cross. Where is it? I need to disable every tracking and recording device."

"I buried it about an hour from here. It's on the side of the road. I couldn't wear it as long as I knew he was watching. Shit, I can't wear it again anyway."

Dope stood. "Let's go get it. He already knows where I live, so let's go back to my place."

"Are you sure?"

"Hell yeah. You're driving though, I need a joint. This shit's been heavy."

I couldn't disagree with him on that. Regret and grief punched me in the gut as I looked around the cabin before we left, realizing I'd walked into the place with three of my best friends and was only leaving with one.

A FEW HOURS LATER, Dope and I arrived at his place and headed downstairs to his dungeon. He immediately started studying the cross, pulling it apart and identifying the cameras and recording devices.

I sat on the couch, my fingers steepled as I watched him. Neither of us spoke until we knew it was safe. Granted, the Pied Piper knew what we were up to, but that was okay. We were taking a stand. Not that he didn't expect us to dismantle the crucifix, but it was the one thing I had control over.

Dope grabbed a hammer from his desk, and with a few swings, he busted the recording devices, sending bits of metal and glass flying in every direction. He leaned back in his chair, finally looking at me. "What do you want to do with the cross?"

"I don't want it. Do what you like with it."

"You sure?"

"Yeah. All it's done is damage. I don't want the reminder anymore."

Dope swiveled in his chair and propped an ankle across the opposite knee. "He'll come around, man. Death has a temper, but we're also the soft spot he has. Ella and us, we're family. Give him some time." Dope snickered. "When he calls you with a body to clean up, you'll know he's forgiven you."

"And you? Ella? Can you guys move past this?"

Dope looked at me like I was speaking a different language. "Dude, you're fucking here with me. I took care of the cross for you. In my opinion, there's nothing to forgive. I'd rather spend my energy on taking the motherfucker down. Him and his organization have done enough damage. Shit, I would siphon all his funds for the Horizon Society. Use his empire to rebuild what he destroyed," Dope added. "That's how we fuck him back. At least the money would go to a good cause helping women and children start over on the bastard's dime." He rubbed his hands together, giddy with the idea. "I like it. I'm going to talk to Death about it."

"Keep me posted, man. On how he's doing. Ella, too, if she can't reach out."

"That's funny. Ella does what the hell she wants to. She stayed behind and hugged you. She's cool. Don't sweat it."

"I just hope it stays that way."

"You'll see. Give him some space. It'll all shake out. In the meantime, go home to Holland and relax. I'll be working to see what else I can find in the meantime."

I stood. "Thanks, Dope. For everything." I approached him and grabbed his shoulder. "Text me if anything comes up."

"Always."

With each step up the stairs, my chest squeezed at the thought of my family falling apart. For tonight, there was nothing else I could do except go see the woman who held my heart in her hands and start our lives together.

53

———

HOLLAND

For the twentieth time, I cleaned my house, waiting to hear from Kip about how the meeting went. I knew him well enough to know he needed a little extra time to process whatever went down, but my nerves were shot. If it weren't for Dog trailing me everywhere, his tail thumping against my leg as he waited for pets, I'm not sure I could have managed the anxiety.

My cell vibrated against the granite countertop, and I nearly jumped over and cleared the island in an attempt to grab it. I groaned as I saw the call wasn't from Kip. I picked it up and answered the FaceTime.

"Hey, Mom and Dad. How's your trip?" I grinned at them as they came into view, the view of two large swimming pools behind them. I tried to sound perky and act as if my world hadn't imploded in the two weeks they'd been gone. My smile was real for them, but just below the surface, I was splintering, waiting for Kip.

"We're driving home tomorrow, honey. It's been wonderful." Mom adjusted her sun hat as she gave Dad a kiss on the cheek. "It's exactly what we needed."

"I'm so happy to hear that."

Mom seemed more relaxed than I'd seen her in years, so something must have gone right. I didn't miss the look in Dad's eyes though as I realized he wanted an update.

"How are you?" he asked, his bushy gray brow arching slightly.

"I'm good. Life seems to be settling in nicely. Work is going well and—" My words cut off as Dog bounded onto the couch, smothering my face with wet kisses. Laughing, I wiped the drool from my cheek.

"Whose dog is that?" Mom asked.

I bit my lower lip. "I met someone. It's his dog. Well, ours."

Mom's mouth dropped open, and she nudged Dad. "Did you hear that? She's met someone!" She turned back to me. "Tell us everything. What's his name? Where did you meet? What's he do?"

Mom's barrage of questions had me giggling. "His name is Kip. We met at Velvet Vortex." There was no way I could tell Mom where we'd really met, but I could give Dad the full story when I had time. He'd be relieved to know that Kip had helped handle Cooper too. As far as the Pied Piper, I wanted to keep my real parents out of it and as safe as possible. Just because I shared blood with a maniac didn't mean he was a parent. Far from it.

"Isn't that the ritzy restaurant and club located downtown?" Dad asked.

"It is. He's part owner."

"How old is he?" both asked in unison.

"We're the same age." I made a mental note to ask Kip when his birthday was.

Our conversation continued as we made plans to all have dinner together. I hadn't asked Kip how he felt about meeting my parents, but I could push out the meeting if I needed to.

Once we said our goodbyes and disconnected the call, I blew out a sigh, my mind returning to Kip again. Seconds later, my doorbell rang, and my heart launched into my throat. For a single awful second, I thought it might be someone else, but then I saw him.

I flipped the bolt and my eyes landed on him. Before he could say a word, I grabbed Kip's wrist and pulled him inside, closing the door behind him. I threw my arms around him, and he wrapped his around my waist, pulling me against him.

"Are you all right?" I asked, my question muffled against his neck. "I've been so worried."

"It's a mixed bag, babe. Death stormed off, but Dope and Ella understood."

I released him, my palms dragging down his muscular chest. "I'm sorry. I think he'll come around though. I mean, you guys have all been so close for so long."

Fear and sadness flashed across Kip's face. "I'll do everything I can to help heal that friendship, but I also need to look ahead ... with you. You're my main focus for the rest of tonight."

"I'll take it." I tilted my head and kissed him softly, his touch sending shivers through me. "Are you hungry?"

"Not for food," he growled against my mouth. "But I could use a break from everything." He nudged my ear with the tip of his nose.

A loud bark shot me out of my skin, and Kip chuckled.

"Hey, Dog." He turned and knelt, giving Dog a dose of love.

"He's missed you." I smiled as Dog's tail wagged, his back feet skipping across the floor. "I need to check his food and water while you two hang out." I squeezed Kip's shoulder as I walked past him and into the kitchen. Apparently, I'd been so distracted while cleaning that I hadn't even checked on Dog's kibbles.

Kip continued to talk to his pet until Dog heard the kibbles hit the bowl, then he practically knocked his owner on the floor to get to his dinner.

"Are you starving my dog, Holland?" A lazy grin slipped into place as Kip took the bag of food and put it in the cabinet, safe from Dog breaking into it later when we weren't looking.

He placed his hands on my waist and walked me backward until my back hit the refrigerator. "I need to touch you and know what we have is real."

Kip's mouth crashed onto mine, his hunger raw and insatiable, as if he'd been wandering in a desert and I was the first drop of rain. He gripped my shoulders, pushing me back against the refrigerator. The cold metal hummed against my shoulder blades, seeping through the thin fabric of my T-shirt.

His calloused palm pressed against the hollow of my throat as his tongue explored my mouth. I could feel his pulse, his urgency, like an electric current surging through my body, so intense it could have lit up the room.

His hand, rough and eager, slid under my shirt, tracing the sensitive skin along my hip, my waist, the curve where my ribs swept down. My head fell back as I let him explore every inch of me, his touch sending waves of heat through me.

I clung to his shirtsleeves, fingers digging into the fabric like I was holding on for dear life.

"You're so beautiful," he whispered. "God, Holland, you have no idea what you do to me."

I kissed him back, tugging at his hair, tracing his jaw, gripping his collar. We had spent the day stressed and worried, and now we were unraveling, our bodies pressing together with an almost violent intensity.

His fingers grazed my stomach as he found the hem of my shirt and pulled it over my head and down my arms. He roamed my body, the cool air from the fridge making my nipples harden beneath my bra. He groaned, his mouth finding the valley between my breasts, teeth grazing the scratchy fabric.

"Bedroom," I managed to gasp. "Come with me—"

He lifted me off the floor with a grunt, his fingers digging into my thighs.

I wrapped my legs around his waist, feeling every step he took vibrate through me. I could feel his heart pounding, his lips hot on my neck, and his hard cock through his jeans.

The bedroom door slammed open, then shut behind us. He fell onto the bed, pinning me to the mattress with his weight. The ceiling fan whirred above us, stirring the warm, still air. My hands traveled over his biceps, his back, pulling at his shirt. I needed to feel his skin, to feel him.

"You drive me crazy, Holland," he said, his voice breaking. "I—fuck, I love you. I love you so much it's killing me."

I tugged his tee over his head, revealing his heaving chest, freckles scattered across his shoulders, muscles taut. His hair was tousled, wild, and his eyes were dark with desire.

He knelt above me, his gaze tracing over every inch. Then he was on me again, his hands and mouth exploring, worshipping.

My bra snapped open, the straps sliding down my shoulders, exposing me to the air. He looked at my breasts like they were a revelation, his mouth finding one nipple, sucking gently, then harder, drawing a gasp from deep within me.

My thighs clenched, and my pussy responded to his touch.

Kip licked and sucked each breast, my back arching off the bed as I threaded my fingers through his hair. I fumbled with the button and his zipper, freeing his thick, hard cock.

I needed him inside me, claiming me, and fucking me until the rest of the world no longer mattered. Nothing else mattered except the two of us.

Kip moved with purpose, kicking free of his jeans, his boxers, his socks. He was all lean, hard muscle, his body a road map of scars and old wounds, every single one a testament to his stubbornness, his refusal to give up.

He loomed over me, his gaze dark with hunger, lips wet and parted. His attention slowly traveled over me, taking in every inch of exposed skin, every shiver and twitch. He bit his lower lip, like he was trying to contain everything he felt, but I could see the need in his expression, in the white-knuckle clench of his fists.

I reached for him, pulled him down, felt the press of his cock hot and heavy against my thigh. He groaned into my mouth, hands cradling my face as if he was afraid that I would disappear.

"I want you so bad it hurts," he said, the words muffled by my lips. "I think about you all the goddamn time."

"Show me," I whispered.

He slid down my body, pushing my panties aside with a single, reverent sweep of his fingers. He spread me with his thumbs, staring at my pussy like it was some sacred text he'd only learned to read. Then he ducked his head and licked a slow, deliberate stripe up my slit.

I gasped, the sensation sharp and electric. He circled my clit with the tip of his tongue, then sucked it into his mouth, rolling it between his lips. I writhed beneath him, thighs shaking, grasping the sheets. Every nerve inside me was a live wire.

He licked me until I was panting his name, until my hips bucked up off the mattress and I begged him for more. He slid two fingers inside me, curling them just right, hitting the spot that sent stars exploding across my vision.

Kip was relentless, his mouth and hands working in perfect tandem, coaxing me toward the brink. I came hard, my body shaking with the force of it.

He didn't stop. He licked me through it, until I was limp and weak, sweat breaking out across my forehead. He crawled up the bed, his chin slick with my orgasm, and kissed me deep. I tasted myself on his tongue and moaned.

"God, Holland," he said, pulling back to look at me. "You're fucking incredible."

I wanted him inside me, needed it so much it almost hurt. I grabbed his cock, guiding him to my entrance. He hesitated, just for a second, like he wanted to memorize how I looked in that moment.

"Are you sure?" he asked, gently.

"I've never been more sure of anything in my life."

He pushed in, slow and steady, filling me inch by perfect inch. The stretch was exquisite, a burn that bordered on pain before melting into pleasure. He braced himself on his forearms, forehead pressed to mine, his breath mingling with mine as he bottomed out. We stayed like that for a moment, locked together, hearts pounding in sync.

My back arched off the mattress as he slid in slow and steady, his cock stretching me wide, each stroke drawing a hot ribbon of fire through my core. My muscles clenched around him, hungry for every inch, every slick thrust that slammed me open.

His eyes locked on mine—intense, determined, like he was sculpting something out of flesh and heat.

He sank so deep I could feel the tip of him pressing against the soft spot I'd never known existed, and a moan slipped out of me. I wrapped my legs around his waist, digging my heels into the curve of his hips to pull him closer. He groaned, jaw tight, the tremor in his voice betraying the effort he made not to come too fast.

"Jesus Christ, Holland," he panted against my collarbone. "You're so—so fucking perfect." He bit down on my pulse point, marking me with his teeth before burying his face in the nape of my neck.

One arm braced him on the edge of the bed, knuckles white against the headboard, while the other moved over my ribs, kneading upward until his fingers found my breast. His thumb curved onto my nipple and rolled it between skin and sweat in time with his thrusts.

My fingernails scored tiny red arcs along his spine, hunting for purchase as wave after wave of pleasure battered me. I felt the damp warmth of our bodies together, the slickness making every angle and movement more acute, more electric.

He shifted his hand lower, brushing my inner thigh before slipping between my folds to seek my clit. When he landed on it, he circled with firm, unrelenting strokes.

My vision blurred and my moans turned into cries. He pulled back just enough to watch me, then slammed back in, hard and fast, as if determined to destroy the world around us with this one collision of flesh.

I came apart around him—fast and loud—my muscles seizing, heat crashing through me like molten metal. My tears streamed down my face, and I tasted the salt of them when he kissed me, his tongue sweeping mine, mirroring the rhythm of his cock. My body shook so violently it rattled the rails, and I felt him shudder as I milked him through my orgasm.

He stilled inside me, his release flooding me until I tasted him warm and heady. He collapsed beside me, arm thrown over my waist, pulling me flush against him. His palm trailed across my hipbone in a slow, gentle caress as he tried to calm the racing of his heart.

Above us, the ceiling fan whirred, its lazy sweep barely stirring the humidity in the air. He pressed a series of soft kisses across my temple and cheek, his lips landing on my jaw as if memorizing every curve.

"I love you," he whispered so quietly I almost missed it, the words fragile, like they needed my promise to believe them.

I curled into him, breathing in the faint scent of sweat and clove from his shampoo. "I love you too," I said, my words muffled but steady.

He laughed—warm, relieved—and tightened his grip. We lay tangled around each other, the aftermath of our bodies slowing down as the fan overhead cast spinning shadows on the walls. After a while, I drifted off to sleep.

When I woke, gold light slanted across the bed, turning every particle of dust into a drifting constellation. Kip propped himself on one elbow, his hair messy, eyes soft with awe. He reached out to brush a strand of hair from my forehead.

"You're even more beautiful than the first time I saw you," he murmured, voice thick with something like wonder.

I smiled, reaching up to touch his jaw. "But now I'm all yours. You own my heart, Kip." I nipped at his lower lip, my chest threatening to burst just from looking at him. If anyone had asked me a year ago what I thought my life would look like, I never would have guessed that the boy who'd saved me would finally come home ... to me.

54

KIP

Three months had passed, and the rainy season had started in the Pacific Northwest. Holland and I had settled into our relationship, and Dope and Ella had welcomed her into the group. As far as Death, I hadn't heard shit from him since the day I'd told him about how the Pied Piper had planted me in his life. I only hoped he wasn't out killing without anyone cleaning up after him, though. Not a day passed that I didn't grieve that friendship.

Thank God I had the woman I loved and the Horizon Society. When Death wasn't around to clean up the sons of bitches who needed to be ended for the abuse and horrible acts they committed, I stepped in. Dope had even joined me a few times to kill. I suspected it gave him a safe place to get rid of his pent-up anger and raw emotion he didn't know how to handle. He'd even slowed down on the weed. Every one of us was worried that our found family might never be the same again. No matter what anyone said, I carried the guilt on my shoulders. It was my fault that we had fallen apart.

Holland was gone for the day, attending a conference with a speaker she was excited about. We spent all our free time together, and I played with the idea of asking her to move in with me. But I wasn't sure it was right yet. Not that we didn't share our places with each other already, but I wanted something new. Ours. A new beginning where neither of our scars and trauma clouded the view.

I pulled up to the house with the for-sale sign on it and killed the engine, letting the quiet settle. Tall pines stood like sentinels around the two-story gray home with black trim and a gravel drive tucked off a sleepy road in the Portland hills. The rain had stopped long enough for the sun to cut through the clouds and bounce off the windows. It wasn't flashy. Wasn't polished. But it was private. Secluded. Safe.

The place looked like it had been waiting for something—or maybe someone—to give it purpose again.

I stepped out and ran my fingers along the hood of my Mustang. My boots crunched the gravel, the air thick with cedar and wet earth. It smelled clean. Like a place that didn't expect blood in the floorboards or secrets in the crawlspace. A place where I didn't have to be the monster anymore.

The Realtor was already waiting by the front door, smiling like she already knew she'd nailed it. And maybe she had.

I stared up at the house again, imagining Holland standing at the top window. Barefoot, with her coffee in hand and her beautiful red hair a mess after I made love to her first thing in the morning. The thought caught me in the chest—too tender, too real—but I didn't shake it off. I let it sit. Because maybe this was what starting over really looked like.

The home had dark lines and quiet bones. It offered enough space to live without hiding.

From the pictures online, there was a room for her to work in. An office with good light and shelves she could fill with the books she never let anyone borrow. There was even a sunroom off the kitchen she could turn into her greenhouse. She would want something green. Something alive. Something that didn't remind her of everything she'd lost.

I didn't know what normal was, but I wanted to build whatever version of it we could find together. Even if it came cracked and crooked, like both of us.

"Ready to see it?" the Realtor asked.

I nodded. "Yeah," I said. "Let's see what home looks like."

The front door opened, and I stepped inside, instinctively scanning the space. Old habits, but there was nothing to fear here.

The entryway was wide and open, leading into a living room with tall windows that pulled in the light. A stone fireplace dominated the far wall, big enough to warm the whole place in winter. It wasn't fancy—nothing polished or overpriced. Just a solid structure and good air.

I could already see Holland curled up on the couch under one of those oversized blankets she pretended not to love. Reading something too dark for her own good with her feet tucked beneath her. Safe. Warm. Mine.

"This way," the Realtor said, gesturing toward the kitchen.

The room had dark oak cabinets with matte-black fixtures. The kind of counters you didn't mind getting scratched. If she didn't like them, I would gut the kitchen and build her anything she wanted, but I had a feeling she would love it the way it was. Holland would have a gas stove, a deep farmhouse sink, and enough room for her to dance barefoot when she thought no one was watching. I ran my hand over the edge of the counter and felt the thought bloom. We could build something here. Not just survive—but live.

The Realtor and I moved toward the back, where a set of French doors opened out to a covered porch that looked out over the trees. A lake shimmered in the distance. Quiet. Unbothered. Like it didn't know anything about blood or trauma or brokenness.

Upstairs, the primary bedroom had tall ceilings and a window seat overlooking the woods. I didn't care much about bedrooms, but this one? I stood there for a long moment, staring at that bench. It was the kind of place she'd stare out at the world from. Think. Heal. Remember who the hell she was.

The hallway led to a second room, smaller but filled with light.

"What do you think of this for an office?" the Realtor asked.

I stepped inside.

Soft cream walls with built-in shelves. A small alcove by the window could easily fit a desk and a lamp, and there was also enough room for Dog to curl up and nap while she worked. It wasn't much. But it could be hers. I pictured her here—hair pulled up in a messy bun, surrounded by stacks of notes and files she'd swear she was going to organize but never would. It felt right.

"She works with people," I said quietly. "Psych trauma. This ... she'd like this."

The Realtor smiled. "Then I think you've found your place."

I walked past her without answering, heading toward the end of the hall where another door stood half open. This one hadn't been in the listing.

It led to a small room—glass ceiling, exposed beams, and warm wood everywhere. Greenhouse, maybe. Or a sunroom waiting to be loved again.

Something in my chest twisted.

This was it.

This was the room I would make hers. Plants. Herbs. A place to breathe without looking over her shoulder. A place she could make beautiful, even if we were both still learning how.

"I'd like to bring her to see it. When can that happen?"

The Realtor tapped her phone screen. "How about tomorrow afternoon?"

"Sounds good. Text me the time, and I'll confirm once I talk to her this evening."

We heard the front door open, followed by footsteps. The Realtor frowned. "Are you expecting anyone?"

"No." Every cell in my body stood on edge, ready for anything.

Black boots appeared around the corner, and my gaze landed on a pair of gray eyes.

"Nice place," Death muttered, eyeing the realtor. "Can you give us a minute?"

She didn't argue but scurried around him and down the stairs. He had that effect on people.

For a second, I thought this was the end. The final judgment. But Death didn't reach for a blade. He reached for me, slapping me on the shoulder.

"I wasn't expecting to see you. How have you been?" I shoved my hands in my pockets, unsure of what to expect with him showing up out of nowhere.

He leaned against the hallway wall. "Bored. It's not the same without you around."

Progress? "You mean Dope isn't a good cleaner?"

The corner of Death's mouth twitched slightly, indicating he was stifling his smile. "Dope is a lot of things, but he's not a cleaner."

Silence filled the space between us. "I'm sor—"

Death held up his hand, silencing me. "I know. It wasn't your fault. It was just too much to process all at once. The fact that the motherfucker has infiltrated us, planned our steps, orchestrated our futures. What the hell do we do with that?"

"I'm still trying to figure that out. Holland and I are taking one step at a time."

"Ella told me the Pied Piper is Holland's bio father."

Shit. Here came the other damn shoe.

"Yeah. No DNA test, but he admitted she's his."

Death rubbed his chin. "Maybe she thinks like him. Maybe she'll be who we need to take the son of a bitch down once and for all." He looked me dead in the eyes. "Together." He extended his hand, and I reached out to shake it. "Up for some hunting?"

"Hell yeah. I just need to let Holland know I'll be home late."

"Take care of her and see the house tomorrow. I'll let you know where to meet me in a few days."

I grinned, relief flooding my system. "Sounds good."

"Oh, one more thing." Death reached into the inside of his jacket and removed something shiny. "Thought you would need a new one."

I froze. For a second, I thought this was it—the final judgment, wrapped in silver. Maybe he'd brought the old one back to remind me who I used to be. My fingers twitched toward the knife I didn't carry anymore. But then. He held it out. A cross. New, shiny, unused. I took it, feeling the weight of it in my palm.

Unlike the other crucifix, it wasn't heavy on one end, but delicately balanced. That's when I saw the sleek, nearly unnoticeable design. I pulled on the edge and popped the blade out, then flipped it over and popped the other out.

"I made sure it had two for you."

"You bought this for me?"

Death cleared his throat. "No, man. I had it handcrafted. I had to make sure no one fucking put a camera in this one."

I chuckled. "Fair." I grinned at him. "Thanks. I can't wait to put it to good use."

"This weekend. Be ready." He paused at the top of the stairs, glancing back once. "You were always one of us, Kip. That never changed." Then he vanished.

I used to think judgment would come with sirens or a noose. But it came wrapped in silence and in my palm. A new cross, forged not from guilt or surveillance, but from choice. This time, no one was watching me. No one was pulling my strings. I didn't wear it to repent. I wore it to remember who I really was—who I chose to be. And that? That was my final judgment.

I turned the cross over several times, noting each curve, each detail, and the intricate design embedded on the crucifix. Death had put thought into every inch of this—each notch, each edge, a message I was finally ready to carry. I closed my eyes briefly, elated that our friendship was still intact. We were good. It was time to celebrate while I could. Before the tides turned once again, and all hell broke loose. But today. Today was good, and that's all that I had.

I closed the blades and held the cross in one hand while I fumbled in my back pocket for my phone. Checking the time, I realized that Holland's conference should be over. I tapped the screen, called her, and then held the phone to my ear.

"There's my favorite person." I could hear the smile in her voice. "Are you home? I'm ready to take your clothes off and worship my monster."

I groaned; images of her with my new cross inside her cunt had my cock throbbing instantly. "No. But I hope it will be soon."

Silence.

"Kip? Are you saying what I think you're saying?" I didn't miss the thread of excitement in her tone.

"I'm standing in a house that I hope you'll love as much as I do."

For several seconds she didn't say a word and then, "You're asking me to move in with you?"

"No, baby. I'm asking you to buy a place with me. Start the next chapter of our lives."

She sniffled, and I realized she was crying. "I want this with you so much. When can we see it? I can meet you there now."

Chuckling, I made my way down the hall to locate the Realtor. "Do you have plans this evening? I would love for Holland to see the place tonight."

She checked her calendar and then confirmed she could stay another hour.

"I'll be there in thirty," Holland said. The engine of her Mercedes purred to life. "Drop me the address."

"Okay. Drive safe. I'll be waiting. I love you."

"Love you too."

Slowly, I walked back inside, sensing the possibilities of a new day. A new start. The woman I loved by my side, and my family reunited.

I tucked the phone into my pocket and looked around once more. Soon it would smell like her shampoo. There'd be coffee cups left on the counter and dog hair on the rug. A real home, finally.

I leaned against the doorframe, hands in my pockets, staring at the filtered light spilling across the floor like a promise.

Yeah. This wasn't just a house. It was a future. Ours.

Holland and I had earned the quiet. For now. But I knew better than to believe in silence. Because somewhere in the dark ... the Pied Piper still played.

And this time, we were listening.

****You thought Kip's story was over*. But monsters don't vanish—they wait in the shadows. In this exclusive bonus scene, Holland finds herself face-to-face with a stranger who knows far too much about her father...and about Ella. And when the Pied Piper's name is whispered, the game changes. Click here for the bonus scene. (Turn the page).

**Have you read the duet that started the series, In the Shadows and Back in the Shadows? Click here to download it for FREE in Kindle Unlimited. Turn the page for the sample.

IN THE SHADOWS SAMPLE

When you finally meet the monster hiding under your bed.

One, two, I'm coming for you.

She's my obsession.

Three, four, kneel on the floor.

I want to possess her in every way.

Five, six, I'm up to my old tricks.

She knows me as The Portland Serial K!ll3r.

Seven, eight, lay in wait.

Little does she know I'm watching her.

Nine, ten, never to be seen again.

Welcome to your worst nightmare, Little Lamb.

Who am I? Let me introduce myself.

I'm Death. And I have found my Queen.

Ella McCloud you're the flicker of light in my dark, dark world.

The color in my grayscale existence.

I yearn for you like the night yearns for the stars.

Dear readers, this ***dark* *romance contains multiple POVs, multiple storylines,* and many exciting moving pieces that come together in one satisfying and unexpected HEA. If you enjoy a single storyline, this book might not be for you.

**In the Shadows is a pitch-black stalker romance and dark vigilante love story with an age gap and an unhinged antihero. Perfect for readers who crave obsessive love, morally gray protector romance, and psychological romantic suspense. Check TW/CW and tropes on the author's website.

"Liberty for wolves is death to the lambs" - Isaiah Berlin

I crept into Ella McCloud's bedroom. Through the parted curtains, the full moon cast a glow on her beautiful curves, and I settled into the grey chair nestled in the corner. Every luscious part of her body was exquisite, and I yearned to feel my knife run along the dips and valleys of her porcelain skin. The possibilities of how I could etch my marks into her flesh flooded my mind until my cock twitched, begging to be inside of her.

She sighed softly and rolled over, exposing her long, toned legs from beneath the blankets. Her neck was poised perfectly and allowed the access I craved. I willed myself not to run my tongue along the curve and taste her.

My dick begged for release while I fantasized that she woke up, terrified. I envisioned her eyes popping wide open as I slipped the knife into her stomach. The cut, as smooth as butter, would steal her breath as she realized what I'd done.

I clenched my jaw and berated myself for allowing my sinful thoughts to consume me. Not my Ella. That wasn't my plan for her. I bathed in my other victims' blood after slicing and dicing them, but not her. Ella was the flicker of light in my dark world, the color in my grayscale existence, and I yearned for her like the night yearns for stars.

The first moment I saw her and spotted her shoulder-length dark hair and piercing green eyes, I had to have her. The gentle touch of water on her face made her skin glisten, and as the droplets clung to her eyelashes, my world came to a standstill. Ella was breathtaking, and the only sound I could hear was my heart pounding in my ears. Her mere presence electrified my heightened senses, resonating deep within my soul and drawing me to her.

As I massaged the back of my neck, the heavenly but faint smell of her peach and vanilla bodywash lingered in the air, imprinting on my mind. Although I'd first seen Ella one year ago, this was the first time I'd entered her house. A thrill surged through me.

Captivated by her beauty, I pressed the flat edge of the blade against my lower lip and slid it back and forth. The cold steel sent shivers down my spine as I gazed at Ella's chest rising and falling, her tightly fitted tank top accentuating her full breasts. The sharp knife grazed my lower lip, drawing a drop of blood that I eagerly licked off with my tongue, savoring its metallic tang.

Life was so fragile—here one second and gone the next. It would be so easy to take away the life she'd built for herself—steal her soul and make it mine for all eternity.

My hand clenched the blade's hilt, the veins in my forearm branching out like a spider's web. I moved closer to her bed, my target oblivious to my proximity.

Her black hair cascaded like a midnight waterfall, deep and enigmatic, reflecting hints of blue or brown under the moonlight. Its richness and depth never failed to captivate me, embodying both the mystery of the night sky and the warmth of a shadowed ember. An overwhelming urge to touch her washed over me. I brushed pieces of hair from her forehead, the strands so delicate and pristine between my fingers.

I reached out my bloodstained fingertip and lightly stroked her cheek with just a whisper of a graze. My little lamb consumed my thoughts. With one glance in my direction, she had become my obsession, and soon I would be hers.

We were meant for each other—even if it meant killing people along the way. I had to have her for my own—no matter what it took because ...

Even Death deserved a Queen.

Read for FREE in Kindle Unlimited.

Behind the Shadows

J.A. OWENBY

Copyright © 2025 by J.A. Owenby

Edited by: Emerald Edits and Lisa Carlisle

Cover Art by: Qamber Designs & Media

First Edition ISBN: 978-1-949414-77-6

FREE PALATE CLEANSER EBOOK

SIGN UP FOR J.A. OWENBY'S NEWSLETTER and download your FREE palate cleanser Ebook, Love & Sins. Stay up to date concerning exclusive bonus scenes, updates on upcoming releases, and more. Visit www.authorjaowenby.com or Click Here.

ALSO BY J.A. OWENBY

The Shadows Series

In the Shadows, book 1 of the duet

Back in the Shadows, book 2 of the duet

Behind the Shadows, a standalone

The Whitmore Elite Series, Dark, Football

Forbidden, a prequel

Illicit Obsession, a standalone novel

Ruthless Obsession, a standalone novel

Sinful Obsession, a standalone novel

Toxic Obsession, a standalone novel

The Beautifully Damaged Series

Beautifully Damaged

Beautifully Broken

Beautifully Shattered

The Love & Ruin Series

Love & Ruin

Love & Deception

Love & Redemption

Love & Consequences, a standalone novel

Love & Corruption, a standalone novel

Love & Revelations, a novella

Love & Seduction, a standalone novel

Love & Vengeance

Love & Retaliation

Love & Betrayal

The Wicked Intentions Series

Dark Intentions

Fractured Intentions

The Torn Series, inspired by True Events

Fading into Her, a prequel novella

Torn

Captured

Freed

Standalone Novels

Where I'll Find You

ABOUT THE AUTHOR

International bestselling author J.A. Owenby grew up in a small backwoods town in Arkansas where she learned how to swear like a sailor and spot water moccasins skimming across the lake.

She finally ditched the south and headed to Oregon. The first winter there, she was literally blown away a few times by ninety mile an hour winds and storms that rolled in off the ocean.

Eventually, she longed for quiet and headed up to snowier pastures. She now resides in Washington state with her hot nerdy husband and three purebred Siberian cats who insist on using her computer as their napping spot. She spends her days coming up with ways to torture characters in a way that either makes you want to throw your book down a flight of stairs or sob hysterically into a pillow.

J.A. Owenby writes new adult and romantic thriller novels. Her books ooze with emotion, angst, and twists that will leave you breathless. Having battled her own demons, she's not afraid to tackle the secrets women are forced to hide. After all, the road to love is paved in the dark.

Her friends describe her as delightfully twisted. She loves fan mail and wine. Please send her all the wine.

You can follow the progress of her upcoming novel on Facebook at Author J.A. Owenby.

Sign up for J.A. Owenby's Newsletter at www.authorjaowenby.com

Like J.A. Owenby's Facebook:
https://www.facebook.com/JAOwenby

*J.A. Owenby's One Page At A Time reader group:*https://www.face
book.com/groups/JAOwenby